RESTORING JUSTICE

Also by Leslie Crocker Snyder:
25 to Life: The Truth, the Whole Truth, and Nothing but the Truth

Also by Matthew Hall:
The Art of Breaking Glass
Nightmare Logic

RESTORING JUSTICE

A THRILLER

JUDGE LESLIE CROCKER SNYDER

MATTHEW HALL

This is a work of fiction. The events described here are imaginary: The names, settings, places, and characters are fictitious and not intended to represent specific 2026 places or persons, living or dead. Any resemblance to actual events or persons is entirely coincidental.

Independently published by Leslie Crocker Snyder and Matthew Hall.

Cover, title-page and back cover art by Caleb Hall.

Snyder Hall Publications
New York

First Edition

Library of Congress Registration: 2026915499

Adobe Stock Image #259598599 Licensed
Adobe Stock Image #316922539 Licensed
Adobe Stock Image #303132792 Licensed
Adobe Stock Image #705902305 Licensed
Adobe Fonts Balboa-Family Licensed
Adobe Fonts Times-New-Roman-Family Licensed

To Fred, Nick, Carla, Doug, Charlotte, Vanessa, Ward, Hunt, Hugh and Webb.

—Leslie Crocker Snyder

For all the fans of my mother, Grayson Hall, who have done so much to keep her memory alive.

—Matthew Hall

PART ONE
Tory

A late September weeknight and the first cold wind of autumn had emptied the restaurant patios and forced drivers, for the first time in months, to close their convertible tops. By 9:00 pm, the streets were empty, and no one saw the white van pull up to 237 K Street, the townhouse that served as the home base, personal offices and occasional sleeping quarters for the judges of the Foreign Intelligence Surveillance Court—America's secret court.

Three men and one woman got out of the Florio's Cleaning Service van. All four wore uniforms and briskly set about pulling out brooms and brushes. Two approached the door; one pushed a key into the door lock while the other tapped the security code into the wall pad. The door opened without a sound.

On the first floor, Judge Kay Breckenridge sat at a Duncan Phyfe desk, intently studying transcripts of top-secret Justice Department wiretaps. She flipped a stray lock of salt-and-pepper hair away from her glasses, ignored the cleaning service in the hallway, didn't pay attention to the uniformed man with long black hair as he stepped quietly into the room, pulled the plastic tip from a syringe, and injected a careful mix of chemicals into her neck. Startled by the sharp pain, she tried to fend him off, and then her heart began to leap about in her chest, and something burst in her head, and she fell. She was dead before she landed on the carpet.

One flight up, Laura Valentino lifted her head and scrunched her eyebrows. There it was again, some kind of thumping noise from down the hall. "What was that?" she asked. Judge Michael O'Shaugnesy, annoyed at the interruption, shifted his hips on the taupe leather sofa. "The cleaners. It's their night. But don't worry—

door's locked, nothing to worry about. Get back to work, there," O'Shaugnesy said to his new law clerk. It was the third week she'd known him and her first week on the job. Laura Valentino buried her head in her boss's crotch.

When she finished, she wiped her mouth with the back of her hand and lifted her gaze, anticipating a satisfied gleam on the judge's face. Instead, Michael O'Shaugnesy was frozen, mouth wide, gaping at something over her left shoulder.

Phfft. Laura felt a thrumming by her right ear, a quick wave of heat as a third eye opened on the judge's forehead. He blinked rapidly, then stopped, blood oozing down his face.

Laura couldn't breathe. She tried to stand as the man with the military crewcut stepped forward, pushed the silenced gun deep into her luxuriant brown hair and pulled the trigger.

On the top floor of the brownstone, Judge Walter Grant had surveillance orders covering his antique mahogany roll-top; the one in his hand was particularly sensitive, but he wasn't reading it. Something was bothering him, and had been for days. Walter's mind kept wandering back to a wiretap transcript he'd read last week. He'd been asked by someone he respected to sit on it, not mention it to anybody until they had more information, and to be honest, he wasn't sure why—if what was in the transcript was true, it would necessitate a fundamental shift in the way the US was fighting the war against drugs.

When the cleaning crew appeared at his door, he barely looked up. "Give me five minutes, will you? " he said. His voice was pleasant, but it carried a military authority.

Grant, a stately African-American in his mid-fifties, had been a Federal judge for thirteen years. He was not accustomed to having his orders ignored. When the dark-haired woman ignored his request and pushed the cart into the room, Walter grew stern. "I said I'd be—where's the regular cleaning woman?" This one, he couldn't help but notice, was singularly attractive, even under the cap. A scar ran through her right eyebrow. "Don't you ignore me, young lady, I'm talking to you." An instant later Walter's heart exploded in his chest, pierced by a slug from the woman's silenced Glock nine millimeter.

The other offices were empty. They had been told to expect one more judge, but there was nothing to be done about that. Lifting fuel canisters from the cart, the man shook gas over Judge Grant's body while the woman opened file cabinet after file cabinet, sloshed the clear flammable liquid over the reams of legal papers. They worked their way back down through the townhouse, stopping at every office; dumping files, pouring gasoline. In each office, the girl set a small gunpowder bomb triggered by a simple kitchen timer. Crude, she knew, but the results would be guaranteed.

The team walked back out to the van. The girl with the scar in her eyebrow would have loved to stay, see the explosion, watch all that paper burn, but she took her seat on the floor and pulled the door shut. The wheelman drove expertly through the night back out toward the highway to DC. When the building went up, they were two miles away, but they heard the explosion very clearly. All of Washington heard it, and soon the rest of America would hear it as well.

* * *

"Fellow justices— my friends—" Merle Drummond, the Chief Justice of the Supreme Court, broke slightly at that last word, closed his eyes, had to steady himself. "My friends," he went on, his voice strained with grief, "we are under attack."

Four fire companies had responded to the roaring fire the night before. The building was a total loss; they had been reduced to hosing the roofs of surrounding structures to keep the flames from spreading. What remained of the four bodies had not been found until daylight. Drummond had adjourned the Supreme Court, sent the justices home for the next few days so he could concentrate exclusively on this crisis. Before him in the chamber sat seven men, one woman, and the 3 empty chairs of the bombing victims. Each was a Federal judge from a different corner of the nation. Each was a member of the most secret court in America. They convened in business attire— never in robes— in a windowless, soundproof room on the top floor of the Department of Justice, across the street from the White House in Washington DC.

In the corridor outside, two tough ex-military Federal Marshals stood armed guard. Three floors below, another marshal stared at two video monitors beaming the same black-and-white picture, opposing angles of the only hallway leading to the rooftop headquarters of the Foreign Intelligence and Surveillance Court, the FISA court, the nation's only antiterrorism court.

By law, the Chief Justice of the Supreme Court is also the leader of FISA, and Merle Drummond, a tall man with a long ecclesiastical face and the bushy silver eyebrows of a biblical prophet, had always taken both charges equally seriously. "I've just come from a meeting across the street—" the assembled judges all knew he meant the Oval Office. "The President is just torn up about the murders of Kay, Michael, Walter and Ms. Valentine." He shook his head. "Just torn up. His family has known Walter Grant for years." Drummond swallowed hard. "I've also been on the Hill this morning, in emergency session with Justice and Oversight, and they've allocated for a replacement for the FISA townhouse—"

"Merle—" the speaker was AO Hart, a lanky Texas judge. "I don't mean to interrupt, but I've got a question for the assembled group here—did anyone see this coming?" He looked around the semicircle at the other justices, at the three empty chairs of the fallen. "We are the antiterrorism court. We're here to handle every wiretap authorization for every terrorism investigation in this country—in any country we choose—and nobody saw a whisper about this? Not even in retrospect?" He looked at Drummond. "I've been racking my brains, trying to think of the one coded phone call, the piece of transcript that might've had some inkling— but I didn't see anything."

Kurt Gunderson, a Los Angeleno who had been a child actor before college and his career in law, shook his head. "90% of my work is middle-eastern subvariants, I see a lot of chatter from the cells. And they talk big— gonna blow up this, bomb that— every time they mention an airplane I worry. But this is too focused, too private."

Jack Riley, a white-haired Federal judge from New York City, was usually the sly wit of the group. Today he looked haggard, with chalky purple bags under his eyes. "I'm not seeing Mideast bad actors here either. This is the kind of thing you'd expect of the mob in Sicily or Latin America, killing judges—"

"Here, mob guys are too busy killing each other." Fenton Kottle of Boston had seen his share of mob work over the years.

Dash Flagler was the scion of an old Florida family. "Lotta countries in South America, it's dangerous being a judge. Drug cartels don't like it when judges get in their way."

Jack Riley nodded his head. "We have big Colombian drug cases in courts all over the country right now. Quantity cocaine, fentanyl— everything they touch turns to rot."

Merle Drummond's sharp voice cut through the conversation. "Gentleman— Madam Justice— this is a court, not a sewing circle. We do not deal in speculation. The FBI and the Marshals are doing their investigation. They'll do their work, and we must do ours." Drummond turned his attention to two stacks of files, each a foot high. "These—" he slapped the first stack with his palm— "are our doomsday candidates. These are judges approved by the Bureau to take our place if we die or are ever decimated by attack." He started passing the folders out amongst the judges. "For the foreseeable future, I will take the place of Judge Grant. If I can be as fine a leader of this court as he was—" he broke off, closed his eyes, the pain obvious. "I will endeavor…" he cleared his throat. "I will endeavor to fill his shoes."

"We are honored to have you," Judge Riley said, and the statement was met with a chorus of agreement from the other judges.

"Thank you all. Now, we need candidates. I want you to go through each file here, see if you know them, if you like them, if you wouldn't work with them no matter what, just give me your gut. I'll take your nominations and make my decisions this afternoon."

Jack Riley opened the first file and thought: *well, that's a touchdown at kickoff.* He took a Post-it and wrote "First Choice Ideal Candidate -JR", stapled it to the front of the file, passed it on and opened the next one, more as a formality than anything else.

* * *

At times, Tory Parker had thought she would never see this day.

The Green Dragons were an uptown heroin gang so large and cocky that 43 murders were attributed to them. Over three years the NYPD had built enough evidence and turned enough informants to chart out the Dragons' organization. The night they shut it down, 130 people were arrested in a citywide sweep. Tory Parker, New York State Supreme Court justice, had been assigned the main trial, eventually whittled to 52 defendants, and had adjudicated countless side-trials and plea bargains as well. At one point she'd had so many defendants in lockdown at The Tombs, the New York City prison, that the cops had taken to calling the 8th floor the Parker Wing. Now, after 9 months of living in the Green Dragons' violent and amoral world, Tory was ready to adjudicate one last remaining matter: People v Shaquille James Jr.

Tory, robed, took the bench, looked out over the empty public seats. Until two days ago they had been packed with victims' and defendants' families and press. Now when she spoke Tory was aware of a slight echo from the far wall. She hadn't heard that echo in months.

Tory didn't use a gavel to begin and end her sessions in court. She'd tried one when she first became a judge, and felt the noise and symbolism more appropriate to an auction than a courtroom. She was signing off on the last of the paperwork being funneled her by Anna, one of her law clerks, and Eddie Mazzuchi, her bridge officer, when she noticed Shaquille James whispering with his lawyer, Bernard Krupnik. Finally Krupnik said out loud: "You're sure?"

"Absolutely." Shaquille James was a tall, thin man in an orange Riker's jumpsuit. Bernard turned and looked at Shaquille's girlfriend, who smiled radiantly. Then he stood. "Your honor, may I approach?"

Tory looked at the ADA's table. "Ms. DeSapio?" One couldn't be there without the other.

“Coming.” The Assistant District Attorney, Veronica DeSapio, joined Bernard at Tory’s bench. "This is not,” she said angrily, "the time to start making new motions."

"Veronica—" Tory's tone stopped her. "Bernard, go on."

"Thank you, Judge. Before he's sentenced, my client wants to get married.”

Tory couldn't help but smile. "Do they have a license?" Bernard handed over the papers.

Tory looked them over. "This won't change his plea agreement," Veronica said.

"It's not going to affect his sentence. He knows that." Then: "They know that," he amended.

Tory turned to Veronica. "Do The People have any objection to counselor's petition?” Then, because she couldn’t resist, “Speak now or forever hold your peace.”

Veronica had to laugh. "No."

"Wait a sec." Anna ran through the door to the cramped clerk's office, came back out with Tory's second law clerk, Thomas. They watched Tory ask: "Mr. James, you'd like to marry your girlfriend?"

Shaquille James smiled his lopsided grin, turned and gestured at a beautiful black girl with carefully ringleted hair. "She's right here."

"I know," Tory said. “She’s been in court every day you testified. It's Takisha, right?"

"Yes, ma'am." The girl was shy, but she was smiling.

“We did the papers weeks ago,” James said, “but the trial made it hard to plan anything.”

“You need two witnesses. Any of your people coming today?”

“I got no family anymore,” Shaquille said quietly. Takisha shook her head.

“Do you mind your lawyer and the ADA?” Shaquille nodded. “Okay. Rings?” she asked.

“Judge,” Shaquille rose up to his full height. “I been at Riker’s ten months. You think I walk in here with rings?”

"I’ve got two." Takisha pulled a ring from her thumb, and another from her index finger, handed him both.

He tried one on. "That's fine," he said.

"Okay, now you give that one back to me." He did.

"That's settled? Okay." Tory came down from the bench, arranged everyone into a proper configuration, stood before the couple. "Shaquille and Takisha, it is my privilege to confer the blessing of the state upon your love for each other. Shaquille, you ran with one of the most vicious drug gangs ever, but the violence got to you, and you cooperated in most of the trials against the Dragons. From the start you knew jail was in your future, but you accepted that. And you, Takisha, I’ve seen that you’ve been a rock for Shaquille, you’ve been in this courtroom every day, giving him the courage to go on in the face of threats from these thugs. You two are a great team. Shaquille, do you take Takisha Vernon to be your lawful wedded wife, to cherish in sickness and in health, so long as you both shall live?"

"I do."

"Takisha, do you take Shaquille James to be your lawful wedded husband, to cherish in sickness and in health, so long as you both shall live?"

“Yes.” Tears were brimming in Takisha’s eyes.

Love always looked so simple to Tory when other people did it.

The couple were entirely focused on each other. "By the power vested in me by the laws of the State of New York," Tory intoned, "I pronounce you husband and wife."

The newlyweds kissed, a long, passionate movie-ending kiss right there in the courtroom. A lump of emotion welled in Tory's throat; she was glad for them. She glanced at Krupnik, who was beaming, then took a quick look at DeSapio. There was a strange light in the ADA's eyes.

Even Mazzuchi, tough old bird with thirty years in the courts, stood to watch, along with Anna and Thomas and the court officers. At last the couple separated, and Tory gently said: "Okay you two, time for the hard part."

She climbed up to the bench, resumed her chair. The courtroom was sealed because of Shaquille James' cooperation agreement. When everybody was in their place, Tory said: "Arraign the defendant for sentence, please." The prosecutor briefly revisited the crimes; the defense touched on his client's assistance to law enforcement. Then it was Tory's turn:

"Shaquille James, as a runner for the Green Dragon Mob, by your own admission you were an active participant in felony criminal activity for four years. But the violence got to you, and you cooperated in most of the trials against the Dragons, and for that you must be commended. From the start, you knew jail was in your future. Pursuant to your cooperation agreement, you pled guilty to criminal sale of a controlled substance in the third degree and use of a firearm in the commission of a felony. The agreement gives me discretion to sentence you up to 25 years in jail. You have already served 10 months. I am going to sentence you to one of the lowest prison sentences pursuant to your cooperation agreement. The sentence of the court is two to four years, with credit for time served—"

"Thank you, Judge," Shaquille said. He'd known exactly what was coming. It could have been so much worse.

"Counsel, please advise your client of his right to appeal. I will instruct Corrections that you are not to be sent to any prison containing any defendants of any trial in which you gave testimony. I expect—" and here she looked at Takisha—"that'll put you pretty far upstate."

Takisha nodded. "Yes, ma'am."

"The two of you can have a life," Tory said. "It'll take a while to get there, but you can be together and have a life. This court is adjourned." She pushed back from the desk, watched as the newlyweds stood and kissed over the barrier. Finally the corrections officers gently separated them, put Shaquille in cuffs and led him to the holding pen door. One long last look at his wife, and he was gone.

Takisha locked eyes with Tory. "Thanks," the girl said, toying with her ring. Then, the emotion too palpable, she walked down the aisle and out the courtroom door.

Tory looked at Anna and Thomas and Eddie. "Guys," she said, amazed, "we're done with the Dragons!"

There was a spontaneous smattering of applause from the little group, months of hard
work successfully completed.

"I think we should go have lunch at Forlini's," said Anna.

"Absolutely," said Tory. "Eddie, you in?"

"I have some shopping to do for my wife. Otherwise—"

"Next time," Tory said, and led her team through the door into her robing room, a cramped office adjacent to the courtroom. Though their official offices were upstairs, most judges decorated these small spaces with framed news clips and photo-op pictures with VIPs.

Tory had none of that, beyond a yellowing *Daily News* headline, "Death Grudge Against Judge," from a trial in which a defendant had threatened her life. But attached to her wall were two pool cue sticks, custom-built Schons she'd worn down years before, and perched on the file cabinet was a dusty trophy, an oversized wood and bronze tower topped by an angel holding crossed pool cues high above her head.

Standing by the file cabinet, perusing the trophy, was a tall, commanding African American woman in a black pantsuit: Tory's boss, Chief Administrative Judge Cornelia Blake.

"Tory, may I speak with you alone? It'll just be a few minutes."

Tory looked at her clerks. "You guys go on, I'll catch up."

"We'll wait," Thomas said, and he and Anna went back out to the courtroom.

Tory hung up her robe. She was wearing cream-colored pants and a fitted black silk shirt. "My God, Cornelia, those FISA judges getting murdered—" she put on a cream jacket, pulled her blonde hair out from under. "God, what that court's been through in the last few years—"

"Until all this, most Americans didn't even know that court existed."

"They do now," Tory's smile had an edge. "Merle Drummond is going to hate that."

"No doubt," Cornelia said. "Now you just ended a huge case, you're probably hoping for a couple weeks of buy-and-busts."

Obviously there were other plans. "What's going on?"

"Baby Nieto." Tory felt her heart sink. Cornelia went on: "It's a monster— it'll make the Green Dragon case look like a car hit a lamp post. You know about it?"

"I remember seeing he got busted." Baby Nieto was the younger brother of Eduardo Nieto, the largest and most important cocaine kingpin in Colombia. Baby had been arrested in connection with seven tractor-trailer shipping containers filled with cocaine that came into New York harbor on a cargo freighter in the Spring. The case was huge.

"Right now we have a few Nieto-related trials going on," Cornelia said.

"I have a friend who's prosecuting a case with Nieto connections." Tory had been seeing Rafe Carr for a few weeks. Whenever he popped in her head, she found herself marveling at how damn handsome he was. She shunted those thoughts aside. "Brooklyn. Task-force case. Mid-level dealer."

"Those trials aren't security risks," Cornelia said. "This one will be. Nieto owned two customs agents in New York. When the boat was busted, they both fled. The feds tracked one, flipped him, and he gave up Baby. Eduardo isn't going to be happy his baby brother is being prosecuted, and he's got resources that worry us."

"Down in Colombia," Tory said. The Colombian government held an uneven grasp over the country's interior, a mountainous region roughly the size of Switzerland. This area contained the ideal soil and climate to grow coca plants, which were then processed into cocaine. It had been ruled for a generation by a paramilitary junta called FARC; throughout the years of political upheavals and paramilitary violence, Eduardo Nieto had wiped out his rivals and consolidated his power to emerge as, essentially, FARC's minister of cocaine, the largest and most feared cocaine exporter in the region. When FARC finally signed a peace agreement and joined the legitimate Colombian government, it merely cemented his power. Despite the United States' ongoing efforts to shut down his supply routes and spray his farmer's coca crops with powerful herbicides that killed every plant they touched, Nieto's drug business had never stopped expanding. Over a decade ago he'd started a lucrative sideline of crystal meth; in the last few years he'd built several labs to produce fentanyl, useful in bulking up cocaine intended for lower-profit US markets.

Cornelia continued: "Nieto's organization has been tied to the killings of judges down in Colombia, and, we suspect, up here as well. And with his baby brother on trial—well, NYPD's going to have to go back to giving you round-the-clock coverage."

"Again." It was surprising how wall-to-wall security somehow became routine.

"Right. So," Cornelia surmised, "it's going to be a huge trial, you'll have protection, there will be danger. By me, you're the best judge for it, but I'll understand if you say no."

Tory took a deep breath. Once more into the breech. "It's a challenge, but yes, let's do it."

"Great." Cornelia opened a square document case, pulled out two fat brown Redwell folders. "Police affidavits, Grand Jury minutes, some wiretap transcripts, this'll get you up to speed. Pretrial conference tomorrow. Sam Walker's prosecuting."

Tory had worked with Sam a lot over the years. "Who's defense?"

There was a pause. "Angelo Schwartz," Cornelia said.

"Really? Angelo Schwartz, crusader for liberty, defending Eduardo Nieto's kid brother?"

Cornelia smiled. "When Baby was busted, the government froze his assets."

Tory shrugged. "They're supposed to allow money for a defense."

"Well, yeah," Cornelia went on, "but no one wants to get on the front page of the *Post* as the judge who opened Baby's drug money vaults."

"Oh for God's sake," Tory said. "The man has a right to a lawyer. That's the system."

"Two judges said no. He was going to go 18B."

“Assigned council?” Tory felt her anger rise. “This case is huge, it's international—"

"The ACLU got involved. They figured they'd make a real statement, get a hotshot to take the case.”

"And they called Angelo— they needed a big gun, and Angelo does a lot of pro bono.” It all clicked in Tory's mind. "I haven't seen him in years," she said, "except him being a talking head on the news."

"And all over social media. Every big juicy trial, he's everywhere. But he knows the law— not like some of those internet bozos." Cornelia turned cool. "You guys had a thing, didn't you?"

Coming from anyone else, Tory would have thought this totally out of bounds. But she'd always liked Cornelia's no-bullshit attitude, and considered the woman a friend.

"Yes," Tory said, "Angelo and I were an item—well, more than two presidential administrations ago. It was—" she considered— "three months max, back when I was still a prosecutor, when he was still a prosecutor—" Abruptly, there he was in her memory: him in her tiny office, charisma to spare, and devastating in court.

Cornelia was watching her. "Is that going to be a problem?"

Tory smiled: "Not at all. I think he only dates underwear models, now."

Cornelia barked out a laugh. "I think you're right." They shook hands, Tory held the door for her, let her through and waved Anna and Thomas back into the room.

"So," Anna said, "Forlini's?"

Tory thumped the Redwells. "We just got Baby Nieto."

There was a stricken pause as the two clerks eyed the fat cases. Anna gulped. "Maybe we should just get Tony's to send up sandwiches?"

Tory opened the first case. "I think," she said, "that might be a good idea."

* * *

Eduardo Nieto sat on the flagstone terrace of his finca in the Colombian Andes with his American friend Dirk Armstrong, a large-framed man with a gym-built body and a well-kept flat-top haircut, looking out over mountains to the horizon. A plate of prosciutto wrapped around figs and grapes and melon had been brought to them, along with two cold luladas, non-alcoholic iced drinks made of mashed lulo fruit. Eduardo popped a perfectly prepared fig in his mouth, savored the interplay of salt and sweet.

"Mariposa worries about my blood pressure from this—" he gestured at the thinly sliced ham. "She wants me to eat all the things she eats—vegetables and grains and fruit."

"On her, they look good," Mr. Armstrong said. "Will we be seeing her while I'm here?"

Eduardo shook his head no, swallowed. "She is in the apartment in Bogota, a shopping trip while we discuss business. Tell me how is Baby, in the prison in New York."

"We have a conduit, somebody who can bring him whatever he needs."

"Trustworthy?"

Armstrong nodded. "I know him from ArrowHawk; he cashed out early, went back to the States. Anything I need done, he's on it."

"Because Baby has always had…appetites, we shall say." He held up his glass. "If today was Saturday, we would have guaro in our drinks."

"Guaro?" the American asked.

"Aguardiente. But it is Wednesday, we are here for serious talk. Baby does not understand this—if he were here now, today, he would have guaro in his drink. Because he is weak."

Armstrong had worked with Baby for three years. The man enjoyed his pleasures, and had an obese body to show for it, but in many ways he had a strong sense of discipline. Armstrong searched for a diplomatic response. "In some areas, yes. In other areas, I see him rise to the challenges—"

Eduardo's eyes narrowed. "My brother needs protection from his hungers." He said it as a statement of fact. "It is your job to get him what he needs, and protect him from what he wants. Now: what are we to do about this trial? We will make it vanish?" Armstrong, juggling responses, said nothing. Eduardo went on: "Maybe being in this trial will light a fire in Baby, make him see that the world is not always soft. Then he will learn something before the trial goes poof and disappears."

Armstrong shifted in his seat. "That's harder to do in America than it is down here."

"Police, lawyers, judges—" Eduardo shrugged. "Those we can't bribe, we kill. Like in that secret court— the FISA court. Poof— no more problem."

Armstrong inhaled deeply. "True," he agreed, and let the next thought— *but sometimes in America that doesn't fix the problem*— go unsaid.

* * *

Frank Dunton's universe was fire and ice, and five days a week, eight hours a day, he walked the margin between them. And when he walked, he whistled.

He was whistling now as he approached tier 2C of the North Infirmary Command, one of the prisons on Riker's Island. "Rock the gate!" he shouted at the glass booth. The first set of bars slid open. He stepped through, holding a plastic supermarket bag and whistling an old Nietzsche Prosthesis song as the bars clanged shut behind him. Then the second set rolled open, and he walked onto the tier.

Televisions were babbling in the common area; immediately Tonton barreled up to him, a big lumbering bruiser, his orange jumpsuit caked with dirt and stench. "Trigger Dog's fucking with my shit. Got this whole place wired, I'll rip out his fucking eyes."

"Trig's in solitary, Tonton." The kid was obviously nuts; he was waiting for some court somewhere to make a ruling. Frank pushed past, whistled loudly as he approached the main group. He figured if they heard him coming, he wouldn't see anything he didn't want to see.

"Yo! Fritz! What you got for me in that bag?"

"Your girlfriend's pussy, dickwipe."

"Aww, that's cold. You a cold motherfucker."

Frank didn't see the big guy there, kept walking. He'd started out regular military, then jumped to ArrowHawk: private contracting, morally in the shitter, way better money. Eventually he'd had enough of these druggistas and came home, took this gig as a prison guard. But if Armstrong and the boys down there needed something, he was always happy to oblige.

Such as today.

Baby Nieto's cell was at the end of the hall. The door was open; the man was so obese he barely fit on the slab of concrete jutting out of the wall as a bed. There were three Latin Players gangbangers not doing much of anything in front of the cell; Baby had hired protection. They stood as Frank approached.

"Hola gents, package for the big guy." One tough punk accepted the supermarket bag, looked inside. He started to take it in.

Frank plucked the bag from the man's hand: "I'll do the honors, scuzzball." He pushed past them, stepped into Baby's cell.

The man was a mountain of flesh, 464 pounds according to the intake forms. It was a wonder, Frank thought, he didn't break toilets when he sat. "Señor Nieto?" Frank asked.

The massive clean-shaven man opened one eye. Then, seeing who it was, he started to raise into a sit, as elaborate a process as a baby elephant standing upright for the first time.

How does he pee? Frank wondered. How does he wipe his ass?

Maybe he pays somebody to do it. "Señor Nieto, I was told you would enjoy these." He waited until the man, panting, had sat up, presented him with the bag.

Baby Nieto opened it, stuck his head inside, greedily pulled out the box of cigars. "Muy bueno," he said, sliced open the paper seal, took out one and smelled it. "Mr. Frank, you are a prince," he said, and pulled the second box out of the bag. "El mazapan— las almendras." He held the cigar in his fat hand, dug out a lurid pink and green log, crammed it into his mouth. His eyes rolled high in his head. "It is like making love to angels," he said. He dug back into the bag, pulled out four Spanish porn magazines, fiery Latinas pouting soulfully with legs wide open. Baby was delighted. "You are no prince. You are the king of the prison!"

Baby Nieto set the cigar aside, gripped Frank's head hard with his meaty hands, and planted a nasty fat kiss right on his lips. Frank started to reach around for his pepper spray but the big man released him. Frank stood to get away.

If Baby Nieto had seen Frank taking offense, he didn't seem to mind. "Mister Frank?" Baby held up one of the magazines. "You bring me someone like her, okay?"

"Wish I could," Frank said, backing out of the cell.

"Don't wish. You are the king, you can make her appear—" he snapped his fingers— "right here." He tapped the empty slab of concrete by his thigh.

Frank backed out, turned past the doormen, walked down the tier. That sonovabitch is crazier than anybody in here, he thought, and then: That sonovabitch is crazier than me.

* * *

Tory sent Anna and Thomas home early in the afternoon, stayed in her office reading the Grand Jury minutes. A question had arisen in her mind: how had they known which shipping containers on which boats were carrying cocaine? The answer was nowhere in the two boxes of papers she'd been given. She had a healthy suspicion what that meant.

It meant FISA, the Foreign Intelligence Surveillance Court. Information had been gathered through surveillance approved by a FISA-authorized court order, but that chain of events had been redacted. The fact that there were no fingerprints meant that FISA's fingerprints were all over it.

Still, what there was was fascinating. Several witnesses had been compelled to aid in piecing together the case against Baby Nieto. Tory was especially intrigued by Barney Lind.

Lind was one of two US Customs officers who had written the manifest and inspection reports on the Nieto shipping containers, signing off on documents stating that they were filled with tiles bound from South America to a nonexistent flooring wholesaler in Long Island City. When the bust went down, both men disappeared, but Lind was eventually found in a hotel near Kennedy Airport. He hadn't left the room in a week; the mounds of cocaine on the coffee table totaled over 10 ounces. In a garbage bag under the bed was $78,000 in loose bills.

Barney Lind had not gone quietly; it had taken eight NYPD officers to extract him.

He'd detoxed on a locked ward at Bellevue before being told by detectives how the system worked. He would get Queen for a Day, during which time he would elucidate as many details of his crimes as he could. A deal would be made that would spare him the full weight of the law. He would testify at trials and if it was later shown he had lied or withheld any incriminating information— about anything at all— during his Queen for a Day, he would go to jail for a long, long time.

His partner in crime at Customs was another officer named Wesley Rexroth, current whereabouts unknown. The cocaine and the money had all come from Eduardo Nieto's people They had promised as much of both as he and Rexroth could ever use, if they took care of the paperwork on certain boats as they entered US waters. Since his arrest, Barney Lind had gone through rehab; unless he strayed from his program he would never see the inside of a jail. He would have to find another line of work, however; the US government was no longer an option.

Most of the time, Tory loved her job. She was in the business of fairness; it was she who balanced the rights of the defendant with the efforts of the prosecution. A great many of Tory's cases over the years had involved drugs and the lethal damage they caused. She saw it every day: people committing unimaginable acts against friends, neighbors, enemies, loved ones, children—nothing in her childhood had prepared her for this stuff. Tory was the eldest of three siblings; her sister Letitia, the baby of the family, had made great headway in her career in the military, and was now posted to Doha, Qatar. Jackson, the middle child, had been a complex boy and had grown into a complex man; brilliant and troubled, he had graduated from MIT and was now working on a fishing boat in Alaska. Every few weeks an email stumbled in from him; they were either fiercely visualized vignettes of shipboard life or incoherent ramblings obviously written very drunk. Tory saved them all and never told her family about the ones that made her worry.

As distant as Jack was, on a boat off Alaska, her father, Emory Parker, could be in the same room, at the same dinner table, and be even more unreachable. Even in the halcyon days before her parents' marriage was gored by her father's infidelities, Tory had seen it as her duty to puzzle her way through the tempestuous maze that was her dad. She spent her childhood looking for the fierce light of love she believed burned somewhere inside him. He shed it easily enough for his work; he shed it unbegrudgingly toward Jackson and, to a lesser extent, to Letitia. Tory only felt his unguarded warmth at unexpected moments— reading her a book from his own childhood, or teaching her how to hold a cue stick at a pool table, tiny little fragments of connectedness that took on monolithic significance in Tory's childhood mind.

Her parents were both academics, her father especially regarded by both colleagues and detractors as brilliant. Charismatic in the classroom, he was both demanding and opaque at home. Every year he came out with a book on a minor historical figure, usually centuries dead and unjustly ignored today. He immersed himself so thoroughly in the historical time period of his research that he often wasn't quite sure what year to write on his checks.

When Tory was 8, her mother was diagnosed with breast cancer. After the mastectomy, confronted by his wife's scarred body and unbridled need for support, Emory Parker had escaped into a relationship with a graduate student.

The fissure in her parents' marriage was not an earthquake, more like an irreparable tear that drained life and love at a slow but steady rate. Though to outward appearances nothing had changed— neither her mother nor her father ever moved out, nor did he give up his lover or the ones that came after— never after had the family been the same.

Tory had grown up in academic housing: a spacious Victorian home just off campus, the type given by universities to their star scholars. There had been a pool table in the basement, left over from some previous tenant. Pool had been a family activity when her mother was still healthy. When the troubles started, each of the children handled their rage differently: Jackson turned inward, a strange boy made even stranger. Letitia, the tomboy, went full jock and became a steely competitor in track and field.

For Tory, pool became an all-abiding fixation. No matter what was happening upstairs, she could go into the basement and chalk up a cue and enter a world of pure physics, of weight and motion and action and reaction, all by trying to make the ball spin the way she wanted it to.

School was an escape from the house as well. Equipped with her father's strength of mind, she had triumphed at college, and then Columbia Law. After graduating from law school, while most of her classmates were trying to find their footing on the corporate ladder, she'd applied to the Manhattan DA's office. The real world was waiting; she wanted to make a dent in it. She became an Assistant District Attorney and began prosecuting people who did bad things.

And, right around then, she met a fellow prosecutor named Angelo Schwartz.

Angelo, sparkling green eyes set in strong Mediterranean cheekbones, was a handsome man. He didn't look perfect, like a model; more like a scrappy fighter, with a slight deviated septum from an early punchout that had never been properly fixed. He'd grown up half Jewish, half Italian in the Bronx, in a Black and Spanish neighborhood. He'd had to use his wits to defuse complications every day. It had made him funnel his considerable intelligence into laser-like charm.

One night Tory and Angelo, working late each on their own cases, started talking about their aspirations as prosecutors. Tory wanted justice for all, everyone equal under the law; Angelo had seen that the system was more equal for those with privilege than for those without. They had ended up in Angelo's small office, electricity mounting between them. She hadn't expected the leap of emotion in her chest when he touched her arm, the sudden sense that what had not seemed possible a moment before was now necessary, even inevitable.

They had made love on the carpet, the first night of what became several months of fantastic sex, emotional turmoil, and a ridiculous amount of effort pretending they were merely coworkers in the office. Finally it became too much for them, too consuming, too forbidden, too damn complicated. Tory had ended it, but that hadn't stuck, and two weeks later Angelo had ended it, and that didn't stick either, and ten days after that Tory had finally ended it for good.

Angelo ultimately had given up the government side entirely and gone into private practice as a defense lawyer. He did a lot of pro bono work, she knew: he had a special interest in cases in which battered wives eventually murdered their abusive husbands, handling every case he could, fighting to keep these women out of jail. Tory had always assumed the high-profile drug cases he took were to fund this more important caseload.

They had both become the people they'd wanted to be, back then. After all this time, Tory thought, it would be good to see the man again. She went back to trying to concentrate of the Grand Jury minutes, but her mind kept drifting. When she'd left Angelo, she'd thought that level of passion would be the baseline of all future relationships.

Well, sometimes, she thought. Her phone buzzed, she snapped out of her reverie and picked up. "Rafe."

"Tor, I'm in Brooklyn, my friend Rob's band is playing tonight. They're excellent."

"Will it get loud?

"Very."

No need to be polite. "I'm really not up for loud, tonight. I just got Baby Nieto."

There was a pause. Then: "No shit really?"

"So we're both doing Nieto trials," she said.

"Yeah, but you have the brother. I just have this mid-level dirtbag moving kilos."

"Stay in Brooklyn, see the band—"

"Ahh, I see these guys all the time. I'd rather be with you."

Tory couldn't help but like that in a man. "Well, I'm going to be boring," she said. "I have my mind fixed on getting a Manhattan and a burger at PJ Clark's—"

"They let degenerates like me into PJ Clark's, now?"

"We'll let 'em know you're a prosecutor."

"Naah, don't, it'll fuck up my image. Forty-five minutes?"

"See you there, goofball."

* * *

PJ Clarke's was a century-old tavern on Third Avenue that had remained unchanged even as the neighborhood around it had grown into skyscrapers. When Tory arrived, she suspected Rafe was going to be late, but there he was standing at the bar, rumpled black hair, rumpled black suit with no tie, piercing blue eyes, an empty shot glass and half a beer in front of him.

He kissed her cheek. "On the way here, I realized I should have asked you if you wanted to play pool."

Many men Tory had dated thought they were good at pool. Most were not. Rafe actually was. "Not that kind of day," Tory said. "I actually did a marriage today. The last Green Dragons defendant. Officiated, pronounced them man and wife, and then sent him to prison."

Rafe raised his beer glass in mild salute. "Apt metaphor," he said, and drank.

She cracked half a smile, ordered a Manhattan, straight up. Rafe gestured at the TV running all-news in the corner. "They're still doing 24/7 coverage of those judges killed in DC."

Tory looked: above a banner— No Suspects Yet in Secret Court Bombing— pundits babbled soundlessly. One of them, she saw, was Angelo. Tory thought what she always thought when she caught him on the tube: he looks well.

Rafe saw him too. "Can that guy get through a day without being in front of a camera?"

Tory laughed. "It must be a terrible burden. He's defending Baby."

"I thought they froze the funds."

"ACLU stepped in."

"And got *Schwartz?"*

"He volunteered."

Rafe sipped his beer. "Jeez, he'll probably win."

He could well, Tory thought, and took a sip of her drink, the ice-cold whiskey turning into tendrils of warmth as it infused her system. They moved to the back, were shown to an empty two-top along the wall. Tory asked for a cheeseburger, rare; Rafe ordered Korean ribs and another beer.

"So," she said finally, "the case you're prosecuting in Brooklyn— has Eduardo Nieto ever come up in testimony?"

"Came up pretrial. The main guy is Colombian, wiretaps caught him bragging about how he knows all these Nieto enforcer guys down there, so yeah."

"The guys who kill judges," Tory said.

"You're thinking there's a Nieto connection with the FISA murders?"

"He's a big enough player that I have no doubt he's a suspect. What I don't get is: why FISA? And if you're going to wipe out FISA, why only do three?"

Rafe's eyebrows knit with concern. "Eduardo wants his baby brother back."

"That can't be the motivation— killing three judges on FISA won't help that." She sipped her drink. "Those three judges died for something."

The burgers came. Tory took a bite; it was precisely as good as she remembered. Rafe requested more hot sauce. "Eat, don't wait," he said, and then: "What do you know about Al Clemente?"

Tory looked at the fries, thought of her treadmill, took one, tasted it and set it down. "He's the judge on your drug case, right?" Rafe nodded. "He's a political hack. He did something for someone— campaign contributions, whatever— and that put him on the bench. Pure political payback." The one time they met, he'd made a pass at her. She debated mentioning it, but Rafe had to work with the man. "I hear he does a lot of wiretaps," she said, "I wouldn't think he has the brain power for it."

Rafe snorted out laughter. "To be honest, I can't get a bead on the guy. The stuff he allows and doesn't allow— I keep trying to find a thread of logic to it, and it keeps eluding me."

Tory considered. "Sometimes with wiretaps I sustain objections because the prosecution is trying to take something out of context. Especially if there's FISA-related material."

Rafe shook his head. "This is weirder than that. I go in to fight my case, and I end up fighting the judge all day." He sipped his beer. "I just can't get a handle on it."

* * *

Tory lived in a stately old building on the upper east side; it wasn't the hippest neighborhood in New York, but she was a block from Carl Schurz Park, right on the river. The penthouse had spacious rooms with wide terraces and great views; she had been there once, for a tenant meeting, but Tory had a rear-facing one-bedroom on the third floor. She led Rafe down the carpeted hallway, worked her keys—Siggy's toenails trotted up to the door on the other side—and pushed it open.

The dog wagged his whole body in ecstasy to have her back, his tail thwacking the coat closet.

He'd been a cute little pound puppy when Tory got him; now he was a sixty-pound black and white sheepdog mixed with God knew what. "Hey ya big mutt!" Tory said, squatting down to rub the excited dog's head. She looked up at Rafe: "Get the leash?" she gestured where it was hanging by the door. "Let's get this guy out."

Siggy pulled them to the elevator, then out of the building, worked his way from lamppost to lamppost, sniffing mightily, leading toward Carl Schurz Park.

The park held the gentle cool of late summer as they entered. Couples strolled by the river, enjoying the view across the water. It looked romantic, but Siggy wasn't interested. "Okay," Tory said, "the dog run." Siggy saw a squirrel flash across the walkway and into the bushes. Tory was holding the leash with her fingertips; when the dog leapt, it tore out of her hand.

"Siggy! No!" Tory called. "Back! NOW!" The terrified squirrel streaked up a tree. "I said NOW!" Tory said calmly, and the dog realized his error and came back, tail down. Tory gently took the dog's muzzle, held his eyes with her own. "I said No." Her tone was forceful.

The dog sat, chastened. Tory stood, and they resumed their walk. "I was holding the leash like he was a Chihuahua," she apologized.

They gave Siggy ten minutes in the dog run, then headed back. In the apartment, as Tory prepared the dog food, Rafe pulled her to him, his urgency palpable. She led him to the bedroom as Siggy sharked down his kibble.

Maybe it was the inevitable result of shooting pool in bars, but Tory had always had a propensity towards bad boys. Guys with motorbikes, guys with pasts, guys in bands. Some of her experiences had been a bit rougher than she'd liked; quite a few turned out not to be so interesting once the initial ardor receded. Rafe combined a certain dark charisma with well-educated intelligence—but what really set him apart was his tongue. Simply put, she'd never had a lover with his oral skillset and innate understanding of female anatomy.

He liked to begin their lovemaking with his head between her thighs. Tory had been thinking about exactly this from the moment he'd called. His expertise was both dependable and always a surprise. He was able to take her to the point of crescendo, then back away and take all her sensations to someplace even greater. Sometimes he'd been able to do this four or five times before an ultimate, mind-blowing orgasm.

He was nearing that first crescendo, the first keen rushes of ecstasy when his cell phone began its irritating staccato ring.

He slowed to a stall. "This'll be Ben."

His co-prosecutor on the drug case. "Ignore it," she told him. It shouldn't have even been an issue.

"I can't." He pushed away to disentangle himself from her thighs. “He’s getting on a flight to California. There's a chain of evidence thing—" he grabbed the phone out of his pants. "Hey, man—"

Tory abruptly felt naked, covered herself with a sheet. Rafe was pacing naked back and forth next to the bed. "So it was a paper mix-up?" he asked. "In the precinct property room? Those idiots." He shook his head at Tory, expecting her to commiserate. She wasn't in the mood. "But it's all cleared up, right?" He listened to the phone. "Well, we can say we never gave them to the defense during discovery because of the paper mix-up—"

Tory froze mid-motion. "You did what?" she asked.

He waved her question away, listening to Ben go on. Tory got out of bed, found her underwear, put it on. She threw on a t-shirt, pulled her hair out from the collar. She watched him, not wanting to stay in this room one second longer, not sure where to go if she left.

Finally he got off the phone, looked at the tempest of anger in her eyes. "What?" he asked, clueless.

"So what was it you never gave the defense during discovery?"

Long pause. "A keychain with a bunch of keys. The cops took it from my defendant when he was busted. None of the keys worked on the locker where he had the cocaine."

"So it's exculpatory?"

"Well— I mean, possibly, with the right lawyer. But it got lost in the property room, it only turned up this morning. Ben was trying to track down what happened." And then he grinned. "If it had stayed lost, that would have been good for us."

Abruptly she saw it clearly. All that charisma, his expertise at pool, even his skills at cunnilingus were all part of a win-at-any-cost attitude. She'd seen glimpses of it before, but never so plainly. Damn, she thought, how could she have been seduced by that? He'd pursued her as vehemently as he'd pursued his convictions: Each was a notch on his belt, and she along with them.

"The point is not to win," she said, trying to keep her voice even. "The point is to find out who did the crime, catch him, and put him cleanly and fairly in jail."

"That *is* winning," he said.

"Justice isn't *winning*," she couldn't believe she had to explain this. "Justice is when the right thing happens to the right person for the right reasons."

Naked, cell phone in hand, he shrugged. "Like with Wachtel— that nonjury trial you did."

The remark, said so casually, hit Tory like a mortar blast. Blood drained from her face, her mouth moved soundlessly, her eyes blinked and blinked. "How dare you." She said it coldly, when she found her voice.

He had obviously not expected her reaction to be so vehement. "We all make mistakes, is what I'm saying—"

Tory had never thought of Wachtel as a mistake; it was a disaster, a lifelong burden of sorrow that never got better no matter how much time had passed. At some point once a day she found herself thinking of that man hanging himself in his cell, of the boy growing up somewhere in this city right now who would never know his father. In a moment of intimacy she had told Rafe the whole story, and now here he was throwing it at her in a fight.

She saw her hand shake as she pointed to the door. She said "out," or started to, but the word was lost by the sharp electric blare of the downstairs buzzer.

Siggy exploded into barking, filled the apartment with frantic alarm. "Siggy! Quiet!" She ran to the intercom, lifted the receiver before the doorman could buzz it again. "Yes?" she asked.

"Mr. Riley here to see you—" the doorman said, and at that moment her cell phone rang. She picked it up: Jack's name and cell number. He was calling from downstairs. She hit the button. "Jack—" she said.

"I wouldn't come like this if it weren't important."

She knew Jack Riley well enough, and trusted him thoroughly enough, to accept the statement on its face. "Right," Tory said. "Let me have five minutes." She hung up. Rafe, naked, came around the doorway, arched one eyebrow.

"It's Jack Riley," she said. "He's downstairs."

"Tory—"

"He wouldn't do this unless he had to."

"I brought up Wachtel to make a point."

"Point made," she said calmly, aware that she was still shaking. "Judge Riley will be here any minute, and you have to leave."

He looked into her eyes, searching for something. She turned her back, threw on jeans, tucked in the T-shirt, sat on the couch. Siggy curled up next to her, his heavy head on her thigh. Rafe emerged, dressed, was about to say something when there was a light tap on the door. Siggy trotted up, a low rumble in his throat. "Siggy!" Tory called, glanced in the hallway mirror. Her hair was a mess; she shook her fingers through it. It would have to do. She opened the door.

However bad she looked, Jack looked worse. His handsome, craggy features were worn and haggard with troubles. His hair, snow white and well-kept by a barber he'd been using for forty years, looked flat and punchy. "Jack—what's wrong?"

He waved the question away, let Siggy smell him. "Been a while," he said, both to her and to the dog. He gave her a quick kiss on the cheek just as Rafe stepped into the room. "I'm sorry, I didn't know you had company. Rafe Carr, right? AUSA in Brooklyn?"

Rafe hadn't expected that. "I'm honored to meet you, Judge Riley."

"You won't be in a minute," Riley quipped as they shook hands. "Please forgive an old man for interrupting your evening—this might take a bit of time."

The three were silent, an uncomfortable pause. Tory broke it: "Rafe was just leaving."

"Let me collect my things." He disappeared down the bedroom hall.

Tory stayed with Jack. He looked at her appraisingly. "You okay?" he asked.

"Fine," she said, too quickly. "Long story. I won't bore you with it."

The concern in his eyes didn't change. His hands were folded at his belt; there was a glint of gold at his wrist, a watch. As Tory noticed it, Jack surreptitiously shifted his coat sleeve to cover it more completely.

Was he hiding it? The gesture puzzled Tory. "New watch?" she asked.

"Oh, uhh–" he seemed startled. "Yes, actually." He held up his wrist, gave her a brief view. "Rolex." It was thick, gold, and looked brand new. "More watch than I need, really."

Jack Riley wearing a new Rolex. He did all right, Tory figured, but not that well. "You deserve it," she said.

Rafe came back. Tory led him out the apartment door into the atrium. The elevator was still there from Jack's arrival. He rang it, held it open. "We should have a conversation—" he said.

“We kind of just did,” she said.

“Pretty one-sided, if you ask me." he said, his voice abruptly snide. It was the first time she'd heard him sound like that, and she didn't like it.

She looked him straight in the eye. "You really should let the defense see that piece of evidence," she said coolly. "I've seen what happens when justice goes off the rails, and let me assure you: nobody wins." She turned and walked back down the hall.

"Tory—" he said, but she kept walking. Behind her, the elevator shut and whirred him away.

Tory went back into her apartment, locked the door. Jack had taken off his trench coat, was looking at a picture of himself and Tory at a Judge's Association dinner a few years back.

He turned to face her. "I haven't been here since that party you threw what— three years ago?"

Tory smiled. "My he-asked-me-to-marry-him-and-I-said-no party."

"A good party," Jack said, "for a good cause. What happened to the pool table?"

"I sold it—it was too big for the room, and it became storage for piles of case work. Jack, what is going on?"

"Got any scotch?"

Tory stood, opened a cabinet, pulled out a bottle. "Great;" he said, "and two glasses."

"I don't want any," Tory said.

"You will," Jack said mordantly. She brought out the bottle, poured him a finger. He opened his briefcase, took out a form letter. "Before I go any further, read this and sign it."

Tory read as Jack sipped his scotch. What began as a boilerplate confidentiality agreement departed from routine in the last paragraph, which authorized the United States government to do a security clearance assessment on the signee. Tory felt a tug of anxiety, looked up sharply at Jack. He presented her with a gold Mont Blanc fountain pen; she signed.

"Okay," Jack started. "The murders last night—"

Tory's breath caught in her chest. Of all the things he might have said, she was expecting this the least. "You mean FISA?"

"Thing is, Tory, if l hadn't missed the shuttle I'd've been there too."

"You?" At once a great many thoughts tumbled and interlocked. "You're a judge on the Foreign Intelligence Surveillance Court." She barely breathed it.

Jack nodded. She looked into her old friend's face. "How long?" she asked.

"Five years. It's a confidential appointment to a secret court. I couldn't tell you. I couldn't tell anyone."

It made sense. Eight years ago, Jack Riley had been instrumental in convincing Tory that she should follow her instincts and become a judge. He'd been her mentor; he'd taken the time and opened the doors. He had made her current life possible. Then, once Tory was on the bench, he had become increasingly more remote.

Though their friendship had never faded, their Guinness-and-burger evenings had gone from twice a month to twice a year.

Now she saw why. She was seeing a parallel world she'd not known. Tory got a second glass from the cabinet, poured herself a finger of scotch. She clicked his glass and they drank.

She had a million questions. "What can I do?" she finally asked.

Jack smiled. "We're down three judges. Drummond's taking the chief's spot, that leaves two. Your name came up. I told them you'd be the perfect candidate."

Tory felt herself blanch. A bolt of adrenaline rushed through her. "Jack— me? I mean, I'm honored, but—" He took a sip of his drink, watched her, waited. "Okay. Let's start from the beginning. FISA court."

Jack smiled. "Established by Carter in 1978. We consider applications from Justice for wiretaps, search warrants, and other investigative tools to collect foreign intelligence—non-US citizens attempting criminal or terroristic acts on US soil—to protect American citizens and institutions. Therefore, the proceedings are ex parte, just the prosecutors and us." He saw something tighten in her face. "You're having a thought."

Tory said nothing for a moment, trying to find the words, trying to be polite. "You know what people say about the FISA court..."

"That we're a rubber stamp? That we never met a wiretap we didn't like?"

"Well, yeah." She hated putting him in this position, but she had to say it. "It's just you and the prosecutors. The fundamental nature of the court means there can never be any advocacy for the defense."

Jack nodded. "Before it existed, there was chaos. Lots of agencies, no due process, no accountability, a huge mess. And yeah, for a long time after 1978, pretty much a rubber stamp. But terrorists are out there, criminal cartels are out there, they want to attack us, they want to hurt our people, and they use phones and computers and we need to know what they're saying. We've caught major players, we've interdicted very bad things, we've stopped some very large and very dangerous plans from killing a lot of US citizens. We serve a critical function.

"And there have been reforms. We pull in subject-matter experts on a lot of topics. That part's fascinating. We have legal advisors and constitutional scholars evaluate some of the trickier cases. And yes, we deny applications— more than before. I know there need to be more reforms. I also know you would be a positive force in making that happen."

A ball of emotion choked Tory's throat. The compliment was so huge she felt humbled by gratitude. "I'd be honored," she said. "But Jack, I'm State. FISA is federal."

"Well, it's interesting." Jack took up the bottle, poured more scotch into both of their glasses. He drank. "Our esteemed elder senator is on the Judicial Oversight committee that funds FISA. He's been looking for an opportunity to put a judge in who would really watch out for New York's interests— a street-wise State judge. Sneaky bastard that he is, he even attached a rider to a spending act to allow it." Then, at the unasked question in her eyes: "I'm not getting any younger, Tory. Term is seven years, only one term per customer, that's the law." Something shifted in him, and he looked away. "You'll be reading wiretaps and interrogation transcripts. They can get pretty rough, but what these people are trying to do is pretty rough, and we're trying to stop them. Tory, I want to recommend you to serve on FISA. Will you do it?"

Tory closed her eyes, sorted through her feelings. Despite her concerns, she felt honor. She felt humility. She could be of service, she could make a difference. "I would like nothing more," she said.

"Excellent," said Jack. "We meet in DC once a month to hear cases. Sometimes twice a month, when there's something urgent that comes up. As the world now knows, there was a townhouse in Georgetown that served as sort of a FISA court dormitory— private bedrooms and offices—so judges didn't have to sleep in hotels or fly long distances twice in a day. I understand they're trying to locate another one."

"Did you stay there?"

"Early on I did. It was very convenient. But—" he seemed oddly hesitant. "I ended up buying a house."

"In DC?"

"A little bit outside."

"I had no idea."

"Nobody does. The place in the Hamptons was never the same after Lucy died. I couldn't stay there. I got the place on the Potomac after my second year on the FISA court."

"Secret court, secret house."

"Very peaceful. Great view of the river. You should come by sometime."

"I'd love that, Jack," Tory said. "If I'm going to DC—perhaps this weekend? Or next?"

He shook his head. "I've got painters coming in. Let me get the place in order, we'll set a date."

"Absolutely. So…what are next steps?"

"You meet with Drummond. He has final approval."

Tory's face fell. "Well, then, I'm screwed." She was serious. "Jack, I went up against Drummond on a news panel last year, a discussion of rape law. I called him 'antediluvian'."

Jack Riley smiled. "He told me. He's actually rather proud of the moniker. That's how conservative he is. Full court's meeting in emergency session tomorrow afternoon. Drummond will want you to be in his office, tomorrow morning, 9:00. Because of the emergency you've already been vetted— signature before was just a formality. If he approves you, you'll join us tomorrow afternoon for your first session. Are you in?"

Tory felt her back straighten. "I'm in," she said, and knocked back the rest of her scotch.

* * *

Judge Al Clemente was at his regular table by the window at the Skyline Club, watching the horses run the oval of Aqueduct racetrack. He'd put a hundred on Sylvan Credo in the fifth but she didn't keep the pace; one horse caught her, then another, and she finished out of the money.

"That's two year olds," said Herb Conover, the Borough President.

"But it won eight of its last nine starts," Al Clemente said, a trifle defensively.

"Then it came to New York—" this was Chuck Bellort, the Nassau County comptroller, a fat man with manicured nails, "and Al bet on it. And halfway through the race, the horse suddenly realizes: *wait a minute— Al Clemente—* and it gets slower, and slower—"

Big laugh all around, Al chuckling along as they turned their attention back to their steaks. Al kept noticing one of the waitresses, a petite blonde with the straight-backed poise of a beautiful child in a ballet class. Chuck followed Al's gaze. "She's young enough to be your daughter, Al—"

"That's never stopped him before—" Herb laughed.

Al wasn't smiling. What did they know, these cronies, these pals? Herb, whom they called Herb Combover behind his back— Al was sure they had some stupid name for him, too. Then his cell phone went; he looked at the caller ID and his heart sank. "Lemme get this." He stood, left his sirloin to cool, walked away from the group at the table.

It was always like this. Eating dinner, in the shower, in the sack with some sweet little tail, his phone would ring, and if Mr. Armstrong's name came up he'd have to stop and answer.

Like Armstrong was the guy's real Goddamn name. When Al was far enough away from the table he hit the button. “Yeah,” he said. He heard the petulance in his voice, didn’t care.

"Al, it's me. I understand you're at Aqueduct."

How did he know that? "Yes." he stepped out the restaurant's door into the hallway.

"What a coincidence," Mr. Armstrong went on. "So am I." And there, leaning against the restaurant entrance, was the big man with the perfectly groomed flat-top. He smiled at Al, hit his phone off. "Let's take a walk," he said.

Al turned off his phone, shaking slightly. This wasn't playing by the rules at all.

They fell to, side by side. Down below the tractors were raking the turf for the next race. "How's your luck been tonight?" the tall man began.

"Piss poor," Al said. No sense lying.

"Well, buddy—" he smiled. "That's about to change. In the next few hours, somebody is going to make you an offer. More power, more work, more money. You'll stay in Brooklyn, our arrangement will stay just the same. But there'll be a new thing on top of it."

To Al, it sounded like a lot of work, and for what? "What if I don't say yes?"

The man flashed him a dark look. "Oh, you'll say yes. You know those clubs you like in DC?" Even as Al blanched, somewhere inside he felt a quickening at the thought. "Only a few places like that in the world, Al. DC's got 'em. And you'll be seeing a lot more of them."

Al stifled his excitement, kept his demeanor professional. "You care to tell me what this is about?" The man didn't say anything. "At least let's get rid of the wiretaps I'm doing." The man was silent. Al had dealt with him long enough to know what that meant. "Okay, what about the drug case I'm running in Brooklyn? Prosecutor's a punk with attitude, he's a pain in the ass."

To Al's surprise, something changed in Armstrong's eyes. "Don't you worry about that case," the large man said. "We'll make it go away—you won't have to lift a finger."

* * *

The next morning, Tory took Siggy out while it was still dark. She entered the dog run, unclipped Siggy's leash and threw a new squeaky ball for the excited dog. But her mind kept racing. She might think the Chief Justice of the Supreme Court's judicial philosophy was out of touch with the realities cops saw every day, but the man was a fastidious legal scholar. She wasn't sure whether to think of this as a job interview or a debate.

Though FISA had been in the news before, it had never had a public persona as it did now, with these murders. She had adjudicated several trials in which secret court warrants had been vital. She understood the need for FISA, but the situation made her worry.

FISA was a closed system, a black box. Even judges like Tory who worked with evidence acquired through FISA had no real understanding of the secret court's internal workings. Though it appeared to be run by men and woman of good will, an innocent person tainted by a FISA-warranted investigation could find government trouble hounding them for the rest of their life, and never know why. There was no way of knowing what exactly was going on in that courtroom.

Now Tory had an opportunity to find out. She went back up to the apartment and fed the dog. Then she stripped, stood in her bathroom, investigated her naked body in the mirror.

She thought she looked horrible; the harsh bathroom light revealed every flaw. She was 36 years old; she watched her diet and tried to get to her treadmill every morning, but even with all that she could plainly see the curves were getting flatter and the flats were growing more curved.

Rafe throwing Wachtel at her, so casually reopening that wound to score a point in a fight. It made her loathe him, even as the memory of Wachtel trying to defend himself in the courtroom made her wince.

Somewhere out there. That boy. How old would he be, now? 5? She looked into the face in the mirror and hated the person she saw.

The judge. She forced herself onto the scale, didn't like what the numbers told her. She'd been lax about the treadmill for a couple of days, and this morning she had a plane to catch. She turned on the shower, hot all the way with a scrinch of cold.

She'd never been to the Supreme Court except as a visitor, a tourist, like any other.

Now she was going to enter its inner sanctum, sit across from the Chief Justice—the soap fumbled out of her hands, hit the floor of the bathtub, shot around as she knelt to retrieve it.

Finally, clean, she stepped out, toweled herself dry. She spent too long on makeup— more than her usual; she had evolved a light hand— and then considered clothes.

A pantsuit, she always felt like a flight attendant when she wore a jacket and skirt. She didn't want this meeting to be about her legs. The black Armani? The pinstripe? Last night she had thought the pinstripe, but today it felt too gaudy.

The Armani, then. Basic black, bought at an outlet store in New Jersey for half what she would have paid in Soho. She selected a simple blouse, light blue, no frills, all business.

It would do. It would have to. She put it on, spent a moment scratching her dog's ears for good luck, called her dog walker, confirmed that the keys would be downstairs with the doorman and left to get a cab to the airport.

* * *

Everyone thought Garry Jenkins was a vet, because of the arm.

He'd been up since sunrise, reading his Bible, bright new day over Washington DC, and his arm had been itching all morning. It itched something awful, even though it had been severed in a car accident in Birmingham when he was 16. People asked him about the missing arm when he hustled the mall near the war memorial, and he always said the same thing: "Arm's doing fine. It's in heaven waiting for me. It's the rest of me down here that needs something to eat."

Jesus was humanity's phantom limb, Gerry knew, living in us even though he was long dead and gone. That was the pain of being a Christian.

Gerry Jenkins kept his stuff under an old railroad bridge by the Potomac. No trains ever ran through it—phantom railroad, Gerry thought. Real railroad had bypassed it long ago.

Three years he'd been doing this, and every day the same. People thought if you were homeless, you didn't have a routine. White nicey-nice tourists would be all scared of you, like you were the prince of lies come to steal their soul, and all you'd be doing was the same thing you did every day. He took two half-full water bottles and a thin bar of soap up the steep hill from the trackbed, performed his ablutions right where he always did. Back at his cart, he shook out a battered plastic Duane Reade bag. He put his Bible in, made his way down the precarious rocks to the bank of the Potomac.

Always something to find. Beer cans, soda cans. Garbage people tossed down, some stuff you could use. He came across two soda bottles, and then some beer cans, put them in his bag. He'd walked half a mile down the embankment when he saw the body in the water.

In one moment his heart was filled with scared bleak sadness. Face down, back to the skies, black hair flowing like seaweed, tangling and curling, like it was reaching for him.

A child. Beautiful little child left like this, water lapping around her like she was moving, like she was going to rise up, climb up on the rocks and continue living, needing him to love her. And he did love her, whoever she was. He dug through the bottles and cans in his bag, came up with the Bible, opened it at random, looked down—Matthew 22— and read to her:

"In the resurrection, therefore, whose wife of the seven will she be? For they all had married her? But Jesus answered and said to them: 'You are mistaken, not understanding scriptures nor the power of God. For in the resurrection they neither marry nor are given in marriage, but are like angels in heaven." He looked at the body in the water, looked back down at the page. What he'd read before had been for her, but this was meant for him: "Then render to Caesar the things that are Caesar's, and to God the things that are God's."

He sat with the body a few minutes longer. He didn't want to leave her, but he knew what the book wanted him to do. Go to Caesar. He repacked his bottles and cans, shouldered the bag and made his way south, looking for a cop.

* * *

The shuttle to DC was half empty. Tory had been up late printing out material on FISA on Lexis and various other legal databases. She went through it all during the flight, and what she saw both fascinated her and made her uncomfortable.

The Foreign Intelligence Surveillance Act, or FISA, had been a response to widespread covert domestic surveillance of civil rights and antiwar activists in the '60s and '70s. The court authorized surveillance of foreign suspects and the American citizens with whom they communicated. It considered applications and evidence from the Office of Intelligence Policy and Review, a shadowy bunch of prosecutors who wrote wiretap warrants exclusively for FISA's judges to adjudicate.

What FISA approved were warrants for audio and video surveillance, physical entry into private property, and the collection of business records. In regular courts, a wiretap warrant had to state probable cause, as required by the Constitution, based on documentable criminal activity. As a judge, Tory had on a number of occasions thrown out wiretap applications lacking probable cause—the Constitution had not given government the right to go on fishing expeditions against anyone it chose.

But FISA was different. Tory could not believe that fair-minded American judges would ignore the Constitution in their daily labors, but at the same time, the increasingly dangerous state of the world had changed the rules. The idea behind FISA was to keep a balance between government intrusion and the need to protect

American citizens. FISA was intended as the arena in which this contradiction was properly addressed.

That was the theory. It would be interesting to see how it worked in practice.

As the plane descended, she could see the mall in the distance, the Washington monument and the White House and the rotunda of Congress. The sight never failed to stir her.

Corny, she knew, but true. The plane landed at Ronald Reagan Airport; United States marshals, charged with protecting all federal judges, met her at the gate and took her to a car.

* * *

Merle Drummond was taller and more imposing than Tory remembered, but she'd only seen him in person twice, once on a stage at a lectern speaking to a room full of newly minted judges and a second time during their rocky TV roundtable encounter. Behind his bushy eyebrows his eyes were intelligent, and surprisingly kindly. He wore a dark suit and grey tie; on his lapel was a small American flag pin. He stood when Tory entered, came around the desk and shook her hand.

"So—" Merle Drummond looked her in the eye. "Antediluvian, eh?"

Tory felt herself blush. "Sir, I sometimes speak from passion—"

"Honest debate is the heart of the law, Judge Parker." He waved the problem away. Tory immediately liked him in a way she never had before. "Have a seat," he said, and sat on the other side of his massive desk. The office was beautiful, deep wood walls and shelves upon shelves of law books. "I'd like to discuss your background." He opened a distressingly thick file. "Your parents are both scholars—your father is quite extensively published."

"My mother is, as well," Tory said. He didn't answer that, turned several pages.

"Tufts BA, Columbia Law." He looked up. "Not schools at which your father taught."

"I didn't want to spend college knowing all the teachers socially through my parents." He seemed to accept that.

"Do you still play pool?"

"Just for me," Tory answered easily. Of course it would have come up on her background check. "I haven't entered an official tournament in years."

"Hmmm," Drummond flipped more pages. Tory abruptly wondered if the man had some inherent prejudice against pool. Finally he grunted. "You began as a prosecutor and spent a lot of your career in the New York County sex crimes unit. You saw some very nasty cases."

"Rapes, sex-slave kidnappings, child molestation—"

"You had a 98% conviction rate."

"That reflects my team, not just me."

"But, successful as you were, you went on to become a judge."

She treaded carefully. "I had seen judges who were incurious. I felt I had more to offer."

"Ambition sometimes overwhelms more virtuous aspects of personal character." Drummond stared her down with his imposing eyes, looked back at her file.

Tory took a breath. The man was, famously, a Christian; he spoke to church groups and anointed himself with oil each day. A pall of hopelessness filled her chest.

Drummond looked up. "Often you've offered first, second, even third-time drug offenders rehab in lieu of incarceration. Rehab programs are fine when they work, but a crime calls for a sentence."

Tory sat up. "I've sentenced drug dealers to triple lifetime sentences without the slightest regret. Nobody can look at my record and say I'm soft on crime."

"Indeed," he said, "they cannot." He turned several pages, pressed his lips together until they were a thin white line. "Now, in the matter of Irving Wachtel— what happened there?"

Tory felt her posture tighten, even as her heart sank. She took a deep breath. "The case was a very nasty rape-murder, it got an enormous amount of attention in the press. Because of that, the defendant asked for a non-jury trial, so it was all up to me. The prosecution's lead witness was a detective I'd worked with before. He ran rings around Wachtel's story. At the time, I went with what I thought was the best decision I could make." She swallowed, cleared her throat. "I was wrong." She looked up into the eyes of the chief justice of the Supreme Court. "I could make excuses, I could say I'd only been a judge for a year, I could blame the detective, in my mind I've done all those things. But that doesn't change the fact that the defendant committed suicide a week after the verdict, another man confessed to the crime, and now Mr. Wachtel's young son is growing up without ever knowing his father." She shook her head. "It's like a hole in me, that case. It doesn't get better. The only thing it's taught me is that at every turn I have to try harder."

Silence in the grand room. Something hard glittered in Chief Justice Drummond's eyes. "We all have things we would do over if we could. We are imperfect beings," he said softly, "and the world is an imperfect place."

Many people had weighed in over the years on what Tory should feel about Wachtel. Nobody had ever said anything quite so simple, or so profound.

"Consider it part of the education of a judge, " he said, and returned to the file before him. The room filled with the quiet sound of pages being turned. At length he looked up. "You've also, on at least two occasions, retained relationships with some of the people who have passed through your court." She thought she detected a scowl in his eyes. "Do you think that's entirely proper?"

Whoever had compiled this file had done a scarily precise job. She took in a deep breath. "I had a case where a little girl's testimony put her father away for the murder of her mother. Extending myself to that girl was the least I could do." That had been post-Wachtel, both in chronology and evolution.

He looked at the file. "There are situations here when you've extended yourself to people less innocent than that. You've retained a relationship with—" he glanced down to get the name right. "Penelope Jefferson."

Penny. "When you and a witness are being threatened by the Glock 9s, a violent drug gang, you bond." She'd thought of calling Penny Jefferson while she was in DC, but figured she wouldn't have the time. This conversation convinced her she should.

Drummond smiled with tight lips. "For the people we adjudicate through FISA, continuing relationships aren't on the agenda."

"I understand that, your honor," Tory was quick to say. "It is ultimately suicidal to be guided by sympathy for those who seek to destroy us."

"We must never be afraid to be ruthless. We do more than merely approve wiretaps, Judge Parker. We are the unseen immune system that keeps the body healthy and whole."

Something about his words sent a shiver up her spine. "I would like very much to be a part of that work," she said, with absolute sureness.

He looked at her a long time, his eyes boring deep into hers. Then, finally, he smiled. "FISA is going to meet at 1:00 at our courtroom at the DOJ on Pennsylvania Avenue. Be in the lobby at 12:45, I'll take you up, show you around before you get sworn in."

Sworn in? Tory raised an eyebrow. "It's really that easy?"

"The President will accept my choice." His smile was dazzling.

Tory found herself so surprised by her own excitement she was at a loss for words. "Mr. Chief Justice, I will work my hardest to fulfill the trust you have given me."

"Jack Riley said you would." They shook hands. "Now, on another matter entirely, I make it a point to spend some social time at least twice a year with each of the Justices I work with. Managerial quirk of mine, you might say— I like transparency." Tory had heard that about the Chief Justice, though she'd never imagined him cracking open his schedule to fit her in. "As it happens," he went on, "at our house we have a pool table in the basement. Doesn't get much use with the boys now in college, but back in law school I will admit I was something of a shark. Be delighted if some evening you would join my wife and me, we'll play a few games."

Of all the things he had said over the course of the meeting, this was by far the most surprising. "I'd like that, Mr. Chief Justice," Tory said. They stood and shook hands.

"I look forward to your contribution to the court." He let her out the door.

* * *

The courtroom, on the top floor of the Department of Justice building on Pennsylvania Avenue, was soundproof, windowless, and swept daily for listening devices. Approaching it, down a long white hall monitored by cameras, Tory had never been more intimidated in her life. Drummond tapped a shielded keypad at the door. "We all have different codes for the alarm system," he explained, "so that the computers can track who is in this room at any time."

Several men and one woman were inside, in quiet conversational clusters. Around them, grouped in a semicircle, were desks. At the center was a high-tech bank of large flat screens and audio equipment, a perfect setup, Tory immediately saw, for the group perusal of surveillance footage and other video evidence.

"You will note," Drummond said, "we do not wear robes. This is shirtsleeves work." And then: "Gentleman—Madam—" Drummond got their attention. "As you know, as chief executive of this court, I will be stepping in indefinitely to carry the workload left when Walter Grant was taken from us. I have selected two capable judges: one is with us right now, and one is downstairs in a meeting; I am confident he will be here soon. Please take your seats—"

As the eight judges went to their assigned desks; Jack Riley passed Tory and whispered: "you made it, kid." Drummond handed her a congressional document that authorized cross-designation of a state judge to this Federal court. Then he produced a bible; Tory lay her hand on it, and Drummond began: "I, New York State Supreme Court Judge Tory Parker—"

She hated the honorific, went with: "I, Tory Parker—"

"Do solemnly swear to uphold the Constitution in my service to this court—"

"Do solemnly swear to uphold the Constitution in my service to this court—"

"So help me God." There was a smattering of applause as Drummond led Tory around to one of the two empty desks. Once she was seated, Drummond went to the central desk, banged a gavel. "The FBI has evidence the murders of our colleagues was a drug cartel operation, Colombian in origin."

Tory gulped. Eduardo Nieto. And she was prosecuting his baby brother. The events of the last two days clicked into place like puzzle pieces. And at that moment a buzzer softly rang, and the door was opened from outside by a United States Marshal, who ushered in the justice who would complete the court.

Tory's mouth dropped open when Al Clemente strode into the room.

* * *

Two hours later, during a break in the proceedings, Al Clemente approached Tory. He was eating a sugar-drizzled pastry. "Judge Parker," he said, his mouth full, his gaze locked at her chest. "You believe this? It's like being inducted into the Judge hall of fame!"

Tory winced. It wasn't like that at all. He was shorter than she remembered, well-fed, thick without being fat. He was wearing too much cologne.

"Hello, Judge Clemente." She offered her hand. He shook it hard, up and down like a politician. "You're currently working with someone I know," Tory went on. "Rafe Carr."

He finished the last bite of pastry. Tory waited for him to stop chewing. "AUSA," he said, and swallowed. "Young guy. Kinda got this pissed-off vibe all the time. You should tell him it never hurts to smile."

She couldn't take his cologne for one more second. "Excuse me, Judge—"

"Al"

"Excuse me Al, but I need to talk to Jack Riley—" she pointed across the room.

"Of course, Tory. It's gonna be a treat, you and me, working shoulder to shoulder."

She forced a smile, slipped by him and sought out Jack.

He was standing in conversation with Judge King, a strong-boned woman with piercing eyes. "Tory—" Jack said as she approached. "Rebekkah King."

"We met before," Tory again shook her dry hand. "Though I didn't get a chance to say how much I enjoy the humor in your decisions."

The older woman's eyes sparkled. "I never think anyone reads them except the parties involved," she said. "And even then, not always."

"Would you mind if I steal Jack from you for a moment?" Then, out of earshot: "Is there a place we can talk?"

"Conference room off to the side." Jack led Tory through one of the doors at the back. They were in a smaller meeting room with an oval table. Tory waited until the door was shut before saying: "Jack," Tory said. "Al Clemente?"

Jack's shoulders went up slightly. "Not my first choice."

"Jack— he's awful. According to Rafe and a lot of other people, he's incompetent."

Jack put his hands up. "There are judges who are poets of the bench, and Al Clemente is not one of them."

"He's a political beast, appointed by someone as a favor to someone else. He owes God knows what to God knows who."

"Tory, we don't like to think politics plays a role at this level of the judiciary, but it does." He took a seat at the conference table. "Because of the murders, once again we are in the public eye. Our chief suspect is Hispanic, and FISA has never had a sitting Hispanic judge."

Tory saw the logic. "But surely there must be better-suited Hispanic judges."

"Drummond calls the shots, but who knows what pressure was brought to bear. There are people in power who look at every crisis as an opportunity." The jovial camaraderie drained from his face. "My advice is, make it work with Judge Clemente. Drummond believes harmony is important, and it would be a shame to break up the team." Tory was aware of the implicit message. "I expect," he went on, "you'll find it'll all work out for the best."

The Secret Court's afternoon session was given over to the presentation of investigations by the Justice Department's Office of Intelligence Policy and Review (OIPR). The OIPR was a governmental office whose bland, wonky title masked a complex mission: when an Assistant Attorney General, or the AG himself, felt that wiretaps— audio or visual surveillance orders—were needed in a secret terrorism investigation, he or she presented the evidence to the OIPR. OIPR then created a brief specifying in detail the person being targeted, the evidence that led the government to request the wiretap, what minimization procedures would be in place to protect the privacy of nontargeted individuals, and why FISA had jurisdiction. These briefs were presented to the Secret Court, either in mailings to each member separately or, in times of crisis, at presentations before the full seated body. The court would then debate the merits of each element of the request and make a ruling. OIPR would go back to the AG with the results.

OIPR were the only prosecutors the FISA judges ever saw.

Over the course of the afternoon, OIPR presented the FISA judges seven cases; four involved Middle-Eastern figures, both in America and abroad, while the fifth involved the murderous inner workings of the Russian mob. The sixth, as it turned out, had special relevance to Tory.

That case was presented by Henry Severn, Chief Prosecutor of OIPR, a sharp-as-tacks vet who had worked his way up from Naval Intelligence. Though older, he was fit, tall, in a pinstripe suit.

Drummond banged the court into session. As Severn's clerks passed out folders of evidence to each judge, Severn read the docket number, and began. "May it please the court." His voice was surprisingly soft. "In the last week two separate FISA-authorized wiretaps, one in Miami and the other in Los Angeles, have yielded corroborating information that an assassin under the employ of Colombian national Eduardo Nieto is now in America. This assassin's identity is unknown to US law enforcement, though the consensus is that he is male, likely a Colombian national who speaks both Spanish and English. His AKAs include El Limpiador, the cleaner, as he 'cleans up' people regarded as problems to the Nieto organization. He is implicated in the killing of several Colombian judges and senators. It is thought by the FBI—" and here, Chief Prosecutor Severn looked directly at Tory— "that he is in America to interfere with the trial of Mr. Nieto's younger brother, about to begin in New York."

Tory felt her breathing change. *This guy kills judges, and he's coming after me.*

Severn went on: "In the intercepted Miami phone call, reference was made to an illicit shipment of two ounces of high-carat Colombian emeralds, intended as payment to this assassin for his expenses and services in America. It was stated that these emeralds had arrived safely in Miami, and were being sent by courier to New York City.

"It is known that Eduardo Nieto has previously used Colombian emeralds as currency in America. In three instances, in Miami, in Los Angeles and in New York, stones were converted into cash by US-licensed gemologists of Colombian extraction. The FBI is reasonably certain that, in the current instance, the emeralds will be converted into cash in New York City. OIPR requests of this court that wiretaps and search warrants for business records be granted against 24 New York-area licensed gemologists named on exhibit 12, in the hopes of intercepting information leading to the arrest of this international fugitive."

Judge Kottle opened the folder. "Is this package complete?" He held up the list of gemologists.

The prosecutor nodded. "Transcripts, indictments and current intel. Judge, this is a time-sensitive matter—"

"Indeed it is." Drummond cleared his throat. "Questions, ladies and gentlemen?"

Tory held up a hand. "Because I'm presiding over Baby Nieto's trial, I'm the most likely target for this man. Thus I feel I must recuse myself from this decision."

"Of course, Judge Parker." Drummond nodded. "Any other questions?"

Judge Hart raised his hand. Tory had noticed him upon first coming in: he was a remarkable looking man, with strong cheekbones and sensitive eyes. "Why would he go through a legal dealer?" he wanted to know.

"He has in the past." Severn went on: Colombia was the world's largest supplier of emeralds; two of the three major mining areas had been nationalized. The third was thought to be connected to cocaine money. "We know Nieto's emeralds have been top quality. Only a gemologist would know he was seeing excellent stones, and pay accordingly."

"But if the stones are that good, the courier could just go into any good jewelry store—"

"Nieto only does business with people he trusts," Severn replied. "Behavioral at Quantico sees a fundamental need for control, especially in financial matters."

"Anybody else?" Drummond asked. No one responded. "Right, then, let's vote."

Severn and his young clerk left the chamber, and Drummond polled the judges. The vote was 10 to authorize, none against, with Tory recusing.

"I hope they get him" Drummond said, when it was over.

"So do I," Tory said, and the tension in her gut didn't dissipate as the court moved on to the next case.

* * *

Washington DC had a reputation for violent crime; dead bodies were fished out of the Potomac with some regularity. Sometimes children died there, drowning in accidents. But in the last three years, four adolescent girls had been found floating in the Potomac whose bodies bore witness to profound and terrible degradations before their demise.

Kelly Kelleher had done autopsies on the previous two; the first had been handled by her predecessor at the DC Medical Examiner's office. Now the fourth was waiting on exam table 5. Kelly sat in her office reviewing her notes on the previous autopsies. The first girl had been found in early Spring; the second a year later; the third this Spring. None had been identified. And now the doer was speeding up. That was never a good thing, Kelly knew.

In the cold room, Kelly Kelleher nodded at her Diener, Morris, a medical student from Georgetown. Morris unzipped the bag as Kelly turned on the voice app to record her impressions. "Floater," she said, "female, 10-13 years of age. No clothing, no ID. Face obliterated by—" she went into the empty eye socket with forceps, dug a lead pellet that had lodged in the bone—" a shotgun blast, leaving pellet in the left orbit. Lower mandible smashed, perhaps to make dental identification more difficult. Ligature marks at the neck, erythema and swelling. Whip marks on the chest, shoulders, buttocks, dorsal thighs. Round burns in profusion—" she counted 23— "around the groin and buttocks—cigar burns," she realized. When the external wounds had been catalogued, she took up the chest saw, cut the Y, went inside. After ascertaining that this was a normal specimen of a pre-adolescent girl, she began to concentrate on the last hours of her life. Kelly photographed the ligature marks at the neck, then cut down to see internal damage.

The windpipe wasn't crushed; the bones of the neck were intact. The girl had been tied, or in a noose, but that hadn't been what killed her. No water in the lungs, but that was true in a third of all drownings: in many people, water hitting the trachea caused a reflex closure of the vocal cords. "Contents of the stomach:" she sliced it open, scraped food remnants into a bowl and weighed them. "Dog or cat food." As in the previous murders. She knew the cops had two theories: either the doer had a dog or cat, and she was stealing the animal's food, or else that's what the doer fed his girls before he killed them. One did not necessarily preclude the other.

Slowly she worked her way down to the genital area, again took photographs before beginning dissection. After a moment, she spoke for the notes: "Lacerations in the lower bowel 2-6 inches above the anus. Lacerations in the vaginal canal-"

"It's like somebody stuck a kitchen knife in there," Morris said.

Kelly agreed. "Consistent with a large-blade unserrated knife." She took more pictures. Morris couldn't stand it. "Doc, shotgun? Drowning? Hanging? How'd she die?"

However she'd died, Kelly could see, she'd had a hellacious time of it. Some sick fuck had used this poor girl as a human sex toy for days, perhaps weeks, and when he no longer needed her, he'd tortured her— slowly, drawing it out for maximum pain— until she died.

* * *

At the end of the day's session, Al Clemente was deep in conversation about the West Coast racing circuit with Judges AO Hart and Fenton Kottle when Tory pasted a smile on her face and deliberately joined the group. After an unamusing anecdote about a betting mishap at Santa Anita, Tory interjected: "Judge Clemente— I'm glad we'll be working together."

Al Clemente looked her up and down as if she were a Lamborghini. "We should have dinner in New York sometime, eh? Just the two of us?"

Tory thought fast. "Maybe we could include Rafe—" she said, "after your current trial ends, of course."

"Right, right." That wasn't his mental image at all.

"Got to run. I have plans to meet a friend here in DC." Thank God she could always claim that excuse. "Nice meeting you all—" Tory shook hands all around and left the room.

Waiting for her outside were three agents from the US Marshal Service. She was introduced to Gar Burton, a slightly older man with a military bearing and a complicated handlebar moustache. "Judge Parker, we've had a request to come with you to New York, do a security analysis." He checked his watch. "Next shuttle's at 7:30."

"I'm meeting a friend for coffee,"

"Where?"

Tory pulled out her cellphone. "El Chuleta d'Oro on Martin Luther King Jr. Boulevard."

One of the Marshals couldn't help himself: "That's a terrible neighborhood," he said.

Gar Burton frowned. "Is this 'friend' someone we might look at as a security risk?"

"Her name is Penelope Jefferson. She's a recovered prostitute and drug addict who turned her life around. I wrote a letter of recommendation to help her get into social work school."

Gar Burton toyed with the ends of his moustache. "Right, then. Orgera and Linser, you go into the diner first, work out sightlines before the judge enters. Judge Parker, they'll sit as diners at the next table, if anything untoward occurs they'll grab you and get you out of there."

"Don't sit too close to us," Tory suggested. "Penny can smell a cop a mile away."

*   *   *

Penelope Jefferson was a dark-skinned woman with strong Nigerian cheekbones and close-cropped hair. Seven years before, Penny had been a prostitute on the streets of Bed Stuy. She had been an invaluable prosecution witness in Tory's first big drug-gang case as a judge.

From her position on the street, and her own purchasing of drugs, Penny had been able to identify virtually all of the members of the Glock 9s. During part of her testimony two men stood in the courtroom, held up pictures of her and her young son, and yelled out her address and the address of his school. Tory yanked her into her robing room and kept her under the protection of her own security team until the situation was cleared. It turned out Penny was a voracious reader; during this enforced time together, they'd ended up talking about Toni Morrison books they'd both read. Two years later Tory was doing one of her talks in the public schools when a handsome young African-American teenager stepped shyly up and said that his mom was manning the cupcake table at the back of the room and wanted to say hi.

Thus had begun one of Tory's more unusual and rewarding friendships, cemented when Penny asked Tory to write a recommendation to help her get into a two-year social work program. Now, a hundred years and a thousand miles from her streetwalking days, Penny had built a new life for herself in Washington, sending her son off to Tulane University while holding down a job as the intake social worker at a health clinic on S Street.

When Tory came into the restaurant, Penny stood, and Tory saw that the statuesque frame had not changed. "The rest of us get older," Tory said as they air-kissed. "You stay the same."

Penny barked out a loud laugh. "Wish that were true." She nodded at the two white men perusing menus two tables away. "You have protection again?"

"It comes and goes—" Tory shrugged it off. They sat.

"Cafe con leches are great here. And the roast pork. And they make their own hot sauce."

They ordered, and then Tory asked: "How's the clinic?"

"It's a little rough right now," Penny sighed. "Our HIV patients are getting older—that's good. But I keep seeing these dual-diagnosis cases, young kids coming in with sexually transmitted diseases and also mental problems they're self-medicating with street drugs, and we're not a mental clinic. We're body, not mind. So we give them a referral and they never go and that becomes a revolving door." She shook her head.

"That's a lot to deal with." Concern stirred in Tory. "And Kendrick's at Tulane—"

"He's doing fine. He joined a frat down there, Alpha something something, I never get it straight. Keeping good grades. I was worried, but he's doing it right."

"That's great to hear. You seeing anyone?"

"Like a shrink?"

"Like a *guy—"* Tory said, and they laughed.

"Aah, it's impossible." Penny shook her head. "At work everyone who comes in the door has some STD. Makes me wonder about the guys I meet socially."

"You know too much."

"Funny thing is—" Penny dropped her voice. "I had so much sex as a kid when I didn't want it, and now I could use some, and there's none around." The coffee came; it was as good as Penny had said. "You catch in the news they pulled another little girl out of the Potomac?"

Tory's eyebrows knotted. "I missed all this."

"It's awful," Penny said with a grimace. "Fourth one in the last three years. Sex crimes. Always, like, ten-year-old Hispanic girls, they think. And nobody ever identifies them." It had been a long time since Tory had worked on the Sex Crimes Unit; she felt her professional instincts narrowing in on the story even as her stomach turned queasy.

"Four Jane Does?"

Penny nodded. "And it's disgusting, what these girls went through."

"The police don't have anything?"

"Nada. See, the theory I keep hearing is, it's like a club of high-level political guys, right? Girls are Hispanic, so it's got to be some big drug guy in South America. They buy her, he sends her up, they rip her apart, ask for another."

"That can't be true," Tory said.

"I've seen a lot of shit in my time," Penny said. "I wouldn't be surprised by anything."

Tory sipped her coffee. At this point in her life, she was inclined to agree.

* * *

Immediately after leaving the Justice Department, the man in the suit drove south, out of DC. He was thinking about the day, how the presentations had gone, the remarkable amount of work OIPR had been able to accomplish. He kept along the Potomac, drove until the city had faded away and all that remained were the long white fences of horse country. When he arrived at the driveway, the house was so dark it was hard to see from the road. He clicked the garage opener, entered the single-car garage, waited for the door to lower completely before getting out. He unlocked the door into the kitchen, stepped through. Out of habit he opened the refrigerator, looked inside at the bare shelves before letting the door slap shut. There was never any food in this house, except when he had one of his visitors.

The decor on the first floor was minimally functional: a couch, a chair, a bare coffee table. Nothing on the walls. The man unlocked the door to the cellar, went down a flight of stairs, unlocked a second door.

Inside was a simple metal bed. This was the room in which the relationships began. He took up the pillow, held it to his face and smelled. The odor of his last girlfriend was fading, now; he spent a moment lost in memory, then set the pillow down and entered the second room.

Here was his camera equipment, the makeup vanity with lights like in a theater dressing room, the racks full of frilly, lacy clothing. This was where the relationships blossomed; just walking through this room was heady with memories of all the girls who'd served him here. He used another key to open the third door.

This room was painted entirely black. Even he found this room chilling: this is where the relationships invariably came to an end. He had watched girls die here. He hated the things he had done here, hated the things that had happened here just weeks before, but he knew himself: the more he thought of the horror those girls had suffered, the more an illicit thrill quickened in his veins, hardening his desire.

But even as the well-ingrained responses rode through him, he couldn't help but think: the things I would have been able to achieve in my life, were it not for this sickness. As it is I have to hide myself like a rat, burrowed deep within the cozy cover of the Justice Department.

He left the room light off, walked directly to a desk against the wall, opened and turned on the laptop by feel alone.

When it had booted, he linked with the ArrowHawk intranet, typed in an access code. This opened up the ArrowHawk Group's proprietary encrypted text program.

The man typed an anonymized address from memory, then took a sheet of paper from his jacket pocket, unfolded it and typed, one by one, the names of the 24 gemologists FISA had placed under surveillance. He paused at the end of the list, and thought; for that I deserve a reward. He typed:

> Last delivery a bit too much fat on the bone. Keep future deliveries lean. Ready for another serving.

No sign-off, no signature; the recipient would know who it was from. The man sent the text, and sat back.

Right now the software was scrambling the text's origin and destination signatures before stripping them off. When Eduardo Nieto received it, it would appear that he had sent it to himself.

The man thought: I really should close up and go home. Instead he found himself scrolling through all the pictures he'd taken of his last girlfriend, down here in the basement. Though she had been a little thick in the middle, the progression of images was so erotic that once again it made him want to burst.

* * *

On the ride to the airport, Tory sat back in the Marshal's black Ford and remembered her days on the sex crimes unit, listening to the stories, corroborating the evidence, putting together the cases. The human quest for sexual pleasure sometimes took extremely sick turns, she knew; working on the unit, it became unsurprising how awful people could be, but it was impossible to become inured.

Four dead girls. Some sick fuck was out there, having his orgasms, getting away with murder.

The evidence pictures of Ariel Daumberg crossed her mind. Tory looked out the tinted window at the dark DC streets, allowed herself to think about Wachtel.

Ariel Daumberg had been a young cellist with the New York Philharmonic, beautiful and by all accounts precociously talented, when she left a Halloween party and joined the ranks of New York's headline-making murder victims. Her body was found, tied and duct-taped, on a garbage-strewn hill above the West Side highway. She had been assaulted in a variety of ways; various words had been cut into her skin with a sharp knife. Her nipples and aureoles had been hacked off, and were missing.

The girl's talent, her photogenicity and the horror of the crime all conspired to make her story national. The pressure on the police to solve the case was immense. Midtown North Detective Jerry Sanmartino, an older cop Tory had always looked up to and respected, had been given whatever resources he required to find the doer.

Six days later Sanmartino arrested Irving Wachtel, the superintendent of Ariel Daumberg's building. Recently married, his wife pregnant, Wachtel had kept the building immaculate for eight years. A search of his premises turned up, among items from other female tenants, underwear and a bra belonging to Daumberg. And the brand of duct tape Wachtel used in his basement workshop was the same as that found gagging the dead girl.

Wachtel's computer was impounded; the NYPD's forensic computer specialists were able to determine that at one time he had a small collection of sadomasochistic pictures downloaded onto his hard drive. Under questioning, he was surprised the police had found them; he had deleted all his porn when his wife became pregnant. Unfortunately, one of the photos the NYPD had been able to recover was a young woman, tied up, with the word BITCH written on her abdomen in lipstick.

One of the words carved into Ariel Daumberg's skin was BITCH.

Sanmartino interrogated Wachtel for 13 hours, at the end of which the super signed a statement that he had been sexually obsessed by the beautiful cellist, that he had entered her apartment surreptitiously when he'd known she was out, had collected clothing items from her wardrobe and had worn and used them in sadomasochistic masturbatory fantasies. He denied committing the murder, claiming he had had a fight with his wife that night, and had taken the subway alone to the Greenwich Village Halloween parade. Sanmartino felt strongly that the alibi didn't stand up.

Tory had been a judge for a year when the trial landed on her desk. In pretrial motions, Wachtel's attorney requested a change of venue. Tory denied the change. The crime had been a national media story, and there had been no death threats against the imprisoned

Wachtel. Tory had assured the defense that she would bend over backwards during voir dire to ensure as impartial a jury as possible.

The next day, the defense, feeling that any jury they encountered would be gunning for vengeance for the horrible things that had happened to this young woman, announced they disagreed with her change of venue ruling. But since that was off the table, they wanted a non-jury trial.

Maybe that had been the mistake, Tory thought, as the black Ford merged seamlessly onto the highway. Maybe a jury would have been able to see through Detective Sanmartino. But in a non-jury trial, the burden of sifting through the evidence and coming up with a decision falls squarely on the judge. It was Tory's responsibility, and her responsibility alone.

The trial was short, but every minute of it had been achingly hard. Tory had known Sanmartino from back when she was an ADA. He was older, and he walked in the door with a certain authority to which some part of her— the part that wanted to be the good daughter to the strong father, despite everything— tended to automatically defer.

He had always been one of the good guys, the kind of rock-solid cop whose word was bond. But as the trial went on, Tory could feel the holes in his story in the pit of her stomach.

They were subtle, but they were there. They kept her up at night.

Jerry Sanmartino knew how to present his material in court. Rather like a teacher, she thought, he led the room through every turn of his discoveries, into the interrogation room where Irving Wachtel, wide-eyed and nervous, talked about his pornography and his wife and his underwear thievery and the fact that some part of him always found the idea of a willing female slave erotic, on and on and on. He said his wife had known about the porn, and then he said she hadn't known about all the porn, just some of it. He said things and then took them back and then contradicted himself and then said things he said he didn't mean.

On the stand, Irving Wachtel, fighting for his life with his pregnant wife in the first row, had been adamant that he had not done this thing to Ariel Daumberg. He had been firm and strong and clear. But Jerry Sanmartino had managed to wrap his testimony around Wachtel like a python.

Tory had taken as much time as she'd needed. She'd thought it all through. She'd come, she felt, to the right decision.

Irving Wachtel was guilty. The bailiff pulled him away from his crying wife.

Two weeks later he was dead, alone in a holding cell, hung from a pair of pants tied into a noose.

Six months after that, a drug snitch told his NYPD handler that this crazy asshole in Bed-Stuy had shown him this little shriveled piece of flesh and said it was Ariel Daumberg's nipple. The cops sent the snitch back in wearing a wire, got a full confession on tape, details nobody else could have known.

When they busted the guy, they found everything they needed to put him away forever.

And Tory Parker lived every day knowing that there was a boy out there somewhere who had never known— would never know— his father. And it was her fault, because she'd let a charismatic man's authority override the little voice in her head that knew all along.

It never got better. Somewhere inside, after Wachtel, something broke in her, some final piece of inhibition that she had long held in check without knowing it was there.

She began to go out at night and find men.

They were always there when she played pool. Leering. Interested. Watching her from behind as she bent over to take her shot.

In high school, she'd been disgusted by them. In college, she'd been amused by them. In law school, she'd let one or two of them get close, briefly, but she had way too much work to do for it to go beyond torrid necking in the backs of bars.

After Wachtel, though, something changed. Part of her didn't care anymore. She told herself she wanted to break free and live, but she knew she actually wanted to break out and plummet.

And plummet she did. One night she'd taken her cues and gone to a pool hall on the Lower East Side, not her usual, because of a man she only knew as Hawk. He'd beaten her in the semifinals of a league she used to be in, and she told herself she wanted a rematch.

That had been a lie. And when she woke up in his shithole apartment, her head pounding with hangover, and saw that the tattoos she'd been all over last night were in fact crude images badly drawn, some obviously from prison, she had to suppress the urge to vomit.

She got out of there without ever learning his real name. In the taxi home, she swore to the heavens above she would not do this again.

Three weeks later she pushed a man named Marcus onto her bed and held him down and had her way with him. All because he'd played amazing harmonica in a bar band on the West side. Amazing enough that she hadn't gone home at the end of the last set, had waited, flirted, bought him a drink, and then another.

In the morning, he'd asked what she did. She told him she was a paralegal. It just wasn't worth explaining in depth.

And so it had gone, once every two or three months, during periods when work was particularly stressful. She told herself it was seasonal—four a year—but she knew it was more. But since she told no one, she figured it didn't matter.

When Rafe had pursued her, he actually seemed to be able to cross between both worlds—he played keyboards in a band and could control both side-spin and back-spin on a cue ball, but he'd also gone to law school at Cardozo and had built a solid track record prosecuting criminals in Brooklyn. And, for Tory, the sex had been off the charts. For a few weeks, he'd seemed ideal.

But his not putting evidence into discovery was unforgivable, in Tory's mind.

She had a weakness, she had come to realize. A certain kind of man could get under her skin, make her lose herself against her better judgment.

But now she'd have to give this up. She looked out the taxi window at the planes rising above Reagan International and thought: here I am, the judge with secrets on the Secret Court.

* * *

The flight back to New York was mercifully free of Al Clemente. Tory sat with Gar Burton and his remarkable moustache while his men covered the aisle. Gar had become a Marshal after a 20-year career in the military; until two days before, he'd worked the detail that handled threat assessment for the Supreme Court. He had been told about Nieto's assassin arriving in America. "We're not going to let anything happen to you, Judge Parker. That I promise."

At Tory's building, a van was parked right in front. Burton knocked on the window and agents loaded equipment on handtrucks as a German Shepherd jumped out of a crate.

Tory led the team up in the small elevator. She forced them to wait, opened her apartment door, leashed the excited Siggy, took him to the hallway as the team trooped into the apartment. When Siggy saw the Shepherd, he dropped down, danced around trying to get her to respond, but the police dog was too well trained to be interested.

Gar stepped up. "Tory, I'd like you to meet Bart Alicia." Tory shook hands with a tall man with jet black hair and taut skin. "Bart's DEA, he's been working undercover on Eduardo Nieto, posing as an American entrepreneur in Medellín. He's been to the man's houses. He knows the man's players."

"Most of 'em, not all. Some by name, some just by face."

Tory shook his hand. "I am always amazed at what you undercover guys do," she said.

His face brightened. "Thank you." Then: "I could never be a judge. I'd be dead set against the guilty guy."

"Bart's gonna be on you 24 hours a day until the trial gets underway."

"Twenty-four hours?" Tory was surprised. "Not in shifts?

"Just until we see their approach." Bart explained. "My bet is Eduardo's already sent a team to get to you. They're going to be watching. All I need to do is see one instance where their cover slips, and we can bring the hammer down."

Gar jumped in: "We'll have the van outside every night. When you sleep, Bart sleeps."

Tory's eyebrows etched high. "What about the rest of your life?" she asked.

Bart shrugged. "In court, you'll be covered security-wise, I may slip out, call my mom, buy socks and underwear. When I take a day off, you'll have coverage from the Marshals. But even then I'll never be far." He let Siggy smell him. "Were you going to walk him? I'll come."

In the elevator, Tory considered Bart. Some women might have found him attractive; he had an easy charm, but that was a tool of the trade. "So—" she said, once they were on the street. "How did you get in with Eduardo Nieto?"

"The man's a gambler. We knew he played occasionally at one casino at Medellín. When we got intel he was going, I'd show up, pretending to be a rich American financier. After a while he invited me to a poker game at his finca. I kept him amused by losing money to him, and then winning it back." He smiled. "Actually, long-term, I came out ahead."

Every undercover cop Tory had ever met had nerves of steel. "What's he like?"

Bart considered. "He's a bastard," he said finally. "He thinks he's king of the world."

"Did Baby ever come up?"

"All the time. See, in his mind, he's an equal to the United States— not the president, presidents come and go, the whole country. He's got this thing about how he wants to speak at the UN." Bart shook his head at the craziness. "When you guys popped Baby, that was the end for me. He felt betrayed by the US, and I was the local representative, out there by the pool." They watched in silence as Siggy figure-eighted back and forth at the base of a lamppost, detecting every nuance of smell. Bart went on: "He's got two teams I know about here in America— a West Coast team and an East Coast team. They're the enforcers. If a drug deal goes bad, if someone tries to rip someone off, they make sure that person dies. If they want it to be quiet, the person dies of a heart attack. If they want to send a message, they take out the person's entire family."

Tory, watching Siggy, felt her stomach twist into scratchy anxiety. She had seen cases like that— entire families killed down to the babies in their cribs, and all the police could ascertain was that it was the result of a drug deal gone bad.

"They're professionals," she said.

"Extremely," Bart said. "A few of these guys are private contractors from companies like The ArrowHawk Group, went down as part of US/Colombian drug eradication efforts, Plan Colombia and the rest of them. They spent too long in-country and went native, got corrupted by the dark side." For more than a generation, the US had spent billions on drug eradication programs with the ever-shifting Colombian government. Tons of herbicide had been sprayed on Colombian coca fields, an ongoing effort that continued to this day. Tory knew there was a United States military presence down there; she'd never thought about US companies sending down their own private armies, but from various deniability and PR standpoints, it made sense. "The East- and West-coast teams I know about," Bart went on, "put together an American ex-military man and a Colombian soldier, regular military or narco-gang paramilitary. The American knows how America works; the Colombian communicates with Nieto's people down South." Standing in the open talking about this, as Siggy sniffed everything along his route, Tory felt vulnerable.

"And you would recognize them?" she asked.

"East Coast guys, yeah. West Coast, there's one guy I heard about but never met. American ex-military. Big balding guy. If he walked up right now, I'd know what to do."

"Do the teams ever work together?"

Bart paused. "Story I heard was that they came together to do those Secret Court judges— but that's just a rumor, I don't know if it's true."

"So—" she heard the squeak in her voice, cleared her throat. "These are the guys who'll be coming after me."

Bart shook his head. "They'd be part of it; I mean, if you were adjudicating a standard mid-level Nieto trial, they probably would be. But since you're the judge in Eduardo's brother's trial, they're probably gonna send someone special for you."

"El Limpiador—The Cleaner."

Bart nodded. "Right. So you know. But don't worry—he'd need the East Coast team to set things up, and I know them. Besides, I met him as well, so I know what he looks like."

"You do?"

"Little runty guy. In it for the money. Trust me, you're gonna be fine."

* * *

When Tory got back to her apartment, her dishes and the food in her cabinets had been set in neat piles on the floor, and all her furniture had been moved away from the walls.

"That Shepherd still here?" Tory asked the nearest Marshal.

"Naah, K9 unit went back down five minutes ago."

"Good," said Tory, and unclipped Siggy's leash. The dog, sniffing mightily, wandered utterly confused from room to room.

Gar stepped up to Tory. "This'll interest you, Judge." He led her through a thicket of electronic equipment to an open laptop. "Reverse directory for this address, cross-indexed with public records. These are your neighbors." He scrolled down the list. "Mrs. Fergusson in 7-F?"

"She's nice," Tory said defensively.

"Thirty years ago she was convicted of vandalizing abortion clinics in Ohio."

"Stop!" Tory pleaded. "I don't want to see these people in the elevator and know this. Is there anyone I have to be actively concerned about?"

"Naah," he said. "Maybe the former gay porn star who embezzled—"

"Gar, leave it."

Half an hour later Tory's furniture and dishes had been put back, a new lock had been installed in her door and Bart was in the van downstairs, ready to race upstairs if she hit the not terribly attractive panic button on the simple silver bracelet they'd given her. She let the last agents out, felt exhausted, but there was one piece of evidence from the Secret Court that she needed to see.

She dug through the boxes of transcripts and recordings and thumb drives, found one labeled 'Guantanamo Interview Excerpts', slid it into the slot on her laptop. This was evidence she would never see if she weren't on FISA; in a standard trial she would get a transcript, often with redactions, and a stipulation from the Government that it represented a true account of the evidence she couldn't see. But this was raw footage of the interrogation that led to the arrest of Baby Nieto. The general public was not allowed to see this, and she would soon know why.

Siggy jumped up and curled next to her on the couch. Tory clicked the video on, sat with a legal pad and a pen, Siggy's heavy head on her knee. There on the screen was a standard interrogation room, the camera looking through a one-way mirror at cinderblock walls, a desk and a chair. A timecode on the tape told Tory this had been videoed 12 months earlier. After twenty seconds, the door opened and two burly GIs in uniform brought in a detainee with a square black bag over his head. They removed the bag, and to Tory's surprise it was a woman, a furious feisty Chicana spitting invective in Spanish at her captors: "You Americans bring me to Guantanamo to put me in a cage forever. You talk of freedom freedom freedom, but it is only freedom for Americans and their companies."

Tory hit pause on her remote, took a deep breath, rubbed Siggy's ears, then rewound a little, played the woman's entrance again. She made notes on her pad as the video streamed.

"We do not recognize this concentration camp you have brought me to. We do not recognize the justice system of Colombia—when the judges get in our way, we kill them. We will gladly export those same techniques to the United States if you do not leave us alone. That is my statement, that is all I will say." With that, she leaned back, crossed her arms, stared boldly into the camera behind the mirror until the interrogator signaled and the two GIs took her away.

The next scene showed another interrogation room. The time code told Tory that eight months had passed. When the door opened, the woman came in freely, no bag on her head, and for a moment Tory didn't recognize her. Her hair was shorn; she was thinner, her fire was gone. My God, Tory thought, and checked again: eight months. What had they done to her?

The questions started, less an interrogation than a conversation. The woman spoke so quietly that Tory had to turn up the volume, but all at once she deciphered what had happened.

Ovarian cancer. She must have had it when they arrested her. And here it came, the interrogator explained: we've offered you treatment at Sloan Kettering, America's best cancer hospital, if you tell us how Nieto gets cocaine into the US. After a long pause the woman said: Shipping containers. On boats. He has customs officers in America who know which containers have the cocaine. Baby oversees the operation in the US. They don't need to disguise the drugs as long as the right customs inspector inspects the containers.

There is it, Tory thought. They gave it to NYPD, let them make the pop on the boat because they didn't want any trace of Guantanamo on the arrest. How did the NYPD know which boat to check? As Cornelia had put it, "a tip".

One question remained. Tory searched through the boxes of materials, couldn't find anything. She looked up at the time: almost 11:23 pm.

Drummond had told her specifically to call him until midnight if she had any questions.

She found his number, dialed it into her brand-new securitized cell phone, thinking how odd it was that she was about to call the Chief Justice of the Supreme Court at home at this hour.

It rang three times. He picked it up himself. "Judge Parker," he said.

"Mr. Chief Justice—" It felt like some strange dream. "I hope it's not too late."

"Anytime until midnight. Sometimes you'll get me, sometimes you won't, and it'll have to wait. How may I be of service to you?"

"Three questions: I've just been reviewing the video of the interrogation of Fernandia Morales. I was wondering whether transcripts of the complete interrogation were available—"

Long pause. "To be honest, I don't see why you need them. What's on the tape is probable cause enough, don't you think?"

"I like to have the whole picture."

He softened. "We'll see. There might be some procedural problems. What else?"

"How did the ArrowHawk Group get tied to Nieto?"

There was a pause. "Not ArrowHawk per se, I don't think," Drummond said. "A tiny fraction of their employees appear to have switched sides. Not the first time we've seen the corruptive influence of cocaine money." Then he chuckled. "It's the kind of thing our friends at the CIA call 'blowback'. When the US began the cocaine interdiction effort, the spraying and all that, they didn't want US forces actively involved in counterintel against the drug overlords. So they brought in one of the private security firms."

Tory nodded. "Like in Iraq."

"Precisely. In fact, it was largely the same companies in both theaters. ArrowHawk is, I believe, a division of Beschmel Group. And, yes, it would appear they had some problems in Colombia with their men getting corrupted by the drug lords. I think they kept a much tighter leash on their boys in the Mideast."

Tory was shocked. "Beschmel's a huge important company. I'm surprised this isn't better known."

"I expect they stamp it out wherever they find it. And besides, as you say, they're quite large. I imagine there are a lot of things that go on that never make it into the *New York Times*. Anything else I can help you with?"

Tory checked her notes. "What happened to Morales? The woman on the tape?"

Long pause. "She was brought up to Sloane Kettering for treatment, and after the police interdicted the boat someone walked into her hospital room, slit her throat, and lit her on fire."

"My God—" Tory's stomach lurched toward nausea.

"We don't know how they knew she was there," Drummond went on. "Perhaps she told a family member, and word got back. All of which proves, once again, that Eduardo Nieto is not someone with whom to trifle."

* * *

The day the boat got busted, Customs Agent Wesley Rexroth had become a fugitive. Eduardo Nieto had promised safe passage to Colombia, and his man Armstrong had delivered. And at first it really had seemed like a tropical paradise: a house on the beach, a girl to clean and cook. But he didn't like the food, he didn't like the people, and, eight months later, he found more than anything that he missed his son.

He'd walked away from a life: a co-op apartment, a girlfriend, a career as a New York harbor Customs Agent with a profitable sideline falsifying the paperwork on shipping containers filled with cocaine. Two months after he disappeared his mother had died in her nursing home; Wesley knew his disappearance had played a part. He hadn't even asked to go to the funeral— that would have been out of the question. Armstrong had ruled that even going back up to see her grave anytime, even years from now, was never going to happen.

But the most galling thing was the thought of his ex-wife raising Ozzie, filling his head with all her bullshit negativity. They day he'd fled the city, he'd taken a quick side trip to his son's school, walked down the hall to his classroom, heart pounding, ready to grab him and get him the hell out of there, but at the last minute he'd chickened out. It would be harder to travel with a six-year old; the media would freak, they'd do a national alert.

He'd turned around and left. He would wait until he had everything in place.

Now he had a new passport, a Colombian one in his new name, courtesy of Eduardo Nieto. And every day for months he had built his plan.

He would go to New York, he would walk down that hallway to the classroom door. He would go through and get his son and bring him down here.

He knew the risks he'd be taking, reentering America and grabbing Ozzie. But the rewards were vast: a new life, just the two of them in a Colombian fishing village on the Pacific, away from his ex-wife and all her lies.

Him and his boy.

Armstrong had said over and over not to even consider going back to the States, but once he'd gone and come back, what could they do?

On the flight north, his one worry was passport control in New York, but he knew: Nieto got people in and out of America all the time. They did rock-solid work with passports. And indeed, upon landing, his passport worked beautifully. The bored flunky behind the counter completely accepted that he was Felix Hoffman, a Colombian national of German ancestry. And with that, he hailed a cab to the Waldorf Hotel in Manhattan.

He had prepaid the room for two weeks with the intention of leaving with the boy the minute the opportunity arose. They would make their way to Florida, buy a used fishing boat, island-jump around the Caribbean to make themselves harder to find, and eventually make their way to Colombia. It would be the perfect father and son adventure— the first of many.

On his third morning at the Waldorf, there was a knock at the door. When he opened it, his heart sank to see Armstrong. He was with a knockout Spanish girl Wesley didn't know, a real heartbreaker with a scar that cut through one eyebrow.

"Wes, Wes, Wes," the big man said. "After all our talks, all the conversations about the rules, not going back to America, here you are in New York."

"I had to do something important."

"Your kid, right? You want one last look?"

Wesley considered his options. The man was here. If he could enlist Armstrong in his mission, a lot of things would go more easily. "Actually, I was thinking of bringing him down."

Armstrong considered, scratched his ear. "All right, let's take a drive."

Armstrong's Caddy was his office; it was where he and Wesley had always talked business, which boats were coming in, which containers needed papers. The girl sat in the back; once they were in motion, Armstrong began: "The cops got your old buddy Barney Lind to tell all."

"I heard."'

"That's going to be a problem," Armstrong said, and then: "Why'd I say I didn't want you to come back to the States?"

A long pause. "That it would be dangerous."

"Dangerous for you, dangerous for me, dangerous for Eduardo. You come up here, get BOLO'd by some goddamn street cop, that's two problems I have, not just one. I don't like it when people don't take my advice."

"I planned this out. I've got everything under control."

"Didn't plan to see me, did you? Girl who cooks and cleans at your beach house tells me you vanished, I called three New York hotels under your passport name, and here we are."

"I can do this. I can get my kid, go down there, no sweat."

"Are you kidding? Every news show in the country is going to run this story. Daddy disappears, then kid disappears—you think that'll pass under the radar? You think I need this shit? You think Eduardo Nieto needs this shit? Esmerelda, do your thing."

"What— wha—?" From the backseat, the beautiful girl jabbed him in the neck with a needle, jammed the plunger down hard. He grabbed her hand too late. "What was that?"

"Nitroglycerine, fentanyl, and amyl nitrate," Armstrong explained. "You really shouldn't mix them."

"What do they do?" His heart was doing some kind of strange tachycardic pounding.

"They shut your blood pressure down. Pretty damn quickly, too, by the look of it."

Wesley felt a great crashing wave hit him, send him spiraling down someplace deep. "My boy—" he said. "I need to get—"

"Shut up and die," Armstrong said. "We've got a busy day ahead of us, making you disappear." But he was talking, he saw, to a corpse.

* * *

When Tory passed out the forms, Anna looked up. "I've never seen one of these."

Thomas finished reading quickly through the document. "Security clearances? Like top secret, eyes only, like that?' Tory nodded. "Any chance you can tell us what this is about?"

Tory smiled. "Nope. Only I wouldn't sign it if there was anything you didn't want the government to know. They're very thorough."

Anna signed without hesitation; the girl was intellectually fearless. Thomas was, like Hamlet, doomed to see every side of any decision. It made him a hell of a clerk— he could think several jumps into the future—but Tory knew his interior life was complex.

He read through it, read through it again. "Can I get back to you on this?"

"Absolutely," Tory said. "Let's start Mr. Nieto's trial." She threw her black robe over her pantsuit, pulled her blonde hair out behind and walked into the courtroom.

The place was packed, reporters and sketch artists vying to get a first look at Baby Nieto. Sam Walker and his team had taken over the prosecution's table; the defendant's was empty save for a young woman, looking fresh out of law school, holding the fort for the big folks.

Tory already didn't like this. "Counselor, where's your team?"

"Good morning, Judge Parker."

Like they were going to chat. "Team, counselor. Where is— " the back door of the courtroom slammed open, and Angelo Schwartz strode in, staffers following in his wake. He stepped to the defense table, thumped box after box and folder after folder— of what, Tory had no idea, but she could plainly see they were all very heavy.

He'd put on muscle since their time together back in the DA's office. Where before he was wiry, now he was lean, trim. Back then, he'd been bursting with energy and new ideas. Now he had an aura of intelligent gravitas. He had developed, she could plainly see, charisma.

The cheekbones were still there, and his green eyes had a lively spark in them. His black hair had grayed slightly at the temples. He had matured into a startlingly attractive man.

Finally he looked up, their eyes met, and Tory felt something jump, correct itself, a lens abruptly coming into focus. She hadn't been expecting that.

He'd been about to speak, but something had stopped him. He blinked the moment away. "Angelo Schwartz," he said finally, "for the defense. May I approach?"

"Come on up," Tory said, then glanced at Sam at the prosecution's table, inviting him as well. Angelo stepped to the bench.

"This isn't about my client, Judge. I just wanted to say long time no see."

There was genuine warmth in his gaze. Tory smiled, happy to have him in her courtroom. "You've become ubiquitous on television," she said.

"That's not me, that's all bullshit," Angelo said. Tory remembered: she'd always liked his candor. "It brings in the interesting cases, so I don't have to take any I don't want."

Sam's gentle Southern accent made even the most cutting remarks mellifluous. "I must say, out of all the cases for the ACLU to get involved with—"

Angelo kept his tone light. "To freeze the man's money and then insist he get some schmo public defender, can't afford dry cleaning much less forensic accountants—that's the state stacking the cards against my client. On a case this large, that's just unfair."

"Plus all the face time you'll be getting in the press, the papers, the tube—"

"Hey— if I wanted to do nothing but Hollywood murders, I could, but I'm here, not making a paycheck for the next few months. Would you prosecute this guy for free?"

Sam didn't even pause. "Yup, I would."

"Well, turn over every paycheck until verdict to the ACLU. Help keep the playing field level." Angelo smiled. "I can give you some names over there, get you started."

"Guys," Tory said, "cut it. Did you have a purpose in coming up here, counselor?"

Angelo smiled. "Actually, I wanted to ask if Siggy is still with us—"

"How do you know Siggy?"

"I ran into you in Carl Schurz Park a few years back? You had this tiny cute puppy—"

Actually, he had. Crisp fall morning. Tory had blocked that, for some reason. "Yes, Siggy, he's considerably larger. He's a loon, but he's very sweet."

"All right, you two," Sam interrupted. "If y'all are gonna catch up on household pets, I'm goin' back. Give a yell if anything important happens up here." He stepped off.

"Did you ever get a dog?" Tory asked. "I remember you wanting a Weimaraner—"

Angelo made a face. "I travel too much, it wouldn't be fair. So, everything's good with you? Things are comfortable in the world of Tory Parker?"

"Reasonably close to it," she said.

"Glad to hear it." Something in his eyes changed. It was an expression she remembered, a sad little bump of remorse, but he got past it. "Hey, umm, I heard they offered you FISA."

Tory felt her heart lurch hard, her face go white. Damnit, she knew, he just saw his answer. "Whether or not that's true, counselor, it's not germane to this trial—"

"Well, unfortunately, your honor, it is, because the evidence against my client came through FISA from Guantanamo."

Tory held up her hand. "Sam—" she gestured. The prosecutor stepped to the bench. "Counselor has brought up the admission of classified evidence."

Sam let out air. "We've had a couple of these cases, and the procedure we hammered out, after everyone and their uncle weighed in, is that the three of us look at the evidence in camera, the judge gives a ruling, and the evidence never gets admitted."

"What a wonderful system," said Angelo dryly. "So free, so transparent—"

Tory looked at Angelo: "It's not that strange a procedure, counselor, as you well know. And you're not going to put FISA on trial here. FISA did not put that cocaine on those shipping boats, and they will not become your scapegoat. Are we clear on that?"

"Clear as crystal, your honor."

Tory wasn't done. "Angelo, I will bend over backwards to be fair, especially because of FISA. But if you feel I cannot adjudicate this trial, you are free to ask that I recuse myself—"

Sam whistled appreciatively. 'Man, you two are better'n Wimbledon."

Angelo's face had changed. "I understand, your honor."

Tory moved the final chess piece: "Do you want to go on the record with a recusal motion at the present time?"

Angelo looked straight into her eyes. "Absolutely not, your honor."

"Well, then, get back to the defense table and let's get this thing started."

When the lawyers were in position, Tory called the court to order. "Is the defendant here?"

There was a flurry of activity, and then the Hats and Bats Squad came out from the holding cells, tough corrections officers in thick black Kevlar and helmets, and at the center was Baby Nieto.

The man was so large, Tory was shocked he could stand and walk unaided. His head was shaved bald, and he was in a charcoal suit, yards of material somehow cut to fit. He came in staring up at the ceiling and humming a song. And then he looked at Tory.

The singing stopped. "It is my birthday?" he asked, in accented English.

Tory thought of nothing so much as Vincent 'The Chin' Gigante, a mobster famous for faking insanity.

"Mr. Nieto, you know as well as I do your birthday's in April."

"But here you are! So it must be my birthday." He flashed a wide, dazzling smile, spread his arms wide and said "Come to Baby."

"Mr. Nieto, sit down."

"You'd look good in boots, you know that?" And then: "Mira! Puss in boots!"

Tory had seen this before. "Mr. Nieto," she began, "if you wish to address this court, you will do so through your counselor. You will only answer questions put directly to you—"

"Boots and a chair, that's how I want you." Baby Nieto growled low in his throat. "Ooh, lady, you're a lion-tamer, and I'm a lion."

"Get him out of here," Tory ordered. "Hook up a speaker, let him listen to his trial in his cell."

As the officers hustled the huge man back through the door he turned to her and shouted: "Wait! If it's my birthday I want cake!"

* * *

Mariposa was, as usual, still lazing in bed when Eduardo Nieto, freshly showered and shaved, stepped into his office to find a carafe of hot coffee at his desk. He turned on the large-screen television and hit mute. A circus scene, beautiful female jugglers and acrobats gyrated around a female singer emoting soundlessly into the early morning light of the office. Eduardo powered up the computer.

He ignored the long list of new emails, went into the ArrowHawk text program, scrolled down to find one he appeared to have sent himself from this computer. This was from a friend—well, an associate—in Washington. The provenance of the message may have been obscured, but what it said was to the point.

Twenty-four gemologists in New York were being watched by order of FISA, at the request of OIPR. He looked down the list, saw some names he recognized, breathed a deep sigh.

And then the message at the end: the greedy bastard wanted another girl. Well, he would get one. But not right away—best to let him sweat.

Eduardo stripped off the man's personal request, encoded the list of gemologists and forwarded it to the team in New York. What busy little monkeys they would be up there today, he thought, and could not suppress a sharp laugh.

Eduardo Nieto knew all about FISA. He had to; he was a businessman, though an American presidential executive order several years before had declared him a terrorist, after his connection was proven to the unfortunate unpleasantness involving the Colombian supreme court. Thereafter, FISA, he had come to learn, had taken a special interest in him, and he, in return, had taken a rather considerable interest in FISA. He, or rather his agents, had found a weak link and had been able to exploit it. He had access to their inner workings; he knew which way they would jump almost as soon as they did. When they acted in ways he found unreasonable, he took steps to correct them; when they came into possession of information he didn't want them to have, he caused them to die.

Allowing Baby to be arrested was unreasonable. Allowing the man to go to trial— that was going to be a problem.

He had to think this newly elevated judge, Tory Parker, was controllable. Certainly, her being on FISA allowed him to monitor her actions in great detail. And if she was malleable, then her presiding over Baby's trial, if trial there had to be, might be a good thing. But if not— if all the effort he'd put into FISA turned out to be for nothing—well then, it was time for another plan, the backup plan. The plan B.

Eduardo picked up the phone, dialed a cell number. Sixty yards away, in a building housing over 5000 assault rifles and a variety of other lethal ordnance, Dr. Reynaldo Torres touched the screen of his phone.

"It's Eduardo. The time has come to replace the fire extinguishers. Are we ready?"

"Of course," said Reynaldo. "We've been ready for months."

* * *

When asked, Esmerelda Marquez told people she had gotten the scar that cut through her eyebrow in a car accident. In fact she had received the wound in hand-to-hand combat at a Colombian paramilitary training compound, and every time she looked in the mirror she was proud.

The text she had received this morning had thrown careful plans into disarray, and now she had to rush, which was what had brought her to this place she'd never seen: an entire street of Jewish diamond merchants. She looked again at the address she had been given, found the correct building and went in.

This was an open space filled with stalls, and each stall was its own business, with racks of gold earrings and diamond rings under glass. She stepped through the hectoring throng, found the elevators at the back and went to the third floor. Down the calm gray hallway she found the office. She rang and was buzzed in.

Two men, both Jewish, wearing hats indoors, were talking. When they saw her they scattered like mice. The receptionist was a dark-haired beauty.

Esmerelda checked her paper. "I am looking to see Mr. Fein?

"Yes." She wavered a moment. "Right this way," she said finally, stood and led Esmerelda through a door into the back.

A man in a fedora was cleaning his desk. "Oh, hi," he said when he saw Esmerelda. She watched as he dumped in a small pile of framed photographs into a desk drawer and shut it. "You're the girl about the emeralds."

Esmerelda took from her bag a ziplocked baggie heavy with green stones, set it on the desk. The man took up a jeweler's loupe, spread a thick swipe of stones onto black velvet, took up a silver tool and gently began sweeping them across the black surface, sizing them as much by feel as by eye.

As he worked through them, Esmerelda noticed a photograph of Mr. Fein, his wife, who appeared to be wearing a wig, and three young children, two boys and a girl. Evidently he had missed it in his hasty cleanup. "These are exceptional," he said as he neared the end of his grading.

"Eight hundred thousand dollars," Esmerelda said, and crossed her long legs.

The man continued his investigations. "I sold some pieces to Baby Nieto," he said.

"Si, I know this." She checked her watch.

"He came to me because I am fair. I was fair to him, and I will be fair to you." He continued grading the stones. When he was done he had three mounds of green stones. He gave her a blunt, direct look. "Six hundred seventy-five," he said.

"Eight hundred thousand dollars," she repeated.

The man pursed his lips. "There is a market for emeralds, it goes up, it goes down—"

"Eight hundred thousand dollars," she said.

He spread the stones with his tool, looked through them again. "Seven. Seven is more than fair, it's an excellent price."

"Eight hundred thousand dollars." As she said it, he realized she was looking at something over his shoulder, on the shelf behind. And with a galvanic shock of awareness he remembered the picture on that shelf. His wife and his boys and girl outside their house—

"All right, eight," he said hastily. Her gaze turned from the picture to him, and she smiled as he swept the emeralds into three separate bags, set them in his wall safe. Then he wrote a note on a post-it, went to the door, opened it slightly, spoke to someone in a language Esmerelda didn't understand. He shut the door, sat back at the desk. "We're getting your money now."

* * *

In Brooklyn, Rafe Carr was in a bad mood. For one thing, Al Clemente had a seemingly inexhaustible supply of peanuts up at the bench; he had spent the last hour of proceedings cracking shells, chewing nuts, shaping shells into an ever-growing pile, and cracking more. Rafe would have loved to tell Tory about it, but she hadn't returned his calls, and now he just thought she was a bitch.

He'd have broken it off eventually, he knew, but it had come as a surprise that she'd gotten there first. And for all her highfaluting bull about ethics and principles— look at this judge, scooping peanuts into his mouth like a pig at a trough. Think he cares about who didn't see what in Discovery?

Rafe glanced at his watch, thought again of the girl in his boxing gym. He'd been lining her up for weeks; tonight he'd get all hangdog on her, let her pry the information that his girlfriend had broken up with him. In his experience, that would be enough for the initial drink.

Rafe was prosecuting a Colombian national named Arturo Hidalgo. It should have been an easy case. Arturo came up in wiretaps of Baby Nieto associates; they discussed, in rather lame code, the purchase of five kilos of cocaine. Evidently he had paid $20,000 for a key to a compartment in a Brooklyn mini-storage warehouse. The defense's argument was that Mr. Hidalgo had thought the key was for a storage locker full of sporting equipment, because that's what the conversation on the wiretap had been about.

Rafe had taken pictures of the storage locker, and blown them up to life-size. He couldn't imagine any sporting equipment that cost $20,000 being able to fit in that small space.

How much was a Super Bowl trophy worth? That would fit. But not much else.

And now, the jury out in the jury room, Clemente was entertaining a motion to disallow Rafe's blown-up photographs, taking forever to look at each one while eating peanut after peanut. Rafe had a sense of time frozen into stasis, moving as slowly as a glacier. He stared out at the sky in disbelief. There was a white ribbon somehow caught on the outside hardware of the window; he watched it dance in the breeze. He tried to ignore the defense attorney's quiet conversation with Hidalgo: "When you get on the stand, I want you to sit up straight, look the jury members in the eye. You must not give them the impression you don't care."

Arturo's smile needed orthodontics. "But I don't," he said, shrugging. "This is all garbage— Eduardo promised I would never stand trial in America. I don't know how, but Eduardo will send someone to rescue me. Trust me, my friend. You'll see."

* * *

Esmerelda had spent days mapping out the Brooklyn building and putting everything in place so that when the man they called El Limpiador arrived, everything would be flawless.

In Colombia he'd used larger teams, but Esmeralda had done her work with great efficiency. She'd worked out ingress and egress. The elevators had security cameras; Esmeralda tripped the stairwell circuit breaker just as the man arrived. He'd never been here before, but he knew, climbing the pitch-black stairs, that each riser had sixteen steps. Other than the dark stairwell, the building was operating entirely normally; no one knew there was a killer climbing up its spine.

At the roof level, the stairs changed exactly the way he'd been told they would. He stopped at the bottom, called out: "El que esté ahí, vayase." *Whoever is there, leave.*

"I live here. You leave." The reply was English. The man didn't need the code to recognize Esmerelda. He hiked the last flight of stairs. She was at the top. He kissed her, and she kissed back. "I got the money for the stones," she whispered in his ear.

"It went well?"

"Si. It's safe. And everything is ready for you here." He nodded. and with one black-gloved hand slammed the bolt open. Light flooded into the stairwell; the man adjusted his sunglasses, stepped into the sunlight.

The roof was tar-paper, empty except for a duffel bag against one wall. The man opened it, pulled out binoculars, looked across the street at the Brooklyn courthouse. Over the past two days, a piece of white ribbon had been glued to the window frame, and a minuscule microphone and low-power frequency sender had been planted in the courtroom, its antenna a single strand of copper wire painted to the wall.

The pale man found the ribbon, aimed his rf receiver toward it. The voices of two men filled his earpiece. When he heard the name Nieto he knew he'd locked onto the right courtroom.

He pulled out a bag filled with sand, laid it on the ledge. Then he extricated the rifle, screwed on the barrel, set it onto the sandbag. He fixed the window with his scope and waited.

In Colombia the justice system was wary. Here he had surprise on his side, as well as infinite patience. He intended to make the best possible use of both.

*   *   *

Judge Clemente ruled that Rafe could use two of the sixteen photographs, and the jury was brought back in. Arturo retook the stand, was reminded he was still under oath.

He sat with one arm slung over the back of the chair as if waiting for a waitress to bring him a cocktail. "Mr. Hidalgo," Rafe began, "In Colombia, did you know Eduardo Nieto?"

Arturo glanced at his lawyer, who shook his head 'no'. "Sure, I worked for Nieto. My mother and father worked for Nieto. Most of my village worked for Nieto."

"What did you do for Mr. Nieto?"

"I was on a road crew. I drove an asphalt spreader. We built roads through the jungle."

"Did you ever, in your employment with Mr. Nieto, encounter any cocaine?"

Arturo Hidalgo smiled. "What Americans don't understand is your market for drugs here has ruined my country. The farms around my village used to plant yucca and coffee and plantains, but now they all plant coca. The farmers mash it up with *cal viva*— what you call lime—"

"Quicklime, the solvent?" Rafe said.

The man nodded. "They make white powder, it is called base, which they sell to the cartels, who refine it into cocaine. But the man from the cartel only comes to each village once a month— so you go to the doctor, you pay in base, the doctor buys fish, he pays in base, the fish man buys fruit, he pays in base. Stores don't have cash registers, they have scales— except in the bordello, you get a girl for a shot glass of base. Then the paramilitaries come with the man from the cartel, and everybody lines up and sells their base for money. And the paramilitaries take 30%. So all the cocaine going to America is what buys guns and jeeps for the paramilitaries. So who should be on trial here?"

"And when you worked on Mr. Nieto's road crew, did you ever see anyone killed?"

Something in Hidalgo's eyes changed, looked hollow. His lawyer rose. "Objection—"

"Sustained," Judge Clemente agreed.

Rafe started again from a different angle. "There's a man in Colombia they call El Limpiador. The cleaner. Who is he?"

"I don't know. Who is he?"

"I remind you there are penalties for lying under oath. You don't know El Limpiador?" Arturo shook his head.

Rafe turned to the jury. "Let me call your attention to People's 32 in evidence, the wiretap transcript numbered 32. Jurors, you should all have it—" much shuffling as the jurors looked through their copies. "Page 29, jurors, please read it to yourselves. Here you say in conversation that you knew El Limpiador, whom you describe as 'Eduardo Nieto's top assassin in Colombia.' On page 30—" he gave everyone time to turn the page. "You say: 'He used to come to my parent's house—he loved my mother's arepas, he'd sit and smoke cigars with my father and me.'" Rafe smiled. "Do you still say you didn't know this man, El Limpiador?"

Arturo hadn't changed his lounge-lizard pose. "Yeah, I knew him."

"Did you know him well enough to know his real name?"

Arturo weighed responses. Finally he said: "Well, his family were from Am—" and as he spoke the window smashed into shards and the first hollow-point slammed into Arturo's head, reduced it to a spray of gristle and slime. The second bullet entered Arturo's side, opened and expanded as it cut through his body, filled a wide vector of the room with pulverized viscera and bone.

The room erupted, everyone running for the courtroom door. Rafe, covered in red, stood in open-mouthed shock for a moment, then turned to flee, slipped on blood and fell. As he tried to get up, get away from the window, Al Clemente, barreling down from the bench, smashed with the full force of panic into Rafe's left knee.

Rafe heard a loud snap, knew immediately something had broken. The pain was white-hot and excruciating. Al Clemente cut out the door, but Rafe couldn't do anything but clutch his knee and scream.

* * *

After the second shot the man on the roof broke down the gun, shoved it and the rest into the duffel. He dropped in the two ejected shells, drew the rope tight. He shouldered the bag.
Esmeralda was still at the door; the man went through and they ran down the dark stairwell together.

At the first-floor landing, no light at all anywhere around them, Esmeralda grabbed the man's shoulder, spun him around and pressed him hard against the wall. She found his lips, kissed him ferociously, lips and teeth and tongue gnashing like predators. After a moment, he pushed her away.

"I have to go," he said.

"Yes," she said, breathless. "You do." She took the duffle, handed him the motorcycle helmet she had left on this landing. He put it on, pulled the mirrored facemask down, and together they ran down the final flight of stairs to the basement.

The man walked out the building to the waiting motorcycle. He started it with one mighty kick. At the first red light he thought of Arturo's parents, that nice couple making arepas back in Colombia. Not their fault their only son never knew when to shut his mouth.

Somewhere behind him by the courthouse police sirens started to wail. He didn't bother to turn and look; he knew they were just beginning their work, and he had already ended his.

When he was back in Manhattan, he left the motorcycle behind in an alley in Chinatown, took out one of the three cell phones he'd had activated the day before and dialed a number. "Si. Hola," he said to the man who answered. "You know the job we spoke of, that judge who's making life so tough for Baby—I want you to make her uncomfortable, let her know she's being watched. Do it precisely the way we discussed. Tomorrow will be fine." The man on the other end agreed.

The Cleaner got off the phone, thought of finally being in this city with Esmeralda as he hailed a cab uptown.

* * *

When Angelo took the Baby Nieto case, quite a few lawyers and consultants offered their services for free to get to work with him. The ACLU had convinced him to use a jury consultant of some renown. The man was here today, and Angelo wasn't listening to a word he said.

Tory liked him for that. These consultants came in at the beginning, overpsychologized tiny nuances of the dress and speech of prospective jurors to read whether they'd convict or acquit, got their check and moved on. Tory had often wondered if there was anything besides anecdotal evidence that any of this helped sway trials, but Baby Nieto, if he'd had access to his money, would no doubt have demanded one, so it was just as well.

Pendleton McGreavy had a strange high voice, and everyone in the courtroom could hear every word of his supposedly discreet advice to Angelo. Sam, the DA, had just finished with a potential juror, Lolita Martanho, an art director from Brazil. As Angelo began to ask his first question, McGreavy loudly suggested he should ask if she had relatives in Colombia.

That was the last straw for Angelo. "She speaks Portuguese, not Spanish. And I think it's time for you to go."

"Really?" the man asked, in his odd high voice.

"Really," Angelo said. There were suppressed titters from the prospects as the man gathered his papers and left. And then the robing room door burst open and Anna emerged, breathless. She went right to Tory, kept her voice low. "There's been a shooting at the Brooklyn courthouse. They're taking Rafe to the hospital."

Shock and worry burst in Tory's heart. "Ten-minute recess," she said loudly and stood. She was aware of Angelo's eyes on her as she left the bench.

"Who called?" she asked Anna.

"Jack Riley. I'm not sure where he heard it." They pushed into the robing room. Tory picked up the phone, punched in Jack's number. "Jack, it's me," she said when she got him.

"Rafe's been injured. His leg. A sniper took out Arturo Hidalgo."

"A *sniper*?" Tory had pictured someone rising from the public area, laying down fire. It was hard to get a gun into a courtroom, but not impossible. "And Rafe was shot?"

"Evidently not, there's some question precisely what happened. But it's his leg, and it appears not to be life-threatening. He was taken to Kingsbrook."

"Thanks, Jack." She got off, punched in Rafe's cell number. He sounded awful when he answered.

"Rafe? It's Tory- I heard you were wounded?"

"My knee—it's all torn up. They've got me all full of painkillers now. I didn't get shot, Al Clemente barreled into my knee."

"Al Clemente?"

"Didn't even apologize. Had a moment by the ambulance where he could've said something, but he didn't. That guy's mother didn't raise him right."

Tory, despite her worry, couldn't help a short, sharp laugh. "How bad's the knee?"

"It's a big swollen mess. Nothing broke the skin, but there's broken bone and torn ligaments. He really did a number. They're going to stabilize the knee, and I'm going to fly out to Colorado." '

'Rafe-" Tory was baffled. "Should you travel? The best hospitals are here—"

"You remember— my uncle? I told you this." The note of snide had returned to his voice. Tory wondered if this phone call had been a mistake.

"You told me he was an assistant something-or-other, a trainee—"

"Not a trainee. A trainer. He's the assistant athletic trainer for the Broncos. He's on their medical team. He'll be able to point me toward the finest resources in the country."

Tory swallowed. She felt like an awkward fool. "Well then," she said, "you'll be in good hands." All at once the distance between them felt unbridgeable. "Is there anything I can do for you here?" she asked. "While you're gone?"

Long pause on the line. "If I think of anything," he said, "I'll give you a call."

That was it; it was over. Tory got off the phone, sat watching steel-gray clouds roll in from the South. Another failed relationship.

"Tory?" It was Anna. "You okay?"

Anna the fearless. "We broke up last weekend. I'm sorry this happened, but—"

"But there's nothing you can do."

Tory knew it was true. She stood, adjusted her robe. "You know what the real lesson of this is? Al Clemente is an even bigger jerk than I thought."

* * *

"I don't trust Colombians." The man speaking was a history teacher at a private high school on Fifth Avenue. He stood at the bench before Tory, sandwiched by Angelo and Sam.

"Why?" Angelo asked.

"I've had Colombian exchange students. In my experience, they don't tell the truth."

Tory sighed. Telling the truth was the point of the 'Voir Dire' process. The words voir dire, from the Old French, meant "to tell the truth". This was the moment for potential jurors to explain any biases that would make it impossible to judge the defendant fairly. But jurors took it as an opportunity to lie like crazy to be excused.

It was hard, she knew: this would be a long trial. They needed 18 people—12 jurors and 6 alternates—who were able to drop out of their lives for all that time. As a rule, people who wanted to serve were either retirees, who tended to walk in with certain long-held opinions, or people who hated their jobs and knew their employers had to pay them indefinitely—office workers, mail carriers, sanitation guys. And this population tended to come with its own prejudices, as opposed to what Tory would expect of elite private high school teachers.

"What areas do you teach?" asked Sam.

"American history, World War I, World War II—"

"Would you give a Colombian student a lower grade because she was Colombian?" The man paused. Tory watched him. There were people in this world— in this city—who would have answered that question with an unqualified yes.

This man wasn't one of them. "No," he said hesitantly, "I could not." He looked defeated, caught in his earlier lies.

"Mr. Abrams, you teach American history. You know the importance of jury duty—"

The man nodded once, quickly, caught in Tory's gaze.

"I understand it's a hardship," Tory went on. "It's also a tremendous opportunity to anyone with a degree of intellectual curiosity." She was getting to him. "So I'll ask again—do you really feel Colombians are all liars?"

There was a pause while he weighed what direction he would go. "We had a Colombian maid," the man said finally. "She stole money from us. She stole bottles of wine—"

"Consent," Angelo said. "Consent," Sam said.

"Mr. Abrams, you're free to go." Tory looked up, took in the room, the crowd of strangers, Baby at the defense table, working on a doodle on a legal pad. Angelo had somehow convinced him to remain uninsane in court, and even to waive his right to be present at the bench during these conferences with prospective jurors. It would have thrown in an extra week or two just to reinterview all these people individually in his presence if he hadn't.

Tory looked down at the paper, found the next name. "Hermione Lockhardt."

"That's me." Ms. Lockhardt was a sharp-featured woman of indeterminate age, dressed as if for apres-ski in a mink vest and black stretch pants and fur boots. She was hugging her Gucci bag to her chest as if Angelo had spent the last half hour trying to wrest it from her.

"Ma'am, as I said earlier, everything you say up here between us is off the record. You said you could not be fair. May I ask why?"

"Because he's guilty."

"And how do you know that?" Tory asked;

"Well, just look at him," the woman hissed. "He's so fat!""

"You can't presume him innocent because he's fat?" Tory was trying to put it together.

"He's fat, he's ugly, he's from Colombia, and we all know what they do down there." And suddenly she had what seemed a brilliant idea. "And that's like a poverty-stricken country, right? Little kids hungry and like that, right? So if he's from Colombia and he's fat, it must mean he's guilty. Because, you know, all the unguilty Colombians would be thin."

Tory opened her mouth, and no words came out. The woman glanced at her diamond-encrusted watch, looked back up at Tory. "So that's it, right? l can go to my manicure now?"

Tory found her words. "No, ma'am, you cannot go to your manicure. You may be excused from this case, but you'll go back into the other room, and rejoin the pool of potential jurors, and we'll try to make sure you get picked for another trial."

The woman didn't like this one bit. "I know some very important people—" she started.

Nothing could have impressed Tory less. "Right now, in this courtroom, I'm the most important person you know. And I just told you to go get back into the juror pool."

The woman huffed down the aisle and slammed out through the two portholed doors. Tory looked again at Baby Nieto. He was still doodling, still seemingly oblivious, but on his face was an unmistakable smile that told Tory he had heard every word.

* * *

El Limpiador didn't like fancy hotels.

It was a quirk of his. He could afford to rent the finest rooms in the best hotels in New York, but he preferred places where the walls were dirty and the sheets were dubious.

Which was precisely what Esmeralda was expecting when she arrived at his latest one, a seedy pit near Bowery. He'd told her the room; she marched right by the drowsing man behind the counter, a game show erupting into applause as she passed. She took a cramped elevator up three flights, walked down a dirty red hallway past door after door to his room. She knocked; the voice inside said "Take off your clothes out there. Then I'll let you in."

Damn him, she thought, it took me forever to dress, even as the sheer perversity of the order triggered something deep inside. She looked up and down the hall, took a deep breath, stripped off her leather jacket, set it on the floor. She reached down, unzipped her boots, slipped them off, left them in a pile with the jacket. She looked up and down the dingy hall, thought: any moment any one of these doors could open, and despite herself some piece of sexual tantalization came to life, made her fingers tremble as she unbuttoned her black silk shirt—it was insane, how this man affected her. She felt electricity in her skin as she pulled the tails out of her black jeans, looked again up and down the hallway, saw no one. In one crisp gesture, like jumping into an icy pool, she whipped the shirt off. In anticipation of their time together, she had not worn a bra; the hallway air felt cool on her exposed breasts. Even as she hated him for this ridiculous game she found herself caught in a strange erotic headiness; no one else could bring this out in her. No one else could get near enough to try. But God damn it, why did he—

A door opened twenty feet down the hall, a grey-haired man shambled out. Esmeralda banged on the door. "There's someone coming."

From inside: "Are you naked?"

"No," she said mournfully, undid her wide leather belt, got her pants open and slid them down her legs. She had not worn panties. The man was older, shuffling down the hallway.

When he saw her, he stopped, and a smile curled on his features. In reply, she banged on the door. "I'm ready," she said.

He opened the door, took one look at her. "Socks," he said, and slammed the door.

The older man was hovering now. She ripped her socks off first one foot and then the other, stood naked and shivering, hating the pale man for this. She banged again.

The man opened the door, looked her up and down, grabbed her and pulled her in. Then he scooped up her clothes, threw them inside and shut the door on the older man.

Esmeralda was shaking. "I can't believe you made me do that— I am so pissed off at you—"

He laughed and laughed. Funniest thing in the damn world.

Esmeralda looked around the room. It was dilapidated, water-stained, functional. On a round coffee table were handcuffs, a horse crop, a leather collar with rings. "I found an interesting store," he said. "I figured payback would be a bitch."

"Oh, it will be," she said, considered the tools before her and then took her black jeans from where he'd thrown them. In one long flash she stripped out her black leather belt, folded it in half, held it by the buckle. She snapped her fingers at him. "Naked," she said, "and turn around." She held up the doubled belt. "Eventually I might fuck you, but first I'm going to make you scream."

* * *

After her final orgasm, Esmeralda rolled off, lay for a while breathing hard and staring at the ceiling. After a while she forced herself out of bed, found her jeans, took out her pocket knife and cut the ropes from the headboard so her lover could drop his arms. They nestled— together, drowsy and satiated. Eventually he shifted, got his watch from the bedside table.

"We have time." He sank back into the bed.

She held him tighter. He had come out of nowhere into her life; all her years in Colombia, dropping out of school to join paramilitaries in the mountains, then working security at one of Nieto's drug labs, she had never thought a relationship like this—with this kind of strange freedom—was possible. All the crazy things they did, all the experiments—every step they'd taken, they'd always been equal.

No matter what she'd achieved, no matter what she would achieve, she knew: the men in her country would never see her as an equal.

This man did. Growing up, she'd had no idea this existed. Had she known, she would not have been able to imagine she'd wanted it.

But now that she had it, she had no intention of ever giving it up. "So," she asked, "the judge in Baby's trial—the woman."

"Mm-hmrnm?"

"When does she go?"

The man rubbed the rope burn on his wrists. "Two schools of thought on that. Armstrong says we should just take her out in a big public way, big enough to scare the next judge into doing what we want. But Don Eduardo seems to think he can control it from long distance."

"How?"

"I don't know his plan," he said. "I just know he's got one."

Esmeralda twisted her hair into a chignon off her neck. "Eduardo's always got a plan. And inside that plan is another plan. And inside that plan is another plan. And that's why, no matter what happens, he always wins."

* * *

Thirty-two people had waited on line to explain to Tory and the lawyers why they could not be fair. Most declared themselves bigots. One woman wanted out on the grounds that only God could dispense justice, and for us to even try was a blasphemy. Tory hadn't heard that argument yet this year. One woman said she felt all drug laws were wrong on philosophical grounds, and that she would vote for nullification of those laws in any trial. Tory commended her on her principles even as she vehemently disagreed with them, and let her go.

That left them with a room full of available potential jurors. Now it was time for Angelo and Sam to engage in the genteel but ruthless battle to put together a jury.

They each wanted people sympathetic to their cause— that was inevitable. And they each had only a certain number of challenges to use to excuse jurors, which meant they had to compromise, which meant they had to keep their agendas as hidden as master poker players.

Thus the questioning began. Have you ever known anyone convicted for drugs? This case is going to include testimony from someone who was caught with drugs, and is testifying in lieu of a harsher sentence. Would this change your opinion of his testimony? On and on, juror after juror, hour after hour. It was, Tory always thought, fascinating to watch— at least in the beginning. Somewhere around the seventh hour, it was anything but.

On any other day, Tory would have worked to convince Angelo and Sam to work late, keep a two-day selection from becoming a three-day ordeal. But as 5:00 came and went, and the crowd in the room began to get antsy, rumors began to circulate about a shooting in a courthouse, and Tory saw it was time to send these people home.

Finally, she called it. "We'll pick up tomorrow," she said, and visible relief stirred through the crowd. "Everybody, same room tomorrow 9:30 AM sharp."

As the jurors shuffled out, Tory waved Bart Alicia over. He held up a hand, waited until the courtroom was empty, then ushered her down the back stairs to the waiting car.

Tory was silent on the ride uptown, and Bart left her to her thoughts. In the elevator of her building, he tried to convince her to let him walk Siggy in her stead.

"The walk will clear my head," Tory insisted. She opened her door and the dog wagged furiously, thumping the walls with his tail. "Let me just get the leash."

* * *

In the park, Siggy was on squirrel patrol, his acute night vision and expert nose allowing him knowledge of the small animals in every bush and up every tree. Bart was impressed. "If we'd gotten him young, I'll bet we could've trained him as a drug-sniffer dog."

"He's focused enough," Tory said, as Bart's cell phone rang. He sat Tory on a bench, stayed standing so he could see anyone coming. Then he answered the phone. "Yes, boss."

Tory scratched the dog's ears, thought about Rafe, thought about Angelo. She hated that he'd been injured, but for all his bad-boy charisma, Rafe had always carried a certain air of entitlement—his casual attitude towards evidence in discovery had clinched something she'd already understood about him. Angelo could appear entitled, especially on TV, but Tory had known him long enough to see that everything he'd become, he'd earned. It was, she thought, a defining trait.

Bart finished his call. "In the Brooklyn thing, NYPD traced bullet trajectories to a rooftop near the courthouse. They say it doesn't look like the shooter could've been aiming for the judge from that angle. It looks like the hit was specifically on the guy in the witness box."

"I wonder what Hidalgo knew that was worth killing him."

Bart Alicia shrugged. "My experience, these guys train themselves to be sociopaths, you don't know which way they'll jump. But I promise this doesn't mean they're going to start killing their own guys now. Baby's trial is the biggest problem Eduardo Nieto has. And when Eduardo has a legal problem—"

"Judges tend to die." Tory smoothed Siggy's coat where she'd ruffled it. "Let's go back to the building." She stood. "It's starting to get cold."

* * *

There was only one man in the world whom Eduardo Nieto truly considered a genius, a man Eduardo was justifiably proud of having as an employee, if one can look up to an employee as one might look up to one's father. For Dr. Reynaldo Torres had made the impossible possible.

Dr. Torres was a chemist, but that term belied the prodigious reach of the man's mind. Eduardo had recruited him from a boring job as a mid-level manager in a pharmaceuticals company to scale up the Nieto production of fentanyl. As that project grew, he'd shown Eduardo how artificial intelligence could be used to cut inefficiencies in every aspect of Nieto's business and even predict safer trade routes into the US and other markets.

And then Nieto had discovered Dr. Torres' true value: if, in a perfect world, there were a Nobel prize for coca production, Dr. Torres would have earned it when he solved the glyphosate problem.

For years, both the United States government and, when politically expedient, the Colombian authorities had decimated coca production in Colombia by spraying glyphosate—a pesticide sold commercially under the name "Roundup"—onto fields of coca plants from low-flying planes. It did its job well—within two weeks, the plants would shrivel and die, wiping out a farmer's year of careful work. Year after year, the spraying had cut down Eduardo's yields, and he'd begun to see the loss as a permanent debit on his balance sheets until Dr. Torres walked into his office and showed him the solution.

Very simply, the doctor had explained, some plants had been conferred immunity to Roundup. Monsanto, the company that made the pesticide, had spliced a gene into soybeans that made them resistant to the chemical. Splice the same gene into coca plants, and the fields wouldn't die when the planes came—in fact, they would thrive, because the US government would do the service of weeding the furrows for the farmers, killing everything else that grew so the coca plants wouldn't have to compete for nutrition.

Eduardo had immediately offered Dr. Torres whatever funds he needed. Within a year test fields were planted in places the government routinely sprayed. The planes came, clouds of poison filled the air, and two weeks later the plants were larger and healthier than before.

Eduardo had sent his best men to harvest those fields and process the leaves into cocaine. Finally the day had come for Eduardo to compare the drug made from the new plants with that of the old. Sitting in Eduardo's office with piles of white powder they had conducted melting point tests, purity tests, every test Eduardo knew.

It melted as cocaine did, it reacted to reagents as cocaine did. But there was one decisive test Eduardo needed to conduct. He took down a mirror from the wall, carved the white powder into cigarette-width rails, and snorted. He felt the familiar hum of warmth in the room, as if the lights had become richer, the colors around him deeper, and then the euphoric overloading of gladness as the drug coursed through his system. But there was something else, too—he felt a spark of aggression, a very subtle tipping towards anger somewhere inside.

There was, in this new drug, an extremely delicate difference. It was as if some tiny fragment of the spirit of the drug had been perverted, but in a way only a connoisseur with decades of experience would begin to comprehend.

To be honest, Eduardo liked the old drug better, but it didn't matter. The government kept spraying, and the crops grew fat, and the cocaine did precisely what it was supposed to do.

Dr. Torres had received a preeminent place in the organization, an extremely generous stipend for overseeing fentanyl production, and an unlimited budget to apply his mind and abilities to whatever aspects of Eduardo's business suited his fancy.

Now, together, they were driving up to their most recent cooperative venture. The road was paved, wide enough for a truck. It led far from Eduardo's main property, through miles of virgin forest over the ridgeline to the other side of the mountain. Finally the road forked; both branches extended another half mile in opposite directions; each ended in a cleared half-acre lot. In each was a barn.

Nieto took the left fork, drove for less than a minute, came to an asphalt lot in front of the windowless barn. Dr. Torres, impaired from an old leg injury, needed assistance to extricate himself from the enormous Land Rover; Eduardo got out, held the man's cane as he guided the fragile scientist to the ground.

No one but bright-plumaged birds saw Eduardo power up the generator outside the barn. As it roared to life, he stepped to the barn door, unlocked it and slid it open.

Inside was a forklift, sinks against one wall, spigots attached to brand-new coiled hoses.

In the middle of the barn floor were two parallel trap doors, steel rectangles at the center of an uninterrupted expanse of gray cement. Eduardo Nieto stepped to the first, flipped it open with a loud metallic clang, stepped to a circuit breaker, flicked all the breakers on.

Electric light poured from the hole, illuminating a wide cement ramp with a handrail on one side. Eduardo Nieto's concrete pourers and construction crew had thought they were building a specialized drug lab here, not too dissimilar to the hundreds they'd built all over Colombia.

They'd been wrong. Nieto gestured to Dr. Torres not to bother following him, walked down the ramp. At the bottom, a short hallway led to a solid metal door.

Nieto slid open the bolts, stepped into a large room of poured concrete in which a smaller room had been created with cement blocks. This inner room had a single steel door and a five-inch-thick bulletproof glass window. Nieto peered through the window at the workbench inside, at the hammers and chisels and saws and vice grips and crowbars, at the electric handsaw, and finally at the wooden shelves on the far wall.

It had taken Eduardo Nieto several years to amass the collection of items resplendent on the shelves, though he had no desire to go into the room and investigate them further. Some had been purchased through cover corporations. Some had been secured with bribes to medical clinics and dental offices. And in some cases, men with guns had gone into hospitals, in Colombia and in other countries as well, and taken them by force.

It was interesting to see the various designs companies had come up with to make the radiological cores of X-ray machines safe and transportable. Each one was essentially a sealed seed pod full of radioactive material. With the right tools, each would yield up its poison.

In the corner, in a large burlap coffee sack, was what until last year had been the pride of the collection, stolen from an American oil company in Venezuela: a powerful yet compact scanner that used americium and beryllium to X-ray oil pipelines for cracks. Had Eduardo's efforts ended there, he would have considered the entire program a great success.

But that was before he'd gotten the item suspended in water in the sealed fish tank.

It was curious, the notion that something so deadly to any living thing in the air around it could be rendered safe merely by surrounding it with water, but that was the basic design of all food irradiation plants. By exposing meats and vegetables to the machine's cobalt 60 and cesium 137 core, all bacteria, viruses and microbes—in essence, all living things—were destroyed. The gamma rays the core produced were deadly to every organism they encountered, but they could not penetrate more than an inch of water.

The three-foot plastic and steel beast suspended in Eduardo Nieto's fish tank had been purchased quite legally, albeit using a series of Brazilian holding companies as a front.

No matter. They had Baby. He had all this. And he was ready to use it.

He exited, locked the steel doors and walked back up the ramp. "The fire extinguishers?" he asked.

"In the other barn," the older man said.

"Let's go," Eduardo said, and led the man back out to the Land Rover.

They drove back to the fork, took the other branch off the single main road. This barn, when they arrived, was identically situated; Nieto unlocked the door, helped the older man into the building.

No trap doors; no mysteries under the cement floor. Two long work tables, a wall of tools. And, against one wall, a pallet of fire extinguishers, all still in their boxes, the entire shipment still encased in a clear skin of plastic.

Eduardo Nieto took a knife from the table, sliced through plastic and cardboard, pulled out one of the extinguishers. These were the very latest dry chemical extinguishers, sleek red torpedoes thick as a man's thigh. He and Dr. Torres looked it over, considered every angle.

Eduardo took the notebook from his back pocket, flipped through to his list, looking for someone appropriate for the job at hand. He circled one name, put the notebook away and led Dr. Torres back to the car.

* * *

There was a slight echo on Tory's phone line, a minuscule time delay, but there usually was when she talked to her sister. Letitia was stationed in Qatar, halfway around the world. Their conversation was bouncing back and forth between God knew how many military and civilian satellites. And what all that technology was allowing Tory to say was "gee, you know, I don't really know."

"Come on, Tor—" Letitia was serious. "Eventually you're going to have to tell them."

Tory knew that. "It's a seven-year term, so, you know, I figure I've got time—"

A world away, Letitia spat out laughter. "Any other family, you getting on the FISA court would be cause for, at the very least, a dinner out. Our family—" she trailed off.

Tory filled in the blank: "We all saw what happened when you joined the military. Dad accused you of trying to abet the American imperium."

"So he's going to love you approving wiretaps." Letitia sighed. "It'll take the heat off me, at least."

"Thanks, sis," Tory said ruefully. After she got off the phone she called Jack Riley again. He hadn't answered any of his phones, the night before. The phone rang and rang.

How odd. She called Bart. He answered on the first ring. "Judge Parker."

"Hey, Bart, I've got a dog here begging me to go out."

"I'll be right up."

Bart arrived three minutes later, gratefully accepted a cup of coffee and the use of Tory's bathroom as she leashed up Siggy. Then, downstairs, Bart became all business. "Van's right out front—" he pointed to a black Econoline with mirrored windows, parked right in front of Tory's building's canopy. "And that guy-" Bart's eyes narrowed—"is still there." He gestured with the slightest nod. There was a worn station wagon. Behind the wheel was a young man reading *El Diario,* the New York Spanish-language daily.

Instantly Tory's senses were at high alert. "Is that someone you recognize?" she asked.

"I know the type," Bart said. "Ignore him. Just keep walking." He opened his jacket to have access to the gun in his shoulder holster.

Okay, Tory thought. Siggy was taking an inordinate amount of time smelling a hydrant. Tory, lost in her own fear, yanked the leash. He held his ground; he never responded to brute force. "Come on, kiddo," she said, and touched his snout. He perked up, trotted along beside.

"So the sniper in Brooklyn—you think that was El Limpiador?"

"Worth a bet, I'd say." Bart had his eye on a maintenance man in a green uniform packing garbage out of an apartment building basement. "Evidently that was a hell of a shot, and I know from experience he's a hell of a shooter."

"Really?"

"He and I went shooting at Eduardo's range, once." Bart shook his head. "Guy was amazing. However tight my groupings were, his were tighter. Like watching a classical musician, or a surgeon— that kind of precision."

"So he could be lining me up right now." Tory looked up at the buildings around them.

Bart cracked a smile. "Naah, he likes to hit people where it'll spread the most fear— like hitting the guy while he's testifying in the courtroom. But that takes research to pull off. Right now I'm looking to see his team here, building a file on you."

Siggy circled, doing the little dance he always did before doing his business. Tory, usually amused by his Chaplinesque earnestness, felt trapped and vulnerable, out in the open.

She had been threatened before, and she hated the way fear would bleach away the joy of the most commonplace moments. Walking her dog, bantering with the woman at the coffee shop, all the little moments of her day became tainted with paranoia, and the end result was a numbness toward the world that turned Tory into someone she didn't recognize.

And here it was again. "OK, this El Limpiador guy—besides being a good shooter, what was he like?"

"Kind of all-business," Bart said. "He didn't gamble—Nieto liked to gamble, so everybody around Nieto gambled, except him. The only way I could get close to him was, you know, shooting, so that's what we did."

A methodical assassin with great skills who didn't take chances. Tory didn't want to know anything more. "When Nieto gambles," she asked, "is he smart, or is he impetuous?"

"Not as smart as he thinks." Bart smiled. "I could always tell if he was bluffing. He'd reward himself—smoke his cigar a certain way, drink his aguardiente. So I'd let him win, then take back my losses, let him win again. Then I finally scored big, took him for sixty grand one night, and he actually liked me better for it. That's when I knew I was in."

They were passing the construction site on 88th street, girders going up behind a wooden partition. Tory was slightly ambivalent because the guys in hardhats always made a big fuss about the dog while checking out her legs. Some of them were nice, though. One or two were even cute.

She wasn't really in the mood today, but one guy always gave Siggy scraps of sandwich, so the beast pulled them right up to the gate.

"He likes this place," Bart said.

"They feed him," Tory explained. No one was about; she touched Siggy's nose to get him to keep walking, and he did. When they came back around the block, the dilapidated car was still there.

"Go in the building," Bart said. "I'll approach, see what happens."

Tory was always amazed by cops, no matter what level of the government they worked for. They did things that no sane person would do, and they did them all the time. "Thanks, Bart," she said, as Siggy pulled her up to her front door.

She went through, watched through the glass as Bart stepped right up to the driver's window. She couldn't quite see the interaction, but suddenly the car squealed out, fishtailed down the street and disappeared. Tory watched as Bart took out a pad, scribbled something, and walked back to the building.

"I don't think we'll see that guy again," he said, "but if we do I know what he looks like, and I got his plates."

* * *

Angelo was electric.

Sam opened the trial, and he was great—calm but never unemotional, both forceful and plaintive as he painted a picture of the boat being stopped in New York harbor and the discovery of the cocaine. From there, he bridged a connection between that boat and Baby Nieto. He built up to an impassioned crescendo as he described Baby's affluent lifestyle, and argued that such lavish excesses could not be afforded by the flower business Baby claimed as his principle source of income. When finally he sat, the courtroom was in thrall.

Then Angelo stood, and at first Tory, on the bench, thought he was making a huge mistake. "Ladies and gentlemen of the jury, my name's Angelo Schwartz, and I'm a lawyer." He stopped, gave a little smile, let anybody who might know the 12-step reference get the joke. "I handle a lot of drug cases. I don't do it because I like drugs—I hate drugs. I've seen the wreckage they do. I've seen dead teenagers, dead ten-year-olds, dead from drugs. And I've seen the violence. The business of drugs is a culture of death. You all know that—we read about it every day, gangs shooting each other, journalists getting killed—you know it."

He stopped, drew himself to his full height. "I hate drugs. But you know what I love? More than anything else? Freedom. The right to be left alone. The right to go about your business without being constantly swarmed by the buzzing flies of suspicion, without the state watching every move you make. Being able to make your own decisions. Being treated like an adult—not a baby." And with that, he looked at the enormous man seated in a waft of dark blue suit at the defense table, the man the jury all knew to be Baby Nieto.

Angelo walked up close to the jury box. "Got a question for you. I say '1970s', what do you picture? Discos, glam rock, punk rock, crazy times, all those subcultures. You know what the standard street price for a gram of cocaine was in 1975? It was $100.00.

"Been a long time since then, right? And we've been fighting a war on drugs this whole time—billions and billions of dollars, wars in South America, wars in Southeast Asia, wars and wars and wars, money and money and more money. It's never stopped, has it? It's. Just. Been. Constant.

"Ladies and gentlemen, do you know the standard street price for a gram of cocaine today? This week, this month, right now?

"Ladies and gentlemen, that price is $100 a gram. Exactly the same as it was in 1975. Exactly. The. Same.

"You know what that tells us? That tells us the war on drugs—all that money, all those wars, all those lives torn apart for all these years—the war on drugs has been a miserable failure. If it was a success, cocaine would be priced so high nobody could afford it! Cocaine would be the rarest commodity in the world! But it's not. It's the same damn price it's always been.

"Ladies and gentlemen of the jury, the US Government is frustrated. Somebody keeps sending tons and tons of cocaine into this country. So they have used every tool of the justice department— and when I say 'every tool' I mean all the tools you know, and some so secret we're not allowed to talk about them here— on this man." He put his hand on Baby's enormous shoulder, a gesture that showed the jury he was completely unafraid of the obese defendant.

Back when she'd been a young DA, Tory had been frightened by the power of theater in a courtroom. She'd had a drug case where the defense attorney had been a dazzling entertainer. Tory had spent sleepless nights wondering how much the jury bought the flamboyant act. They laughed all the way through, and then they looked at the evidence and convicted the defendant.

Which was not to say it had no effect. The courtroom was, like it or not, a theater; the jury was the audience, the rules of law and of evidence defined the narrative. Guns that appeared in the first act invariably went off in the third.

Once one accepted the theatricality of the courtroom, the judge's role made sense. The judge was the director, shepherding the production along, making sure the jury was able to see, as much as possible, both sides of every story.

In Tory's courtrooms, overt theatricality tended not to be indulged. But it was, at times, fun to watch. And Angelo, to be honest about it, had become among the best she'd ever seen. "...so they went with the easiest target they could— Ricardo Nieto." Angelo flourished a gracious hand toward his client. "A man tortured with health problems, some of his own making, some not. A man with several entirely legitimate businesses— papers filed, employees with dental plans, taxes paid— here in New York. A man, ladies and gentleman, who has not been in Colombia *in four years."* Angelo held up four fingers. "If you were a partner in an ongoing billion-dollar international business, you'd go back to the home office every once in a while. But if you had seen that world, and seen how it consumed your brother, turned him into some kind of monster, seen how it damaged him, seen how it damaged *you*, if you'd made a choice to move to a new country, settle in a new city and build a new life and not— once— looked— back," He bowed his head, took a deep breath, gentled himself: "Then you'd be my client, Ricardo Nieto."

Tory realized she wasn't breathing. She could see the handsome, ambitious kid she'd known all those years ago, and she could see he'd grown into the lion before her.

He'd fulfilled his promise, and he'd done it better than anyone she'd ever known.

* * *

Angelo had clocked his opening perfectly—when he was done, it was time for lunch. Tory declared a recess. Then, knowing full well the weeks of order-in tuna sandwiches which awaited them, she turned to Anna: "Forlini's? To make up for last time?"

When they arrived, the place was crowded and noisy. Joe, the owner at the door, greeted Tory with a hug—they'd known each other since she was a baby DA. He immediately understood Bart's presence. Bart asked to be seated between Tory's table and the door.

After a moment of reconfiguring, Bart was offered a small table ten feet from Tory's regular booth. She had barely sat when Angelo made his way across the restaurant to say hello.

They shook hands. His grip was firm. "Good opening today, counselor," said Tory.

"You think? I thought Sam had me on points."

Tory introduced Angelo to Anna and Thomas, handshakes all around. "See," Angelo told them, "I know judges who wouldn't bother introducing their clerks."

Anna smiled. "We all know judges who wouldn't bother introducing their clerks." Big laugh at the table. Angelo looked around.

"I haven't been to this place in years."

"It hasn't changed," Tory said.

"Some things never do," Angelo said, and Tory was aware of his focused gaze, how it excluded everyone else in the world but her. As quickly as it had come, the moment passed. "Lovely meeting you all," he said with a wide smile; and headed back to his table.

Tory ordered her usual, a Forlini salad, Anna the same. Thomas opted for a big pasta. Tory noticed Bart ordering without ever opening his menu. Focused, she thought, and turned her attention back to Thomas, who was telling a story about his most recent round of dating. "So I tell her I clerk for a judge, and she asks: oh, does that mean you do his laundry—"

Anna burst out laughing: "Sometimes I think the public has no idea what we do."

"They get it all from cop shows," Thomas opined.

Tory wasn't listening. There was a man at the door whom Tory found familiar; he was looking all around the restaurant until he found her. He brushed past Joe and abruptly Tory knew: the car, this morning, the glimpse she'd had through the window. The same man.

He'd followed her here. Panic galloped through Tory. She wanted to get away but there were customers standing in the aisle, she was trapped—and Bart stood, pushed past waiters just as the man reached into his coat. In one motion Tory saw the gray glint of smooth metal.

"GUN!" Bart Alicia yelled it as he launched himself at the man, slammed him in the chest with his shoulder. Bart grabbed the man's gun wrist in one mighty hand, held it crushingly tight as he barreled him out the door of the restaurant. After a few seconds the entire room convulsed at the unmistakable BLAM of a gunshot, close and loud, just outside.

Bart walked in, blood on his sleeves, holding a wad of white handkerchief. "You're safe now," he said, as much to the room as to Tory. He went to her, opened the handkerchief. Inside was the man's revolver, the cylinder open, five chambers loaded, one empty.

Tory looked up to Bart's eyes. "Thank you," she said, her voice thick with emotion. Bart nodded as Angelo rushed up, his face creased with concern. "Tory— are you okay?

"Yes," she said, and a strange wave of shocked emotion washed through her; part of it was nausea at what had happened, and part of it was a flood of fierce relief.

*   *   *

The dead man had been removed uptown to the morgue; the cops had spoken to Tory and her team, taken their statements and let them go on with their day. The jury, cooling their heels in the deliberation room, were not to be told.

On the phone, Jack Riley was formal. "You're sure you can do this, Tory?" he asked.

Tory was pacing back and forth in the robing room. Bart, Anna and Thomas were all drained, as still as statues. "Yes, Jack," Tory said, "I'm sure."

"Because you can take the day off. Hell, you can recuse, turn down the damn trial—"

"I've had death threats before. They didn't stop trials then; they won't now."

"Good to see you haven't changed," Jack said. "Call me if there's anything I can do."

"Right," said Tory, and got off the phone. Thomas stood, a piece of paper in his hands.

"This security clearance thing you gave us yesterday—" his voice was quiet. "It's about Nieto?"

"Amongst other things, yes," Tory said.

He took a pen from his breast pocket, signed and dated the document. "Whatever we have to do to stop these bastards, I'm in," he said, and gave the paper to Tory.

"Thank you, Thomas." She put on her black robe. "Ready?" she asked.

"I go first," said Bart, and, walking point, led her into the courtroom.

* * *

For nine years, Judge Lucy Ocindo had presided over the worst drug cases in Los Angeles Country. An attractive, buxom brunette of Mexican heritage, she flaunted her dark good looks and drop-dead figure everywhere but in her courtroom, where she had fallen into the habit of wearing oversized robes in order to keep leering defense attorneys and defendants at bay. Outside the courtroom, however, it was a different story. Twice divorced, currently single, and on the wrong side of 45, Lucy still made quite an impression on men. It was happening again tonight: various men, some of them quite attractive, had made their interest plain. But there was one man in particular she was waiting for—Francisco, a tall, elegant Latin American man with long black hair.

She had been to Zinc the weekend before with her best friend, Lola Ontiverres. The two of them—large-breasted, raven-haired, fearless dancers— often hit these clubs together, cutting a wide swath through the evening. That weekend, they had met Francisco and his tall American friend. Lucy and Francisco had immediately been sympatico; Lola had not been interested in the balding American. At some point Francisco had pulled Lucy aside and suggested they meet there next Saturday night, it will be our secret, just you and me. There was something romantic and seductive about the man's proposal— so much more intriguing than merely asking for a phone number. Lucy had thought about little else all week. When Lola called with invitations to a film premiere party for this evening, Lucy had begged off, claiming a headache.

Now here she was, dressed to enthrall, the ice was melting in her mojito, and disappointment was corrupting her mood. She had staked her evening's happiness on a promise, and two divorces should have taught her precisely what the promises of men were worth. She finished her drink, crunched an ice cube, debated calling Lola's cell phone. She would claim a miraculous recovery, wonder if it wasn't too late to join her friend at the party, hobnob with the stars.

Then she saw him, and all thoughts of escape popped like soap bubbles. His hair was down to his shoulders, his suit was Armani, he had that lean frame she always found so admirable. When he saw her, his dark eyes seemed to smolder and a half-smile played on his face and the part of her that had always had a thing for bad boys just melted.

He was alone. She was alone. They drank mojitos and he seemed fascinated to hear her speak about her job, about her cases, about whatever came into her increasingly drunken mind.

The club was crowded, but it was as if there was no one in the place except the two of them. At some point, after her third drink, she became flushed, excused herself and went to the ladies' room to pee and check her makeup.

There was a strong smell of marijuana in the lady's room, a smell not entirely unpleasant to Lucy, though she had not indulged in many years. Somehow it managed to increase the heady sense of danger that permeated the evening. And it made it seem only natural when, reapplying lipstick in the mirror, she saw the dark-haired Francisco loom up beside her.

She pulled him quickly into a stall, almost girlishly afraid that someone would see.

They grappled for a moment in the small, dimly lit space. At first, she didn't understand what he was doing, he told her to sit and then squatted before her. She opened her thighs to him, looked down and licked her lips. In reply, he took something from his jacket pocket, passed it from hand to hand, and then she felt a sharp needle enter the fold behind her left knee. Abruptly, her blood pressure seemed to change; her heart was missing beats, shaking with a tremor she'd never felt before. She looked at the handsome longhaired man and tried to form words, tried to ask what? And why?

The words never came. "Adios, judge" was the last thing she heard before she died.

* * *

Tory got home at 8:00 that night, dead tired but filled with tension. Reporters—those few who had her private number—had been calling since right after the murder attempt at Forlini's; she hadn't responded to any. Then the story hit all the news aggregators on the Internet, and her phone had blown up.

She silenced it, and she and Bart walked Siggy. Then, back home, she sat on her couch and went through the messages. Most she ignored—reporters, old friends she didn't want to talk to. Her sister. Her father. Her mother, separately, from an alternative wellness center she often visited in Montana. Not Rafe, who was, she was sure, too occupied with his own troubles to bother. Not her brother, the one person she wanted to talk to, if she'd known where he was.

She stood debating whom to call first—not her father, not yet—when the phone burst into ringing in her hand, making her jump. She checked the screen, hit the button. "Hello?"

Penny down in DC. "Tory Parker, what is going on up there? I turn on the news, some guy tried to hit you in a restaurant?"

"I'm fine," she said.

"Really?"

"A little freaked out. But fine. I mean, I went straight back to work, and all."

"And that sniper thing? In Brooklyn? Was that guy got injured same guy you dumped the other night? I mean how many Brooklyn prosecutors named Rafe—"

"You've been watching too much news," Tory said.

"I know it." Penny didn't laugh. "Ever since Kendrick went to college—" she was interrupted by an incoming call on Tory's phone.

"Penny, I'm fine, but that's my dad calling in."

"You take it. You must have a zillion calls to make."

"I'll be down there later this month, we'll talk." Tory said goodbye and clicked the phone just as the incoming call hung up. She held her thumb over her father's number, stopped, took a deep breath. She was operating on autopilot. She put down the phone, debated what she wanted.

She wanted to go to a seedy bar with a pool table, pick up a guy. Any guy. Drink too much and wake up in somebody's bed smelling like booze and cigarettes and sex.

Bad idea. A drink was tempting, sink into the warm subjective fuzz, but she decided against it. She had to keep sharp; if anything happened, she wanted to be able to move quickly.

She put on an old pink terrycloth robe, made an enormous bowl of granola, opened a little metal screw-topped house full of maple syrup that had been on her shelf for months, glugged in more than was socially acceptable. Siggy was watching her every move, but he didn't criticize, and she loved him for that. She sat on the couch, Siggy next to her with his chin on her thigh, ate granola, gave in to the urge to scroll through all the social media. Everything from factual reporting to conspiracy theories. She watched a couple, couldn't bear them, clicked on videos of baby goats jumping around in people's living rooms and chipped away at her granola.

Finally, the bowl empty, she dialed her father's number. It rang three times, and Maritzka answered.

She wasn't the original student with whom her father had had the affair. She was the latest in a long line. Some of them had been younger than Tory; this one, she was pretty sure, wasn't. "Is my father there?"

"He just tried to call you." The accent was Norwegian. "Emory, it's Victoria."

"Just Tory is fine," she said, false cheer through gritted teeth. Her mother used to call her Victoria when she was particularly angry. Maritzka had no right, but it wasn't worth a fight.

Her father's booming voice took over the phone. "Tory," he said. "What happened?" She'd had the thought of telling him about FISA, but now, she knew, was not the time. She took him through the man being stopped in the restaurant, waiting for the reaction, and inevitably it came:

"Do all the other judges live with bodyguards trial after trial?"

Tory was at a loss what to say. "I'm good at what I do, dad," she said finally

"You're good at things that don't involve people trying to kill you over lunch."

"Dad, I'm privileged to be in the position I'm in."

"Your sister's in the military, and I worry more about you than her."

Tory sucked her lips together, unable to come up with a response. Funny how her father could checkmate her in three moves. "This is what comes of you being the tool of a failed government drug policy—"

"Dad, somebody tried to kill me, today. I'm really not up for the lecture."

"Spraying poison onto all the plants in Colombia— it gets into the soil, it gets into the streams—"

"Dad— Stop it!" She hadn't meant to yell, but inescapably she had.

A long pause. "Tory." His voice was softer. "This drug war creates nothing but victims," he said. "I just don't want you to be one."

At last something they could agree upon. "Neither do I, dad. Neither do I."

*   *   *

Penelope Jefferson had come to hate leaving work.

She handled the social work intake desk at her clinic, trying to sort out what people were appropriate for which programs, trying to ease their way through the labyrinth of bureaucracy. She was the last one in the office because she had been elevated to manager; she had to do the nightly report after everyone left.

Sometimes she thought the real point of this clinic was the creation of a mountain of paper where all these reports and applications and coding requirements ultimately would end up, eventually to be burned in a great conflagration. The bonfire at the end of the world.

It was a job. She finished her email, sent it to a list of seven people in the building, shut down her computer. She put on her coat and made her way through the waiting room, the last few patients getting their meds. She smiled when she saw them, dropped the smile once she was past. She said take care to the security guard, walked out into the chilly night.

Halfway to the bus stop she passed a convivial bar, music and warm lights and beer signs in the window. Not her speed, not her style, and besides, they all looked so young.

She got to the bus stop, peered down the street. No bus, not yet. She had the thought, as she always did, that she really had to change her bus route; the other one was longer, this was more direct, got her home quicker, but on this one she always had to pass the building.

A bus rumbled to a stop. Penny got on, gave in to temptation and took a seat on the right side. Back when Kendrick was still in high school they'd taken this bus together; Penny had been aware of the building, but hadn't wanted her son to see it, so it had been easy to avoid.

But now the boy was in college, and Penny was alone. The bus pressed forward, the neighborhood deteriorating as it went, boarded-up shops and crumbling buildings getting worse at every stop. A block away she saw the first lookouts, tough men in leather jackets talking into cell phones. After the light, the building itself. a tenement, music blasting from somewhere, boys in basketball jerseys, girls in painted-on jeans, all just mingling. Street life. Funny, she thought, the groups at NA meetings and the groups in front of drug houses all looked the same.

She couldn't resist glancing to see who was covering the door: the tattooed muscle guy.

Sometimes it was a skinny nervous guy. The tattooed guy seemed more approachable.

The bus built up speed, left the building behind, and Penny shook her head: Jeez, girl, you're a damn Social Worker, you're 33, son in college, haven't had a cigarette in 4 years, and now you're debating which door guy looks nice at the dope house: Get your ass to a meeting.

That's it, she thought. Tomorrow night I'm switching routes.

*   *   *

The next morning, Eduardo Nieto was at his desk early. Before him, spread in piles, were his files on the best uniformed men at his disposal, along with a handful of the worst. He drew up a list, took it down the hall to the first man he saw. "Get these people here in an hour," he said, and walked out towards the stables.

Diego was in Darth Vader's stall. He hadn't finished mucking out the straw and horseshit; the horse still needed to be groomed. He looked surprised when Eduardo arrived.

"Señor Nieto—I'm sorry, I wasn't expecting you yet."

"I'll ride later," the man said. "It's Diego, yes?"

"Yes, sir." The young man nervously rubbed the downy hair on his chin.

"Come, Diego. I have a special job for you." And he led the young man out of the barn.

* * *

Eduardo Nieto clanged open the barn's metal trap door, led Diego down the ramp. "The job is simple," he said, and led him to the glass window. "On the shelves in back, you see the plastic and metal cases?" Diego nodded. "Each of those contains a rare and precious material. In some cases it is solid, in others powder. I want you to get it out. Don't worry about preserving the casings, you'll have to destroy them to get to what's inside. When you get to the material, be very careful. Don't spill a speck of it. I need even the smallest amount. If it's solid, use the band saw to cut it into tiny pieces. Put all the material in that bowl—" he pointed to a large metal bowl on the wall. "Mix it very well, and then fill those long plastic bags with it. Don't pack it in tight, they should bend without breaking. When you're done, open that drawer—" he pointed to a metal drawer set into the wall inside. "Put the full bags in, shut it and ring that bell. We'll come get you. Got all that?"

"Yes sir," Diego said. "I just want to thank you for giving me this chance."

"No, I thank you," Eduardo said, opening the door to the inner sanctum. Diego went in and Eduardo relocked the door, smiled at the man through the thick glass and went upstairs.

Behind the glass, Diego took up the first piece of machinery, flipped open a vice on the workbench, screwed it in tight, took up a hammer and chisel. He stripped away a black plastic outer shell, revealing an oblong metal canister. He unscrewed the vice, repositioned the metal case and began to attack the welded seam. After much sweaty work in the airless room, he cut his way to a thick ceramic rod at the center, stripped it out. He held this in his hands, debating the best way to proceed, turned on the band saw and carefully began shaving the ceramic core into the finest slivers he could manage. These he threw into the bowl. He started a garbage pile for metal and plastic remnants, then turned his attention to the next item on the shelf.

The last item, the long case in the fish tank, had been especially difficult to open. Diego had to attack it with the handsaw. When it broke apart, powder had sprayed across the room. He'd gone down on his knees, making little piles with his hands, wetting the tip of his finger with his tongue to pick up individual specks. When he was done, he sat for a moment looked at the bowl filled with powder and band-sawed ceramic chunks.

The room was hot and airless, and he couldn't wait to get out of there. He took up the plastic bags, was surprised to find they were long and thin, rather like snakes. He found a funnel, rubber-banded the first bag on, and began filling it with the mixed powder and slivers.

When a piece was too big, he smashed it in the mortar and pestle to get it to fit. He couldn't touch the stuff without chalky white dust rising into the air.

He figured this was base, some kind of special extra-strong base that came in these casings. He had been noticing a rash on his hands where he touched the material, like a sunburn, but indoors. Now blisters were forming on his fingers, on his lips, on the inside of his nose.

He thought of Don Eduardo's horse— seeing him run in the fields was a beautiful sight. He thought of his parents, his brothers. He remembered a section of fence he had to rebuild.

Each bag was two feet long; he kept filling them until he was out of material. His lungs were beginning to hurt, now, and he was feeling nauseous. He knotted the long bags, opened the metal drawer in the wall and dropped them in. He shut the drawer and rang the buzzer.

He had made plans to see Hortensia tomorrow night. He hoped this rash would clear up by then. He thought he heard noises on the other side of the drawer, tried to open it to talk to whoever was there, but it was locked now. He banged on it, rang the bell again, finally gave up and sat.

Someone would come down and get him. He was sure of it. All he had to do was wait.

* * *

Dr. Torres had not worn a chem-bio-nuclear suit and respirator since setting up the most recent fentanyl lab, and he never liked how hot and cumbersome they were. When the bell rang, he pulled the headgear on, opened the second trap door. He stepped carefully down a second ramp. To his left, behind a cement-block wall, was the boy Eduardo had picked to handle the radioactive material. Dr. Torres could not see or hear him, but the buzzer he was ringing was insistent and irritating.

Then, finally, it stopped. Dr. Torres puckered his lips in mild concern, set about the business of pulling the lead-lined box out from his side of the wall. He made sure all the latches were completely sealed, set it into a larger wheeled box filled with water, latched down a cover on that, attached a rope to a handle on one side. He let out rope as he climbed the ramp, then pulled the box up the ramp into the barn. Then he lifted the heavy metal trap door and let it slam shut.

Evidently the boy in the radioactive lab had heard that, because the buzzer from the underground lab began ringing again. Dr. Torres found the noise interruptive and irritating. He took up a saw from a workbench, made his way to the buzzer, sliced the wire with two cuts of the saw blade, silencing the noise instantly.

Much better.

He walked out the back of the barn, took off the hazmat suit, dumped it in a deep hole dug in the ground. Then, very slowly, he made his way back around to the front.

His car stood between a pickup truck and an idling cement mixer, its massive tumbler rolling. He stepped up to the pickup, spoke to the first of Eduardo's soldiers he saw.

"There's a box on the floor in there. Pull it out with the forklift, put it on the pickup truck, take it to the other barn down the road. And whatever you do, don't drop it. Don Eduardo would be very displeased."

Dr. Torres lit a cigar, waited. Finally the lead-lined box was tied to the back of the truck. The men threw a tarp over it, drove slowly out of the barn, disappeared around the bend.

When they were gone, Dr. Torres approached the cement truck, saw the driver was asleep. He took up his cane, rapped hard on the window.

"We're ready for you," Dr. Torres said. The cement man had the ruddy face of a drinker; he was not, the doctor knew, one of Eduardo's favorites. Dr. Torres got into his car, rolled up the windows as the cement truck backed into the barn. Torres watched intently through the barn door as the cement man went in to unscrew the vent pipe. He seated the wooden funnel over the pipe, shifted some gears on his truck and started the slurry of cement down the chute.

Dr. Torres had seen enough. He started his car, headed down the road. He thought briefly about the man in the underground room, but he didn't bother to look back.

* * *

In the underground cell, Diego was lying on the floor too sick to extricate himself from his own vomit when the globs of cement began to spew down. At first he thought it was mud, and it meant somebody was in the barn, somebody was digging through to find him, and his heart filled with hope. Then some landed near him, and he touched it with his fingers, knew instantly that this was cement.

He sat up, got out of the way of the vent hole in the ceiling of the room. Wet cement was splattering down on the table, on the chair and the pile of plastic and metal discards from his work. He stood, again banged on the door, crossed the room and jammed the buzzer with his finger, ran across again and banged on the door, and all the while cement kept raining down.

He fought to make as much noise as possible, but as the thick grey paste reached his ankles, he sat in it and hugged his knees and wept, because he realized this wasn't a mistake. This was how he was going to die. Cement would fill the room, and solidify, and no one would ever find him, his parents and his brothers and his sister would never know what had happened to him, the life he had imagined for himself would never be, he would never marry, he would never meet the love of his life, he would never be an old man in a garden with grandchildren.

And all, he knew, because he had been late, once, in saddling Eduardo Nieto's horse.

*　　*　　*

A mile away in the other barn, Eduardo's plastic explosives crew had just about finished their careful work. They took an empty fire extinguisher, brought it and the explosive trigger to Eduardo. "We found several different cell-phone motherboards which suited our size requirements," Dr. Torres explained proudly. "The metal in the extinguisher valve acts as our antenna. The signal comes through the antenna, turns on the motherboard, the motherboard sends a pulse to the blasting cap in the plastic explosive—" the doctor made a flourish of his hand. "Et voila."

"Let's see if it works," Eduardo growled.

The extinguisher nozzle, plastic explosive and trigger rode in the front of the jeep next to the driver. The empty extinguisher was in the back. When the man was seventy yards from the barn, he stopped, gingerly screwed the nozzle assembly into the extinguisher, set it on the ground, roared the jeep away.

Eduardo Nieto took out his cell phone, dialed a number. He waited a moment while the cell connection was made. Then the number began to ring.

The second the ringtone began, the bottle in the middle of the field burst into an angry red nimbus of shrapnel and fire.

* * *

A gray fall morning in Washington DC, the city and its monuments banked by clouds, and black town cars with government plates filled the street.

"If I was Nieto," Tory said, "and I saw all these, I'd know something was up."

"Ahh, just another day at Justice," Bart said, and shrugged. Tory entered the building, took the elevator up, showed her badge to the Marshals, typed in her code and was let through the door into the chambers of the Secret Court. Inside, the place felt like any office before the workday begins: little groups of people drinking coffee from the cart in the corner.

Everyone was extremely solicitous to her about the assassination attempt. And then Al Clemente arrived, bursting with his story of being shot at through the window of his courtroom. Tory and Jack stood on the sidelines as he unspooled a narrative larded with self-aggrandizing heroics. Afterwards, Jack approached her. "With Clemente, that's not how it went, right?"

"Not at all," she answered. "It must be interesting, going through life with no shame."

"I wish I could," Riley said. And with that, Chief Justice Drummond stood from the papers he'd been perusing and called the Foreign Intelligence and Surveillance Court to order.

"One housekeeping note. The Justice Department has secured a new safe house for us, once again in Georgetown. I had the pleasure of visiting it last night, and I think it'll meet our needs perfectly. As before, each of you will have your own chambers to use when you're in town. The Marshals will assist you with keys and codes. All right, let's get to business."

One by one the judges gave updates on their cases. Tory found this fascinating— the kind of colloquy one thought one would get from a room full of judges, but all too rarely did. The majority were involved in the efforts against Mexican fentanyl gangs and Middle Eastern terrorist groups. There were, Tory learned, several cases either in pretrial or trial involving US real estate being purchased by foreign organizations for money-laundering. The amount of money these cases had uncovered was frighteningly large.

Drummond, when his turn came, looked at Tory. "I spoke to Director Severn late last night: I regret to say there has been no movement in the case involving emeralds being shipped to Eduardo Nieto's hired killer in New York. To be honest, I was hoping for better news."

"We did what we could," said Tory.

"Not enough, I'm afraid," Drummond said sadly. Then OIPR, in the form of a bullet-headed ex-JAG named Theodore Vasco, made their first presentation of the day.

"May it please the court," Vasco began. "On the date of October 13, in the city of Los Angeles, County of Los Angeles, California State Supreme Court Judge Lucy Ocindo was found dead in a nightclub bathroom. Preliminary toxicology suggests she was injected, likely with fentanyl." This did not come as a surprise to most of the judges in the room; the lurid details of Judge Ocindo's demise had received national attention. "This fits the pattern seen in two recent, similar cases.

"On February 8 of last year, Nevada Superior Court Judge Hiram Canute died of an apparent heart attack in a restaurant bathroom in Las Vegas. On July 16, Pennsylvania Criminal Judge

Brenda Pell was found dead in her car in a movie theater parking lot. Cause of death was also listed as a heart attack.

"In all three cases, these judges had recently presided over, and convicted, known members of the Eduardo Nieto crime organization involved in large-scale cocaine transactions. The causes of death indicated for both Judge Canute and Judge Pell were not challenged until the Ocindo toxicology results were made known, at which point Justice Department officials began to connect the dots.

"The FBI is continuing its investigation of Ocindo, and at the same time reopening the cases of Canute and Pell. The likely mastermind of this linked series of murders, if linked series of murders they prove to be, is Eduardo Nieto. Mr. Nieto is a resident of Colombia; thus he is per se a foreign agent, and under Executive Order 416255 is officially classified by our government as a terrorist. Thus the actions of Mr. Nieto and any agents under his employ or influence do in fact fall under the purview of this court as defined by the FISA Act and the PATRIOT Act. OIPR, in its application before this court today, requests authority to wiretap and search the business records of any agents serving under the authority of Eduardo Nieto, who may have information about the commission of these crimes." The former military man, ramrod straight as he spoke, broke character for a moment, looked at each judge in turn. "In Colombia, Nieto has a long history of killing judges who convict his boys. It's made the conviction rate drop precipitously. It would seem he's trying to apply the same pressure up here." Then the man's posture, without ever appearing to have relaxed, seemed to become somehow even straighter: "OIPR asks these applications be granted with the maximum haste that prudent deliberation will allow." He bowed his head once, curtly, and then stepped back.

Drummond took over. "Timely and succinct, Mr. Vasco. Thank you." He looked at the judges arrayed in a semicircle around him. "Are we all content with this, as presented? Or does anyone need further supporting documentation?"

Tory raised a hand. "I would be interested in seeing the expanded package."

"I thought you might, Judge Parker," Drummond said kindly. "Do you need that in order to pass judgment in the matter before us today?"

"I see no reason to allow my personal curiosity to hold up this investigation. I'm prepared to vote right now."

"Excellent." Drummond nodded at Vasco. "Please ensure that Judge Parker is given all supplementary documentation in this matter by end of day today." Then, to Tory: "That good enough?"

"Couldn't be better," she said. "Anyone else have something to say?"

Rebekkah King raised her palm to the sky. "I knew Hiram Canute. We were in law school together. He was a wonderful man." Something broke inside her, but she held it in·. "He had three children in diapers when he died." The silence in the room turned to a pall. She cleared her throat. "Because of this personal connection, I will recuse myself from voting in the matter of Hiram's death. I will, however, be more than happy to vote in the matters of Judges Ocindo and Pell."

"Very well, then," Drummond said, "we'll break them up. Anyone else? No?"

A few minutes later, the Secret Court voted to grant their full ration of powers to the FBI investigators looking into the deaths of Judges Ocindo, Pell and Canute.

* * *

After the fourth case of the morning, Drummond looked at the cases remaining on his docket and suggested that in lieu of a proper lunch break, a collation of sandwiches be sent up from the DOJ cafeteria. When they arrived, Tory selected a turkey club and an iced tea and watched as Fenton Kottle searched until he found roast beef. She had been looking for a moment alone with him.

"Judge Kottle," she plunged. "I was very impressed by your Family Court book."

Kottle turned, pleasantly surprised. He was an avuncular man, taller than Tory, with a fierce intelligence behind mild New England Wasp looks.

"Please— Fenton." He spoke in a Boston accent. "Glad to hear that book still has a life."

"It really speaks to how the legal system interacts with children."

"I would see kids walk in the courtroom innocent, and then they'd grow up and I'd see them again and again, each time worse. I tried to help— sometimes you intervene personally. But after a while I had to get out of that world." He smiled thinly. "So now I'm in this one." His tone was ambivalent.

"Is this one better?" she asked.

He considered. "Something about knowing there was an innocent child at the heart of a case made it worth fighting for. Though what we do here is important, it's also much more abstract. I find I do miss the kids," he said, and then, as if afraid of showing an excess of emotion, he began rummaging through the iced cans of soda, looking for one he liked.

* * *

Baby Nieto hated lines.

There was a line everywhere at Riker's Island. To eat food, there was a line. To shower, a line. To use the payphone, a line. It was always like waiting to be let in to some big summer action movie, except with no movie at the end and no pretty girls to look at while you waited.

The payphone was in a corridor of white-painted cinderblock. Corrections officers had a desk at one end of the corridor, so they could keep things orderly. Around the phone there was a black halo of numbers and doodles. Each person was allowed ten minutes, and no chairs to sit. Baby was supposed to make the call at 11:00; he was leaning against the wall, two dead-faced gentlemen he'd hired from the Latin Players gang at either side.

On the clock, the second hand swept around and around. The young black man using the phone was making cooing sounds at his little son on the other end. He was in the eleventh minute. Baby was willing to wait. It was nice, the man had a son, but Chivo, the taller of his two bodyguards, wasn't happy. Finally he could stand it no longer, stepped around, pointed at the clock, and made a quick slashing gesture with his thumbnail down the man's cheek.

The man immediately hung up the phone, hurried away. Baby dialed in the number he'd been given. There was a sign in English above the phone he had been warned about, Calls Made On This Phone Are Subject To Monitoring, but he wasn't overly concerned about that. They wouldn't let him have a cell phone, and he had to assume they'd been monitoring his calls, one way or another, for years.

The phone rang, the man picked up. "Brazo Fuerte Dry Cleaners."

They spoke in English. "Yes," Baby said, "I am having trouble with this shirt— the customs-made shirt."

"My boss was concerned about that custom shirt, too. It has a stain that needs cleaning?"

"If your boss thinks so, then I think so to."

"Just the custom? None of the other shirts?"

"No, only the one, I think, will be enough."

"For now, at least."

"Right."

"Very well then, we'll take care of it."

"Right," Baby said. "Thank you," and got off the phone.

* * *

At the end of the day, Drummond invited all the FISA judges to tour the new townhouse in Georgetown; only Judge Hart begged off, saying he had an appointment in DC.

Tory, back in the car with Bart, marveled as DC commuters pulled aside for fleets of black town cars all rushing to make the same light. In New York, the line would have been cut to pieces by some cabby making a turn.

The townhouse was lovely, a stately red-brick building with a well-scrubbed collegiate faculty-housing feel to it. Tory had grown up in places like this. Walking in, she was surprised by an odd coupling of mixed emotions: perfect outsides often housed imperfect tribes within.

The furnishings, desks and fold-out couches were basic but serviceable. Drummond cleared his throat, and his authority cut through the hubbub. "I've taken the liberty of assigning rooms. Tory and Rebekkah, I've put you on the third floor, more private up there. All the men, I've divvied up the rest by seniority; you'll find names on doors. I know many of you have purchased homes in the area—" he nodded at Judge Hart— "but please don't forget what a tremendous resource a place like this is. You'll have conversations over morning coffee that'll change the future of this country."

Names on the doors, thought Tory as she made her way upstairs. Was it just her, or did that seem perhaps just a mite over-controlling? Still, when she saw the view from the high window of her room, she thought: well, this is actually very nice indeed.

* * *

As the judges settled into their new building, Drummond stepped up to Tory, asked if he could speak to her, and led her to a private conference room on the first floor.

Tory followed, heart in throat, searching her mind for what she might have done to deserve a private rebuke, but when Drummond came in, he merely said: "I was wondering if tonight was a good night to come over, shoot some pool. If you're not busy."

Tory, instantly relieved, took a deep breath. "I thought I was being called on the carpet."

"Have you done anything I should be concerned about?"

"No— no, that's not what I meant."

"Well, then— come, meet Irma, I'm not a drinking man but I expect we could rustle up a bottle of beer, if that's to your liking—"

Tory had had a plan to see Penny Jefferson. She'd called Penny earlier, and hadn't heard anything back. "I would be honored," she said. "Let me make one quick phone call."

* * *

Penny Jefferson had stopped at a bar on her way home; she hated bars but now, back in her apartment, she liked the way she felt. She stood over the answering machine in her living room for an unsteady moment, looking at the blinking light before jabbing the button.

Evelyn, her downstairs neighbor, complaining about some damn thing with the heat. She skipped to the next one.

Her son Kendrick, down in New Orleans. Just checking in. It sounded like he'd been drinking—he had that chortle in his voice he got when he was drinking.

She really didn't want to talk to him. Not right now. The third message was Tory Parker: "Hey Penny, I called your office—listen, we had a plan to get together, but I didn't hear from you, so I'm going to duck out, if you don't mind. You're not going to believe this, but Merle Drummond, the guardian of morals himself, plays pool. I'll let you know if he's good."

Whoa, Penny thought. Girlfriend is shooting pool with the Chief Justice of the Supreme Court, and meanwhile over here in my life all I want to do is get high.

* * *

When they entered Drummond's Tudor home, two King Charles spaniels barked in a furry squall around Tory's ankles. "Irma!" Drummond yelled, "Call the dogs!"

"That's all right," Tory said quickly, and knelt to play with the excited little beasts. They were joined shortly by Irma: blonde, a perfect ski-jump nose, a classic American type. There had been a press binge when she married Drummond a decade before. He'd been in his fifties, she still in her twenties. Tory shook her hand, saw she had hearing aids in each ear.

Tory had forgotten about the hearing aids, but now it was all coming back. "Judge Parker here is said to play a mean game of pool," Drummond said.

"Well, thank goodness for that!" the woman said in a soft Southern voice. "Merle's too good for me. I haven't beaten him in years."

"Your house is gorgeous," Tory said. The walls were covered with judicial paraphernalia—degrees, awards, gavels in wooden frames with bronze plaques stating what trial they'd banged open. Tory didn't immediately see anything that suggested Irma lived here at all.

Miss America. She hadn't won, but she'd made it into the final ten. That's why the press had worked themselves into a frenzy of glee when she'd married Drummond.

"If you ladies could excuse me—one quick phone call." Drummond headed upstairs.

"Let me give you the tour," Irma said, and led Tory through the dining room, the library, the solarium. In the kitchen was a large official portrait of Irma in an evening gown with a sash— Miss Tennessee. The hearing aids were discreet but unmistakable. There was a fullness to her face in the picture which had been pared down by life and gym trainers. "It's funny how women 18, 19, 20 are celebrated for their looks," Tory attempted, aware she might stumble, "but I think girls at that age often still look slightly unformed—"

"Like puppies," Irma said, and Tory was immediately relieved the woman understood what she was trying to say. "They haven't completely grown into their feet yet."

Drummond came in, rubbing his hands. "Ready for a little game of pool?"

The table was regulation size. "Had I known, I'd've brought my sticks," Tory said. She found a well-balanced hardwood with onyx inlays, a solid shooting stick.

"8 ball?" Tory agreed. "You break," Drummond said, lifting the triangle away.

Tory liked breaking. She liked showing other players that she had force. She selected a heavier stick, slammed it hard, got a decent spread, dropped the 4 ball. She sunk her next shot, a tricky bank to the middle pocket, then put the 3 in the right corner, did a slow fade to the far-left corner with the 2, and then kissed the edge of the hole with the 7.

The ball didn't go in. Just as well, she thought, give the old guy a chance. Drummond did a clean sharp drop with the 11 ball, then a long hard slice that had the English to curve across the table and drop into the far-right corner. Tory remained poker-faced, thinking: good shot. He did a beautiful Y shot that sunk two more balls in two different pockets. Then he got trapped in her defense and missed a shot Tory could easily have made.

He's good enough, she decided, *I'm not going to worry about letting him win.*

* * *

Tory won five out of seven; one of her losses was out of reach and the other was a gimme. Then they'd had a brief meal: leg of lamb, mint jelly, some kind of boring zucchini side. Drummond waxed animatedly about Tory's bona fides as a pro-law enforcement judge: "Jack Riley said you'd be tough," he enthused, "and I'm pleased to see he was right." Throughout this, Irma seemed slightly spacy, not as funny as she'd been before. Tory wondered if she was on some kind of medication, or if she'd simply turned down her hearing aids.

After a simple dish of vanilla ice cream with chocolate syrup, Drummond excused himself: he had work to do. With grateful thanks, Tory took her leave.

Back in Georgetown Al Clemente was reading a hardback thriller in the communal meeting room, stocking feet on the glass coffee table. He looked up when Tory entered. "Drummond tells me you play a mean game of pool."

So that's how it works, Tory thought. "I just came from his house," she said blithely.

"Someday you've got to give me some pointers."

"Absolutely," Tory said, and got upstairs as quickly as possible.

* * *

A perfect blue-skied autumn day in New York, gentle winds blowing swirls of leaves on dry streets. Tory, accompanied by Bart, gave Siggy a long walk around the Central Park reservoir, then let him drag her over to the construction site, where the weekend guard gave him a bite of bagel. Then, back in the apartment, the dog asleep against her thigh on the couch, Tory opened the large packet of documentation on Judges Ocindo, Canute and Pell.

A month before her death, Lucy Ocindo had finished adjudicating a long drug case with multiple defendants. Tory recognized the species: the prosecutors had relied heavily on government wiretaps showing the route of the cocaine all the way from the coca farmers and homegrown labs in Colombia through the posh gated community of Bel Air. She was surprised to see that the main defense lawyer had been none other than Angelo Schwartz.

Well, she thought, that's how he can afford to do the battered women cases and these ACLU freebies like Baby Nieto. She turned her attention to Hiram Canute: another big multi-defendant drug case, lots of wiretaps. There, listed as co-counsel, was Angelo Schwartz.

Tory's heart sank, and anxiety curled the edges of her stomach. She put down the Canute material, reached immediately for the Pell documents. Pell's most recent case before her death had been a big heroin case; Angelo had had no part of it. Tory was relieved until she saw that, two cases before that, Pell had adjudicated a large

Nieto-related drug case. It only took a moment to find it: lead counsel, Angelo Schwartz.

Tory closed her eyes, felt something wither and sicken inside. Three cases, three dead judges, and the common thread was Angelo. And here she was, all set up to be number 4.

Suddenly nothing in the room was any comfort to her, not her dog, not her books, not the art on the walls or the furniture she'd collected over the years. None of it helped her feel safe.

She poured a shot of whiskey, sipped the liquid and felt the false warmth in her stomach and looked out her window at the New York night and thought: Angelo, what are you doing? You keep taking these drug cases, making money hand over fist, and you've left behind a string of dead judges. Hiram Canute's kids will never know him, and for what? Lucy Ocindo and Brenda Pell— for what?

And now you've interjected yourself into my case. Should I be scared? Logically, yes, but you're the same Angelo I knew all those years ago. Aren't you?

Aren't you?

* * *

When FISA authorized a thorough investigation into an agent of a foreign national, the full force of the United States' data collection and counterintelligence structures were put into play. In searching for the killers of Ocindo, Canute and Pell, the first step was the enormous Cray and IBM supercomputers kept in carefully controlled atmospheric conditions at the National Security Agency in Fort Meade, Maryland.

The NSA was the nation's— and, arguably, the world's— premium eavesdropping center. On those rare occasions when its leaders were subjected to the inquiries of congressional committees, they always spoke of data collection and processing, as if they were doing something as routine as credit card applications. What they were collecting, recording, transcribing, and translating, were telephone calls, cell phone calls, emails, text messages, and any other kind of human communication that went over a wire or a wave or a beam. In Menwith Hill, Britain, in Alice Springs, Australia, and in a hundred places in between, the NSA had acres of real estate filled with the world's most sophisticated antennae. These, and the satellites that communicated with them, allowed the United States to listen in on any conversation anywhere on Earth.

The problem was knowing which ones were important. The answer was to save them all, subject them to ever-improving AI algorithms that would break them into hierarchies of threat levels for different regions of the globe.

Though it was Sunday, the supercomputers were working at full speed, and the staff that fed, watered and cultivated the data they spat out was at full strength. Mo Rheza, working weekends so he could cover his kids while his wife taught a class on Monday and Wednesday, was in place that morning to receive the order from the Secret Court. It had priority Alpha-Sigma, which meant it went to the head of any queue of Justice Department-related searches, though Defense-related requests could supersede. Mo, in his carrel, sat at his terminal, quickly turned the FISA request into logic strings the AI wouldn't misinterpret. When he'd set the parameters correctly, he entered the request, then reorganized all the paper all over his desk back into the request file. He put that in the Out bin, turned his attention to the next request, from the DIA on another matter entirely.

Inside the supercomputer, two searches were being carried out simultaneously. The first parsed phone calls by region, cell tower usage, or satellite link packet. In the delineated geographic search regions, the first request was to look for key words: Ocindo, Canute, Pell, judge, juez, togado, juzgar, and on and on in English, Spanish, outliers, and area-specific regional dialects. This search included an algorithm of known and surmised slang and code terms specific to the region and enterprise being investigated. The second, parallel search looked for patterns of phone use among known Nieto associates, up to and including Nieto himself. It went under the assumption, seen again and again, that there will be a flurry of calls leading up to the date of each murder, and then one more, the "valedictory" call, and silence. One dead giveaway was that phones used during the commission of a crime tended to get dumped immediately after; this pattern occurred enough, in various criminal and terrorist enterprises, that the AI had become adept at finding it when it occurred.

In less than 2 minutes, the enormous computer system had cracked open all the data to find everything that fit the pattern and had pulled together a list of phone calls and phone numbers under those parameters. These results were forwarded to the Analysis section, where a report would be made to go along with the sum total of the computer's findings. This was the raw data the OIPR had requested; what they did with it was entirely up to them.

* * *

Dale Anderscoggen loved Los Angeles sunsets. He knew, as all Los Angelinos did, that it was smog and car exhaust that bathed the setting sun in brilliant oranges and purples. But as he and his boyfriend Arthur sat on the deck of their home in Santa Monica, the sight never failed to stir him. He reached over, apropos of nothing, and gripped Arthur's hand.

They were sitting like that when Dale's cellphone chirped. Louisa Santiago, his boss.

He let Arthur go, answered it. "Hey, Lu."

"Dale, a FISA order just came in from Meade. It looks like a real number cruncher. They sent a huge chunk online directly to our office. I know you've done these in the past—"

"—and God they're fun—"

"I was wondering if you could start tonight."

Dale looked at Arthur. Arthur was a medical resident at Cedar's; for the two years they'd been a couple, interruptions because of work had been the rule, not the exception. A lot of relationships wouldn't have survived, he knew. "Who am I," he asked, "to deny the power of FISA?" He got off the phone, looked at Arthur.

Arthur knew. "You have to go be a Special Agent?"

"Looks that way."

"What about *Murder in Cairo?"*

"See it without me."

Arthur shrugged. "It can wait."

Dale checked his Timex. "I should jump in the shower." He stood.

"Got five minutes?"

"What did you have in mind?"

Arthur smiled. "As much as we can do in five minutes," he said, and led Dale back into the apartment.

* * *

Dale Anderscoggen had never met Lucy Ocindo, but he'd felt sorry for her. By dying in public, loaded with drugs, she'd gone from a respected judge to a punchline. As both a gay man and an FBI Special Agent, Dale had seen some spectacular self-destructive flameouts in his time; perhaps it was the conservative values of his parents, but he never went in for schadenfreude. As it said in both Matthew and Luke: Cast out first the beam out of thine own eye, and then shalt thou see clearly to pull out the mote that is in thy brother's eye.

The social media and the morning DJs had all had way too much fun with Judge Ocindo's demise, which was why Dale, ten minutes after arriving at his desk at the federal office building on Wilshire Boulevard, found himself immediately and completely wound up in the case. If Lucy Ocindo had been murdered, along with two other judges, then something would be vindicated and all those snarky media twits would have to eat their words.

But first, he was looking at a mountain of work. It was one thing for the NSA's Crays to suggest that a cluster of phone calls was an identifiable pattern. It was another thing entirely to prove it in court, and for that he would need to subpoena records from— he counted— 12 different phone companies, half here and half in Latin America.

American phone companies, he knew, were great about this stuff. Getting foreign companies to cough up detailed information was, in his experience, like trying to herd cats. Requests had to go through the State Department to local justice officials. Sometimes you got what you asked for, sometimes you didn't; sometimes this was a matter of policy, sometimes it was a matter of ineptitude.

The slow-motion chaos of the Colombian authorities tended not to help, especially when requesting info on powerful figures like Nieto. Within an hour of arriving at the office, Dale had three people attached to this project, and they had begun the international paperwork; better to get it in gear before turning his attention to the US companies.

By 1:45 AM, the subpoena requests for all the telcos were finished; the foreign ones were on their way to the State Department; the US list would be seen by a local judge first thing in the morning. Dale thanked the special agents helping him, sent them home, and then stayed at his carrel until 3:15 AM, poring through the data set, trying to find footholds that would allow him to climb in.

* * *

In New York, Monday dawned to a shock of cold, the first frigid blast of winter. When Tory walked into the courtroom that morning, the first eyes she met were Angelo's, vulnerable with concern before he blinked it away.

What did that mean? She was in no mood to play guessing games. "Mr. Schwartz, Mr. Walker, I'd like to see you both *in camera."*

They followed her into a small conference room. Angelo, as they walked in, could not refrain: "I just want to say how anxious I've been for you—"

Tory didn't answer, shut the door, sat across from them both. "Lucy Ocindo," she stated flatly.

"I was so sorry to hear she died," Angelo said. Sam's eyes shot back and forth, trying to decipher what was going on.

"Hiram Canute. Brenda Pell."

Angelo didn't immediately put it together. "I've had cases in front of all three," he said.

"And they're all dead. I am half a minute from throwing you off this case, declaring a mistrial and getting out of this situation, but I can't just walk away and let the target land on the next judge that gets picked." She turned to Sam. "A pattern has emerged of judges of big Nieto-related drug trials being killed after guilty verdicts. The FBI opened an investigation this weekend."

Sam gestured at Angelo. "And he was on those Nieto trials?"

"All three," Tory said.

"Now wait a minute, I was co-counsel—"

"All three," Tory said again, and something in her tone told Angelo she wasn't interested in subtleties.

Sam shifted in his chair to size up Angelo. "Why do you take these big-ticket drug cases anyway? Is the money so good it doesn't matter that it's dripping blood?"

Angelo kept Sam level in his gaze. "That's not it at all," he said, and his tone was calm, rational, even pleasant. "These cases are wiretap-heavy. I'm interested in fighting governmental overreach. To do that I have to take on the cases where the government overreaches the most."

Sam waved the comment away with a scowl, but Tory thought: Actually, that makes sense. That's the Angelo I remember.

* * *

The first witness was Jonas Richter, a police captain with the harbor and shipping squad, who described the flotilla of NYPD boats and helicopters that greeted the containerized cargo ship *Firmin* as it entered New York harbor. The ship was boarded, and seven twenty-foot metal transport Truck Equivalent Units, or TEUs, were opened by the NYPD. They were found to contain wooden crates filled with wrapped briefcase-sized packages of cocaine. Each package weighed a kilo, or 2.2 pounds; each crate had 100 packages; there was room for 6 crates on the TEU, and the boat had 7 TEUs filled with coke. At a street price of $100 a gram, that made the total catch worth more than $420 million.

The cocaine, all 9,240 pounds of it, was now in police custody; after the trial, it would be incinerated. The thing that struck Captain Richter was the utter lack of guile. In the past, drugs had been smuggled in TEUs with false bottoms, or hidden in innocent-looking items like bowling balls or cans of food. This was the first time in Captain Richter's knowledge that smugglers hadn't bothered to disguise their load. Presumably, they'd had too much to move.

Next up was NYPD narcotics detective John Vasquez, a tough young cop with a blunt haircut. He explained that the *Firmin* had been interdicted because of intelligence received from anonymous sources suggesting that certain Customs Agents were on the payroll of the Nieto drug smuggling organization. Two months before the *Firmin* sailed into New York harbor, NYPD began surveillance on several area customs agents, but settled quickly on two men: Wesley Rexroth and Barney Lind, both of whose spending patterns suggested unreported income. Rexroth disappeared and has never been found; Lind became aware he was being surveilled, and, using an elaborate ruse, disappeared as well. He was found three weeks later in a motel near Kennedy Airport in the midst of a cocaine binge. He was placed under arrest, and elected to cooperate with the NYPD.

But all of this was just a preamble. Tory was glad to see she had enough time before the lunch break to get Barney Lind sworn and talking. She told Sam to call the next witness.

Barney Lind wasn't attractive. His cheeks were pitted with acne scars and he didn't have much of a chin. But there was an earthy intelligence in his eyes, and he had charm.

"Do you promise to tell the truth, the whole truth, and nothing but the truth?" the bailiff asked.

"Absolutely," the man said, and his abrupt forthrightness made a few on the jury laugh. Then Tory saw Bart Alicia cut through the main doors, come around the side of the gallery.

Something had happened. Angelo felt it too; he glanced over, aware of a flurry of activity. One of the COs left Bart and came up the short steps to the bench.

"Adjourn for the day and get 'em out quick," he said, "but don't panic 'em. We just got a bomb scare called in. They're emptying the whole building."

* * *

The stairwells were filled with jittery people trying to make their way down flight after flight of steps, it was like trying to leave the blue seats at the Garden after a Knicks game.

For Barney, it felt like a curious mix of death sentence and reprieve. Arturo Hidalgo had sat down on the witness stand, and Nieto had killed him, just as sure as if he'd pulled the trigger all the way down in Colombia. Wesley Rexroth had dropped off the face of the earth, which, knowing Nieto, didn't bode well for his health. And this afternoon Barney was going to tell everything he knew about Baby's involvement with the boat full of cocaine, and suddenly there's a bomb scare. What was he supposed to think?

Barney made his way out of the building, stood in the middle of a cluster of uniformed cops and the two plainclothesmen assigned to keep him alive. Barney was heartily sick of them—big guys, professional about their job without an ounce of well-meaning. They were waiting for an unmarked car to pull up.

"So what happens now?" Barney asked Paul, the taller of the two.

Paul looked at Ben, his partner, who shrugged. "Back to the hotel room," Paul decided.

"Guys—" Barney was wheedling. "Drugs are out. Drink is out. Last guy who testified against Nieto got shot by a sniper, and we just had a Goddamn bomb scare. I'm sorry, another day in the hotel eating crap food and streaming shitty movies isn't going to cut it for me." The two cops stood stone-faced. "Can we at least go to Burger Haven or Black Top, one of those places, and have a real burger, not a fast-food burger?"

There was a crack in the facade, a moment of weakening resolve. Barney leaped in: "Come on, guys— I'm working my ass off for you, here—"

Paul finally caved in. "Right, yeah, okay. There's a Black Top on Chambers."

"That'd be great," Barney said, oblivious to the helmeted motorcycle rider watching the streams of people exit the stairwell.

All those cops surround that ugly little man, Esmerelda thought. It had to be him. Just to be sure, she took up a cellphone, punched redial with one gloved finger, watched as the man with no chin jumped to dig out his phone. As he started to answer, she broke the connection, roared the motorcycle to life and waited to see where they would go.

*   *   *

Barney and his two guardians were seated at a checkerboard-tableclothed table, burgers in baskets and pint glasses of soda before them, enormous screens showing football and basketball and golf at every turn. The place was half empty: older couples and office workers ate lunch at tables while demoralized men watched sports at the bar. There were even a few single female patrons; one had come in after, and was seated a few yards away, directly in Barney's line of vision. She was prettier than the waitresses, a brunette with a scar through one eyebrow, but it didn't make her ugly— it made her exotic, an interesting woman who had lived a life. And she kept making eyes at Barney— not in an obvious way: a long gaze, then an embarrassed head down, but then her eyes would flash up to make sure he was still looking.

Barney glanced at his tablemates; Paul was locked on the game; Ben's gaze was drifting from waitress to waitress. Barney looked back at the girl. She was holding something in her hands, now. A slight white square. A note? Maybe it was a note, she wanted to give him her number. Then she touched the small square to her nose, glanced over at the bathroom, and all at once he understood, and his stomach dropped out even as his heart instantly began pounding.

Coke. It was a bindle. Rehab, all of that, abruptly went to hell. He wanted it. He wanted her, and he wanted it. He stood, the chair squeaked when he pushed it out. The men looked up. "Bathroom," he said, he was aware he was shaking. He forced a smile, walked right past the beauty, she had him with her eyes. He stood in the men's room, unsure what to do. He went pointlessly to the urinal, started to unzip when the door opened and the beauty walked in. She looked under the two stall doors to see they were alone.

"Come here," she said, grabbed his jacket and pulled him into the stall.

"You have—? I saw—?" She smiled, handed him the bindle. He unfolded it greedily, his hands shaking, took a pinch of white powder with three fingers and snorted it hard up his left nostril. The sensation was immediate, good coke, pleasure mounting in powerful sureness through and around him, and she was undoing his belt, evidently she was going to blow him, this was like a dream. He filled the other nostril with cocaine, and she'd opened his pants, she had his penis out. Then he felt a sharp piercing pain in the delicate skin behind his scrotum.

"Owww!" he tried to pull away, trying not to spill the overfull bindle. "What— what—" He swallowed, suddenly very afraid.

"Cocaine and fentanyl."

"What's it do?" Barney was not unwilling.

"It makes your blood pressure— how do you say? Crash." Suddenly he got it, and his face turned milk white. "It is a little gift," she went on, "from Eduardo Nieto." His heart was doing something wrong, something tachycardic. He tried to push past her, slammed against the tile wall, banged his elbow and his forehead on the ceramic as he landed. Then something exploded inside, something became eclipsed in his thinking, and he was dead before she walked out the door.

* * *

Tory had learned to relax and ignore bomb scares. Perhaps because no bombs had actually blown up in recent memory, most of the court's workers took them as pleasant little interruptions of the daily grind. But this time was different.

This time, she felt uncomfortable in her skin. Anna and Thomas had convinced her to go to Hop Sing, an old Chinatown favorite of theirs behind the courts buildings, and she sat, staring at her plate of razor clams and hot chili and coriander, and nothing felt right.

It was funny: whenever she was busy, whenever her time was truly not her own, she found herself wishing above all else that she could sneak away from everything and find a pool hall and shoot some pool. In her mental imagining, the place was empty, and she always played alone. And then, whenever her schedule relaxed a bit, did she go shoot pool?

Not nearly enough. Today, she decided, she would. Bart had spent most of the meal on his cell, calling various people to find out what was going on at the courthouse. Anna and Thomas were engaged in their ongoing discussion of the copyright issues surrounding AI. Then Bart's cell rang again, and he answered it, and Tory watched as his eyes blinked rapidly, as he covered one ear to block out the restaurant noise.

Finally he held the phone away from his cheek. "Barney Lind is dead."

A shrill burst of panic opened in Tory's chest, stayed there. "Evidently," he went on, "he had a heart attack in a restaurant bathroom, they found him with cocaine."

"Barney—" she said softly. "It's murder. It has to be murder."

"They don't want to commit until they do the autopsy."

"It's murder," Tory said again, sure of it. Eduardo or Baby, reaching their long arm into her trial, taking out witnesses like so many chess pieces on a board. Suddenly her food was no longer attractive, the restaurant felt oppressive, and she felt a strong need to get out at once.

She took a deep breath. Some calm inner part of herself could see she was acting panicky. All right, she thought: don't run away. These are the variables. What's the shot?

She took out her cell phone, dialed Sam's cell, got his voicemail and left a message saying that Lind was dead. She assumed he'd want a *Sirois* hearing, as early as tomorrow. In the meantime there was nothing further to be done with the jury today except make sure they didn't learn of Lind's death until she was ready to tell them.

"We'll head back to the courthouse," Tory told the group. "The bomb scare was to get Lind out. It worked. Right now we've got a hearing to prep for, and that building is probably the safest place in Manhattan." And with that, she signaled for the check.

* * *

Three hours later, Tory had sent Anna and Thomas home, and was typing up her notes for tomorrow when Bart knocked at her office door and stuck his head in.

"Car's ready when you are, Judge Parker."

"Thanks," Tory said turned off the computer and got her coat. She thought about the pile of FISA wiretaps she had waiting at home. She looked up. "Do you play pool, Bart?"

Bart shrugged. "I'm all right. I mean, I'm not the best player you've ever seen." Then: "I've seen that trophy in the robing room. That's pretty intimidating."

“If I wanted to intimidate people I'd put it in chambers, not the robing room. That's there to ground me when things get intense during a trial."

"Remind you that skells aren't all there is in life—"

"Right." She walked back into the office, pulled out her keychain, unlocked one of the bottom row of extra-wide grey file cabinets that lined one wall. She pulled out a leather case almost three feet long, slung it over her shoulder and locked the cabinet back up.

Her cue sticks. "Okay," Bart said. "Now I'm intimidated."

* * *

Most of the pools halls in New York had music and alcohol and red-cheeked young bankers who thought they were better than they were. Tory loathed those places. What she wanted in a pool hall was silence and privacy, and a sense that she had all the time in the world.

Knox's was such a place, a second-story emporium west of Chelsea. She requested a table away from the players by the window. As she was walking to it, Mr. Knox, a grey-haired man, stepped up. "Long time no see, Judge." They shook hands. "What'd Ronnie give you?"

"18."

"Take 23. Better table, in the corner."

The table was perfect. Tory unzipped her case, slid out her custom-built Lyons cues, Gabon ebony and bloodwood, with malachite inlays.

"Wow, you got two in there?" Bart asked. "Can I use one?"

"One's a game cue, one's just for breaking and hitting jump shots," Tory explained as she locked the first stick's shaft onto its butt. "It's heavier. You don't want to play a game with it—it's too powerful. We can trade off my game cue," she offered. "Just try not to drop it."

"Expensive?"

"You don't want to know."

Bart considered. "I'll just use one of these on the wall, if you don't mind."

Tory tried to keep her wins against Bart gentle, coaching him as they went along, but after three games he asked to sit one out, and she got to the solo drills she'd come for. Losing herself in problems of force and speed, action and reaction, the tensions of the day drained away. After a time she felt a razor-sharp clarity, a pungent emotion she experienced in other areas of her life, but never so cleanly as when she was laying down combination shots on green felt.

Was she hiding from her life, as her mother had once accused her? No, she was living it. She lined up a row of balls down the center of the table, worked on bank shots, her stroke even, her rhythms coming back as they always did.

Solo practice was like tai chi, or swimming laps: a chance to communicate with oneself, to find out, as the mental noise faded away, what one was really thinking. And this evening, the grey autumn sky slipping into night, she found herself thinking about Angelo.

She hadn't called him with the news of Lind's death; she'd had Thomas call his office. She had felt the formality appropriate, but now she wondered if something hadn't been behind it.

In truth, she realized, she held Barney Lind against him. Angelo probably had no more to do with Barney's death than Mr. Knox or Bart Alicia— but the man was dead, probably being autopsied right this minute, and Angelo's client was the chief benefactor. And Angelo—

Well, Angelo wasn't responsible at all. Just like he wasn't responsible for Ocindo. Or Canute. Or Pell.

Unless he was. Tory realigned the balls, went around the other side and began working on kick shots—shooting the cue ball against the rail to hit her desired ball. But he couldn't be, she thought. Then Detective Jerry Sanmartino popped into her head, using charm like a bulldozer to crush Irving Wachtel. She stubbed the cue ball, sent it careening unintended around the table.

Useless. Pointless.

Some men had a certain kind of charisma that made Tory suspend disbelief about their motives. Her father had it. Jerry Sanmartino had had it.

And Angelo had it, as well. Did that mean she couldn't trust him? She shouldn't trust him?

She took a deep breath, set the cue ball back into position. Three ball, side pocket. Four ball, side pocket. Five ball, side pocket. Six ball dinged the pocket corner and skittered across the table.

Damn. She finished the rack, set them up again in the same formation, again missed the six.

She was making the same mistake over and over, she saw. She needed to break the problem down to its components, figure out what was wrong, and rebuild it from the ground up.

PART TWO
Maria

The village of La Plata lies in thes Colombian Andes, one hundred miles north of the equator. La Plata, remote as Tibet until Eduardo Nieto put in a two-lane blacktop, was not a stop on any tourist map, but it was beautiful: a high plateau backed by mountains and cut through with streams, with rich soil and wild orchids climbing rock walls.

La Plata was of little importance to anyone who didn't live there. The presence of any Colombian governmental authority was nominal; the local power structure, dominated by Eduardo Nieto, was represented locally by self-important teenagers with machine guns who acted like they'd seen the world, though they'd never been as far as Ibague, much less Medellin or Bogota.

It was morning in La Plata, equatorial sunlight waking chickens to another day. Maria Gonzalez got out of bed slowly so as not to wake her brother Hector, and went out to scare up eggs from the hens. She loaded wood into the stove, started a fire. She went to her mother's room, watched her and the baby in the crib at her bedside. The more sleep her mother got, the less pain she had, or so it seemed to Maria. She quietly opened her mother's tin box, took out the plastic bag of cocaine base.

In the kitchen she dug in with a table spoon, used a knife to level the excess. She dumped the tablespoon into a plastic cup, quietly put the bag back in the box. Then she hosed out a plastic milk jug, took it and the base up the road to the Ortegas.

Señor Ortega was milking his cows; his wife left her baby in his high chair, filled Maria's jug with milk and dumped Maria's cocaine base into her own big bag of white powder.

When Maria got home, she broke eggs into a bowl, mixed in milk and cornmeal and more sugar than her mother usually used, and made arepas as the house began to wake.

Maria's father worked in a banana plantation two days walk away; he got back once a month or so, less during harvest. Often he was paid in base. Maria's mother had been a washerwoman before the pain had slowed her down. Now she didn't have energy to pick up and deliver, much less handle the big tubs of water and laundry that used to fill the backyard.

Maria helped her mother change the baby. She used the outhouse, scrubbed her hands before changing into her green dress. She'd meant to sew the hem where it had opened, but didn't have time now to fix it. She and Hector kissed their mother and walked to school.

Boys in dusty jeeps banged down the roads, guns sticking out. Maria hated those boys.

At the school Maria went into the girls' door; Hector went in the boys'. She arrived just as Mr. Robles lead the class in the national anthem. After, he started writing English sentences on the board: *I have five sheep in the barn*. Then below it: *she___five sheep in the barn.*

"Have!" somebody blurted. "Have!" someone else seconded. Maria knew they were wrong. Quietly, under her breath, she said: "Has." Mr. Robles kept writing: *I___five sheep, but now they are gone.* He turned to the class. "Present and past," he started to explain, and the classroom door slammed open, and four fighters in uniform, automatic weapons pointing to the ceiling, marched in and took positions at the door and the windows.

They were older than any of the narco paramilitaries Maria had seen; they were better dressed, and they had better guns. Another man entered the room, obviously the leader. Mr. Robles stepped up to him, furious. "What is this? You can't just force your way in here—"

"Girls," the older soldier said, "line up, please."

"Class, stay where you are." Robles held his ground. 'Tm sorry, you will have to leave."

The older man shot a quick glance at the soldier by the window, who took two steps into the room and bashed Mr. Robles across the face with his rifle butt.

Mr. Robles went down, and the soldier smashed him again. The chief watched all this serenely, then turned back to the class.

"Girls, please— line up," he said. A brief, scared pause in the room, and then one girl stood, and another, and they all took places along the back wall.

Maria, heart pounding, made her way to the back. Were they doing this in Hector's classroom too? Men with guns— did they need more soldiers?

Two girls were crying. Mr. Robles was moaning on the floor, blood slathering his shirt.

The chief walked up the line, stopped at Rosa, the girl Maria had always thought of as the prettiest in the class. He looked her up and down like he was buying a horse.

"How old are you?"

Rosa was so scared tears were leaking from her eyes. "Eleven" she said.

He nodded, kept walking. He stopped, looked at Nita, another beauty. He reached over, massaged Nita's upper arm in his meaty hand, dropped it and moved to the next.

Maria snuck a glance at Nita, at her arm. Her arms were chubby. Evidently that wasn't good. Maria wished her own arms were chubby, but they weren't.

The man stopped before her. Maria felt her heart in her throat. "How old?" he asked. "Ten," Maria answered.

He nodded, looked at his soldiers. "This one," he said.

"No— I have my mother— and the babies—" One soldier raised his rifle butt, and the chief caught his arm.

"Just get her out," he said, and the soldiers marched her out of the classroom.

*   *   *

This was not the usual jeep. This was a strange vehicle she had never seen before, a jeep all grown up, flat top, huge tires, the seats high off the ground. It was enormous.

The car made Maria think these were soldiers from somewhere else. "I'm not rich," she told them. "My mother is sick, my father works at a banana farm—"

"Your parents will be compensated for your time," the soldier said, and turned away.

What did that mean? Money? They would get a new daughter? Maria kept her gaze out the window. She was further away from her home than she had ever been.

After an hour, the car went through gates, started to climb. Another set of gates, armed guards everywhere. A plane flew overhead, huge and noisy, close enough to touch the trees.

After one final gate they turned up the drive. At the end of a field so vast it would have contained Maria's entire village sat the largest and finest house she had ever seen.

There was an enormous bird running across the field, long legs and a feathery ball of a body and a long neck and a small bald head. An ostrich.

An actual ostrich. She'd only seen pictures. They didn't have them in Colombia, but there it was.

She twisted around, followed it with her eyes until it was out of sight. They drove to the house; soldiers scrambled out; one gestured with his rifle. "Out. And stay with us."

They led her into the house, down a hallway to a small room. There was a bed, a box in the corner, no window.

"Go." The soldier pushed her in and locked the door from outside.

She was alone. She wondered if Hector knew yet, if he'd gone to tell their mother. And then the little box by the bed began to shake and hum. She jumped, but fear gave way to curiosity. She pulled the handle open, felt cold air on her hand.

She'd seen refrigerators at school, but never this small. Inside were cans of American soda, and piles of chocolate bars. She looked furtively about; she knew she shouldn't, it was bad, but they had so many. She took one, unwrapped the foil, broke off a corner and ate it.

It was delicious, sweet and crunchy. Hector and Ramon would love this. Her mother would like the chocolate, but she would love the refrigerator more. She finished the bar, rolled the wrapper into a little ball, slid it under the bed. Then she noticed the ripped hem of her green dress.

Only two inches were torn. The rest was a secret pocket that would fit a chocolate bar.

She took another bar, slid it into the hem— it fit. She stood; the dress was hanging too low on her right. She took a third bar, slid it in the other side. She walked around; the dress looked normal, from what she could tell.

She heard voices in the hallway; the door unlocked from the outside and swung open. A different man, older, with bad skin. "You are a pretty one, aren't you?" he said. "Come."

Maria followed him up two flights of stairs, the chocolate bars bumping against her shins. He led her into a long wooden room with a picture window and a desk and the largest television Maria had ever seen. On it was some kind of strange jumpy movie, sexy women and fire and tigers. Someone was singing, she realized, but the sound was off.

The man at the desk was on the phone. "That will all have to wait until we get Baby back," he said, and then: "Soon. Look, someone's here." He hung up, turned to Maria.

When she saw him, her fear diverted into a strange new sensation: this man could help her. This man could find out what medicine her mother needed. Her mouth was abruptly dry.

"Do you know who I am?" the man asked.

"The Roadbuilder?" She hated the way she'd said it. "Don Nieto?"

He had no reaction. "How old are you?"

"Ten. My mother—"

"No 'your mother.' Are you a virgin?" he asked.

The question so shocked Maria that she blushed deep crimson. She shook her head yes, her black hair shimmying down her back.

"Let me see," Don Nieto said, stepped forward and lifted her dress. She was so terrified he'd seen the chocolate bars that she was entirely unprepared for his rough hand peeling down her underpants, his huge fingers probing her sex.

This was bad, very bad, she couldn't stop it, and she didn't know what to do. Tears rimmed her eyelids, the room was swimming in tears. Finally he dropped her skirt and stood.

"I'm going to send you to the north to meet an important man. You will do everything you can to please him. Whatever he wants. Do you understand?"

Maria was shaking, tears spreading down her cheeks. "If you do this for me, your family will receive this." He took out his wallet, showed her a fat sheaf of pesos, more money in one place than Maria had ever seen.

The sight of the money made her talk. "My mother is sick," she said quickly. "The X-ray machine is broken at our clinic, the doctor said to go to the hospital in Ibague, but my mother can't walk to Ibague, she has too much pain—"

Don Nieto smiled a toothy smile, handed her a pad and pen. "Write down your mother's name and your town, I'll make sure she gets treatment." He knew there wasn't a functioning X-ray machine at lbague either. Maria wrote in big clear letters, handed it back. He set it down without looking. "Now, the man in the north— do not make trouble for this man, do what he asks. Don't eat too much— he doesn't like that. Don't cut your hair."

She could still feel the way the rough hand had touched her. Her stomach quaked with rising vomit, and she steeled hard against it. "Can I see my mother before I go?"

"No, you're leaving right now. Don't worry about your mother, I'll handle everything." Her mother would be okay. The man with bad skin tugged her toward the door.

There was one thing that seemed important to say. "My name," she said, "is Maria Gonzalez." It wasn't a declaration; it was something important that had been missing from the transaction. She went out the door with the man.

Eduardo took up one of his phones. Several calls later, he noticed the girl's address on his pad. He tore off the page, threw it in the garbage and didn't give it another thought.

* * *

It was going to be tough, telling the jury that Barney Lind was dead. It was going to have an impact, and its impact could be permanent and immeasurable.

But first, before the jury heard anything, Sam had requested a *Sirois* bearing, as Tory had known he would. Named after a state case in which a witness was killed before testifying, *Sirois* set the standard for how New York State courts handled these matters. The hearing was held in the courtroom without the jury; Sam and Angelo were at their tables, along with Loretta the court reporter. "We are here at the People's request," Tory began, "for a *Sirois* hearing to see if Barney Lind's Grand Jury testimony should be allowed into evidence at trial. That will depend on whether his murder can be traced, by clear and convincing evidence, to this defendant or anyone acting on his behalf."

Angelo was pissed off. "This hearing is unnecessary." Sam Walker just stared at him. "Come on, Sam," Angelo went on. "Sixth Amendment, the right to confront your accuser. Guy's dead, coke'll do that, sad thing, but there it is—"

Sam met his anger with disdain. His Southern accent managed to keep his tone gentlemanly. *"Sirois* says that by participating in any way in the murder of his accuser, Baby waived his right to that constitutional protection."

"Are you even 100% sure it *was* murder?" Angelo asked.

Sam smiled. "Physical exam. They found a fresh puncture wound. They think it's fentanyl or something else." Sam leaned in. "He had cocaine all over his fingers. Meanwhile somebody injected something behind his scrotum. Took the syringe, too. Unless Barney Lind had a third hand, it's murder."

Angelo wasn't done. "Okay, if somebody killed him, it doesn't mean that Baby—"

Sam grew harsh: "Bomb threat just when the guy gets sworn in, and then boom he's dead an hour later. You think maybe there's a serial killer out there? Maybe that's his MO? Maybe we should look at other bomb scares in other courthouses in other states—"

"Gentlemen." Tory cut through. "Enough. There are ample legal grounds for a hearing. Let's get to it." Angelo, Tory could see, was not happy.

The jury box was empty. The Hats and Bats squad brought Baby in; he leaned back in his chair, stared hard at the ceiling as if it contained the answers to universal mysteries. Tory looked at Sam. "Call your first witness," she said, and the court reporter began her quiet, coded typing.

Sam had three. The first, Detective Paul Brinzana described the bomb scare and the decision to go to lunch. His affect was flat as he told of thinking his man was taking too long in the bathroom, going in, finding Barney Lind on the floor.

On cross, Angelo was bracing: this man had been charged with keeping Barney Lind alive, and he had failed. How sad.

Next up was Wallace Forstmann, the Medical Examiner for the County of New York, who described Barney Lind's autopsy and the finding of the puncture wound. Though full toxicology reports were not yet in, a blood test in the lab suggested fentanyl. Mr. Lind's autopsy revealed no heart disease; Mr. Lind's records during his rehab and incarceration contained no prescriptions for heart medicine or prescription pain management.

Sam then called Riker's prison warden Lewis Clapp, a surprisingly small man to be chief of corrections at a place like

Riker's. When he spoke, he commanded great authority. "We monitor the payphones intermittently," he explained after being sworn in. "Anything that sounds like code, we take a second look."

"And on the afternoon of the 14th, your office monitored this conversation between the defendant and an unnamed coconspirator?" Sam handed the man a sheet of paper.

Clapp looked it over. "Yes, that is correct."

"Your honor, at this time the People would like to admit and mark as People's exhibit 103 the transcript of a phone call taped at Riker's Island prison facility." Sam handed sheets to Tory and Angelo. Tory noticed that Baby Nieto was sitting up with a hooded look in his eyes.

Angelo spoke first. "Objection— this conversation is about dry cleaning."

"Overruled," Tory said, "but I want to hear how this relates."

Sam turned back to Clapp. "Mr. Nieto placed this call?"

"Yes he did, the man said.

"Did he call a dry cleaner?"

"No, he did not. The call was placed to a payphone at Grand Central in Manhattan."

"To a dry cleaner's shop at the train station?"

"There are no dry cleaners at Grand Central. We checked."

Sam finished his questions soon after, handed the witness to the defense. When Angelo stood for cross, it was apparent he was ready to do battle.

"When a dry cleaner leaves his shop," he asked, "it's legal for him to conduct business, right? Even from payphones?"

"Objection—" Sam said tiredly.

"Never mind," Angelo allowed. He took up the transcript. "Could you point to me where, in this conversation about dry cleaning, Mr. Nieto makes the request that Barney Lind be killed with a mixture of cocaine and fentanyl?"

Clapp held his own. "Well, it doesn't say that."

"I'm glad you admit that," Angelo said scathingly. "It makes a request relating to the laundering of a shirt. When was it decided this was a solicitation for murder?"

"After Lind died, we went back and took a look—"

"So you didn't see it before Lind died? I mean, if it's so obvious, why didn't you jump on it right away? Why didn't you immediately do something to save Mr. Lind's life?"

"It only became obvious in retrospect."

"Ahhhhhhhhhh," Angelo turned to Tory. "This is innuendo, it is beneath the dignity of this court. I move that this conversation about dry cleaning be stricken from the record."

There was one thing that bothered Tory that neither side had picked up on. "I know you both stipulated to use the transcript at this hearing, but I'd like to hear the tape."

Two minutes later, the recorded conversation came hissing through speakers:

> *"Brazo Fuerte dry cleaners."* The man sounded American.
>
> *"Yes."* No question this second voice was Baby's. *"I am having trouble with this shirt— the customs-made shirt."*
>
> *"My boss was concerned about that custom shirt as well. It has a stain that needs cleaning?"*
>
> *"If your boss thinks so, then I think so too."*
>
> *"Just the custom? None of the other shirts?*
>
> *"No, only the one, I think, will be enough."*

> *"For now, at least."*
> *"Right.".*
> *"Very well then, we'll take care of it."*
> *"Right,"* Baby closed the conversation: *"Thank you."*

Tory looked up. She thought she'd heard it, but she wanted to be sure. "Again, please."

The technician replayed the audio file. The second time, Tory was positive. What was on the transcript was exactly what the man had said.

He'd said 'customs-made'. Not 'custom-made'. Barney Lind had been a Customs agent.

The hearing continued, but nothing substantially changed Tory's opinion. Finally she made her ruling: "I find clear and convincing evidence of this defendant's complicity in Barney Lind's murder," she said, "and I'm going to allow Lind's grand jury testimony into evidence."

* * *

As a matter of law, the connection between Baby's phone call and Lind's death would never be revealed to the jury in this trial. Lind's grand jury testimony would be admitted into evidence and read to them, despite the fact that Lind could never be subjected to cross-examination by the defense. In effect, Baby had waived his right to object, having been an active participant in the conspiracy that led to the murder.

Tory ordered the jury back into the courtroom. They trundled in, took their seats. "Members of the jury," Tory began, "the next witness scheduled to appear was Barney Lind. However, as some of you may have heard or read, Mr. Lind died last night. There has been speculation in the media about his death, but I charge and instruct you as follows:

"Do not speculate as to the cause of his death, and draw no inference whatsoever from his death with regard to any issue at this trial. As jurors, you are not permitted to do so. Mr. Lind's grand jury testimony will now be read to you, as the law permits. Remember, however, that Mr. Lind was never subject to cross-examination, and that cross-examination could have changed his testimony or made you see it in a different light. Now I need the assurance of every one of you that you can follow these instructions and be fair to both sides. Juror no. 1?"

The man said yes. Tory went through the two rows of jurors, not stopping at a nod, soliciting verbal agreement. Then she reminded them all to refrain from reading, watching, or listening to any accounts in any media about Lind or the trial.

"Remember, jurors, "she finished, "you will judge the credibility of Mr. Lind from his testimony before the grand jury, as well as all the other testimony in this case, and determine whether you accept it or reject it, in whole or in part. As always, that is strictly up to you." The jurors were handed the transcripts. Tory accepted one as well. Two of the DA's office's Trial Preparation Assistants read Sam's questions and Lind's answers out loud:

> LIND: I was snorting so much cocaine, I'd have nosebleeds every day at work. Told people I was on blood thinners. I'd be on the job talking to some of the other customs guys, my nose would go, and I'd excuse myself, go to the bathroom and snort more blow. The nosebleeds became a good thing because it meant I had an excuse to go do more cocaine.

ADA: Had you always done this much coke?

LIND: Hell no. Back before all this started, I had a guy I'd go to, score a bag of weed every couple of months.

ADA: A drug dealer.

LIND: Yeah. In the beginning I'd just buy marijuana from him, maybe a little cocaine twice a year, you know, my birthday, Christmas. He knew I was a customs agent. But it's not like I was the guy's biggest customer—I was totally recreational. I was holding down my job, I was doing okay. And then one day I'm over there, and my guy says this guy he knows wants to meet me.

ADA: That was Mr. Armstrong? State yes or no for the record, please.

LIND: Yes. Mr. Armstrong. I don't think that's his real name. He came in twenty minutes later, sits down, starts carving these fat lines of pink cocaine—I'd never seen pink cocaine. I thought I knew cocaine, but that was special.

ADA: What happened next?

LIND: We took a drive, we ended up back at my place. We did more of that coke. We talked about my job. It was weird. He already knew all about my job. He knew how the docks worked. He knew how Customs worked. Anyway, he made me an offer. He'd give me ten grand for these basic records, blank forms we use all the time. He asked for a whole bunch of things. Later I figured out all he was really interested in was how we sign off on TEUs.

ADA: Truck Equivalent Units, the metal shipping containers they load and unload onto boats?

LIND: Yes. We seal them with stickers after we check them. He wanted to get some of the stickers. That's where it began— ten grand and all the pink cocaine I could snort for some stickers. Then I got Wesley Rexroth involved. And now I don't know where the hell Wes is and here I am today.

Tory looked over at the jury. They were engrossed. The sad thing was the man had obviously gone through hell and come out the other side, telling everything he knew, and no one would ever be able to look him in the eye and thank him for his cooperation.

*   *   *

A day of blinding brightness in Los Angeles, glary to the point of irritation under a high blue sky. Dale's telco subpoenas had born fruit; he and his team had spent hours hunched over the lists of phone callers and recipients, slowly building a timeline for each cluster of calls. If cell phone A and cell phone B, purchased in Los Angeles around the same time, exchanged calls for three weeks and then abruptly stopped, one then had to look for cell phones C and D; purchased the day before A and B went dead, which used coverage from the same cell towers and kept up the same call frequency. Three weeks later these would be changed for cell phones E and F.

Even if you only used it for 3 weeks, purchasing a prepaid cell phone required an address.

Dale's team was flashing badges and checking records at low-budget cell-phone stores. Dale was looking at apartment buildings within the cell coverage area in which the majority of these calls had been placed. The apartment building he had assigned himself was 5 stories of pink stucco above a two-story parking garage. Useless little balconies littered the building's sides. To be honest, it was a better class of hovel than his terrorist suspects tended to rent—cocaine created more money to spread around; terror had to rely on contributions. It might have looked swinging once, in a rat-pack early '60s kind of way, but now it looked sun-blasted and hideous.

Dale walked through the open gate, paced up and down the open central courtyard looking at doors until he found one labeled SUPER. He rang and waited. Presently a bald man, Indian or Pakistani or possibly Malaysian, answered the door.

Dale flipped open his wallet, showed his badge, let him look at it as long as he wanted. "FBI. This your building?"

"I work here." His accent wasn't Indian. "I have my work papers—"

"I'm not here about you," Dale said quickly. There was a slight smell of incense emanating from inside. The guy didn't look like a weedhead, but if he was, this conversation would be considerably more difficult. "I'm trying to track down a tenant or tenants who may have lived here. I'm looking for a Fred Martin and Tomas Espinosa."

The man had no reaction.

"There are other names they may have used: Ed Palm and Otto Veracruz."

The man stirred. "Well, that's what I was thinking. Two guys in the same apartment. Ed Palm and Tony Madrid. American and a Spanish man. They left last week."

Dale began to feel excited. "When did they move in?"

"Come in." Dale was grateful to get past the door. He stepped into a tidy space, worn but not unpleasant furniture, a small Buddhist altar in a corner, live punks of incense sticking out of sand. "I am Sayeed Manumar."

"Dale Anderscoggen." Dale saw no reason to Special Agent him. They shook hands.

He waited as the man burrowed into an aging metal file cabinet, came out with a thick file. "This year's leases," he explained, and started to flip through. "Sit, sit," he gestured.

Dale sat. "Two men," Manumar went on. "They came in July, they paid for 4 months, cash up front. Not monthly."

"All at once."

"Yes." He shrugged. "They still have a little time, but they left last week. Here it is." He handed Dale a standard lease, signed messily with two indistinguishable signatures.

"These are unreadable," Dale said.

"In America, everybody writes likes birds." He described them: a tall American man, and a skinny Spanish man with straight shoulder-length hair.

Dale made notes. "They give any job references, bank references, anything like that?"

"They paid four months cash up front. Why should I need bank references?"

Valid, Dale thought. "Were they a couple?" he asked.

"A couple of what?"

"Two men living together. Were they gay?"

The man thought. "Not that kind. The American, I think he once said he was a Marine."

Dale had known a number of gay Marines over the years, but that was irrelevant. "Visitors?"

"I only hear about visitors when somebody complains."

"Nobody complained?" The man shook his head. "They pay utilities?"

"Not like the lights went out— I assume they did."

"What about cars?" Dale asked.

"That I have—everybody has to fill out a form to use the garage, and we write down the car make and plates and take a photocopy of their driver's license."

"Can I see that?"

"Sure." The bald man stood, opened a file cabinet, flipped through and pulled out a thick file. Inside was a two-inch thick stack of letter-sized paper. He paged through the top few.

"This is Ed," he said, handed over a sheet, white except for the photocopy of the card in the middle. Dale looked at a not great image of a big, blocky balding guy. Underneath, in handwriting, it said Gray/black Subaru California WCN-713.

Dale looked at the picture and thought: you judge-killing sonofabitch, you're mine. "Has the apartment been rented yet?"

"Not yet. You know anyone who wants it?"

"I'd like to see it," Dale said. Mr. Manumar led him up two flights of stairs. The door was unlocked; the apartment was bare. "I thought it was furnished," Dale said.

"We take it all out to paint. Then the new tenant comes, they pick and choose from the basement."

Dale stood in the living room on a blue shag rug, considered the white walls and ceiling. Well, okay, he thought: with some color, the right accents, would this place work? Naah, it would still be a horrible dump. "We have a cleaning service," Mr. Manumar explained. "They come in, scrub everything down before the painters come. We used to have a service that was shoddy. These people are very thorough."

"And they've been here?"

"Two days ago."

Why was nothing ever easy? "Well, I'd still like to send a fingerprint team in. You never know."

* * *

The plane was old, with Mexican Air Force markings. It had been leased to the Colombian government to aid in drug interdiction. Eduardo Nieto had wanted his friends in the government to lease an older USAF cargo plane from the Americans, but they wouldn't do it without a crew in the package. The Mexican government had no such qualms.

Maria, belted and cuffed to a seat, felt like Jonás in the belly of the whale, a vast silver tube with metal ribs, with wires and pipes running along the walls. She was near a door with a round window through which she could see a tiny view of trucks and trees.

There were wooden crates belted into place all around her, just as she was belted in. "It's for your protection," the man had said when he cuffed her hand to the armrest. But he hadn't looked in her eyes.

Maria had stuffed some of her green dress between the cuff and her wrist to keep it from hurting. She kept going back to the way Don Nieto had touched her. It made her want to die.

After a long time of waiting, a machine sound started, like a generator but much louder. Maria could feel everything vibrating. The noise went up in pitch, and the plane began to roll forward. The way was bumpy; out the little window the trees rushed by. Maria pressed her free hand to her handcuffed one, started to pray. The noise got louder and everything was shuddering like it was all going to split apart any second. Then the front tilted up before her, immense weight pressing her into her seat, and her ears hurt, her eyes darting everywhere— and out the window— out the window—

They were looking down at the tree tops, they were in the air above them, and the curve of the world fell beyond. Maria's jaw dropped because they were actually in the air, and she could see great distances out the little window as they roared up toward the clouds.

* * *

Ed Palm's driver's license was a forgery.

To Dale Anderscoggen, this in itself was interesting. It had become evident, over the years, that Eduardo Nieto's organization used a great many well-crafted personal documents— passports, green cards, driver's licenses and such— to cover their people in the United States.

Dale had the photo image lab guys take the man's picture off the photocopy of the license and pass it through an AI program to clean it up. What came out was a decent black and white image the size of an index card. Dale thumbtacked the picture to the wall of his carrel, stared hard at it for three solid minutes.

Fred Brown. Ed Palm. The first names sounded the same. That would make sense, Dale thought; guy picked pseudonyms that rhymed with his real name, it cut down his reaction time.

If he was dumb enough to not be able to remember his pseudonym. That said something about him right there.

So: first name sounded like Ed. This was obviously a large man. Mr. Manumar, the super, had put him about 6'4". Dale could see it in the thick cheek bones and forehead.

His hair was tight-shaved on the sides: modified jarhead. Balding tough guy, about 30, with a military background, not current but part of his identity.

Looked like he went through the military, then, stateside, joined up with DEA, DHS, one of the 3-letter agencies trying to stop people and drugs coming in across the border. Eventually got to Colombia and learned that being an enforcer for Nieto brought in the big money.

Which meant he'd have guns. Great, Dale thought: big, ex-military, contract killer, not too bright, guns. Just the guy you want to have running around loose in your city. The phone on his desk started in; he grabbed it.

"Anderscoggen."

"Dale." It was Louisa, his boss. "DMV found your guy's car. Used Subaru hatchback, purchased June 14, in cash, in Reseda. Plates were issued to a company: First Holding. Address is a box in a Mailbox store in Ventura."

"It's a dummy," he said. "How it usually works."

"I'll bet they dumped it after the Ocindo hit. Drove it to Compton, left it on the street for the bangers to strip down."

He got off the phone, slid his stack of photos into a vellum envelope, went down to his car. He drove straight to the pink stucco monstrosity where the dubiously named Ed Palm had lived, found Mr. Manumar sweeping the concrete.

"Yes," he said, "he looked like that. That is very good."

Dale thanked him, drove around the neighborhood, debating what stores and businesses would appeal to him if he were a 6'4' ex-military nutjob. He parked at a CalAmerica Bank, went in and requested the manager, flashed his badge and asked if he could show the pictures around. This took 40 minutes and didn't achieve a thing.

He tried a gas station, and another, and a third, before switching to liquor stores. The first one was big on wine; no dice. The second, tucked away two blocks from the pink building, didn't much care for new adventures in Zinfandel. The guy behind the register was wide and flushed red like a boiled lobster.

"Once, twice a week," he said when he saw the picture. "Boulton's Bourbon."

"How'd he pay?"

"Cash."

"No cards? No checks?" The man thought about it, shook his head. "Get his name?"

"Naah." Dale wandered over to the bourbon section, found Boulton's Super Premium, hand-distilled, $59 a bottle.

"There a check-cashing place around here?"

"Next block up." Dale walked it, had the uncanny sense that at some point Ed the Jarhead had walked along this same sidewalk. Sometimes those senses meant something, Dale knew, but it was better to treat them like they didn't.

The check-cashing store had a cheery front and a back covered with bulletproof Lucite. Dale waited on a short line, showed his badge to the lady behind the thick plastic. "I need to talk to the manager," he said, slowly and distinctly, into the little microphone.

After several minutes a young Asian man in a polyester shirt and tie came through the security door. He spent a long time looking at Dale's badge and ID, then took up his cell phone and called the FBI field office on Wilshire. Only after somebody there attested that Dale was legitimate did he introduce himself as Mr. Kim and escort Dale back to his office.

The office was bare save for a poster of a whale breaching the water. There was a strange acrid smell, but Mr. Kim didn't seem to mind. He didn't recognize the man in the photo, but a quick search of his records said that Ed Palm had in fact cashed checks here. Dale asked for a printout.

Mr. Kim looked shocked: "Don't you need a subpoena?"

"Yes," Dale said, not smiling. "I suppose we do."

* * *

Esmeralda was still quaking from her orgasm when the pale man took a combat knife from the table, cut the ropes that fixed her hands to the headboard.

"Wow," she said.

"Glad you liked it," he said.

She nodded, still catching her breath. He crossed to the kitchen area of the dingy hotel room, took a pair of bottled waters from the counter, opened one for her and one for himself. She accepted it, drank off a third of it, sat up. "So all that effort with

Barney Lind," she said, "and that bitch judge puts in his old testimony?"

He drank water, sat naked in an overstuffed chair. "They have all sorts of rules that allow them to basically do anything they want."

"So the trial continues?"

"I'm afraid so."

Esmeralda stood, looked in the mirror, straightened her hair into a plait. "I don't like it when I do work, and it is for nothing." She saw the combat knife, took it up.

"What are you going to do?" he asked.

"Show her that her decisions have consequences."

The pale man sighed. "I suggest you leave it alone."

She tapped the flat blade against her palm. "I suggest you don't know me as well as you think." He stood, came up behind her, held her and smelled the back of her neck.

"I know you well enough to know I can't stop you. Just don't do anything to piss off Eduardo."

She turned in his arms and pressed the point of the knife to his throat. "Put on your clothes and go," she said, and kissed him open-mouthed, the knife tip holding him in place.

* * *

The plane landed someplace dry and dusty; Maria saw brown dirt mountains through the tiny window in the door. Men got on, rough and sweaty, joking and grunting as they took crate after crate off, and she'd tried to be polite: Excuse me, do you have any water? Excuse me— and when they heard her, they fell silent, turned their backs to shut her out.

Like they couldn't even see her, like she was a ghost that made people shudder when she spoke. When the men finished they turned out the lights, shut the little door, and she was alone.

After a while the plane began its throbbing squeal, started forward and picked up speed, jouncing down the runway faster and faster. She closed her eyes and bit her lips and when she felt the ground give way under her she screamed into the roaring empty noise.

Nobody could hear her. The plane leveled out, entered a fog of gray clouds.

* * *

The next leg of the trip was longer; Maria had been in the air so long her panic gave way to a grueling boredom. She ate one of her chocolate bars and half the other before exhaustion took over. She slept for jagged fragments of time, always waking with a stab of fear as she came alert and saw that nothing had changed.

Eventually she was awakened by a sharp pain in her ears, worse than any she'd yet felt, and the engines went from their steady dull roar to a keen whine, higher and higher, and she realized they were going back down to the earth.

Through the tiny window in the door she could see it was night; there were electric lights down there, lots of them in little squares that went on forever. The plane got lower and lower, and she watched as trees and buildings became their proper sizes, and then with a skidding thunk she felt the ground underneath her. The noise roared higher, then slowly faded back to nothing. Then nothing happened for a long time; out the window, there were other planes and funny little trucks. Then the lights blinked on, shocking her eyes.

The man who'd belted and cuffed her to the chair now came down the center of the plane. Without a word he unlocked the handcuff from the armrest, grabbed her free arm and locked the cuff around it. Then he jerked her to her feet, led her up to the open door, held her arm tightly as they stepped out into the night and down a flight of steps to the hard black ground.

This place was freezing, boxy buildings all lit up in the distance. There was a police car a few meters away, black with red and yellow lights flashing on the roof. As they approached, a man got out, a tall Anglo with very short hair, cut flat at the top of his head.

He opened the rear door for her, put his hand on her head, and bent her forcefully into the car in such a way that she didn't bump the metal. Then he slammed the door.

The back seat was a cage. She went for the door handle with both hands, but there was none. She tried to find the knob to roll down the window, but it was gone.

She lay on her back, tried to bash through the side window with her sandals. The haircut man got behind the wheel, held a handgun up against his side of the cage.

"Do you see this?" He said it in Spanish. Maria froze mid-motion. "That glass is not going to break. If somehow you get out, I will shoot you before you run ten feet. Now sit up like a good girl and don't make a sound. We don't have far to go."

He drove to a gate, slowed and held up a wallet at the man in the booth, who waved them through. Then it was confusing, a lot of fast traffic on a huge wide road. Maria watched the green signs come and go. They were in English; they went by so quickly it was hard to read them, sounding them out in her mind as they passed.

Then she saw two words she instantly recognized. Hope leapt in her heart; it stayed alive when she saw them again, and a third time. She remembered where it had been on the map in last year's schoolroom. If anyone could help her, fix this situation and get her home it would be someone here in the main city of the government of North America.

Washington DC.

* * *

In the previous year, Sam Walker had been through a rough divorce. Tory had known him long enough to be concerned for him, but had not wanted to touch on such a sensitive topic. Now, jammed into an elevator with him and Bart Alicia at the end of a busy day in court, she saw an in: "How's your daughter?" she asked.

"She's a hoot," Sam said. "Fifth grade, and way smarter than I was at that age." He smiled. "It's my weekend with her, I'm on my way to pick her up right now." Then: "You have a dog, right? She wants a dog. Mom won't let her have one, so of course she asks me."

The elevator disgorged. Bart took up his position on one side of Tory, scanned the faces as she and Sam walked through the lobby.

"Okay, but do you?" she asked.

"I love dogs. It'd be a change, but it'd be great. 1 was thinking a pound dog, just to show her that side of how the world works."

"I've always had pound dogs," Tory said. "CACC on 110th street. But I warn you, you walk into that building, especially with a fifth grader, you're going to leave with a dog."

"I'd had that thought," Sam said. Bart went through the door, held it open for Tory and Sam. The car was parked 10 feet up the street. "This way, Judge—" he gestured, stepped to it and opened the door.

"I know a great trainer—specializes in pound dogs. I can put you in touch—" She didn't hear his reply because of the roar of the motorcycle coming up fast behind them. Her first thought was: that's crazy, going so fast on a crowded sidewalk, and then she saw the knife.

Sam saw it too, and his response was atavistic: he pushed himself in front of Tory, got between her and the oncoming bike. The helmeted rider was steering with his left hand; in his right was a long thin hunting knife, like a bayonet. The knife cut across Sam's upper arm, right over the bicep.

He grabbed at the rider, got a piece of fabric and held on, then lost his grip.

The knife clattered to the ground; the bike wobbled, then screeched down the street, jumped the curb into moving traffic, turned a corner and was gone.

Bart ran up, grabbed the knife off the sidewalk. "Into the car. Now." He bodily shoved Sam into the back seat. "Now!" he barked at Tory, who jammed herself in with Sam and slammed the door. Bart ran to the driver's seat, started the car and jerked it into motion. "I am so sorry," he said, with more fury than contrition.

"Bart, we're safe, that's all that matters. Sam, are you okay?"

"I'm fine," he said. "Got my adrenaline pumping."

"Your coat—" Tory gestured. There was a straight slice over the arm of Sam's ski jacket.

He took it off. The blade's edge hadn't gone all the way through the padding. His suit jacket was untouched. "Look at that," he said, holding up his coat.

"Get a PBA patch, one of those iron-on things, nobody will ever know."

"Or a ski patch," Sam said. He looked up at Bart. "You get the knife?"

"Yes, sir." He held it up.

"Any point in giving it to them to pull prints?"

"We can try," Bart said. "I should have been more careful when I grabbed it. I just wanted to get it off the playing field."

"You did the right thing, Bart," said Tory. "Sam—thank you."

Sam leaned back in the seat. "You know the interesting thing? I thought the rider was a man until I touched him. It was a woman."

"Really?" Bart said. "That's the East Coast team, Judge Parker. That's Nieto. Evidently he just wanted to reach out and touch you."

* * *

Maria had never seen a place like this. The highways, everything roaring, millions of cars, shiny and clean and fast. No rusted trucks, no jeeps filled with boys with rifles. At one point she kneeled to look out the back, but the man told her to sit with her feet on the floor.

Now they were off the wide road, passing house after house, each one different, all with two and even three levels. No chickens in the yards, no pigs blocking their progress. She wanted a house like this for her mother: no disorder, no chaos, a perfect world.

The car turned down a long dirt driveway up to a house that Maria thought looked a little like a castle in a storybook— not so large, but lots of windows and round towers and different kinds of roofs. The car pulled into an attached garage; the man got out, pulled down a wide door so she couldn't escape. He was joined by another man, an Anglo.

The second man opened the car door. "Come out, my dear," he smiled. "Vamanos." Maria, frozen in the back seat, didn't like this at all. This was obviously the man she was supposed to please. He looked like a vampire in some old movie.

"You must be hungry," he said. "I have cake and candies and pizza." The man pulled out a ring of keys and got into the car next to Maria. "We can take these off, now—" he said, gently. took Maria's hands and unlocked each cuff from her wrist.

"My mother is sick," Maria said.

"You speak English!"

"In my school they teach it."

"Great," he said in English, and in Spanish: "That will make things so much easier."

"My mother needs me to help her."

"Shhhh-shhhh shhh." He put his finger to his lips, reached across and touched hers, very gently. "There'll be time for that. Come in, eat, and then we'll talk."

Gingerly, seeing no other way, Maria slid out of the car, stood rubbing her wrists, raw from hours in the cuffs. "We'll get cream for that," the man said. "You must need a bathroom."

Maria nodded. The man put his arm over her shoulders, led her through a kitchen filled with gleaming white appliances, opened a door to an indoor bathroom, a toilet and a sink, no window. "Go right in," he said. She entered; he locked her in, went back out to the garage.

The brush-cut man was waiting by the car. "You like?" the man asked.

"I think she may be the prettiest one yet. Thank you, Mr. Armstrong."

"A pleasure." The man got in the car. "Give me a call when you're done."

* * *

The next day found Tory back in Washington. Over coffee before the session began, Fenton Kottle told about being stalked by the father of a young girl whose case he'd had to adjudicate in Family Court. The man took it personally that he had lost custody of his daughter, and everywhere Judge Kottle went, there he was, calling him a child molester in restaurants and theaters. Eventually the man had been institutionalized, and the trouble had ended.

Then Drummond took his seat, called the session to order. The first thing he did was ask Henry Severn, OIPR's chief prosecutor, for an update on Ocindo, Canute and Pell.

Severn was in a charcoal pinstripe suit. "I'm pleased to report," Henry began, "that we have identified a suspect. An FBI agent in LA tracked a phone to an apartment building where two tenants had left the week before. The place had been cleaned and painted, but the agents out there were able to pull prints from inside the closet. We are now looking for a man named Ned Bjorn. And the happy thing is, there's tons of documentation on this guy— he was USMC, he gave that up to go private as a contractor with ArrowHawk in Colombia, and we surmise he gave that up to work for Eduardo Nieto. He shared the apartment with an unsub, a Spanish gentleman, which would fit the intelligence we've gotten about Nieto's hit squads in the US. So we've got a national alert on this guy Bjorn. Evidently he's 6'4", so he'll be hard to hide."

Spontaneous applause filled the air. Tory wasn't sure who started it, but it was as if the constant tension of being in this room with this power had broken for a moment, and a ray of light had shone down.

Everyone around the semicircle was smiling.

Tory, for the first time in weeks, felt a lightness in her heart, a glimmer of hope: maybe, just maybe, there was a chance she would come through this.

It almost seemed too much to ask.

Five minutes later, Henry Severn began to present OIPR's first case of the day. "Recently the Justice Department learned that contacts had been made between the radical Maoist guerilla organization Tierra Libre Gente Libre— in English, Free Land Free People— and various high-level authorities in Colombia. TLGL, as it is commonly known, began in Peru as a drug-production cartel with a Marxist ideological perspective and a willingness to use violence to achieve both drug enterprise and political aims. Over the past decade, their political program has evolved to the legalization and nationalization of all South American drug production in every country in the region, with the ultimate goal of uniting South America into one Communist nation funded by marijuana, cocaine, and other illicit drug production, as well as traditional exports like oil and agricultural products. They envision the current countries functioning as semi-independent states. They are responsible for the deaths of more than 11,500 cartel rivals, soldiers, politicians, farmers and business owners. Their leader, Esteban Espinoza, was killed last year in a shootout with military forces in Costa Rica. There had been hope this decapitation would put the organization into disarray.

"A new charismatic leader has emerged," Severn went on. "He calls himself Artemio. And he has been reaching out to various influential figures in Colombia, Ecuador, Costa Rica, and other countries. In the last two weeks, he has found a willing audience in some of the more radical figures in Colombian political circles. NSA cell-phone captures tell us that meetings have been set up between Artemio and various Colombian business leaders, among them Eduardo Nieto, who has similarly called for legalization of cocaine in his country and throughout the world, though our evidence suggests he does not share TLGL's Marxist ideology. We have assets in place; unfortunately they would be compromised were Artemio to be arrested or harmed." Tory sat up, thinking of Bart Alicia. If he'd still been down there, he'd've been the asset in place. Severn went on: "However, these assets are in a position to extract maximal information through Humint and Sigint." Human intelligence and signal intelligence. "We request the court grant warrants to allow our agents to monitor this meeting through audio, video, and satellite surveillance pursuant to the application before you."

Drummond leaned forward in his leather chair. "TLGL are cocaine-funded terrorist killers. Nieto's organization are cocaine-funded terrorist killers. Them in the same room talking about domination of the drug industry throughout the southern hemisphere, I'd say that warrants our concern." He etched an eyebrow high in his forehead, looked around at the other justices. "Questions?" he asked.

“I have one," Tory said. "If I were Eduardo Nieto, I might have an opinion about anyone trying to nationalize my business."

Severn cleared his throat. "One of the respondents in the NSA tapes was surprised that Nieto offered to send a plane for Artemio. As Artemio is traveling under other arrangements, it was not deemed relevant. I can get you a transcript of that exchange in half an hour, Judge Parker."

"I'd like to see it," Tory said.

Drummond was solicitous. "Do you need it to decide on the warrants in this case?"

"No, Tory said, "no. I'm ready to vote right now."

"Anyone else have any questions?" Jack Riley did, and AO Hart did, as did Rebekkah King. Al Clemente, Tory saw, sat there, not saying a word, hunched in his chair like a frog. Finally, Drummond closed the questions, sent the prosecution team out, and took his poll.

Tory was happy to cast her vote, was unsurprised when the decision was unanimous.

When TLGL and Eduardo Nieto had their revolutionary summit in the Colombian mountains, America would be listening.

* * *

It had been a long day at the Department of Justice, and now the man driving to the Potomac house had to force himself not to speed. But the needle kept pushing into the 70s and he had to make himself calm down, slow down, take deep breaths, keep his eyes on the road.

At last, the safety of the driveway into the woods. He drove slowly through the trees, fished out the garage door opener from under the dashboard, pressed the button and waited as the door rose. When he was back inside he ran through the kitchen to the cellar stairs, unlocked the door and relocked it behind him, trotted down the steps and unlocked the door into the girl's bedroom. Just before he entered he hit the lights from outside.

She gave a startled animal cry, sat up on the bed, eyes winced shut, the chain still around the ankle. "Excuse me—" she said, "excuse me—" but he ignored her, unlocked the second door, went into the camera room and shut and locked it behind. He crossed the little studio, opened the door on the far wall, entered the black room. He didn't turn on the lights. He sat at the desk, turned the laptop on by feel. When it was booted, he opened the ArrowHawk text message anonymization program.

Artemio, the Los Angeles situation, there was so much to tell his patron, Eduardo Nieto, that he wasn't sure where to start. At the beginning, he thought, and typed the first sentence:

> The FBI is looking for an ex-Marine, ex-ArrowHawk vet Ned Bjorne. They have fingerprints, they know he was involved in Ocindo. He will be

> arrested on sight. He has a partner, identity currently unknown.

The man had debated not saying anything about Artemio; the US had assets in place, and this would likely blow them; there was every reason to suspect they might be killed if Nieto found out who they were. But then he thought of the beautiful child in the other room, thought of the weeks with her that were to follow, and he knew he had to make his report complete.

When he had finished sending the text he locked up the black room, went back to the bedroom. The girl had dried tears on her cheeks; the man always found that resonant. He squatted next to the bed. "Were you lonely when I was gone?"

The girl said nothing. She was a beauty— strong bones, great eyes, but still a child. As beautiful as a faun. "It's okay to be lonely," he said. "It's okay to be sad."

Her hands covered her pubis, guarding herself. Against him, he always found himself asking, or against her own unknown desires? That was what he had learned as a boy: it may start as a shock, an assault, but soon the child realizes they likes this, they want more. And that realization leads from being powerless to having all the power in the world.

He stood, came around the bed, sat at the edge. "I just want to lie here," he said. "I won't touch you. I just want to lie down." Gently he unfolded his long frame onto the mattress, smoothed his hair back, lay with his head on the pillow. "I'll put my hands behind my head, just relaxing. You lie down too— that's a good girl," he said, as she lay back stiffly. This, he well knew, was how it always began. "That's it," he went on, "just relax. We'll just lie here, and we don't have to say a word."

*   *   *

The next day, New York was grey and humid. On the way to work, Tory debated whether or not to mention the previous day's proceedings to Bart. He would be interested, she thought, in the meeting with Artemio, and his security clearance was high enough to allow it.

"Eduardo's a businessman," Bart said, after she gave him the basic set-up. "He hates all that Marxo-Lenino-mumbo-jumbo."

"Evidently he's warm to the visit, at least in the intel I saw."

"Really?" Bart glanced at Tory. "Well, he must be getting something out of it."

When Tory came back to the peeling institutional paint of her robing room, Anna was ready with a sheaf of messages. Prominently at the top was one from AO Hart, fellow judge on FISA. Anna had asked if it was urgent, and Hart had said yes.

Tory kicked Anna and Thomas out of the robing room, dialed the long-distance number.

The man answered. "Judge Hart, Tory Parker," she said.

"Judge Parker. Hello." His voice was deep and clear, in its way as attractive as his face.

"Your message said urgent. I've got to step into court in a minute, but should we talk on the securitized phone line?"

"Please, Judge, it's not that kind of urgent. I've been in DC on court business for months, now I've got an opportunity to come up to New York, get out of the house for an overnight. And I've got an invite to a charity masked ball, big Halloween thing thrown every year by the Trial Lawyer's Society. Finally this year I'm up here and I'm free, but I hate going to this sort of thing alone. Now I know we only just met, but I was wondering if you could see your way clear to—well, if we were in high school, it'd be a date."

She'd liked him in court. He'd been funny, and when necessary he'd been strong, trying to cut through to the truth. And the fact that he'd been blessed with remarkable cheekbones didn't hurt.

"Is this the Anonymous Ball?" Even as she asked, she realized it had to be. "Big social whoop-de-do, whatever money is raised is given to charity?"

"In a lump sum, and the donor is listed as anonymous. Anonymous good works—a way that lawyers can warm their egos with the thought that they're not so egotistical after all."

Tory let out a laugh. "I've heard of this for years, but I've never been invited. I figured I must have pissed off some lawyer in my courtroom who made sure I was blackballed."

"Well, that's the beauty of it—it's a masked ball, so nobody'll even know it's you unless you want them to. We'll be like two spies, sneaking through with our secrets intact."

"It sounds fun," she said, and pulled over her desk calendar. "When would this be?"

"This Saturday. I know it's short notice."

"Actually," Tory said, "I'm free."

"Excellent," said Judge Hart. "I'll be staying at the Carlyle; I'll pick you up at 7:00. It'll be fun. And if it isn't fun, we'll skip out of there, do something else."

Tory thanked him, got off the phone. Back in the courtroom, she was surrounded by Anna and Thomas, long faces filled with deep concern. Thomas spoke for them both: "I know there are secrecy issues in your work that you can't share with us—"

"He asked me for a date," Tory cut through their solicitude. Thomas rolled his eyes, immediately disinterested.

"What'd you say?" Anna asked.

Tory offered a light shrug. "I said yes," she said, and Anna cracked a smile.

* * *

"A masked ball?" Bart Alicia said. "You want me to figure security for a *masked ball?"* Tory winced. Bart had been unflappable in extreme circumstances. She hadn't realized she was giving him a problem. "I'm only good to you because I know faces. If I can't see faces—"

Tory felt like an idiot. "I hadn't thought of that," she said quietly.

"Well, hold it," Bart said. "This Judge Hart—he's FISA too, right?" Tory nodded. "So he'll have his own security I could coordinate with."

"He's only got basic Marshals security. It's not like he's on a case like Baby Nieto."

"So no 24-7. So it'll just be me."

"I won't go," she said. "I'll call him and cancel." In some weird part of her brain she felt like she was talking to her father. She pushed the strange tangle of thoughts out of her head.

"Listen," Bart stood for a moment, thinking. "This'll have a guest list, security, all that stuff, right? Let me take a look at it, do an assessment. Meanwhile, what would you wear"?

"I hadn't thought about it," she lied. What she hadn't done was decide on anything.

"Can I suggest— nothing too elaborate, no—hoop skirts, no, I don't know, bear costumes, nothing you can't run in. I don't want to lose track of you in a crowd."

She had a red dress she'd worn once, it'd been sitting in a dry-cleaning bag ever since. Red dress to the floor and a red mardi gras mask, if she could find one. Not too shabby.

If Bart let her go, of course.

* * *

The next day, Tory safely ensconced at court, Bart drove to the New York Athletic Club, an immense stone building on Central Park South that hosted the Anonymous Ball every year. He parked in front, left the Police Business placard on the dash, went into the lobby.

This was a New York members-only institution, founded soon after the Civil War and more reminiscent of the era of robber barons than of rubber yoga mats, with 300 guest bedrooms, a 30' by 75' swimming pool, and vast equipment rooms overlooking the park. Bart was met at the front desk by Judd Carr, chief of security, a spry older man who obviously used the facilities.

"The ball takes place every year in our card room," Carr explained as they rode up in the luxuriously appointed elevator.

Bart perked up. "Card room? Is it just Bridge? Or—"

"Our members play whatever private games they choose." On the ninth floor, Carr walked Bart into a spectacular long room half full of old men with chips at green felt tables. "The ceiling is considered a masterpiece."

Bart glanced up, nodded. He and a decent partner could start on opposite walls, pick this place clean by the time they met in the middle.

He pried his attention from the ageing card sharks. "Orchestra? Jazz band? I assume not a DJ."

"Orchestra or big band—15 to 20 pieces. We set them up against the wall. Bar stations and food along the sides." He pointed.

"Security?" Bart asked.

"Two guest lists, downstairs and at the door. We've had bodyguards in full costume, we've had them in black tie—even dressed as waiters. Now—the Loggia." Carl led Bart onto a vast stone terrace, larger than Tory's apartment, open along one side to Seventh Avenue. "When the orchestra takes breaks, everyone comes out here to cool off. It gets quite crowded."

Bart walked to the parapet, looked out over the city, at the modern building across the street, He shook his head. He didn't like it, but it would have to do.

* * *

Three nights later, Tory was changing earrings for the third time when the buzzer rang from downstairs. Siggy barked furiously as Tory ran to the intercom. "Siggy! Sit! No bark!" She touched his snout and he quieted. She hit the button.

"Got Judge Hart here for you." Mario, the doorman, sounded puzzled.

"Send him up." Tory caught sight of her earrings in the hallway mirror, held up the mask and decided that dangly was good. She tried to tie the mask's ribbons behind her head, gave up as the doorbell rang.

She opened the door to Mark Twain, white suit, a shock of white hair and a fulsome moustache. Even under the camouflage, however, AO Hart's handsome features managed to shine through.

"You look great," Tory said.

"I look like Mark Twain. You, you're a vision."

"Thanks," Tory said, suddenly modest in a dress that didn't support modesty well. He kissed her cheek, the moustache bristly against her makeup. "Come in, come in—the moustache is so realistic-"

"I had it made for me by a Broadway makeup artist—came to the hotel this afternoon and fixed me up."

"A friend?"

"No, I hired him specially for this." Wow, Tory thought, either you're a total nerd or you're really really rich. He went on: "Twain's always been my favorite writer. The older I get, the wiser he seems. Are you being a specific person? Or are you just going as The Most Beautiful Woman In The Room?"

"That's very sweet," Tory said, and touched his arm. "I'm going as a girl who has a red dress she loves but doesn't get to wear much." Then she smiled: "and a mask." She held up the feathered papier mâché shell.

"Well, if anyone asks, we'll just tell 'em you're Aphrodite or Helen of Troy and be done with it." And then: "You haven't introduced me to your dog."

*   *   *

Two thousand miles south, the ostrich stood at the edge of the clearing, afraid of the music, watching the men and women mingle on the stone deck of the house. After a while she grew bored, turned her attention to carefully nibbling the heads of flowers.

Eduardo Nieto was making sure everyone had enough aguardiente. The guest of honor did not drink; alcohol was capitalist poison. Eduardo assumed, as he always did when people didn't drink, that his young guest was an alcoholic and felt less for him as a result.

A real man engaged in life's pleasures without ever giving up control over them.

His brother flashed in his mind, how absurd that Baby wasn't here today. It was a crime, this disrespect of the Americans for Eduardo, a man so crucial to the international economy.

He would show them. He knew they were watching. He had received a text from his friend the American that told him everything.

He would get Baby out of their clutches. Tonight would be a first step.

Mariposa looked lovely this evening in a sleek black dress with lots of cleavage. Nieto saw clearly that Artemio was quite taken with her,

Mariposa was always fond of an appreciative audience. Nieto walked over, drew Mariposa close and whispered in her ear: "Go find out if the General's wife really is a lesbian."

Mariposa giggled, waved at Artemio, clicked across the flagstone in her heels.

Eduardo turned to the young man. "So, you wish for us all to join in business."

Artemio emphatically shook his head. "The vision I have is so much more than simply doing business. I know you have a long-held dream of legalizing coca in Colombia, the way marijuana is increasingly legal all over the world."

Nieto smiled. "I think it would make Colombia the premier tourist destination in Latin America."

"You said just that in an editorial you wrote in *El Tiempo* some years ago." He closed his eyes, recited from memory: "'There is no reason the tourists who flock to the hashish cafes of Amsterdam could not also enjoy the finest cocaine, entirely legal and free of pollutants, served on mirrors in nightclubs in Cartagena or Medellín.'"

Nieto nodded in acknowledgement. "You've done your homework."

"I envision a united Latin America in which all states would be free to sort their affairs as they pleased. Colombia would be free to remake its society as it pleases, same with Brazil, same with Peru and Ecuador and the rest. As it is now, each country—each government—has to negotiate with the United States, its banks, its businesses, its law enforcement and its military. Each has to make compromises against the soul of its people, because of the endless demands of the United States. But by uniting into one economic force—a continental bloc of country-states all under one banner—our continent could free its people and craft its own destiny." Nieto started to speak, but Artemio held up his hand. "If you had your dream of Colombia, the United States would do everything in their power to undermine it, yes?"

"Of course they would," Nieto agreed.

"And that power would include a military projection of force."

"Inevitably."

"What if the standing army of a united South America could engage them, defeat them, drive them out? What if, when they flew in to spray your fields, you could declare it a military invasion and call in fighter jets from a united South American air force to shoot down their planes?"

Nieto sat back, a smile on his face. Emboldened, Artemio pressed on. "America is united, the European Common Market is united, and we are divided, fighting each other when we could be the vanguard that drives the world."

Nieto sipped his aguardiente. "And who will run this united continent? Who will force this great remaking of society?"

"The people."

"In the form of an organization such as yours."

"There must always be a cadre leading the revolution. The process will be gradual, but as each nation-state joins us, the individual governments will wither away, will attend to purely internal matters."

"And what if the people like their governments? What if they rose up against you?"

Artemio shrugged. "There will always be revanchists who stand in the way of progress. But it is the will of the people who make the revolution, the restructuring of society, inevitable."

"And in this society, would I still have my house?" Eduardo Nieto said. "And my horses? And would Mariposa still have her dress that you so admired?"

The young man gave a long, thoughtful pause. "Things would be different," he said finally. "The structures would be different. And that difference would make a better world."

Eduardo Nieto smiled. "You are a tremendous romantic, I see. Your parents are alive?"

"My mother. In Lima.

"Eduardo took his notebook from his jacket pocket, clicked open a pen. "Tell me her address. I'd like to send her a present."

* * *

Tory had never been to a masked ball before, and she had to say, it was spectacular. People were wearing their fantasies of themselves for all the world to see. Wealthy lawyers had chosen to express their inner self as Churchill, or Stalin, or Mahatma Gandhi.

Most didn't take off their masks once they made an entrance, so she left hers on.

But what surprised her more was that AO Hart knew how to dance.

He'd wanted to the minute they walked in; the band, brassy and amplified, was playing a song she'd loved in college, and he'd led her immediately to the dancefloor. At first they'd done the standard rock-generation shuffle, two people finding a rhythm a foot away from each other. Then the song changed into something slow, and Mark Twain took her into his arms, led her expertly through coordinated movements she'd have never attempted on her own.

In the car they'd talked about the death penalty. Now, as he held her, he returned to their conversation. "That's a harsh standard," he said.

"Not as harsh as executing someone and finding exculpatory evidence after the fact.'"

"True," Hart said. "These DNA-based reversals for people who've been on death row for 20 years— you have to pay attention to that." He pulled away, twirled her, pulled her back.

The song came to an end; Tory wouldn't have minded sitting– her red high heels were beginning to get to her– but AO Hart was waiting for the next song. Reprieve came when his phone began to vibrate. He looked at the incoming number.

"Let me take this," he said.

"Go, go," Tory said. The band was starting up again. "I could use some water." Hart escorted Tory to one of the bar lines, then stepped out of the noisy room to take his phone call.

She'd been waiting a minute when someone tapped her on the shoulder. She turned to see an eye-patched face bedecked in a tricorn hat, an elaborate military jacket over a loose white shirt, a cutlass in his belt, and boots to his knees. "Angelo!" she smiled.

"Tory!" He lowered his voice. "Best not to tell all these lawyers there's a judge here."

"I'm incognito," she said, and then: "I guess the blonde hair gave me away–"

"Well, no, actually–" suddenly he was shy. "You have a birthmark on your lower back."

She met his tone. "You remembered that?"

He nodded, changed the subject. "Your first time at this shindig?" Tory said yes. Angelo went on: "I look forward to it every year, it fulfills my childhood dream to wear a sword in public."

Judge Hart returned; Tory introduced: "Angelo Schwartz, I'd like you to meet Judge Arvin Osbelt Hart."

"Call me AO," Hart said. "Arvin isn't a name, it's a curse parents lay on bad children. Mr. Schwartz, I see you on my TV all the time."

"Every once in a while I say something intelligent."

"I'll grant you that," Hart said.

Tory stepped up to the bar. "Guys, what are we drinking?"

"Champagne," said Angelo. "Bourbon rocks," said Hart.

Tory faced the bartender. "Two champagnes and a bourbon–" she said, just as a blonde in a fitted gold breastplate and Valkyrie horns descended on Angelo. "There you are! There's someone you have to meet–"

Angelo introduced the girl as Willow; they all shook hands before she dragged him off.

"That girl looked very familiar," Hart said.

"She's a model, I think. I mean, I think I've seen her in ads." Then: "The band's ending their set. If we go out right now, we can beat the crowd onto the balcony."

* * *

In Colombia, Eduardo Nieto's cocktail reception was winding down. Artemio was chatting with Mariposa about how his organization, Tierra Libre Gente Libre, had doubled in size over the last year when Eduardo came out with a gun belt, pistols at either side. "Artemio," he called. "Do you shoot?"

The young man smiled. "I wouldn't be very useful for the revolution if I could not."

"I have a range. We will see who shoots better, the capitalist or the communist."

Artemio rose to the bait. "I have the advantage, because you've been drinking."

"I have the advantage, because you have not." Nieto put an arm around the young man, led him off around the house to the shooting range. A fleeting moment of concern brushed across Mariposa's face, but she pushed it away and rose to refill her drink.Nieto entered the shed, flipped on the lights. At the far end was a cement wall angled to prevent ricochets. Nieto loaded paper targets onto the pulleys, sent them down on their long ropes. The two men put on ear protection, and Nieto handed Artemio one of his revolvers. "Six shot Ruger .357. Let's see what you can do."

The young man took the gun, opened it expertly to check the load, slapped it shut. He fired six shots in rapid succession, set the gun down, pulled the rope that brought the target up.

A nice grouping, not too much spread, no wild shots. Very respectable.

"My turn," Eduardo said, braced his arm and shot carefully, five times. On the sixth, he swung around, put the muzzle up to Artemio's temple and put a bullet through his brain.

The young man slammed dead to the floor. "I don't need revolutionaries stirring up my peasants," Eduardo explained to the bleeding corpse. He holstered the guns, pulled up the target to see how he'd done.

His grouping was tighter.

Good. He walked out of the shed, called over the first servant he saw. "There's a body at the shooting range," he said. "Get some men, cut it up, wrap each piece in plastic, put it in a box, and send it to this address." He took out his notebook, ripped out the young man's mother's address in Lima.

Walking back to the party, he glanced up at the sky, thought about the satellites peering down, smiled. The Americans could not help but recognize the global stature of his leadership in ensuring that Tierra Libre Gente Libre's new young lion was no longer a concern.

* * *

The balcony, Tory thought, was remarkable. The size of a decent college pool, it looked out over Seventh Avenue and the base of Central Park. The night was mild; Hart had cut through the crowd to get prime real estate on the balustrade, though now they were gradually being hemmed in by other masked partygoers.

"Been divorced for five years," Hart was explaining. "Got a daughter in college in Maryland, that's why I bought the house south of DC, I'm there all the time these days, but when I'm not she takes it over with her boyfriend."

"Do you like him?"

"He could have more tattoos, I suppose." A photographer and assistant working their way through the crowd approached them: "Would you like your picture taken?"

"No," Tory and Hart said at the same time: The man looked at them oddly, moved on.

"We're the most anonymous people at this thing," Hart said, and Tory had to laugh, because it was true.

* * *

Across Seventh avenue from the masked ball, Mrs. Leiben was finding that the ropes had cut off circulation in her hands, and now pins and needles were setting in. She hadn't seen the people in her apartment when she came home from the supermarket; they had put the pillowcase over her head so quickly she'd barely seen anything. She believed there were two of them, though neither had said a word, even as they were tying her to the chair.

The television was on loud. Mrs. Leiben was fairly sure she was alone in the living room, that meant whoever was here was in the bedroom, or out on the terrace.

How this could happen she didn't understand. This was a good building, a modern building, with a doorman and decent people and wrap-around terraces on every floor.

In the bedroom, his mind utterly unconcerned with Mrs. Leiben's discomforts, El Limpiador focused his rifle's scope on the masked revelers across the street. The orchestra had stopped playing; the terrace was filling up. He found his prey easily: the woman with the red mask of sequins and feathers stood with Mark Twain at the edge of the parapet.

Compared to the shot he'd taken in Brooklyn, this would, he saw, be a simple matter. He held her in his scope, shifted minutely to adjust his stance. He had her lined up perfectly. A shame, really— an attractive woman— but in one way that added to the thrill of the hunt.

He stilled his breath, counted his heartbeats and began to squeeze the trigger.

*   *   *

The man behind Tory was very drunk. He was wearing a kilt, and he kept jostling Tory without apologizing. The third time he did it, he knocked off her mask.

She stooped to get it, heard the unmistakable crack of a rifle from across the street, felt the air-ripping thrum of a bullet directly above her, and the kilted man's head burst like a watermelon dropped from a bridge.

Screams went up; instantly there was a discombobulated rush for the exits. Tory dove for the floor; Hart threw himself over her.

"You're bleeding? Or—"

"I'm okay," she said, though honestly she couldn't be sure.

"Follow me," he said, and together, keeping low, they made their way with the crowd to the door inside. Tory looked back at the kilted man's body on the terrace, the head gone, a pool of blood tramped by footprints.

"That was meant to be me," she said simply.

"Yes," Hart said, blinked his eyes as though dizzy. "Yes. If you hadn't bent down—"

The crush of two hundred people all trying to leave as quickly as possible made for panic around the elevator and chaos in the stairwells. Tory and Hart took the stairwell down, Tory in stocking feet, holding her heels. In the lobby she saw Bart searching the crowd for her.

He was furious at himself. "I knew this was a mistake," he said, when they got to him. "I knew it." He led them out to the waiting car, jumped them in and sped off into the night.

*   *   *

"What I don't understand is how many people knew I would be there." Tory was pacing back and forth in her living room, on the phone with Jack Riley. She had sent Judge Hart back to his hotel, come up to her apartment alone and stripped off the red dress and turned on the shower to get the lawyer's blood off her body. There she had begun to cry uncontrollably. Every decision she made, even the most commonplace, ended with someone getting killed.

She was overwhelmed. She had no idea what to do. She had called Jack because he wouldn't care if she cried.

A deep hissing silence from Jack. "Well, who'd you tell?"

"You—"

"Who else? What about your clerks?"

Something hardened in Tory, something plain and flat and ugly, and she didn't like it. "I trust Anna and Thomas more than I trust anybody on the Secret Court."

"Tory, I understand you're angry—"

Angry? Her fear had transmuted into fury. "The people I've known for years don't suddenly want to kill me, Jack. The people I've just met—"

"Tory, cool down."

"What if there's a mole?" There. She'd said it. "Someone on that court who's been corrupted— someone with a different agenda than anyone else in that room."

Jack was silent. "Tory, I've been on FISA a lot longer than you—"

"Three judges are dead, Jack!" she pulled her hair back with a tense fist. "They've tried to kill me twice. If a wife gets murdered, the first person the cops talk to is the husband because nine out of ten times nobody else has any reason to kill her. That's what this is, Jack— this isn't foreign, it's domestic. This isn't assassination, this is fratricide."

"That's absurd, Tory." Now Jack was angry.

"Maybe Eduardo Nieto is giving someone on the court whatever it is he wants. Just like he did with Barney Lind."

"You're not saying Judge Hart—""I don't know who," Tory said, though her suspicions were mounting. "But if you look at the idea that someone on FISA is behind all this, then everything makes a lot more sense."

Ten minutes later, the conversation remained mired in stalemate. After she got off, she could not believe Jack Riley— Jack Riley!— was being so obdurate.

Impossible, she thought. But still, it made her wonder.

* * *

"I can't tell you how sorry I am for what happened," Judge Hart was saying. Tory had spent a terrible sleepless night, had been wide awake before dawn. "I'm checking out of the hotel," Hart went on. "Got stuff waiting for me in DC. I left you a bunch of messages."

"I got them," Tory said.

Judge Hart pressed on: "I just hate that it was me put you in this situation."

Tory tried to come up with words to say, but all she could think was: *he's from the Secret Court, he invites me to this party, and someone tries to kill me. So he has to be the mole.*

She cut him off. "I've got to walk my dog. Go back to DC. Let's talk in a few days."

"Right." He sounded defeated. The thing was, his remorse sounded genuine— but maybe it would, if he'd set up the hit. Tory got off the phone. What she wanted was to be on a beach alone with Siggy, somewhere with wind and water and sand and no people for miles.

But even if she'd been able to snap her fingers and transport herself there, even then, she knew, she still wouldn't feel safe.

* * *

Maria had been naked and alone in the dark for what felt like days. She'd been shackled to the bed, a chain attached to a black leather cuff on her ankle, with a padlock sealing it shut. If she'd had a scissors, she might have been able to cut through the leather.

If she had a scissors.

She could walk about the room but it was safer to crawl because there was no light. There was a seat with a hole in it and a bucket underneath for a toilet; she had used it and now the room stank. She'd also found a large plastic box filled with melting ice and bottles of soda and tubs of milky goop she'd never seen before, wetter than cheese, not as sweet as dulce de leche. It left her fingers sticky and got in her hair, but Maria ate it. She chewed the ice, but after a long sleep she awoke to find it had all changed to water.

What if the man didn't come back? After this food was gone, what then? Abruptly she wanted to see him again. Which, she was prescient enough to know, was exactly his plan.

In her dreams she was playing soccer in La Plata, running and running. Her mother was getting better, doctors coming to the house. Then she'd wake up in this dark room chained to this bed and begin crying all over again.

When the door slammed somewhere above her, instantly she was fully alert. She heard someone walking down a flight of stairs, closer and closer, then the scratch of a key in a lock. Just before the door opened, an overhead lamp flooded the room with light so bright it was painful. She shut her eyes tight as the man stepped in the room, locked the door behind him.

He sat on the bed without touching her, and spoke in Spanish: "It's okay, I know the light must've hurt you. Take your time and let your eyes get used to it. I'll be right here."

She kept her eyes closed, covered her groin. "I see you worked your way through a lot of food, here– do you like yogurt?" He held up one of the empty plastic tubs of sweet cheese.

She squinted to see what he was talking about, shook her head, very slightly, 'no'.

"I'll find something else. I brought us sandwiches. Turkey and ham and roast beef. Here." He set a basket before her. "You choose."

Maria took a sandwich in one hand, kept herself covered. It was chewy but good. He wasn't a bad looking man, she thought. He had aged better than the men in her village.

Abruptly she was full. "Another sandwich?" he asked. "No?" He set the basket aside. "Want to get dressed? Let me unlock the cuff." His keys were on a chain that retracted into a fob on his belt. "It feels good to get that off, doesn't it? But when you get used to it, it feels good to get it back on." He stepped to the room's second door, worked another key, went in.

Maria ran quickly to the first door, tried the knob. It was locked.

"No, no, this way," said the man.

The second room was white. There was a table against one wall, with lightbulbs all around the edges of a mirror. There was a rack of clothes on hangers. And there was a camera on three long spindly legs.

She opened her mouth to talk, and it was like she'd forgotten how. She had to actively force her mouth to make the sounds: "My mother is sick. When do I go home to her?"

"That depends on you." She wanted to believe him. "Consider this—" he gestured at the room—"like a school. If you learn well, anything is possible. If not, certain lessons will have to be repeated. Let's get clothes for you." He patted the chair. "Sit."

Maria, naked in the doorway, held back. "Do you like chocolate? Other girls have sat in the chair for me, and they got a chocolate." Maria seemed frozen, glued to the spot. "If you want to see your family again, then it's a good idea right now to get in the chair." Gone was the soft, gentle tone, revealing something hard and angry underneath.

Maria crossed the room, sat in the chair.

The man wheeled the rack of clothes closer. "Look at all these pretty clothes," he said. "White stockings and shiny shoes. Try them on if you like."

Maria again had to force the words out: "Do you have a shirt? Or a robe?"

"Why, yes." The man pulled out something black and frilly. "Would you like to see it?" Maria reached for it. The man pulled it away. "Uh-uh-uh. First you have to eat a chocolate."

Maria took one, ate it. It melted deliciously. It was the best chocolate she'd ever had.

"Good, right?" Maria nodded. "Let's try the robe." Maria obediently stood. It was made of very soft material that fluttered like butterfly wings. "You look beautiful." And as he said it, Maria saw he was stroking his groin.

"When I came here, we passed a sign for Washington DC. Are we close?"

He blinked rapidly, several times. "Not so close," he said finally.

"Because in school we studied Washington DC. Could we go there?"

He licked his lips. "Would you like that?"

"Yes, please."

A smile sneaked across his face. "If you're very good, and you do what I say, then maybe." Then: "You'd make me so happy if you put these stockings on," he went on. "You want to make me happy, right? And I want to make you happy."

He took the white stockings off their hanger. "I'll help you with these," he said, "and then perhaps we can take some pictures."

* * *

Tory was reading FISA transcripts in her apartment, Siggy snoring at her feet, when the phone rang. She picked it up, checked the incoming number.

Bart. "I'm outside your door, I didn't want to ring the bell, make you jump." She got up, opened the door, Siggy barking twice until he saw it was Bart. "This just arrived by messenger service," he said, and handed her a small envelope.

"Thank you, Bart." Angelo's handwriting on the front. Funny how she always knew it when she saw it. "Need anything?"

"I'm good," Bart said, and left her alone.

She sat on the couch. The envelope was tucked but not sealed. She pulled out a card, a photo of Times Square in the rain on the front. Inside, he had filled the blank space with his orderly, expansive handwriting:

> Tory,
> I know, I know: middle of a trial, no private communications with the judge. But I hope it's not out of place

to say, apropos last night, thank God you're all right. Please believe me: I will do everything in my power to help you stay that way. If there's ever any way I can help, please ask.

Angelo

Tory held the card and looked out the window at the gray, windswept afternoon and gave in to the sensation of wanting Angelo in the room, his solid tangible presence. Holding the card, his absence was palpable. And even as that animal desire bloomed in her, intellectually she knew all the problems that forestalled it.

All of which left her alone. She pulled out the trial phone list, found his cell, dialed it.

It rang once. She thought: Ocindo, Canute and Pell. What am I doing? She hung up immediately. *Guy sends a card and I turn into oatmeal.* And just as she thought it the phone in her hand started to buzz.

She waited, saw Angelo's name pop up. Of course it was him. She hit the button. "Hello."

"Tory. You called."

Just hearing his voice, something in her melted. "I got your card," she said, after a pause. "Thank you."

"I can't tell you how demoralized I feel, Tor. I don't know what to say—"

"Stop," Tory said.

"I'm worried about you. 1 want to just grab you and fly somewhere far away."

A lump formed in her throat. Was it a lie? He'd always been able to play an elemental decency. It was one of the things that worked well for him in court: on a very deep level, it was absolutely convincing.

But still, there were too many questions. "Angelo, the first day of the trial— how did you know I was on FlSA?"

He was taken aback. "It was an educated guess," he explained. "I knew Jack Riley was on the court, and he's been a mentor to you. When those judges in DC died, you adjourned the trial. My guess was that had to relate to the FISA vacancies."

He'd never been dumb. "Who have you told?" Tory said.

"No one. It was a little piece of conjecture between you and me." He was momentarily unsteady. "I really did mean it when I said 'congratulations,'" he said.

"No you didn't,' Tory said. Her tone wasn't harsh, just honest. "You threw it at me to get me off balance."

"I wanted to see if I was right," he said. "Okay, if I didn't say it properly then, I'll say it now: congratulations. You're the right judge for that job."

That, Tory thought, remains to be seen. "Did you tell Baby?"

A long unsteady pause. Then: "Absolutely not. I'd have no reason on Earth to do that."

He'd been surprised by the question, she was sure of it. "No one else?"

"Tory, I told no one. No one in my office, no one in my personal life. No one." As he said it, she could hear the little boy he must have been, defending himself against unfair accusations. "That guy Hart," he went on, "he's on the Secret Court, too, right?"

Tory hesitated. "You know I can't answer that," she said, and immediately hated herself: she'd done it again, giving the answer by evading the question.

"Do you trust him?" he asked.

"I'd like to think I can," Tory answered.

"Well, I'd consider the question."

Tory thanked him again for the note, got off the phone.

Consider Hart, he'd said. In truth, she hadn't been able to consider anything else.

* * *

Tory needed to see for herself if Hart had set her up to be killed. She needed to look him in the eye and listen to him speak and trust her instincts. And if he was the cause of these attempts on her life, then she and Bart needed to see how it worked in action.

Finally, at the end of a long day of prosecution witnesses, Tory went back to her office, got online and began doing searches.

Judge Hart, the only child of wealthy parents, had started his career as a two-term Texas state legislator; during his years in elected office he had fought for state education money to be spent on girls' sports, and not just boys; he had also been an advocate of state-sponsored gun safety lessons for Girl Scout groups.

After his second term, he was appointed as a judge to the First Circuit Court of Appeals, and had worked his way up from there. He had been married twice, first to a woman he met in college, then to a daughter of Houston oil money. Tory plunged into his judicial decisions, collected in an online legal database. What she'd found was interesting: in environmental versus big business cases, big business didn't always win. They didn't always lose, but the man obviously cared enough about the environment to not just give it away in the cause of rising corporate balance sheets.

He was, in most of his press accounts, described as an avid hunter. Tory sat back, looked out her office window at the gathering night, and considered.

A hunter. Camouflaged, strategic, relentless in his pursuit. She could see that in him.

And what if she were his prey? She took a deep breath, dialed the first 9 numbers of Judge Hart's phone, just as she had before. Then, very deliberately, she pressed the tenth.

The phone rang twice, and a machine answered. Some part of her gladdened with relief.

"Arvin, it's Tory," she said, trying to keep the tone light. "Sorry it's taken so long to get back to you. If you'd like to come up to New York and have dinner, I'd love that. I'm free any day this week." She said goodbye, hung up and sat back in her chair.

Right now she felt a pungent need for the weight of a cold loaded sidearm under her Donna Karan jacket.

* * *

The man had told Maria to call him Papi. She called her father Papi.

This half-naked man bringing her sandwiches twice a day was not her father, and she found herself unable to say it. Which only made him angry.

Most days he came in the morning for a short period, and then hours later in the evening for longer. She'd asked for books, but he'd brought her Spanish picture books for little kids. She read them because she had nothing else to do, chained by the ankle to the bed frame.

He said he didn't want to force anything on her, that he understood how traumatic and wrenching all this had been, that he wanted to protect her. But then he would touch her between the legs, he would ask her to open his pants, he would expose himself to her.

She had seen naked men before; her brothers, sometimes her father for a brief moment in the mornings. But she'd never seen one so red, angry and insistent, like a club or a rolling pin. The man said it was a great compliment to her, that she did this to him. It took a couple of sessions before he convinced her to touch it, to take it into her hands. The first time he'd had an orgasm, she'd been absolutely shocked, and then terrified he'd be angry.

He hadn't been. He'd been gentler than she'd ever seen. The next session he got her to do it again, and then suggested she put her mouth to it. The thought of that made the food in her stomach erupt and shoot out all over his naked lap.

He'd jumped up, cursing, drying himself. And later, after he yelled and chained her to the bed and stormed out, she knew that something had turned.

Now she knew what it looked like when things didn't go his way.

* * *

Hours passed, the house silent. Maria was cold and hungry, too worried to sleep.

Usually he left her food, but this time he'd taken it after he chained her. Finally she heard his feet on the wooden steps, his key in the door. He relocked the door from the inside.

Something was different about him. She sensed it instantly. His gestures were sharp. "I've been patient," he said. "I wanted to do this gently, on your terms. But you're just a tease. And the time for teasing has come to an end."

"Wait," she was halfway up when he knocked her back on the bed.

"Do you know what happens to girls who make me angry? Do you?"

She thought he was going to climb on the bed, but instead he pulled the keys from his belt, unlocked her ankle chain. Then he grabbed her roughly by the arm and forced her into the photography room. He strode across to the only other door, the door he had never opened.

"This is the room where the bad girls go." He unlocked the door, hit on the light. The room was painted black. On one wall was a desk and a chair. On the other side, a black leather armchair faced a platform. Above the platform, hanging from a pipe, was a rope noose.

All at once, Maria saw how this was going to end. She was here to be his plaything, and when he got bored of her, he would bring her here and watch her die.

In one convulsive shock she wanted to lash out, go directly for his eyes with her fingers, but instead she very calmly said: "Let's go back." And taking his smooth hand, she pulled him out of the black room. He shut the door.

"Stand there," she said, knelt before him, shook her long hair away from her face. She opened his trousers, pulled them and his underwear down in one motion, waited as he stepped away from his clothes. He was exposed. She went in close, started to unbutton his shirt, adjusted her stance until she knew she had leverage. She took one step back, kicked his pendulous genitals as hard as she'd ever kicked any soccer ball.

He went down, clutching himself in blind fury. She kicked him again and again, making contact with the ball of her foot until he was bleating in pain. She grabbed his pants, ran with them out past her bed to the door, found the ring of keys. She tried one, tried another— it went in, but didn't turn— and now he was bellowing from the other room, he was lurching to his feet, his hands still clutching his crotch, and a fourth key didn't work. He was in the bedroom when the fifth key turned; she pulled it out, ran up the wooden stairs.

He was making his way up the stairs when she got to the door at the top. It was open. She thanked God, came through and slammed it hard behind. There was a thick black deadbolt; she shot it home just as he started shaking the door from the other side.

He was banging so hard she thought he was going to tear the whole door down. On the kitchen counter was a loaf of bread in a plastic bag. She grabbed it, ran naked out the front door into the night.

* * *

Damn, he thought, when he heard the deadbolt shut, when he heard her leave and silence enveloped the house. Damn it all, this was not going to be met well.

He went back downstairs through the empty basement, kicked furious into the black room and turned on the laptop. He slapped out an encrypted text to Armstrong explaining his predicament, took a deep breath and paced like a caged animal through the basement, trying to think.

Finally he sat back at the computer, began to compose a text to Eduardo. The man in Colombia was going to find out about this; it would be better, he thought, if it came from him.

* * *

Penny Jefferson hadn't been to this particular funeral parlor before, and she thought she'd been to every damn one in DC. But death always found new homes.

Gloria Pomfroy had had a wicked sense of humor. Penny had first met her four years before, when she'd come to the clinic as a new patient. She'd ended up temping there, one of her many part-time gigs in the wake of her husband's heroin overdose. She got clean— she even stopped smoking— and was talking about going back to school when a constellation of symptoms was diagnosed as ovarian cancer. Less than a year later, here she was.

Penny looked at the shrunken figure in the casket, tried to send up a prayer, couldn't imagine a deity capable of doing this to someone when they were just beginning to shine.

She sent up a prayer for Gloria, not for God. Then she looked around for Gloria's son.

Penny had seen the ten-year-old boy when she'd walked in; she had met him a few times. Now he was in a suit and tie, with his grandparents, holding his grandma's hand.

Grandparents raising grandchildren. It was always so wrong. She approached the outer edges of the group of well-wishers, was immediately seen by Imelda, Gloria's zaftig mother.

"Penny–" the woman turned to the boy. "Luis— it's Penny."

"Sure," the boy looked just like his mom. "From the clinic." He stuck out his hand.

Penny wanted to hug him, but they shook. "Your mother told me to look out for you," she said, took her wallet from her bag, came up with a single battered business card. She wished it was in better shape. "Here," she said, and wrote her number on the back. "If you ever want to talk about anything at all, give a call. Your mom was a wonderful person."

The boy accepted the card, looked like he was going to cry. "Aww, honey," his grandmother said, and the boy hid in her ample shoulder, silent tears coming easily.

A curious elation crept over Penny, as if she were going to faint, and all at once she had a revelation: it wasn't her in the coffin; it wasn't her mother trying to comfort Kendrick. She'd survived, and Kendrick was an adult, he wasn't this slip of a boy in a suit at his mama's funeral.

She'd never thought of it that way before. She wondered what her friends would think— Tory Parker popped into mind. Tory was good at seeing the other sides of things. Gloria's mother, still holding the boy, looking at Penny. "Gloria said you were like a rock to her."

Like a rock. Penny licked her lips ineffectively. How many funerals was somebody going to say this to her? Over and over again, every few months: Penny, you're a rock. Strong, silent, unmoving, no emotions, no mistakes, can't afford any mistakes. Not human.

Got that rock. Penny took a long breath in. "I'm going to miss your daughter," she said.

"Sit, sit." the large woman tapped a chair.

"I'm sorry," she said, and as she said it she was shocked at her own boldness, all the times she'd wanted to say this at a funeral and never had: "I really have to go."

* * *

The first decision came at a Metro stop a block away from the funeral parlor. Penny breezed right past it. It wasn't dangerous to skip a Metro stop. People did it all the time.

Instead she walked seven blocks into a crumbling neighborhood, stood for ten minutes waiting for the bus, crossing back and forth between denial and desire.

The bus finally rumbled up; she got on and sat. She discreetly counted her money: $68.

Okay, well, she had money.

The bus lumbered along its route; she passed the clinic, the stop she usually got on, and now the view was familiar, every storefront and window the same she'd seen a thousand times. But a spirit of keening excitement she had kept tightly locked inside had found its way out.

I've gone to too many funerals, she thought, and I've cracked. I never went to the one I was most afraid of, she thought, and now it doesn't matter.

It took forever to get to the lookouts, clusters of guys standing around with cell phones on abandoned street corners. Then the girls, all so young, all so hard.

She was shaking. She was almost nauseous with excitement. She knew what that building could give, and the anticipation was a state of agony and ecstasy with only one cure.

Her hand was shaking as she reached out, touched the plastic strip that rang the bell. She was 35 years old, for God's sakes, she knew better than to even contemplate getting off this bus and going into that building, but even more strongly she knew that it was inevitable, it had been inevitable from the first time she'd recognized the place for what it was. Every neuron in her brain knew exactly what that house could give. She stood, hoisted her bag, surprised at the heaving in her chest and the nerve ticking in her left eyelid, and walked to the back door.

The bus huffed to a stop. She touched the door and it hissed open and she got out. She always knew she would get high again. Stoned men sat in hazes or stutter-walked past her, and she hated them because she was no better, and she loved them for that. Sitting on a folding chair was the tattooed man she'd seen from the bus. There was, in his eyes, a combination of curiosity and wariness at this thirty-something office worker in her matching black skirt and jacket.

Penny reached one shaking hand into her purse, took out her wallet, splayed it open before him. He looked at it, saw the need in her eyes, nodded slightly and let her in.

*   *   *

Maria spent the night naked in a copse of trees in the middle of a field; she'd awakened early to the sound of voices, and had kept hidden. This was beautiful land, she saw: rolling hills and short green grass. She was surprised some farmer hadn't put in coca, but instead there were men driving around in odd little cars, getting out to hit small white balls.

She couldn't walk around naked, she knew. She ate a piece of bread from the bag.

A little car filled with men rolled across the field and she flattened herself in the leaves. They stopped and got out, sticks over their shoulders, to look out over the land.

There were jackets draped over the seats in the car. She looked at the men, all clustered together with their sticks, talking and laughing. She made her move.

Her hair was caught in brambles. She spent a furious moment extricating herself, looked again. Now one of the men had put a ball on the ground, was taking a position over it to hit it.She kept low, sprinted up behind the car, looked around the side. The man was still standing over the ball, almost hitting it over and over, stopping each time.

Maria kept the car between her and the men, made her way around to the seats. She slipped a white zip-up jacket off the driver's chair, turned and ran hell-bent back to the woods.

The men hadn't seen her. The jacket must have belonged to the fat one; when she put it on, it came down to her mid-thigh. She checked the pockets, pulled out a solid gold lighter, four dollar bills and some change— she had no idea how much the money was worth— and a roll of candies. She immediately ate one, hated it, it tasted like medicine.

The lighter was beautiful, heavy and cool in her hand. She flicked it, and a flame came on. She let it go out, flicked it again, and again, staring in wonder at the blue glow of fire.

She zipped up the jacket. She took up the dwindling bag of bread, knotted it shut. Then, while the men were still busy with their balls and sticks, she crept to the far end of the little clump of trees, ran hard and fast across the broad field to the line of trees in the distance.

She would go to Washington DC, she decided as she ran. It could not be too far. Surely, when she got there, someone in the ministries of the American government would be able to help.

*　　*　　*

It was midmorning when Armstrong drove up to the house. The front door was open—not a good sign. He stepped inside, banged on the cellar door. "Hello? You okay in there?"

In reply were footsteps up the cellar stairs and the older man yelling: "Thank you! Thank you for coming!"

Armstrong shot the bolt, and the man came tumbling out. "Any sign of her?" he asked.

"She's gone."

"What do we do now?"

"I've been thinking of that," Armstrong said, "and I believe I have an answer." He took up his cell phone, started to type an anonymized text.

"Who are you texting?"

"The West coast boys. Don't worry, they're ArrowHawk."

"The big guy is wanted by the FBI," the older man said.

"So I heard. Which means they're not doing much of anything out there. Change of theater might do them good." And at that,

Armstrong's cell phone rang. He answered it: "Trojo, you and Ned okay?" He listened to a reply. "Good, good," he said, and then: "Listen, how quickly can you boys get to DC? There's somebody here I need you to find."

* * *

Tory Parker loved her job. There was nothing more exciting than a trial with all the engines fine-tuned and running, talented people using evidence, intelligence and wit to fight their battles. In the hands of lesser lawyers it could plod, but when combatants like Sam and Angelo stepped into the ring– well, the jury was rapt, and so was she.

The prosecution's witness in the box was Paul Resnais, Baby's personal chef, who had lived in his townhouse for a year and a half before moving on. Sam had slowly been building the examination toward a crescendo. "Did Mr. Nieto ever mention his wholesale flower business?"

"It was one of the businesses he was involved with."

"You cooked all of Mr. Nieto's meals while you worked for him?"

"Most weekdays. Breakfast and dinner."

"He have dinner alone a lot?"

"No, sir. Mr. Nieto loved to entertain."

"So he had parties, people over— would you say every night?"

Paul nodded. "He would have dinners for 20 people Thursday through Sunday, and smaller groups during the week. Sometimes it would just be him and one or two of his girls."

"What wines would be served at these dinners?"

"Dom Perignon champagne exclusively. It was the only thing he drank."

A less disciplined prosecutor would have gone off-tangent, lured by the prospect of cocaine-kingpin sexcapades. But Tory knew

Sam: he'd used the Dom Perignon as a marker. He'd get to the salacious when it was time. "At any of these nightly dinners for guests, did fresh-cut flowers ever make an appearance?"

The witness hadn't known where this was going, and suddenly he got it. Tory watched as Angelo did, too. He scribbled a note and slid it to one of his junior attorneys.

"No," said the witness slowly. "I never saw fresh-cut flowers."

"Didn't see any delivered, didn't see any put in vases on tables, didn't see any as centerpieces, didn't see any at all?"

"No, sir."

Sam wore a quizzical look. "Would you think a man who owned a business importing fresh-cut flowers, and who entertained as lavishly as Mr. Nieto— would you expect him to show off his wares to the clients who came to his house? Have the freshest—"

"Objection–" Angelo thundered. "Speculative and misleading."

"Sustained," Tory said. Not that it mattered; Sam had made his point.

He didn't seem to mind. "Not a single fresh flower, in the time you cooked for him?"

"Not a one," Paul Resnais said.

Sam turned, smiled softly at Angelo. "Your witness, counselor," and sat back down.

Angelo stood slowly, took his time crossing to the witness box. "Mr. Resnais, as Mr. Nieto's personal chef, his diet— and thus his health— was your daily concern, was it not?"

Paul scratched his ear. "Mr. Nieto was very demanding about what foods he wanted. That said, yes, we tried to deal with his weight. Actually, in the time I was there, he lost weight."

"How much?"

"About fifteen, twenty pounds."

Angelo raised a world-weary eyebrow. "Fifteen, twenty– call it eighteen. In 18 months he lost 18 pounds. At that rate he'd get into fighting trim in, oh, twenty-five years."

"I'm not a dietician. I'm a chef," Paul said defensively.

"And a good one, I'm sure," Angelo said, and glanced over at his client, who looked like nothing so much as a skinless boiled potato. "Did Mr. Nieto ever discuss any allergies?"

Paul hesitated. "We didn't use any nuts," he said. "Mr. Nieto said they gave him aftas."

"Aftas?"

"Canker sores in the mouth."

"Was that the only allergy you took precautions against?"

"As I remember it, yes."

"Were you aware he had sleep apnea? So bad that a doctor had recommended a therapy machine to improve his breathing?" Paul was silent, thinking. "I can't be sure."

"Were you aware Mr. Nieto had asthma as a child?"

"Actually, yes, I do remember that."

"Are there foods one avoids if one has breathing problems?"

Paul shrugged. "I've heard of milk and milk products having some connection."

"How about flowers?" Angelo went in for the kill. "If you had trouble breathing, and you had a history of apnea and asthma, would you want a lot of flowers around?" And then: "Ah, I withdraw the question, it's plainly beyond your field of expertise." He turned his back on Paul. "No further questions, your honor," he said, and sat back down.

* * *

Late that evening an old rattletrap Mexican Air Force cargo plane arrived at Reagan International, was met on the tarmac by a black undercover police car, red and blue lights flashing discretely in the front grill and at the back. Trojo and Ned deboarded, were ushered into the back seat by Armstrong. Esmeralda smiled at Trojo, was as neutral as possible to Ned.

Armstrong got behind the wheel, looked into the rear-seat cage. "Nice to have you assholes back," he said, and made his way to the highway.

He drove them all to a dark bar and grill on the edge of DC. They took a booth in the back. When they had beers and the travelers had ordered some food, Armstrong put money into the jukebox, punched songs he thought would be loud, and then went back and took out the pictures.

"We're looking for this girl." He passed the first one around, watched the men's faces. Ned didn't seem to register. Trojo looked grim. Then he hit them with the second photo.

Trojo couldn't hide his disgust. "How old is she?"

"10."

"And she ran away? Makes sense to me."

Armstrong was not amused. "Look, the guy who took these pictures is very important. This girl knows stuff that could cause a lot of trouble. Find her and kill her before she talks, come in with proof, and there'll be ArrowHawk combat-level bonuses for you both. Got that?"

He looked at the two fuckups from Los Angeles, privately wondered if they were even worth the bother. But he couldn't do everything himself, and here they were. He pulled out a map. "She ran away from a house here–" he made a mark, circled it. "She was asking questions about how far is DC, so the logic is that's where she's headed."

"She could head home," said Ned.

"Home is Colombia. She was brought here special. She has no idea where she is."

Esmeralda cut in: "She's got no clothing, she's got no money, she's never been in America before—"

"And she barely speaks English," Armstrong capped it. "So I don't think we need to watch the airports," He sipped his beer. "And Ned—"

"What?" the big man said defensively.

"You're a wanted man. I wouldn't fucking use you except we need the fucking manpower. Don't go and fuck everything up for the rest of us, okay? You get nervous, you get the sense something's going down, just go, get, scat, you're on your own. We can do a money drop, no problem, if it comes to it. But if you stay and share cigarettes with the authorities and tell them your life story, that would not go down well with Eduardo. Got that, big guy?"

"Uh-huh," the man said, and drank his beer.

* * *

It had been hours and hours of walking along highways, and Maria's feet were cracked and bleeding, but it was all worth it that night when Maria walked across the bridge into the city and found the park with the famous tower Washington's Needle.

It was the tallest thing she'd ever seen; it seemed to puncture the clouds as they sailed by.

She was standing on a long field of green. At the far end was the needle; she was close to an immense building, very familiar, with a huge round roof at the center and a statue on top. She'd seen pictures of this building, she knew; it had to be where the President lived.

The large building was lit; it was probably full of people. She pictured grand halls, a huge throne, something out of a story. She was strengthening herself to climb the stairs and knock on the door and try to explain her problem to whoever answered, but as she approached she saw a great many policemen loitering about at the entrances or sitting in police cars precisely like the one that had taken her from the airplane to the man.

Abruptly her stomach veered into despair. She sat on a bench, looking up at the doors, and had no idea how to reach the people inside. Then a policeman looked over at her, and she forced herself up, headed away from him into the night.

If she could find someone who spoke Spanish, she decided, maybe they might have an idea what she should do next.

* * *

The next morning dawned clear and ice cold in Washington DC. Esmeralda was driving a Ford Taurus, Trojo next to her in the passenger seat, Ned in a baseball cap in the back, his beard coming in scratchy and adolescent. As they drove along the mall, Trojo craned his head around, taking in every building and monument.

"This city is fantastic!" he said as they passed the windows of the Air and Space Museum. "In Bogota the mountains make everything small. Here it is so open, so more impressive—"

"That's not saying much," said Ned, from the back.

Trojo ignored him. "I would spend a week, go to all these museums and exhibits—"

"Americans always need to feel how great they are." Esmeralda slowed for a light. "Just look at the social media." She thought of the pale man sitting in that shithole in his off-time, doom-scrolling on his phone.

"But the Capitol up there—" Trojo gestured. "Whatever you say, it's a beautiful building."

Ned gazed flatly out. "I came here on a class trip when I was a kid," he said. "I'd been raised to believe we were God's nation. I remember being here and thinking the Capitol was like the Vatican, or, like, Mecca, or something. A place where God lived. Now I look at it," he shook his head. "Just a bunch of assholes in suits trying to get reelected."

Esmeralda drove forward, realized he'd given her exactly what she needed. "Alright, Ned, churches and soup kitchens, si?"

"Yeah." They thought it'd be harder to fuck up.

"Trojo and I will handle going into offices, dealing with the bureaucrats— the guys in suits."

Long pause. "Fine," Ned said. He was getting used to this shit.

Good, Esmeralda thought. Much better than having to spend the day fending off his advances.

* * *

On the flight to Washington, Tory had felt in a state of calm readiness for what lay ahead. Someone connected to the court had sold his soul to the enemy, she was absolutely sure of it, and she was primed to be in the room with all of them, watch their faces, listen to their voices, wait for the half-second of hesitation, the one comment too heartily cajoled.

She hadn't called Penny Jefferson. She had work to do.

Today Bart was taking a day off; Gordon Charlop, his backup man, was covering security for her on this trip. He was a professional, curly hair just beginning to turn grey, had been in the Marshals since getting out of the Navy. He made sure she was the last person on and the first person off the DC shuttle.

Tory was driven to Justice in a standard Federal Marshall black Ford, went up to the FISA courtroom, mingled with the others, gave each judge the same courteous smile, watched their reactions behind a mask of amiable complacency. With that, the workday began.

The first case was interesting: a Yemeni medical student in Michigan on an education visa had been caught by sigint talking to Yusof Famdi, a Lebanese whose ties to Hamas were already under investigation by the FBI. The conversation, about sending books to children in Yemen, may have been legitimate, and may have been in code; Famdi had used similar codes in the past. The Yemeni student was an unknown; the Justice Department, through OIPR, was requesting authority to wiretap his family and social contacts in

Yemen to see if children were truly going to receive books, or if something more sinister was afoot.

Tory had no problem voting yes. Famdi was at the center of a fruitful investigation, and Yemen was a tricky place for the FBI to go knocking on doors. If a bunch of schoolchildren turned out to have brand new books, the matter would be dropped.

The second case was a little darker. An Iranian national picked up in a money-laundering investigation in Boston had, upon interrogation, said that Brotherhood of Jihad, a Syrian terror group, had forged a contact with an ex-MIT scientist who had done his graduate work in bacterial biowarfare. The fact that someone from Brotherhood of Jihad even knew this guy's name, much less his resume, was spooky. Justice wanted to wiretap the contact. So did Tory, and she voted for it, along with the rest of the court.

Then the third case of the day came up, and that was where Tory got into trouble.

The OTPR prosecutor presenting this one was a young fellow, Sean Fehr, Tory had not yet encountered. There was a lazy arrogance in his manner that she found unfortunate. He explained his case: as part of their ongoing investigation into Moslem charities, the Justice Department was asking OIPR to request FISA warrants to search the home of and wiretap the telephones of Michael Bashear, the President of Moslems In America, Inc., a family-run organization founded in St. Louis in 1924. Established by Mr. Bashear's great-grandfather, the organization had long served as a "welcome wagon" for new Moslem immigrants, publishing a weekly newsletter of job-finding tips and ESL classes. Fehr explained that the company had recently been audited by the IRS; though everything appeared in order, an informer was insistent that they were a front to deliver death-benefit funds to the families of suicide bombers.

Drummond turned to the panel for questions. Tory immediately shot up her hand.

"When did the informer first make these accusations?"

"Two years ago."

"And last year the IRS found nothing." Tory didn't like this. "Has any of this informer's other intel proven productive?"

Fehr spent a moment whispering with his second. "We're still trying to evaluate that."

"No arrests? No convictions?" Fehr shook his head 'no'. "Is the informant getting paid?"

Fehr grimaced. "One way or another," he said, "informants always get paid."

Tory felt her anger rising. "You need something of substance, and I'm not seeing it here." She looked around the room at her fellow judges, expecting to see– well, she wasn't even sure what. A smile from someone, a raised eyebrow, something. But that wasn't what she got.

What she got was silence, deaf as a stone.

Drummond was staring straight ahead. Judge Kottle was investigating the wood grain on his desk. Al Clemente was busy plowing a furrow through his earwax with his pinkie.

Arvin Hart was looking right at her, eyes blazing, a smile on his lips. He'd never looked more attractive than he did right then. "I second Judge Parker's logic, here," he said, and tension in the room broke. "IRS took a crack at them, they're not breaking any laws, let's leave them be, follow up with conventional law enforcement, and see what happens."

Drummond didn't like that one bit. "Anyone else?" he asked, one eyebrow raised.

Rebekkah King raised her hand. "I'm not in love with it," she said, "but I'll approve. Either they are or they aren't, and this'll end it. If they aren't—" and she looked at Fehr— "I strongly urge you never to listen to this informer again."

Drummond put the matter to a vote. The motion passed, 9 to 2, to approve the search.

During the next break, Tory went up to Hart. "Thanks for backing me up," she said.

"Least I could do," he replied, and she wondered: had the gesture been chivalry? Or did it reflect what he actually believed?

Or was it guilt that drove him, after he'd set her up for the assassin's bullet in New York?

*   *   *

"This is her on Halloween," Trojo showed the man behind the desk the less ideal of the two pictures. "She dressed up in all her Mami's clothes. Look, she is so serious—"

The man was bald. He kept running his fingers through the hair above his ears. "You talk to all her school friends?"

"They didn't know anything," Esmeralda said.

"Go to the police," the man didn't look at them. "Give them the full description—"

Trojo wasn't quick enough with an answer. Esmeralda jumped in: "They sent us to you," she retorted.

The man found that highly improbable. Children's Services got a phone call when kids were found, not when they were lost.

Either these people were idiots or liars. He'd seen both, coming in spouting all sorts of complex crapola. But these two were an attractive young couple, which threw him off.

"Go back to the police," he said. "Here— let me give you a number of someone to call."

He changed screens on his desktop, found what he was looking for and wrote it on the back of one of his cards. Esmeralda thanked the man, took the card, led Trojo out before he could say anything more.

*   *   *

Alice Malice's feet were hurting, better than yesterday but still in pain. The pain was like ice crystals forming in her blood, spreading throughout her body. Why people would do this to her she didn't know, turn her blood into ice crystals, but they had been for years.

She turned down the alley, this was one of the places she came to pee, everybody used it. Plus, there were lidded garbage dumpsters, worth a stop. She squatted, hiked up her dresses, was about to let go when she saw the girl.

At first she thought she was dead, it took a long time but finally the girl breathed. That was good; Alice hated finding dead people. Dead people made everything inside turn to ice. As she finished peeing, the girl stirred and sat up. She wasn't wearing enough clothing, Alice saw, for the cold.

The girl tried to stand, reverted to all fours, heaved and heaved until finally vomit came. Alice turned away, remembering her daughters when they were sick, it was always wrenching to watch. The girl finished, collapsed onto the ground. Alice approached her.

"Feels better, right?"

The girl opened one eye, looked at her.

"Good to get the poison out of your system. That's what I always say." The girl couldn't answer. "You need food. Maybe not now, but you will."

"Food—" the girl said.

Alice Malice opened one of her shopping bags, clawed through it. That hadn't always been her name— that was a name somebody made up on the wards, years ago. Her real name wasn't her name, it was her mother's name, and she didn't like when she entered her head. She found half a buttered bagel oiling its brown paper bag, held it up. "You want this?"

The girl forced herself up. Her hands were shaking when she took it. She didn't eat it right away— she held it and closed her eyes and breathed, waiting for the nausea to completely pass. Then she took a bite, chewed and chewed and chewed.

"I'm Alice," Alice said.

"Maria," said the girl. She had vomit in her hair.

"You know what you need? Ginger ale. I used to give my girls ginger ale when they were sick." Then: "It's a drink. You drink it." Alice imitated drinking.

"I have no—" Maria said. "I'll get you some. With my girls, when they were little, it always worked."

Her girls. It had been two years, but she still hated herself for how much she drank the last time she saw Mavis and her husband. All the things she said— the ice ran through her, contaminating all it touched. She needed to drink, now, so it would melt.

But still: her girls, when they were little. The apartment on South Street, bank account, bills every month, internet on the computer. Taking them to Catholic school every morning. "I'll get you ginger ale," she said, and stood. "You stay here, eat the bagel. I'll be back."

* * *

Maria ate the bagel slowly, small bites, occasionally unsure she could keep it down. She curled into a ball to help it stay and fell asleep again. When she woke up it was later, the sun had shifted. She looked for the lady, but there was no sign of her.

Maria felt hot and shivery at the same time, a strange roiling sensation she had known before when she'd had high temperatures. She needed to be inside. She didn't care how or where, she just knew it was true.

She stood, breathed cold air deep into her lungs, walked forward. She had a completely real sensation that she was invisible, a spirit trapped in an open-air prison, people stared right through her, she could go anywhere in any direction but she could never leave.

After four blocks she came to a restaurant with Spanish in lights in the window: Café con leche, Corona. Through the window she saw bathrooms at the back; she stepped in, walked quickly through the tables. No one looked at her, no one could see her. At the back she went into the Damas room.

She used paper towels and pink liquid soap to try and wash herself. As she was cleaning her feet, the nausea returned. She went into the little booth, bolted the door and crouched at the bowl, shivering as she waited for the pain to pass.

* * *

The priest was in corduroy pants and a sweater. He was wearing the collar, though.

"Her name's Maria," Ned said as the priest looked at the top photo, the bottom, the top again, the bottom. "That's Halloween. That's, like, the most recent picture."

"She doesn't look happy."

"Well, her goldfish had died. We were trying to cheer her up. You know, go into Mami's closet, pull out whatever you like—" Ned had the sense the priest wasn't swallowing this. "Anyway, she's run off, and we're really worried about her. If you see her, if she comes into your church, call my cell number there."

The priest set the photos on his desk. "We've had some success in situations like this. We'd be pleased to help."

"Thank you. Is there anyone else I should talk to?"

"Evidently you've talked to several members of my staff already."

Long pause, Ned checking the impulse to hit this irritating twerp. "Well then," he asked, "Can you point me in the direction of any other churches around here that have soup kitchens?"

"Saint Agnes,' the priest said, standing. "Seven blocks over. They have a strong outreach program with runaways—you really should go talk to them."

* * *

At the end of a full day of FISA, Arvin said he had to run, and took off. Tory called Penny from an office off the courtroom, not because she felt like being social, but more to avoid sharing a shuttle flight with Al Clemente.

Penny's answering machine at the clinic had a voice message saying that she would be out of the office Wednesday; that message was four days out of date. Tory thought that was weird, called her home number, got her machine and left a message there.

Well, just because she couldn't find Penny didn't mean she had to take the shuttle with Al. She left the courtroom quietly, not looking anybody in the eye.

* * *

The girl in the long white golf jacket was sitting on the curb sobbing. That was the second thing Benno noticed. The first thing he saw, when he came upon her, was opportunity.

Benno was a bulky man in a sparkling new Lakers jersey and personalized Nike TBX sneakers. He wore his hair cut straight across; somebody had said his haircut looked like Julius Caesar, and he'd liked that; he'd been getting it cut that way ever since. The vanity plates on his Escalade said CAESAR II; he had seen every Caesar movie that came out. He was 28, but because of something in his eyes he looked younger.

He sat right down next to her, as if he'd known her all her life and she was sitting alone at a Christmas party. "Hey hon," he said in Spanish, "folks threw you out?"

The girl looked up at him, too caught in her misery to answer the question. Instantly he revised his mental scenario. This wasn't fight with Moms. This was somebody had died.

"Hey—" he kept his tone filled with love. "Do you have someplace I can take you?"

She didn't say a word. "When was the last time you ate?"

The girl looked at him. "I am very hungry," she said.

He stood. "Then let's go," he said, and offered her his tattooed hand.

Warily, she took it in, pulled herself up off the sidewalk. Only then did he realize: Oh, shit, she's a baby. He put his hand on her forehead. "Girl, you're burning up."

"I slept outside last night." Sleeping in the open and the girl still looks like an angel. Even sick, even hungry, that face was worth something.

He walked her up the block to the Escalade. "You like Burger King? Mickey Dee's?" She didn't answer. He opened the passenger door, started to help her up into the high seat. He didn't see the crazy lady coming, but all at once this bitch out of nowhere was yelling "You leave her alone!"

Bitch could barely stand. Benno stepped between them. "Fuck you, you drunk bitch—"

"Don't you get in that car with that man, little girl. I'm sorry I didn't bring ginger ale, I fucked up, I'm sorry I'm sorry I'm sorry, we'll go find some—"

Benno touched the girl's cheek. "Fuck that shit, get in the car, I'll get you some real food." He lifted her, put her in the white leather seat of the Escalade, shut the door.

The old woman was yelling "No no no no no," panicky shouts, hitting the window, the whole fucking neighborhood was watching. He pushed by her, went around to the driver's side, got in and hit the button to lock all the doors and roared the engine to life, roared out of the parking space into traffic. The girl was looking behind at the woman. Like she had some connection.

"I don't know what that bitch wanted," Benno said, "but I'm going to take care of you, and that bitch can't barely take care of herself."

The girl didn't say a word. He drove a mile to the McDonalds, but by the time they got there, she was sound asleep in the soft white leather.

Fuck it, he thought, wheeled around and bought her back to the house.

* * *

The next day, back in New York, Tory was sitting in her office with a pile of work when the phone rang. "Tory Parker," she answered, not taking her eyes off the transcript on her desk.

"Judge Parker, Judge Hart." Immediately she felt anxiety clawing at her neck.

"Arvin— hello!"

"Forgive me, I've been rude. You called last week, but I've been up to my neck in a few things— and then we didn't get to talk at all in DC–"

"I really did appreciate you taking my side yesterday."

"Least I could do."

"But you ran off so quickly— are you okay?"

He gave a deep sigh. "To be honest, the last couple days I've been wanting to escape somewhere. Place I rent by the river just feels claustrophobic. Take my hunting rifles, get out to the wilderness— Montana, or Wyoming— put up a tent, stay for a month."

"Leave all this behind," Tory said. She'd never gone hunting in her life, but the wilderness aspect of it sounded appealing. And at the same time she thought: fantasies of escape. Is that the sign of a guilty conscience?

"Well," she said, "I thought maybe, if you ever come to New York again, we might have dinner." It sounded more seductive than she'd intended.

Hissing static filled the space between them. "Thank you, Tory. I wasn't sure you'd want to talk to me after our last encounter."

"Well, if it happens again I'll be extremely angry."

"If it happens again, I'll take the bullet," he said. Instantly Tory thought: it can't be him.

Or was that exactly what somebody in his position would say?

* * *

That afternoon, driving with Bart up the east side from the court house, Tory explained that Judge Hart was coming to dinner. "Where?" "I figured we'd be safest at my place."

Bart considered. "Probably right. When?"

"Friday." As she said it, she saw a new problem open up. "But Friday's your day off, right? I usually get Gordon on Friday."

"That's all right," Bart said quickly.

"No. I'll call him, try to reschedule."

"Leave it Friday," Bart decided. "I'll be there. Based on what happened last time—"

"That's what I was thinking. It'll be interesting to see what happens while he's here."

"Interesting?" Bart's eyebrows knit. "You mean, if somebody's trying to kill you?"

"It'll give you a chance to look for unusual activity," Tory said, and then: "Don't worry. We're not going ice skating in Central Park. We're having takeout at my place."

"Then I'll put Gordon on-site and I'll cover from the van. You gonna walk the dog?"

"Of course I'm going to walk the dog," Tory said. "You know that." Walking the dog tended to bring most business-related social evenings to a natural end. "Besides," she said, "how are wc going to see if anything unusual happens if I just sit in my apartment?"

"Tory—"

"I'm walking Siggy, we 're going to go to the park and come back around, just like I do every night. I know you guys will keep me safe."

* * *

Morning in Washington found Penny Jefferson awake, having lived through two hours of hard, sweaty half-sleep. When it came time to get up, heart pounding in her chest, she didn't think about her job, her son, her friends, her responsibilities to her clients at the clinic.

What drove her out of bed was the fact that she had dropped a rock onto the carpet.

She'd looked for it last night. She'd come home with a vial, had smoked it up on her couch. At some point she'd knocked over the vial and a chunk had dropped out.

She'd gone over the carpet like it was a holy book. Eventually she'd given up and smoked more.

The best feeling she knew. Then the rush would start to slip, you couldn't hold onto it no matter how you tried, and eventually the world and all its mundane agonies would return.

She wasn't exactly sure if she'd used up all her vacation days, but she knew she was damn close. And her son, down in New Orleans— if he walked in right now—

Just the thought of it would make her reach for the glass pipe, dig another rock out of the vial, fire up the jet-flame lighter, the sharp steady dart of red heat turning another white rock into smoke. And there it was again: the best feeling in the world.

She had done that until the crack was gone, and then attempted to get some rest for the workday ahead. Now, two hours later, she was turning her coffee table upside down, checking for rock in the carpet indents.

Nothing. She stood, took up one end of the couch, lifted it over and pushed it into the center of her living room. She looked where the feet had been, looked carefully at the dust.

This was crazy: she was going to rip apart her apartment looking for a speck of rock. She lifted the other side of the couch away from the wall, got on her hands and knees.

She should stop this. She should get in the shower, put on clothes, take the damn bus to work. Serve her right for this craziness. Sit at her desk, tell the people over and over that they didn't perform abortions, find out if they needed a social worker, try to decipher what programs might help, what programs weren't worth mentioning.

Then, to her coworkers: she had the flu, insomnia, a rough patch. She needed the job, she needed the money. And then she saw the rock.

At the edge of the carpet, the size of a match head. She dabbed it with her finger, got the glass pipe and the jet lighter, slid the rock in the bowl and fired up the steady red flame.

It would be enough to get her out of the house. Maybe on her way to work she could go buy more.

* * *

Penny was at her desk drinking Dr. Pepper when Benno and two of his girls walked in. In her experience, Benno treated his girls reasonably well, for a pimp— they didn't show up with bruises or broken bones or the same clothes every time. If he got popped off the street he would be replaced by someone who, odds were, wouldn't routinely bring his girls to a health clinic.

Thus, Penny kept a note of jocularity in her voice when she addressed him. As long as he kept bringing his girls here she could give them condoms, talk to them about getting out of the life, keep tabs on their general welfare.

"Hey, Nursie," the large man said, cutting the line.

"Hey Benno," Penny smiled. "What can I do you for?"

"Got a sick girl, throwing up, fever, she needs some antibiotics–"

"Is she here?" Penny saw Benno's girls Joanne and Stephanie by the soda machine.

"Naah, she's too sick to come in."

"How do you expect Dr. Chatwal to diagnose her?" Penny asked. "ESP?" That cracked Benno up. "If she's not better tomorrow, bring her in, okay? Promise?"

"Sure," he said, looking away. And then: "Also, Joanne needs more of that cyclevir. And Steph's out of birth control pills."

Penny had instituted a rule that doctors were to write nonrenewable prescriptions to the clinic's prostitute population, so they got seen with some regularity. "Okay," Penny said, "we'll take Steph first, and then Joanne. What do you want to do, go grab a bite?"

"I'll wait."

Too bad, Penny thought, the girls tended to be more open when their pimps weren't around. "Get 'em over here," she said, "we need to fill out some forms."

* * *

Armstrong was eating beef jerky, ripping it with his teeth, the salted meat making his breath smell like carrion. "He's always late, he's drunk every night."

Trojo cracked the car window as they sat. "He does his work," he said.

"He's been a pain in the ass from the start." They watched Ned shamble out of a deli with a small grocery sack. He walked up to the car, got in the back, pulled out a bottle of Gatorade, opened it and immediately drank half.

"Little dehydrated there, big guy?" Armstrong asked.

"Fuck you," Ned kept his tone reasonably amiable, and drank more orange liquid. Then: "Where's Esmeralda?"

"Thing came up in New York. She'll be back when she's done." Ned said nothing, lost in thought of being with Esmeralda in New York, him romancing her, candlelight restaurants, fancy hotels with chandeliers, treat her real classy and gentle. That would be a lot better than running around DC trying to find some bigwig's little sex toy.

He ripped the strip on the box of donuts, ate one quickly. With Esmeralda, if he were ever lucky enough to be with her, he knew it would be hot.

* * *

Something about Jack Riley was amiss, Tory thought. She'd never sat across from him over dinner at a restaurant and seen him so miserable.

She'd wanted to ask him about the court's vote to unleash the full power of the government surveillance apparatus on a fourth-generation Muslim/American with a newsletter. But he only smiled and said: "Yeah, OIPR usually gets what it wants." And then apropos of nothing: "I got locked out of the new house a couple days ago in DC." They were at a table at McFarrel's pub; Gordon Charlop, filling in for Bart this evening, was covering security.

"Stupidest thing," he went on. "Contractor changed the locks, and I couldn't find the key. And I didn't want to pay a locksmith to break the brand-new locks. And my cell phone was dead. I ended up being locked out until the next day."

"Where'd you sleep?" Tory asked.

"Shithole motel about ten minutes away."

"You should have gone to the FISA house in Georgetown."

"Talking shop with judges? I'd rather sleep in a shithole motel room." Tory laughed— that was the Jack she knew. "Listen," his voice lowered. "Your thought of a mole—" he drank an inch off his beer. "What if it's not anybody on FISA?" he asked. "Why couldn't it be one of the prosecutors at OIPR?"

"Interesting," Tory said. "They have the same access we do."

"Just about," Jack agreed. "What if somebody turned rogue? What if Walter Grant or one of the other ones they killed found out?" He saw her hesitation. "We're looking for a weak link," he said. "They're the only people we have any dealings with. And they're just as secretive as we are," He drank more beer. "Be interesting to see if any of them have any unexplained income."

Tory flashed on Henry Severn's taste in expensive suits, and then, more darkly, remembered Jack's reticence about his new Rolex: This was all profoundly troubling.

Jack drained his beer, looked at Tory. "You done?"

Tory considered the rind of her hamburger. "Just about." She finished her Guinness.

"Let's go somewhere we can get a real drink," Jack said. "How 'bout your place?"

"We're closer to yours," Tory suggested sensibly.

"It's a mess," Jack said. "My bachelorhood is not a pretty sight."

"Sure, my place would be fine," Tory said, swallowing the inchoate discomfort he had somehow sparked in her.

Outside the bar, the city was dark; a cold winter wind filled the streets. "I'm sad to see autumn go," Jack said, and Tory thought: how strange— Jack Riley, wistful for lost seasons. Gordon bundled them both into the black Ford.

The problem with Jack's hypothesis was simple, she thought: he had said he was supposed to be at the FISA safehouse the night those judges were killed. If someone at OIPR had done this, why wasn't he dead now? Why hadn't they come back to finish the job?

And why had he insisted on coming to her apartment?

She was becoming paranoid. At her building, Gordon entered first. Tory watched as he spoke to the doorman, went out of sight into the lobby. Presently he came back out to the car.

"Do you know a little girl named Paz Ramon?"

"Is she in there? She's not a problem," Tory said, and she and Jack entered the lobby. On the bench a young dark-haired girl in a winter coat, very short but very pretty behind her glasses, was doing problems from a math book. She looked up. "Hi, Judge Parker."

"Paz—" Tory sat down beside her. "Things ok at home?"

"My grandma's fighting with her boyfriend again. I got in the middle and he hit me." She slipped out of the heavy coat, showed a wide yellow-blue welt on her neck.

"That's gonna be a nasty one," said Tory. "You want to stay here tonight?"

She nodded. "'Cause I have a math test."

Tory stood. "Come on up. You eat yet? We can get something delivered."

Jack Riley stepped up. "Tory, you haven't introduced me to your friend."

"How rude of me. This is Jack Riley, he's a judge." The little girl held out her hand, shook his very formally. "And this is Gordon Charlop–"

"You're her bodyguard, right?"

Gordon smiled. "I have the honor of serving in that position, yes."

"They should assign bodyguards, you know? To families."

Tory's smile froze on her face. "You know," she said, "sometimes they should."

In the elevator, Jack said "Paz—that means peace." She smiled. "How old are you?"

"Thirteen."

"My goodness, yes," Jack Riley said. The elevator opened.

"Siggy will be happy to see you," Tory said. Gordon used Tory's keys, let Siggy come bounding out into the hallway as he quickly checked the apartment. Then he let them all in, Paz romping with Siggy from room to room.

"What's her story?" Jack asked, when she was out of earshot.

"I put her father away for killing her mother. She was the only witness. She's got an IQ of 158." she gave a slight, unapologetic shrug. "I told her I would always be there for her." Jack's eyes were glued on the delighted girl scrambling with the dog on the hardwood floor.

"She's exceptional," he said. Tory agreed, but at the same time she wasn't sure exactly what he meant.

* * *

The hardest thing had been getting the rats.

The pale man had come up with some nasty ideas before, but this one, he thought, beat them all. Scientific supply houses guaranteed 24-four delivery on live specimens; he'd had Esmeralda buy from every scientific supply house capable of meeting their demand.

Esmeralda had outdone herself. The day after she'd hit the phones, crates full of mature live retired breeder rats had been express-overnighted from fourteen different firms. The animals were a variety of different breeds and sizes: Sprague-Dawleys, Brown Norways, Witstar Hannover rats and CD-1 mice, with a healthy measure of smaller inbred and hybrid mice thrown in. The packages smelled pet-store polite when they arrived.

The animals were dumped into three large wooden crates; the pale man used a drill to make air holes in the lids and hammered them on. Each contained over one hundred furious, hungry, writhing rodents. By the next morning some were dead, fighting was near constant, and the smell was turning vehemently for the worse.

The pale man had the judge's schedule. He knew where she would be, and at approximately what time. He was furious at not having nailed the judge with his single shot at the masked ball, but there'd been too many people around, too many variables. Luck had not been with him.

This time, luck would not be an element in the equation.

* * *

Maria was sick for two days, in a little bed on the second floor of Benno's house, and whenever she woke up, day and night, the television was always blaring from downstairs.

Outside her window were trees with beautiful red and yellow leaves; she'd never seen colors like that in a tree. Across the paved street were houses; one had swings and a plastic slide that Maria wished she could get for her brothers back home.

Benno lived here with five ladies. They would fight downstairs, screaming matches. Everybody had two names; Angie and Stephanie, whose other names were Amber and Star, brought her ice cream. Benno brought hamburgers and sodas and pills for diarrhea.

There seemed to be no men but Benno, and everybody seemed to sleep during the day. There was a mean woman named Joanne who completely ignored Maria, and two girls, Bonnie and Mave, who were always together, and who fought more than anyone.

None of it made a lot of sense, but when Maria woke up the third morning, she felt substantially better, and padded downstairs in the overlong soccer shirt Benno had given her.

The TV was on, a man in front of a weather map that showed the US as if it were an island surrounded entirely by water.

Joanne was asleep on the couch. She was wearing a tight shirt which showed her boobies; there was a plastic syringe on a plate and a little plastic bag of powder, whiter and finer than base. Maria turned down the TV, went into the kitchen.

She pulled out bread and peanut butter. The sink was full of dirty plates and pans; she would wash them after she ate. She made a sandwich, was finishing it when Benno stepped in.

"Hey! Look who's up! You feeling better?"

"I am better," Maria said. "Muchas gracias."

"Anything you need?"

She hesitated. "To go to my family."

"We'll get you there." Benno was smiling, but there was something she didn't like in his eyes. "But that's going to cost money, and right now you have a debt to settle."

"A debt?"

"A deuda. With me," Benno said. "I fed you, got you back to health— salud—"

Maria blinked rapidly, again and again, Of course, she thought, of course. Nothing is for free. "You're a virgin." He said it factually, as if, at some point he'd checked.

"You want me?" She realized: if that was the price to go home, she was willing.

That was new. That was something she'd never thought of before.

"Baby—" his eyes filled with tenderness. "I would love to be your first. I would be honorado. But that's not going to do you any good. There are guys out there who would pay good money to be your first. Mucho dinero por una virgen."

She was speechless for a long moment, and then she swallowed. "Is true?"

"And not just ugly fucks. Nice guys. Cabaleros. Guys you'd give it up to on your own."

Her heart beat hard in her chest. Why was he being so reasonable about this? Did he understand what he was suggesting? "This is all to help you," he went on. "Ask the other girls about it. They like it so much, they do it for a living. That's how we all make our money."

Maria kept silent. All day long they complained about the men, the weather, what they had to do. She pushed her hair back. "I go with a man one time, and I fly home?" she asked.

Benno shrugged. "Depends how much he'll pay. Maybe you'll do a few."

Fear clouded her eyes. "How much deuda?"

Benno's smile was dazzling. "Depends on how long you're here, doesn't it? But the sooner you can get started, the sooner you'll be on that plane, leaving this all behind."

* * *

Paz had spent the night on Tory's couch, gone to school the next morning and left a note thanking Tory for everything. Tory, on the bench avoiding Baby Nieto's fixed gaze as Sam built his case brick by brick, found herself alternating between being sanguine about the upcoming evening with Hart, and being absurdly panicky.

At the end of the day, after the jury filed out and the courtroom emptied, she got into a long conversation at the bench with Eddie Mazzuchi, her bridge officer. There were a couple of bailiffs about, finishing up their work.

Angelo swept in, stopped when he saw her. "Judge Parker—" he said, and came through the gate into the well of the courtroom. "I left a file folder." He looked under the defense table. "There it is." He held it up.

She debated not saying it but he had been so solicitous, after the masked ball. "You asked about Judge Hart," she said, and he knew immediately what she meant. "It might interest you to know," she continued, "that he's coming to my house this evening. I felt that was the safest. If anything happens, my security team will be right there."

Angelo thought about it. "You let the security people walk your dog?"

"Not so much. They're not servants."

"Right. Well, be careful."

"Thank you, Angelo." She returned to her conversation with Eddie.

Angelo watched her for a moment, and then walked down the aisle. At the portholed door, he stopped, wanted to say something more, but she didn't look up, and instead he pushed through.

* * *

That evening, Bart and Gordon were in position when Judge AO Hart arrived at Tory's apartment door. Bart was running coordination from the van; Gordon had set up a folding chair in the hall outside Tory's apartment. Siggy, at the bell, started barking. "Sit, kiddo." Tory said, and cracked the door. "Hello, Arvin."

"Tory–" he leaned in, kissed her cheek. "I'm so pleased to see you again."

"It's nice to have you at the door, and not Mark Twain."

"I'd rather have Twain than me, I assure you." He knelt to pet the dog, who wagged his tail vociferously.

"Drink?" she asked.

"Beer, if you have it." Tory brought him a Brooklyn Lager, poured herself club soda to keep her edge. Then she pulled up a website for New York restaurant deliveries. "There's a decent steakhouse, a couple of good Thai places—" After a couple of false starts, they settled on Chinese, clicked to send in the order. "So," she said when that was done, "you hunt."

"Always have." He settled on the couch. "In Texas, growing up, that's what you did." He sipped his beer. "Not like I go to Kenya and shoot rhinos— Hemingway could get away with stuff like that; nobody else should try. But a mule deer or pronghorn in the fall— fill the freezer with steaks, eat them all winter long."

"Sounds great," Tory said.

"As long as you know how to cook," he smiled, and when he did, his whole face illuminated. He was really, Tory thought, quite an attractive man.

Over shrimp with garlic sauce and General Tso's chicken they talked about the odd discordance of their jobs. "Amazing that we have this machinery in place to order wiretaps and surveillance on terrorists," Tory was saying. "We'll even approve a wiretap 72 hours after it's placed if the justification is good enough— and even with all that, there are times when the executive branch does its best to bypass us."

Arvin put down his chopsticks. "Anybody who doesn't worry that contradiction like a sore tooth shouldn't be in this business."

Something inside Tory relaxed for the first time since he'd walked into the apartment. "It's almost," she said, "as if the real work of a FISA judge is to carry two separate and contradictory thoughts in your head at all times—"

"The Constitution giveth rights, and our court taketh them away." He drank beer.

Tory leaned back in her chair. "Sometimes I think we are the bulwark against completely unchecked state power, and sometimes I think we're just another crack in the wall of liberty, another fracture in the dam—"

"Hey—" Hart set down his chopsticks. "Governments *are* power. Throughout history, they've done anything they want. What FISA does is provide legal oversight, so someone somewhere knows what these guys are doing, and why."

"But what if there were a mole?" Tory managed to make it sound casual, though everything she'd said all evening had led to this. "Someone with a hidden agenda—"

Something haunted passed over Judge Hart's eyes. "Wouldn't matter," he said finally, "for the same reason: on our court the majority rules." Then: "Are you saying the murders—?"

Tension filled Tory. "There are eleven of us. Kill enough people, you'll get a majority."

"Yes," Judge Hart admitted. "I've thought of that." His voice came out small. He cleared his throat: "And I don't like it one bit."

* * *

The night was autumnal and crisp as Gordon escorted Tory, Hart and Siggy into Carl Schurz park. Tory showed Hart the promenade, the serenely deceptive East River, the Bronx on the far side. "I used to think New York was unlivable," Arvin said. "Now I see how people can make a life."

Tory had the sense he was talking about her. Then, out of the shadows, a figure rose up from a park bench, walked toward them. "Good evening, Judge."

Gordon smoothly drew his gun, posited himself between Tory and the stranger. Tory saw who it was, felt a rush of warmth: Angelo. Of course he'd be here. That's why he'd asked about her security guys walking the dog. "That's all right, Gordon. I know this character."

Arvin knew him, too. "I'm beginning to see you in person more than I see you on TV."

"Last time I saw you, somebody tried to shoot my girl here."

"Boys, boys—" Tory said. "This isn't a schoolyard, and it isn't the wild west. Angelo, fancy meeting you here."

"You know me, I love this park." He rubbed Siggy's cheeks, the dog pressing his heavy head against Angelo in pleasure. "Since I have you, I wanted to tell you something, and the phone seemed inappropriate." He let the dog go, stepped slightly away. "May I have a word?"

"Go right ahead," Arvin said, pulling a cigar case from his jacket. "If you don't mind, I'll have a smoke."

Angelo stepped a few feet up the promenade; Tory joined him as Gordon discreetly positioned himself between them and the rest of the city. "You didn't have to come," Tory said.

"I couldn't stay away. How's it going?"

Tory hesitated, kept her voice low. "He's nice," she said. Siggy, abruptly aware of squirrels in the bushes, leapt to the end of his leash, straining. "Siggy! Sit!" The dog reluctantly obeyed, his attention focused on motion amidst the leaves. "Okay," Tory said, "what's up?"

"I was talking to Baby today and he said something troubling. Evidently Eduardo regularly sends underage Colombian girls up to DC to service high-up government officials."

From Penny, when she'd said it, this story had seemed far-fetched. From Angelo, it was like finding out he spent his spare time researching the sightlines of the Texas Book Depository. Angelo went on: "He sends soldiers into a school to pick the prettiest one, takes her away, nobody sees her again. The thing is, there have been underage Jane Doe DOAs in DC."

"Four of them," Tory said. "My friend Penny's been following this."

"Then you know. I asked Baby who the government officials were. He said Justice Department officials. I asked how high up. He said 'all the way.'"

"Think he'd flip for a good deal?" she asked.

Angelo shook his head. "He's a gambler. Right now all his money's on red and the wheel's spinning. He's not gonna make another play until he knows how this one goes down."

Tory smelled cigar smoke. By the river railing, the red ash from AO Hart's cigar glowed bright. "Arvin," she said, "Could you come here a second?"

Angelo whispered "Tory, no—" but it was too late.

Judge Hart blew out smoke as he stepped up. Tory asked: "Have you ever heard about underage girls being shipped from Colombia for high-up Justice Department officials?"

"It's a bucket of dung," he said. "Narco-state propaganda turned into an urban legend."

"You've heard it before?" Tory watched him intently.

"DC's all about rumor. That one's been making the rounds—some kind of cocaine kingpin pedophile ring sends girls up. I haven't seen a scanty scintilla of proof."

Angelo persisted: "Four DOA sex crimes, all young girls, same method of disposal—"

"So it has to be some high-up at Justice." He exhaled. "Mr. Schwartz, all due respect, you're a liberal. You'll believe anything that makes the leaders of this country look bad."

A glint sharpened in Angelo's eye. "On certain issues," Angelo said, "I'm more conservative than you, Judge Hart. Like, for instance, the Constitution."

"Stop it." Tory interjected herself between the two men. "Both of you. Now."

Gordon stepped up. "I suggest we keep moving."

"Excellent idea," Angelo said, and kept pace with them as they walked. "Judge Hart, forgive me, I can get a little impassioned." They were coming up on the dog run. Tory tightened her grip on

Siggy's leash. "Sorry, kiddo," she said, and touched his snout. She led the group out of the park by the north entrance, her regular nightly walk. She had thought Angelo might peel off when they got to the street, but as they went the debate continued. "Look, the guy's fighting for his life—" Angelo said, walking with Arvin behind Tory, Gordon and the dog. "He may be in a unique position to tell us things we'd otherwise never know."

They were approaching the midblock construction project; Siggy pulled forward; there was never anyone to give him food on the late-night walks, but he was fundamentally a creature of hope. He strained at the leash, she checked him with a pull; usually that was enough, but not tonight. Siggy reared his head, ears back, extremely alert.

Something's in there, Tory thought, as a large rat ran out, dashed across the sidewalk.

Siggy lunged; Tory held the leash, tried to get him beyond the open plywood truck entrance. Two more rats darted out, one saw the dog, shot back into the dark construction site.

Siggy hurled himself after the rat, and the leash snapped out of Tory's hand. Her yell was controlled: "Siggy, come!" but the dog was inside the site barking as more rats cascaded out—brown ones, white ones, all different sizes. Tory had never seen so many rats.

Gordon was at her side. "Tory—go!"

"I have to get my dog."

"Tory—" she started to head in. He caught her arm. "I don't like this."

"I don't want him covered in rat bites." By this time Angelo and Arvin had run up. Gordon took an automatic from under his jacket, flipped off the safety and pulled the slide.

Arvin saw that, threw his cigar in the gutter. "I'll go in with you."

"We all will," Angelo seconded. Gordon led the group through the open door. They made their way through a maze of forklifts and lumber and cement mixers, the dog barking mightily somewhere in the darkness as Tory called and called. Rats ran over every surface, jumping and scampering around ankles as they got deeper into the construction.

Finally, forty feet in, they came to a large empty space. Above them, girders with partial flooring rose four stories into the nightlit sky. "Spread out," Tory said. "If he comes near you, step on his leash." Then she caught sight of the boxes at the center. "Guys—look."

Before them were three large wooden crates, squirming masses of rats climbing over each other to get out, the air filled with short-throated animal screams. "It's a setup," Gordon declared.

There was the sharp air-splitting thrum of a silenced bullet from somewhere above, and Gordon was hit, slammed to the rough concrete floor.

"Get DOWN!" Angelo said, and yanked Tory's arm.

"Oh God," Gordon was writhing, "Oh God—oh God—"Arvin scooped up Gordon's gun from where he dropped it, was looking up at the girders and platforms above them. Angelo stripped off his jacket, crammed it into a ball and jammed it into the wound. "Press that down. Hold it there."

"He's moving," Arvin said, entirely focused on the high platforms.

"Where's backup?" Tory asked.

"Bart's covering–" Gordon coughed. "God," he said, blood sluicing down his chin.

Arvin stood, held the gun with both hands and fired two shots into the girders. "Get her out—Now!" he barked at Angelo.

"I'm not leaving you here to get shot—" said Tory.

Angelo grabbed Tory's shoulders; "Cement bags." He pointed a few feet away. "Help me." He grabbed Gordon from behind, arms locked around his chest, Tory hugged both legs.

Arvin saw what they were doing, fired another shot into the sky. "Now!" Angelo said, and they bundled the wounded man across, bullets zinging around them from the high girders. They got behind the stacked bags of cement, let Gordon onto the ground. "Sonovabitch was going for my heart," Gordon said. "He got the angle wrong, shooting from above."

In the near distance, Siggy's barking turned to plaintive yelps. Tory instinctively shot her head up at the noise: "Siggy COME!" Another shot rang out, puffed out a cloud of paper and powdered cement. "Tory stay DOWN—" Angelo was furious.

Arvin ran across the open space, slid down to their position. "He's closer," he said.

Tory fished her cellphone out. "I'm calling the police."

"Does this place have an address?" asked Angelo.

"Shit," said Tory.

"Gordon, do you have a backup weapon?" Arvin asked.

"Two," Gordon gasped. "One in the fanny pack, one—" he gestured at his ankle.

Tory unzipped the fanny pack, pulled out a small automatic as Angelo pulled up the man's trouser leg, revealed a snub-nose revolver in an ankle holster.

"Either of you shoot?" Arvin asked.

"Not since the service," Angelo said.

Arvin cocked an eyebrow. "What branch?"

"Marines."

"Why didn't you say so?" Arvin said. "Take the automatic." He pointed towards the box. "Perimeter," he gestured. "Triangulation of fire. I'll take the right flank, Angelo takes the left. Tory—" he handed her the snub-nose. "No safety. Both hands. Point and shoot." He cocked the hammer back. "Ready." He folded her hands around the gun.

"Can we make a break for the door?"

"He'll pick us off at the door. It's probably what he wants," Angelo said.

"It's what I'd do," Arvin agreed. "Angelo and I will get into position. Tory, call the cops, and then call your dog."

"Right," said Tory. Arvin cut to the right, found a place behind rolls of steel mesh.

Angelo made his way left, took up a position behind a pallet of cement blocks. Tory dialed 911. "This is State Supreme Court Judge Tory Parker," she said quietly to the woman who answered. "I'm in the middle of a shootout in a construction site mid-block on 88th street—" she gave the cross streets, clicked off the phone, poked her head up. "Siggy! Come! NOW."

Nothing. "Come on, Siggy—" she put her finger and thumb between her lips and whistled, an piercing shriek that could stop taxis in their tracks, and usually bought Siggy in from afar. At the sound, the dog came barreling across the floor past the rat box, ears back and tail down, and her heart leapt to her throat: if that asshole shot her dog—

He wouldn't. He was waiting to see where she was.

This really was about her, she knew then. Siggy turned the corner, panic in his eyes. He dug his head into her stomach, almost knocked her over with his longing. Tory grabbed his head, hugged him, undid her belt and looped it through the leash handle. She was rebuckling her belt when she heard a well-oiled metallic click from behind.

She fumbled for the gun, turned, the leash now crossing her, holding her in check. She knelt, gun out before her, trying to see anything in the darkness. She didn't, and then she did.

A flash of motion. A white glint she immediately understood to be a wrist. She didn't wait; she fired once, and then again; at the second shot she heard a snarled grunt of pain. The guns on either side of her exploded, the two men firing a barrage. When it was over, there was the distinct sound of a man in agony saying "Motherfucking shit— motherfucking shit— Oh Christ in heaven, motherfucking shit—"

Tory knew the voice. She saw Arvin run up past her, gun forward. Angelo ran to her, hugged her hard, completely involuntary. "Are you okay?"

"I know him," she said simply.

Arvin, from up ahead, called: "He's down, I've got his gun." Tory tried to tug Siggy forward; the dog was quaking with fear.

Tory undid her belt, tied the leash to a cement mixer, kept low as they made their way to Arvin and the shooter.

The man on the floor had worn black; he had a hood and a set of night-vision goggles. "My legs," he was saying over and over in a small voice, "I can't feel my fucking legs."

Tory knelt in the man's blood, stripped off the goggles, wrestled the hood over the man's head. She looked down at the broad, pale face of Bart Alicia.

"Hey, Tory," he said, like it was a normal day between them.

"I trusted you," she said. "You saved my life at Forlini's."

"That was something, wasn't it?" Bart said, and licked his lips. "Hire a straw man, take him down, make you think I was the answer to all your problems."

Tory swallowed, swallowed again. "You bastard," she said softly, aware of the gun heavy and pregnant in her hand. She could shoot him now, she knew. She could shoot him now and neither of these men would ever say a word.

She turned, handed the gun to Angelo, looked back down at Bart. "Why?" she asked.

He turned away. "You'd never understand."

"Try me," Tory said, and then: "What was it? You and Eduardo Nieto are lovers?"

"Fuck you, that's not it at all." She'd said it to get his ire, and she'd gotten it.

"Then explain it to me, Bart," she said patiently.

Bart said nothing for a long while. Tory was aware of the blood spreading beyond her feet. "Whatever you want, he can give it to you," he finally managed. "Whatever you want."

"And what did you want, Bart? You took that shot at the ball?" Bart nodded. "We liked each other, Bart. What could he give you that was worth this elaborate setup to kill me?"

Bart said nothing, his eyes blinking, looking everywhere except at her. "When I was a kid," there was a crack in his voice, "somebody told me about Swiss bank accounts. The anonymous ones." He licked his lips. "I wanted one." His eyes, Tory realized, were moist. "Eduardo knew I was a gambler. He knew— he knew— " he licked his lips. "Now I got one, I go to Zurich six times a year with suitcases full of cash, and I can't feel my legs–"

"You shot Rafe's perp, Hidalgo, in thar courtroom." Bart nodded. Tory put it together. "You 're the cleaner— El Limpiador."

Bart licked his lips "He's a gambler. I'm a gambler. He called me El Limpiador because I could clean out any table. But to everyone else—" his breathing was beginning to buck up unnaturally. Outside, sirens started wailing in the distance. "I'm not going to fucking die," Bart said, "I'm not going to fucking—"

"How far does the corruption go?" Tory asked. "How far up?"

"All the way up your precious asshole, Judge." He caught his breath. "I'm not going to fucking die. I have a Swiss bank account, I'm not going to—" he was having trouble getting air.

"Bart—" Tory tried again. The sirens were getting louder. "Who? Tell me who–?"

"Fuck you," Bart gasped. "Fuck you all," he said, and he died with his eyes wide open.

* * *

Esmeralda, waiting in the van, had immediately seen that there was a fourth person attached to the judge as she approached the construction site. Her first instinct had been to warn Bart, inside, but he was well-positioned with night vision equipment; he'd see it clearly enough. He had dealt with much worse surprises in the past.

Still, the tension was unbearable. Finally, she heard the first shot: that was Bart. She'd followed the dialogue of gunfire back and forth, finishing with the final fusillade of shots, and her heart tightened in her chest because the final explosions should have been

Bart's guns, and they weren't. Beside herself with emotion, furious that she'd allowed him to convince her to cover the car, she'd run across, entered the site, listened to Bart's voice breaking, his body broken, his life draining away, listened to the judge he'd been guarding, strong and healthy, asking him question after question as if he owed her a thing in this world.

She listened to him die. Then the sirens had started to wail, louder and louder, and she thought: no, not now. Take your time, do it right. She backed away, left the construction site, walked down the street and turned the corner just as the first two police cars arrived.

* * *

The ambulance took Gordon to New York hospital on 68th Street; the cops took Tory, Angelo and Arvin to the 19th precinct house on 67th street. Because of Tory and Arvin's connection to the Secret Court, all the press got was that a shooting had occurred, one man had been killed and an investigation was ongoing.

When, finally, they left the cop shop, NYPD had mustered a four-man security detail to cover Tory. Arvin and Angelo were prepared to take Tory home, but she insisted she had to go to the hospital. And so they did, neither man willing to leave her in the care of the other.

Twenty minutes later, Gar Burton arrived with a crew of eight US Marshals. Tory was relieved to see his handlebar moustache. He listened to the evening's events, apologized on behalf of the Marshal's service to all three of them, then sent Angelo and Judge Hart out, talked privately with Tory.

"My instinct said not to bring in a DEA guy," he said. "But the line was, he'd been undercover, he knew Nieto, he knew the players. Now we know why."

"He had me fooled," said Tory. That was the most humbling thing about it all: she'd liked Bart; she'd assumed he liked her as well. How could she have been so far off?

The weirdest thing was, she was profoundly glad he had never touched her pool cues. She would have had to burn them and get Mr. Lyons to make her a new set.

"He had us all fooled, Judge Parker," Gar said. "For the next few days I'm going to be handling your security personally. And I assure you, I've never been to Colombia, I don't want to go to Colombia, I have no hidden agenda other than to see that you live to a ripe old age. I know you probably don't trust anyone right now—" Tory said nothing; he continued: "—that's why I want you to pick your team. Any NYPD guys you like, let's get them involved."

"Thank you, Gar. I appreciate that. And I think the time has come for me to buy a gun and learn to shoot it."

"Absolutely, Judge," Gar Burton said. "We'll start tomorrow."

* * *

Angelo and Arvin were trading war stories in the lounge when Gar brought in Tory. Angelo immediately stood. "If you want to recuse— and I think maybe you should—"

Tory sat, took a deep breath. "Bart trying to kill me is not a part of this case. The jury will never know, and there's no need for them to know."

"Tory—"

"They'll be fair. I'll be fair– I know I can be."

Arvin said: "Problem is, if you recuse, you're putting the target on the next judge's back."

Tory shook her head. "That's not going to happen. Eduardo Nieto doesn't dictate judicial policy." She looked at them both. "I'm seeing this through."

* * *

Half an hour later, the doctors came in and told them Gordon was out of surgery, and there was no reason to think his recovery wouldn't be complete. Angelo, hearing the news, declared himself exhausted, told Tory she'd be safe with her small army of bodyguards, and left.

Tory had been waiting for an opportunity alone with Arvin. There was something she wanted to say.

"Your friend the TV star is a good man," Arvin said.

"He always has been," she said, and then: Why was this always so difficult? Tory forced the words out: "Arvin, you're a good man, yourself. A decent man. I think of you as a friend. But that's as much as it will ever be."

He frowned. "We've been through a hell of a night, you don't have to make any decisions—"

"No." Tory looked him in the eyes, her face serious. "You're brave, you're funny, you're intelligent, but I just don't feel that spark—"

Arvin looked down, rubbing his forehead. "I was hoping you might."

"I take that as a huge compliment, believe me."

Arvin sighed. "When you're my age, all the interesting women are married. The ones that aren't, I can't even explain to 'em what I do for a living."

"It's tough," Tory commiserated.

"I don't need a 20-year-old. I'm not dating models. I want someone to share my life."

"You deserve that," Tory said.

There was a pregnant pause. "Well, I suppose I'll just head back to the hotel, then."

"I'll be safe. I'm probably the safest person in New York right now," she said.

"Yeah." He stood, took a deep breath, offered his hand.

He deserved more than that. She hugged him, then looked into his eyes. "You go," she said. "I want to write a note to Gordon, for when he wakes up."

"See you in court, " he said.

"See you in court," she said, and watched him leave.

* * *

"She killed him," Esmeralda said into the cell phone. "I want her dead."

Armstrong sighed. It was one in the morning. Someday he hoped God would give him back all the time he'd spent handling problems on cell phones in the middle of the night.

"First of all," he said, "doing her now would be a death trap. After this she'll have security she doesn't even know about."

"I can get her. Bart told me her habits." Just saying his name summoned him into being for her, brought back the thick sweet smell of him in bed.

Esmeralda was the most professional person Armstrong had, and suddenly she was acting like an amateur. "This is why ArrowHawk discourages employee relations, in Colombia or Iraq or in Covert Services or with us, it's all the same. We go to funerals, Esmeralda, and we don't fuck the corpse."

Asshole. "It was purely a bad chance—"

"Sounds to me like he got outdrawn, Essy. He thought he had it nailed down, and he didn't." Bart had too much mythos going on, of course he was going to blow an easy one. He believed all that El Limpiador legend shit that had served Eduardo so well. But Armstrong wasn't going to say that to her, not with her in Dead Martyr Widow mode. "Look. In our business, emotional loyalty is emotional liability."

Esmeralda looked at the cell phone, wanted to hurl it against the wall. "I just want her dead. So did he. That was the plan, wasn't it?"

"It may not be the plan anymore. Bart's failure changes the horoscope, alright? We have to go back to the source on this."

"But she killed Bart!" Armstrong heard the anger: she was beautiful when she was angry. He had treated her like a daughter for two years, but that didn't mean he was immune.

"Don't do this," he said. "Let me talk to our friend down south. Wait for instructions."

Great, Esmeralda thought: do nothing while that bitch Tory Parker goes on living and Bart goes unavenged. But: "You're right," she said. "I'll wait. You talk to Eduardo."

"Good girl," he said, and didn't trust her in the slightest.

* * *

When the alarm went off at 7:00 the next morning, Tory was awake and bone-tired. She'd battled insomnia all night, betrayal around every bend of her thought. Her arm muscles still ached from the recoil of the handgun.

She was alone in this great empty bed, her dog on his back, belly exposed to the world, dreaming happily on the carpet below the window. She stood, tottered unevenly to the bathroom, peed and looked hard into the mirror. She found nothing comforting in her bed-matted hair, in the fine skein of wrinkles that tracked out from the corners of her eyes.

She forced herself to ignore herself, padded naked across the apartment, drank cold water from the fridge. She set up the coffeemaker, more for the ritual than because she actually desired coffee. The machine started to hiss and burp; she put on the TV, forced herself onto the treadmill, ran hard for fifteen minutes without getting anywhere.

NY1 was reporting shots fired, one dead, under investigation. Her name never came up.

Usually the treadmill primed her, cut through the cobwebs. Today, fear filled her like a lightning bolt frozen in her chest. It never melted, and the fog in her mind never dispelled.

She climbed off after her allotted time, gulped down coffee, jumped in the shower. When she came out, Siggy was waiting, his optimism showing as the morning progressed toward his walk. She spent a moment doing her makeup, then dialed a cell number.

"Yes, Judge Parker," Gar answered.

"I'd like to walk my dog."

"We can do it for you—"

"No, it's something I'd like to do."

A pause, as he considered. "We'll be right up."

"Thank you," Tory said, and went to get changed.

*   *   *

Every morning when Baby Nieto arrived from Riker's he was brought to the main criminal courthouse holding pen; from there he was escorted upstairs to the small cells directly off the courtroom. He usually didn't see his lawyer until the judge called him in. But today, as he pulled his bulk up the final flight of stairs, Angelo was waiting to greet him.

"Hello, Mister Major General, sir!" He stood for a moment at the landing, regaining his breath. "If I had known you were coming, I would have made them paint a nicer color."

Angelo didn't smile, glared at the guard until he moved away. "I wanted you to know there was another attempt on Judge Parker's life last night."

Baby's face turned as implacable as a stone Buddha. "She is very unlucky, this judge."

"She was lucky last night. She shot the man who attacked her. Killed him dead." Angelo watched Nieto's eyes. "His name was Bart Alicia. Some people knew him as El Limpiador–"

Baby's eyebrows narrowed sharply at Bart's name. "This will stop the trial, no?" he asked.

"In America, the judge doesn't decide your fate. The jury does. This judge has had a lot of death threats over the years. It's never stopped her before." Then Angelo got in close. "If you have any information on this, I feel a deal could be arranged. You'd have to plead guilty—"

For the first time Angelo saw the man hesitate. Then he said: "No plea. We move on."

But in the courtroom, for the first time since the trial began, Baby was paying attention.

* * *

Armstrong had only one phone on which he ever dialed Eduardo Nieto. It was an ArrowHawk special, a dedicated satellite line with scramblers and digital encoding. He was glad he was separated by 2000 miles from the voice on the other end.

"The judge shot him?" Eduardo asked again.

"Her and her security team."

"But he's dead." There was a long silence as Eduardo Nieto wrapped his mind around that. Bart had always seemed invincible.

"Esmeralda wants to finish the job herself." There was silence on the phone. "I don't know if that would be the best thing for Baby."

"No," Eduardo said finally. "No. The time has come to do something from here."

Eduardo Nieto got off the phone, sat in his office chair, looked out the window at the ostrich pecking slowly through the bushes at the far end of the field.

The Americans had the advantage of power, and power brought its own special kind of luck. Eduardo took up the remote, changed the silent music video to American news. He watched for twenty minutes without seeing a mention of any death in New York.

He grew bored of the recurring self-important trivia from America, switched back to videos, checked his texts, then his securitized direct messages. There was one. The message was short:

> This isn't Colombia. You're not going to win by killing her. You're only going to get what you want by controlling her, by making releasing Baby the lesser of two evils.

Eduardo had already seen that inherent truth, but it was good to have his logic confirmed. All right, then, if that's the way they wanted to play it, he would give them something to mention on their newscasts.

He picked up the phone, dialed Dr. Torres. "The extinguishers are up north?"

"In a warehouse in Maryland."

"Come over. Let's decide how to deploy them so they'll do the most good for Baby."

* * *

"The word from the man," Armstrong said, "is no."

Esmeralda stood on a windy avenue west of Chelsea, cell phone to her ear, shivering in the cold. The city was gray under a gathering threat of low clouds. "Because I can do it—"

"He has no doubts you could accomplish the thing," Armstrong said, the signal in the phone hissing slightly. "That's not the point. He has resources to handle this that are bigger than anything you or I could come up with."

"But it would be so simple. She refuses to let her agents walk her dog."

"No, Essy. That's from the man himself. Don't worry— you know he's got a plan within a plan within a plan. That's always true."

"Right."

"Just come back down to DC and help us finish what we're trying to do here. I want you back in this city by 10:00 tonight. Do you read me?"

"Yessir," she said, and got off the phone. *Fuck him*, she thought. Bart was dead and Armstrong just wanted to keep the bullshit going. It was fundamentally unfair.

She had been watching the storage mini-warehouse for an hour, waiting for the call. She hadn't seen any police presence; they may have killed Bart, but it didn't look like they'd figured out anything about his life. She'd seen the way police worked in this city; when they had something, they sent every police car in the area, all at once.

She crossed the street, walked into the office, her heart pounding. Signs up everywhere and a thick American woman with double chins behind a counter. "Can I help you?"

"Just going to my locker," Esmeralda said, walked quickly to the elevator. When it came she went to the 4th floor, searched the row of storage lockers until she found Bart's.

She opened it reverently, not knowing what she would find, aware that there could be things in here that would hurt her, mementoes of other women or something equally private. She didn't care. He had had a life before she met him; there was very little from him she could imagine being shocked by.

Four suitcases, 3 with wheels, one a thin briefcase.

She retrieved a large wheeled cart by the elevator, pushed it noisily back to the locker. The first suitcase was heavy, and had a particular rattle that she immediately knew meant it was full of handguns. She loaded it onto the cart, loaded a second that she felt sure was filled with ammunition. The next suitcase was so heavy she could barely budge it. Gold, she thought, slid it across the floor and managed to upend it onto the cart. Then the item she'd known had to be here: the skinny black suitcase, surprisingly light when she lifted it.

Bart's sniper rifle. His plan for the rat shoot had been to get closer in. He hadn't thought he'd needed it.

She needed it now.

* * *

Throughout Tory's childhood, Thanksgiving had been difficult. Before her mother's illness, her father had always thrown a big open table for any students still on campus during the break. Once she was sick, and knew of his infidelities, that tradition abruptly ended; Thanksgiving, her father declared, should be spent in service to the community. When Tory first got to New York, she'd disobeyed his dictum and had potluck holidays with law-school friends. Then, one year, in a funk after Angelo, she volunteered for an NYPD program that fed people at armories all over the city. She hadn't expected cooking turkeys with cops and firefighters to be a blast, but it was. She'd done it every year since.

Late afternoon the day before Thanksgiving, the jury had been sent home, Baby was on his way back to Riker's and Tory was at the bench sorting papers when Angelo, slipping into his cashmere coat, stepped up to the bench: "So— what are you doing for Thanksgiving? Your family's kind of spread out, isn't it?"

Tory was surprised to feel a very slight high-schoolish quake in her chest. It had sounded like the prelude to an invitation. But that was absurd— not a defense lawyer, not a judge, not during a trial. "Yeah. We're all over the map. I volunteer at the armory thing in the Bronx every year."

"That's good of you," he said, impressed.

"It's selfish. Firemen know how to cook." Then: "You must have a zillion invitations–"

Angelo shrugged. "Law partners. It's not exactly homey."

"Neither is chopping up a few twenty-pound bags of onions with cops and firefighters ."

He hesitated, as if there was something more to be said. "Well, have a happy Thanksgiving," he offered finally.

"You too," she said, and watched him make his way out of the courtroom. Sometimes she thought he was just making polite conversation. Sometimes she knew he wasn't. And sometimes she didn't allow herself to pretend to know.

* * *

When the alarm went off at 4:30, Tory forced herself out of bed and into the shower. She kept her makeup simple, threw on jeans and an old shirt, called downstairs to rouse her protection team and walked her dog. Then she put a change of clothes in a shoulder bag. Siggy would get the dog walker for the rest of the day; she wouldn't be home until late.

In the car they headed north, Josiah Ficht driving. Ficht was the marshal Gar had hand- picked to be Tory's day man. He had already been commended on a number of tough jobs.

Once they crossed out of Manhattan, the dilapidation was everywhere. "Thanksgiving in the South Bronx," Josiah said in his Utah drawl. "sight I'd never thought I'd see."

"What was Thanksgiving at home?"

"It's gotten easier, now they've introduced wild turkeys into Utah. When I was in high school l bagged a moose with a bow and arrow."

"Really?"

Josiah nodded. "Gave us Thanksgiving and Christmas dinner, too."

The armory was a huge brick fortress, gothic and forbidding. The sun wasn't up yet, but already parking was tight. They found a space, ran through the cold into the building.

Inside was noisy, convivial, full of cops drinking coffee, folding chairs being clanged into position around long tables. "Great,

Tory, good to see you!" Phil Ruskin, an FDNYveteran who ran it every year, pumped her hand. “Who'd you bring?"

"Josiah Ficht. He's my security guy." Tory never knew how to explain the relationship.

"Can he work?" Ruskin asked.

"Can you work?" Tory asked.

"Sure," Josiah said, "beats sitting around watching other people do stuff."

Tory led Josiah into the large kitchen, already filled with brawny cops and firefighters wrestling enormous turkeys into ovens. Tory took the first 20-pound bag of onions from the floor and flopped it on the table. "Got any plans later? Like a date or something?"

"No, ma'am," Josiah said.

"Good," Tory smiled, "because by the end of today, you're going to smell."

* * *

An hour later Tory's back was hurting and her fingernails were jammed with onion meat. Josiah Ficht, was a fast and efficient kitchen worker, adept with a knife. Onions finished, they turned their attention to apples, Tory peeling and coring and Josiah chopping, when Ruskin came in and asked "Can you use help on stuffing?"

"The more the merrier," Tory said.

"Stuffing it is," Ruskin said.

"Great," a familiar voice said. Tory looked up.

"Angelo!" Her first emotion was elation. He was wearing jeans and sneakers and a well-worn flannel shirt, and somehow the casual clothes made him even more attractive. "You blew off you law partner?"

"I had a better offer," he said, and there was a spark of delight in his eyes at seeing her. Josiah Ficht looked from one to the other. They were smiling like fools.

"Well, get to work," Tory handed him a peeler. "We're making stuffing for 600."

Angelo was organized and tireless, and quickly the table fell into a natural rhythm. Angelo peeled, Tory cored, destemmed and deseeded, and Josiah chopped. "I haven't worked this hard since the Marines," Angelo said.

"Semper fi," Josiah said, smiling. "Where were you stationed?"

Angelo smiled. "I was actually assigned to the Department of State," he said.

"I thought you were in Africa–" Tory said.

"I was," Angelo replied. "Quick six months."

"And the Mideast–" Tory prompted.

"That was longer. But it was a while back." It was interesting, she thought: when she'd first met him, he'd had a lot of funny stories about the Marines, it was a part of his identity. But he'd since achieved so much, his service experiences had faded from a fire in his belly to a warm ember.

Josiah looked at Tory. "Did you ever think of a career in the military, Judge Parker?"

Tory looked over the hundreds of apples they'd reduced to rubble, held up her corer and paring knife. "I think I'm having one right now," she said, to laughter all around.

* * *

Later, plates loaded high with turkey and marshmallow sweet potatoes and truly excellent cornbread stuffing, Tory and Angelo found a quiet corner and talked.

"Actually," Angelo was saying. "Thanksgiving was a big deal for my folks. We were the house the family came to every year." Angelo's mother had died of a heart attack at 76; his father had passed away five months later. "The holidays were always this huge obligation." Interesting word, Tory thought: she had expected him to say 'celebration'. Angelo went on: "The last thing 1 wanted was to carry on those rituals."

"So you went in the opposite direction."

"Exactly." Angelo took another bite of turkey and cranberry, washed it down with water from a plastic cup. "I went through my 'lobsters and champagne for Thanksgiving' phase."

Tory lifted up her fork. "I like turkey," she said. "Don't get me wrong, I like lobster too, but turkey, Thanksgiving, it's just one of those things."

"Traditional girl," Angelo said; Tory remembered: he'd chided her that way years ago.

"Yes and no," Tory said, and realized something: "You used to say that, and I always felt it was a pigeonhole you were putting me into. I knew you were wrong but I didn't know why. Angelo— if I were the traditional girl you said, would I be here?" She looked around at the tables of homeless men, at the single mothers feeding sweet potatoes to their toddlers. "I'd be married to some banker with a house in Connecticut." Angelo had a strange intensity in his eyes. "I wouldn't be serially dating at 36, I wouldn't be living with 24-hour bodyguards–"

Angelo put up his hands. "You're right," he said, "you're absolutely right." He blinked at her, mouth slightly open. It was an unusual look for him, she thought, not knowing what to say next. Finally, he swallowed. "I used that as shorthand for why it wouldn't work between us," he said. "You were so traditional, and I was going to go on and do all these great things– "

"But you have," Tory said. "I've never known anyone who became so precisely what they wanted to become."

"See, I could say that about you." And then: "I was an arrogant little twit, back then. Thinking I could read everybody like a book." He shook his head. "How embarrassing."

"Hey," Tory said, "it's the people who don't learn who ultimately aren't interesting."

"What did you think about me, back then?" he asked.

Tory leaned back, considered. "That if you could do half the things you said you could, you'd go far." She dropped her voice down. "Also, that you were the best lover I'd ever had."

He had the grace to blush. "That still true?"

"Nope," Tory said, and ate a forkful of turkey.

* * *

The next morning found Esmeralda in a battered Honda driving north up the Taconic to a place Bart had mentioned once. Tiger Gun and Bow Range was an outdoor gun club that had gone out of business; the land was for sale, but the berms, backstops and wooden posts to hold targets were still in place.

She got off the narrow parkway, took twisting roads into the hills. She passed the cutoff twice before she found it. Untouched snow in the driveway; no cars or tire tracks in the lot or at the clubhouse. The place was quiet.

She took out the thin suitcase and one of the clear garbage bags of soda cans she had bought off a homeless man on the street in Chelsea, followed a path around the clubhouse to a long open shed. There were signs at the edge of the field demarcating 50', 100', 200', 300', all the way to 1000'. Esmeralda set up rows of soda cans at various distances, most standing in the snow, some on the wooden posts and fences. She went back to the shed, opened the suitcase and screwed the rifle together.

She affixed one of Bart's machine-drilled silencers, shot a round at a can pushed into the snow atop a distant post. She adjusted the scope, shot another, made more adjustments, liked the third shot. Then she started in on the cans.

It took her a moment to find her rhythm. The rifle was lighter than she was used to, it seemed to want to dance in her arms, but within minutes her old touch had returned. She decimated the cans at 300 feet and had little trouble with the ones at 500. 700' proved a challenge; after several frustrating stray shots, she took a deep breath, slowed her rhythm, forced herself to relax her muscles. The first shot sent a Miller Light can flying.

She was realizing why Bart had loved this gun. Simple, honest and clean. The rest, once she'd relaxed, were easy. She had problems with tremor at 1000', tuned into the rhythms of her heart, shot between beats to compensate.

When she'd gotten them all, she walked out with the smelly plastic garbage bag, set out more rows, and started in again. Every so often she would dump the silencer and screw in a new one; they wore out quickly with steady firing. She worked with the rifle until she ran through almost all the boxes of Bart's rifle loads, and then turned her attention to the pistols.

* * *

Gar Burton and Josiah Fitch were trying to be helpful, Tory knew, but at that moment all she felt was frustration. Tory had pictured herself with an automatic, mostly because the silhouette was slimmer if one had to wear the damn thing, but she had been vetoed by the experts. The autos had more moving parts that could get jammed, and critical seconds could be wasted clicking the safety off and working the slide. A revolver, as Gar put it, was much more user-friendly.

Having decided that, the questions of size, comfort, caliber and relative stopping power came into play. To that end, four guns had been laid on the shelf of the NYPD shooting gallery on 20th street. Tory liked the feel of the Colt .45, but the thing was unwieldy. After firing several rounds in comparison, she became enamored of a snub-nosed .32.

A new target, the standard burly man with a gun, was wheeled into place at the end of the lane. Tory adjusted her eye protection, held the gun with both hands, aimed for the chest, squeezed the trigger six times.

One in the paper off the neck, one in the left arm, one in the paper down in the lower left corner, and the other three somewhere in the back of the alley, having left no physical evidence of their flight.

"Actually," Tory said, "with Bart, I did better than that. I saw a flash of white and I shot at it. But now I'm overthinking everything."

This was met by a short silence. "With a gun in your hand, it's probably better to think," said Gar.

"I was wondering," Josiah said gently, "if we might work on your stance."

* * *

Siggy was being intransigent.

Tory had seen it before. He wasn't dumb; drag him past the dog run three nights in a row and he became resistant, electing to take a stand the next time it came up. It wasn't his fault that Tory's life currently was hell. Even though it was 10:30 at night, he just wanted to be dog, catch balls in full gallop and sniff other dogs' butts.

There were a few diehards in the dog run, people Tory knew but hadn't spoken to in weeks. Emboldened by the late hour and the .32 in a shoulder holster under her coat, Tory turned to Josiah. "Can we give him a quick run?"

"I'd rather we didn't," but Siggy had accepted the momentary pause as acquiescence, and pulled her to the gate.

"Just for a minute," she said, and flipped up the catch. Josiah was quick to follow. Tory opened the second gate, and Siggy pulled her through. She unclipped his leash, let him romp, the dog immediately overjoyed, pronking like a springbok.

"You wouldn't think that dog would be so fast," Josiah said, and the first shot drilled past. Tory heard no report but felt the thrum of the bullet, felt the shockwave in her ear before noticing the chaff of fabric in the vision of her left eye, an awareness of fibers abruptly liberated and in play in the air. The bullet had gone through the shoulder of her winter coat, she realized, and at that moment Josiah tackled her, smashed her into the soft woodchips that covered the dog run. Fuck, she thought, agony coalescing in a pit in her stomach, not again.

She was in the wide open and somebody was shooting at her. She had a great many thoughts all at once— draw the gun, run, leap over the fence, get underneath something. Josiah was up immediately, pointing a small submachine gun up into the trees. "Silencer," he said, and then two more shots hit the ground around her, and she realized: the only reason I'm alive is that my coat matches the dogrun wood chips.

People were screaming, she realized now, and running toward the one exit. "NO!" She yelled, and was up in an instant. She ran the other way, towards a bench on the far edge of the run. She used the bench to leap over the short basketball fence, pulled the .32 out from under her jacket, stood for a moment, turning in a circle, looking up at the trees, the buildings across the street, the promenade next to the river. "I'M HERE!" she yelled into the night, her heart careening in her chest. Anything to keep the shooter from the people and animals bottlenecked at the exit of the dog run.

In response another shot rained down, but this time she saw the flash of light, dove into
bushes as the bullet plowed into the dirt.

On her back, she pointed the .32 at the spot the flash had come from, both hands together. She thought of pool, forced her mind to clear, fired two shots. Noisy as hell compared to the silenced rounds. Then the returning salvo, two quick shots in succession. A different gun. She crumpled into a fetal position, heard the bullets land around her, and then pure adrenaline overtook her and she was up and running straight forward, gun in both hands towards the promenade.

There was a woman there, dressed in black. The first thing Tory saw was the rifle slung behind her back. The second thing she saw was the pistol in her hands, sighting her as she came into range. Tory fired once, her gun offsetting the woman as she got off a shot.

Tory fired two more times, and at the same time a blare of automatic gunfire came from Tory's right.

The woman seemed to blast apart. She fell and rolled, and there were pieces of her missing as she came to a stop. Josiah ran past Tory, kicked the woman in the head, pointed the gun and said "Freeze!"

It didn't matter. She was dead.

* * *

At the precinct house they were very nice about Tory keeping Siggy with her. Even as they questioned her, the dog sniffed the edges of the room. The detective kept looking at him as if he were about to pee, but Tory knew he never would indoors.

Once they'd established who Tory was, the questioning didn't take long. But they warned her that the press had gotten hold of the story, and to expect tabloid covers the next day.

Tory had always hated those moments when she was in the papers, but she didn't mind tabloid coverage this time, she supposed, as long as she was around the next day to read them.

And so she went home. Josiah, weapons ready, slept on her couch; Siggy, afforded a privilege rarely allowed, slept next to her on her bed.

When she woke up the next morning, her first thought was a blow-by-blow recount of the events of the night before. Only after she'd relived it completely did she allow herself to think: I really have to put in a lot more time at the shooting range.

The dog next to her roused himself at her motion, got in close and touched his cold nose to her cheek. *Okay*, she thought, *I'll take that as agreement.*

* * *

By Monday, Tory's splash of headline ink had more or less passed; it had been kept to a somewhat murky one-day story, One Dead In Shooting In Park, and FISA had not been mentioned at all.

At the start of the workday, everyone had expressed concern, but once the proceedings began, the give and take of the trial became all-consuming.

Angelo was indignant. He and Sam Walker were at the bench; Sam wanted to introduce a new witness. "I included Mr. Izquierra during discovery. The fact that I couldn't find him until now–"

Angelo wasn't buying it. "You front-loaded the list so you could start pulling rabbits out of hats when your case started to crater."

Sam looked Angelo square in the eye. "Oh, you know that trick, do you?"

Tory said "Gentlemen!" sharply enough to silence the room. "Is Izquierra here now?"

Sam looked. "Back row, dark-haired man next to my associate Megan."

Tory shrugged. "The guy's on the list, he's entitled." She saw Thomas come in from the robing room with a FedEx. Whatever problem he had, right now she wished he'd take care of it himself. "Angelo, if you have a substantive argument about why Sam can't put this guy on—"

"He's a Colombian under threat of deportation. He'll be cinders by the time I'm done."

"That's not substantive," Tory said.

"Excuse me— Judge Parker?" Thomas was on the first step up to the bench.

Tory turned around, sharp: "Thomas, what?" she asked.

"I think you need to see this," he said, and handed the FedEx up to her.

His hands were shaking. The FedEx envelope, addressed to her from Miami, had already been opened. Inside was a single sheet of paper. She put her hand up to still the conversation, took out the sheet, read the first line.

Adrenaline burst in her chest, her heart began galloping. She looked out at the court.

"Tory–" Angelo said, "are you all right?"

"Recess," Tory said, and then again, louder. "Recess. Fifteen minutes." She stalked off the bench with the FedEx into her robing room, Angelo and Sam staring mutely behind.

Thomas had stayed lockstep with her, tried to make himself unobtrusive as she sat at her desk and read the letter. The single sheet was a printout from a computer:

> We have radiological explosive ordnance that will release americium, beryllium, cobalt 60 and cesium 137, among other isotopes, capable of killing all life in a large area and making it uninhabitable for centuries. At three o'clock this afternoon, the defense will, per your explicit and private instructions, ask you to declare a mistrial. You will comply, and immediately release Baby Nieto free of charges by 4:00 today, or we will demonstrate our power at a time and location of our choosing. We have many bombs. This will be the first. It is your choice, and your

choice alone, whether or not
it will be the last.

"It's a hoax," said Thomas. "It has to be."

"It may not be," Tory said quietly, and picked up the phone. Anna came in chipper from an errand, immediately sensed the tension. "Cornelia," Tory said when her administrative judge picked up. "I've got a situation here," she said, and read the letter. When she hung up, she looked at Thomas and Anna, now visibly pale with fear.

"First of all, not a word to anyone," Tory said. "Tell my security guys to get in here. no one else, and then guard the doors." When she was alone, she fished the securitized cell phone out of her bag, called Drummond and read him the letter.

There was a long pause on the phone. "And it came from Miami?" he asked.

"Yes, sir." Tory did not immediately see how that was germane to her main concerns.

Another long pause. "It's a hoax. Nieto's too smart for this," Drummond said finally.

"I don't know if it's Nieto or not, sir," she said, though if this was real she could not imagine who else might be behind it. "My question is: what do we do about it?"

"We alert the NEST teams, we alert FEMA, we start the nuclear emergency chain of command. What are you going to do in that courtroom?"

Tory felt her throat dry up. "I'm trying to figure that out, sir."

"You're scared. Go with your gut, Judge Parker. That's the best advice I can give you."

"Yes, sir." Someone was knocking on the door. "Security's here," she said.

"I'll let you go. Anything you need from me, just call."

"Right," Tory said, hung up and unlocked the door. Cornelia was there, along with Mike Leavall, a large, blunt detective who had been NYPD chief of counterterrorism for years. Leavall put on latex gloves from his briefcase, read the letter. "How many people have touched it?"

"Just Thomas and me." She looked to Thomas for verification. He nodded.

Leavall slid the letter into a zip-lock bag, ran off a single photocopy and gave it to Tory. He put the original in his case. "I wouldn't make a million copies of this," he said. "If it ends up on the front page of the Post—" He pulled out a larger plastic bag, began the same procedure for the FedEx envelope when he was interrupted by the entrance of Special Agents Jerzy Poldak and Bronwyn Taggart. "Judge Parker," Jerzy said, “can I see the letter?"

"It's a copy. NYPD got here first." Tory handed it to him. Poldak read it, didn't flinch.

He looked up at Leavall. "We're going to need the original."

"Just like that?" Leavall was furious. "You just walk in here and say that? This is an NYPD case, hotshot. This is a state court. We have jurisdiction."

Jerzy wasn't a lightweight. "Come on— a dirty bomb goes off anywhere west of 12th Avenue, you want those headlines? 'NYPD sat on evidence that could have prevented—'"

"For God's sakes—" Tory had heard enough. "This isn't some guy selling guns out of a car on Broadway, this is a dirty bomb. If it's real, people will die. Work together. Please."

A chastened silence in the room. Mike Leavall opened his briefcase, handed the originals to Special Agent Taggart. "Here," he said.

"Thank you." She turned and left the room.

"Let me go call the commissioner on this," Leavall said, and slipped out after her.

Tory shook her head. Interagency cooperation was never what it was cracked up to be. "Now," she said, "what does the FBI suggest we do?"

Jerzy considered. "Recess the trial. Buy us time while we investigate the hell out of it—"

"Look at the letter." Tory took up the copy. "It's to be a demonstration. That's why the time frame is ridiculous. He's itching to blow something up, show us his new toys."

"Then the real negotiations begin," said Jerzy.

"So what do we do?" asked Thomas.

Tory took a deep breath. "Eduardo Nieto does not force the decisions of the American justice system. We resume the trial immediately."

Jerzy shook his head. "I'm sorry, Judge Parker, I can't."

"Why not?"

"Because we have to pull Baby Nieto out of there and ask him what he knows about Big Brother's dirty bomb capabilities."

Tory considered. "Okay, then, let's bring Angelo and Sam in, they have to know." Thomas slipped out, returned from the courtroom with the two lawyers. She handed them copies of the letter.

As Angelo read it, his eyebrows peaked high in his forehead. When he finished the color had drained from his cheeks. "I think I need to sit down."

Sam read it. "We're not going to release him." There was no question in his voice.

"Of course we're not going to release him," Tory said. "The question is, do we acknowledge? Do we have Angelo ask for a mistrial? Or do we ignore?"

"Ignore," Sam elected. "It buys more time."

"Ignore," Angelo agreed. "Let him stew in his own juices."

"Done," said Tory.

*　　*　　*

When Judge Parker returned to the bench, she sent the jury to the jury room. When they were gone, Baby Nieto abruptly found himself at the center of a dense circle of black-clad hats and bats. Angelo interjected himself between them. "Nobody questions my client without me present."

"Of course," Tory said. "If Mr. Nieto wishes, you have the right." Tory ignored a sharp look from Jerzy Poldak. Alone with cops, Baby might clam up, but with Angelo there he would feel he could negotiate.

The black-clad cops guided Baby back through the door to the cells. They hustled him down countless stairs— he had to stop and catch his breath at the end of every flight— until they came to a corridor of doors. He was marched into a little room with a desk and two chairs and a mirror on one wall. The white paint was scuffed and the air smelled like dirty laundry.

Poldak pushed past into the interrogation room, Angelo right behind. As he walked in, Angelo said: "They're not charging you with any crime. You don't have to answer a thing. That said, if you are helpful, they will remember."

Poldak grimaced. He hadn't agreed to anything like that, but he wasn't about to counter it. "Mr. Nieto," he said, "we need to know if your brother has access to radioactive materials."

Baby's face popped wide. He spoke slowly: "Eduardo, if he wants something, he has it."

Poldak leaned forward. "Have you ever heard him mention the Atucha nuclear power plant in Argentina? Or the Angra plant in Brazil?"

Baby looked pale, greenish under the fluorescent light. "He goes to gamble in Brazil sometimes. He used to. I don't see him in four years."

"Did he go to Itaorna? Or have any contacts with anyone at the Itaorna nuclear site?"

"On the coast? Near Rio?" The way Baby said it, something in Angelo froze. "He used to go to the ocean at Itaorna. I said Why? We have ocean at Colombia."

Angelo's eyes briefly met Poldak's. The Special Agent went on: "Do you know if he has any X-ray machine parts? Anything radioactive he keeps in a special place?"

"Anything he wants to get, he gets." Baby was becoming more agitated.

"Did you ever hear him talk about radioactive things? X rays, gamma rays, americium, beryllium, cobalt, cesium, plutonium, tritium–"

"We don't talk!" Baby wailed. "He does what he wants! If he wants this, then he has it." And then: "You want to know if he is planning an attack, I say yes, it is him. Maybe Eduardo would say he is doing this for me, but I promise you— anything Eduardo does, he does for himself alone."

* * *

"A dirty bomb?" Jack Riley said over the phone. "Eduardo doesn't have the facilities."

"It's not like building a nuke," Tory said. "You don't need to process plutonium—"

"It's not a line I thought he'd cross," Jack said, and then: "Listen, I have people to call."

Tory got off the phone, sat staring out the window. Sickly gray clouds had coalesced over the city, sweeping the sidewalks with cold wind. Not releasing Baby was the only decision possible. She closed her eyes for a moment, hoping it was also the right decision.

Tory took a deep breath, went out into the courtroom to continue Baby's trial. She called the jury back in, reconfirmed her decision about Sam's last-minute witness.

Mr. Izquierra, a sharp little man with delighted eyes and a Nietzschean moustache, took the stand at 3:27 PM. His English was imperfect, but serviceable.

"I was a driver for Mr. Baby Nieto," he explained, to Sam's gentle coaxing.

"Where did you usually take Mr. Nieto?"

"One man he would meet in the car every day. Mr. Brazo Fuerte. Mr. Armstrong."

"And what was Mr. Armstrong's relationship to the defendant?"

"He was the man between Baby and Eduardo. Everyone thinks Baby was the contact to Eduardo in America. To me, Baby was like the embajador, the face that sees the public. Sympatico. Mr. Armstrong was like your CIA, the hidden antipatico that does the bad work."

Tory remembered Barney Lind's grand jury testimony, felt a quiver of excitement underneath all the black dread in her chest. Barney Lind had talked about Mr. Armstrong. She looked out over the jury, saw that some of them were putting it together as well. "So," Sam went on. "Did this Mr. Armstrong have anything to do with the importation of cocaine?"

Angelo was blasé: "Objection, your honor, hearsay–"

"Sustained," Tory said.

Sam smiled. "Did you see or hear Mr. Armstrong and Mr. Nieto discuss cocaine?"

"Yes I did," Mr. Izquierra said. "I used to drive them around, and they'd talk."

"Tell us, please, what conversations you overheard."

Angelo sat up. "Objection, still hearsay, your honor."

Tory shook her head. "No, I've previously ruled these are admissible as exceptions to that rule, as co-conspirator statements. Overruled. You may answer the question, Mr. Izquierra."

The man nodded. "They talk about ships coming in, judges they bribe, customs agents—"

"Do you remember any names you might have heard?"

Izquierra shook his head. "This was two years ago. I remember Armstrong. I remember Lind. I remember a judge they called Fredo, like the Godfather movie. They would look for a weakness, then go in and feed it."

"Like with Barney Lind?" Sam asked.

"With Lind it was pink cocaine. Sex, gambling— I would listen to them plan. This police chief has a mistress, that Senator likes girls to whip him. So, they could use these people."

Tory, listening, caught sight of her watch, and instantly her heart plunged back into the thick bleak hell she'd carried inside all afternoon.

3:58. Two minutes to Eduardo's deadline. When she glanced up, Baby was searching out her eyes, but when she met his, he looked away.

He's nervous, she thought, and then realized: so am I.

* * *

The sixteenth hole at the Augusta National Golf Club is played almost entirely over water. A pond, built in 1947, separates the tee from the hole. Not the most famous landmark on the storied course— that would be the Eisenhower tree, which interrupts the fairway on the 17th, and so infuriated the 35th president that he campaigned to have it removed— the pond is, nevertheless, where innumerable golfers' hopes of winning have disappeared without a bubble.

When the bomb at the bottom of the pond exploded, it sent a radioactive plume of aerosolized water and dirt and steaming golf balls in all directions. Wind-borne radioactive particles spread across the acres of loblolly pines and magnolias, over the clubhouse and the horseshoe of cottages, over the restaurant and parking lot. It settled into Rae's Creek, which threaded one end of the course, and carried down through red-dirt Georgia farmlands, spreading death everywhere it touched. Insects soon started to die; squirrels and birds shortly followed.

The golfers on the links, businessmen who had reached the exalted level where taking clients to the most important golf club in America was an accepted part of their weekday labor, reacted with mixed emotions to the fiery eruption and the column of dirt and smoke. The more steadfast thought perhaps a transformer had blown or a gas line ruptured, and played through.

The Vice President's secret service men did not react so lackadaisically. The Veep was not actually on the links; he was in the pro shop, considering glove designs, when the men with earpieces swarmed in and braced him back out to his car.

Privately, his doctors would tell him not to worry, his exposure was minimal. Fourteen months later, cancer vigorous inside him, he would be dead.

The Masters' Tournament would go on, but not here. It would take a long time for many Americans to heal. It would take even longer for the people of Georgia.

And for some—those who had been there, those who had loved them, and buried them, and a cluster of law enforcement officials in Atlanta and Washington and New York— it would be a mark in their lives when things had changed: before Augusta, and after.

* * *

That night, Tory was reading FISA briefs as the Jets got pummeled by the Colts on her TV when the securitized cell phone rang. She hit it on. "Judge Parker," she said.

Drummond sounded exhausted. "Have you seen anything about that explosion in Georgia?"

"The golf course?" It had been an item on the news. "Transformer fire or something."

"It was a dirty bomb. " Tory sat bolt upright. Drummond went on: "It had precisely the elements mentioned in the letter you got this morning."

Tory felt tight in her skin, her heart racing. She scrambled for the remote, hit the television off. "My God," she said.

"Georgia governor and the AG will announce it in an hour. We have a NEST team on site, that's how we know the particles.

We've got FEMA and the CDC setting up field quarantines and a morgue truck. Any chance you've got another FedEx from Eduardo Nieto?"

"I think that bomb is all the communication we're likely to see right now. He's proven he's got the upper hand. Now it's to us to decide what to do."

"How does this affect the trial?"

Tory took a deep breath. "It doesn't at all. It might have an impact on Baby."

"I hope so," Drummond said. "I hope to God they pull something out of that boy."

* * *

When the crowd of corrections officers arrived at the door of Baby Nieto's cell at Riker's, Baby saw that his friend the whistling guard was part of the group. But when Nieto tried to catch his eye, the man didn't crack a smile.

Something had happened. Baby, surrounded by a phalanx of uniforms, was marched down the hall. They brought him to a small room he had not seen before, covered with graffiti. Waiting for Baby in the room was Special Agent Poldak.

Baby didn't sit. "I do not talk without my abogado— my lawyer. Mr. Angelo Schwartz."

Poldak wasn't impressed. "You see the news?" he asked.

"TV is junk. I do not watch."

"Bomb went off." Poldak watched him intently. "Just like your brother said it would."

Baby blinked rapidly, rubbed his lips with his finger. "Is bad?" he asked.

"It's a fucking dirty bomb, Baby. Fucking radiological fucking bomb. They set up a mobile morgue unit to handle the bodies. Yeah, I'd say it's pretty fucking bad."

Baby had gone pale, grey-green around the eyes, as if he would topple at any moment.

Poldak went on: "Why don't you start by telling me where this happened."

Baby put his hands on the table. They were white, his fingers like slugs. "I don't know—"

"BULLSHIT!" Poldak slammed the table so hard that Baby's huge hands jumped in alarm. "He's doing all this for you, right? It's a simple fucking question. I know where he put the bomb, and you know where he put the bomb—"

"I don't know any place he put any bomb," Baby said, his voice high and reedy.

"Man, you are such a fucking liar."

"I don't know!" Baby wailed it. Poldak watched him carefully.

"Guess," he finally said.

Baby swallowed and swallowed. "The courthouse where we are in the trial."

"Guess again."

"White House."

"Guess again."

Baby thought about it. "Supreme court?" he asked.

He was trying. Poldak could see it. "How 'bout Augusta National?"

"What is that?" Baby said, and then he interrupted himself. "The golf course?" Something in his eyes had changed, Poldak saw: now he looked querulous and haunted. He leaned back, seemed to deflate. "Si," he said, nodding his head, "is logical."

"Why?" Poldak tried to keep the anger out of his voice.

"My father— Eduardo's father. At 19, he came to America, he worked at August National golf club. He worked on the flowers. They said he stole money— he didn't, he always said he didn't— but they sent him back to Colombia." Poldak nodded. "Augusta golf course." Baby shook his head. "I should have been able to say."

"How do we get him to stop?" Poldak said.

"No one stops Eduardo," Baby replied. "Not me, not you. Eduardo gets a sore tooth, he likes to pull it out of his mouth himself." Baby searched for words. "No one stops him," he said again. "I came to America to get away from Eduardo—" he looked down, shook his head. "But now here he is."

Poldak was surprised to see Baby's eyes swimming in tears.

* * *

Climbing up hill, Darth Vader solid as marble between his legs, Eduardo Nieto began again to think of the statue: himself on the big black horse, rearing off the ground. A present to the people of Cartagena, to be placed on the street where he grew up.

He had destroyed the American golf course that had caused the deportation of his father. It had been Hector Nieto's great regret in life— thrown forever out of America, the country he had loved since childhood, for money another man stole.

But this was about more than honor. It took a special man to avenge his father and brother against the most powerful nation on earth. It took a world-historic figure like himself.

Transnational power. The United States refused to acknowledge the sovereignty of the World Court in The Hague? Well he, Eduardo Nieto, refused to acknowledge the American court's sovereignty over his brother. They had no right to hold Baby, as he had made abundantly clear.

He knew how it would play: the jury would hand the scared bitch judge their verdict, she would open the paper and pronounce Baby innocent, no matter what the jurors had written.

Baby would fly back to a national holiday, roast pigs and beer and music in every village. And the world would know Eduardo Nieto was a man with whom governments were not to trifle.

Europe, Asia, Africa, they would all have to listen. There was no reason the chief export of Colombia had to be illegal in every nation. And now, with his labs producing fentanyl, he could begin to weaponize his product. He could deal death to the US and any other nation who fought him, all the while blaming the illegal channels the drugs had to take to enter those countries. Meanwhile, the countries who understood his vision would get the cleanest, safest, finest connoisseur cocaine on the planet.

Countries around the world had all but legalized marijuana, and were reaping the benefits of taxation. When countries all over the Earth realized the tax revenues to be gained from government-regulated coca products, they'd wipe out their national debts and build more schools than they had teachers to staff them.

All it would take was one farsighted individual, one fearless nation, and the tide would turn.

* * *

Benno had found a customer for Maria.

They were in the car again, Stephanie smoking and staring out the window, Angie telling a long story about one of her guys last night. Maria had a sodden lump of pain in her throat that had been there all morning, Finally Benno saw the address. "We're here," he said, and swiped across three lanes of traffic to a building.

He turned to Maria. "First thing—" he pulled a round pink case from his pocket, punched a small pill through the foil.

Steph rolled her eyes. "Not like she needs that yet," she said.

"You never know," he replied. She grunted, exhaled smoke against the glass window.

Benno handed Maria the pill. "Take this, it'll keep you from getting pregnant."

Pregnant. Oh, Lord God in heaven. Gingerly Maria took the small pill, put it on her tongue like a communion wafer. He handed her an open Pepsi and she washed it down. "You're in luck," Benno went on, "this guy doesn't want to use a condom, and that costs extra. So, you know, that's good for you." He got out, opened her door.

Maria was shivering as she descended to the street. She felt she was going to vomit, but she couldn't because of the pill.

"You look great," Benno said. She was in an itchy plaid skirt and a black T-shirt that said *Foxy* in little sparkles. Benno punched a number. "Yeah, we're downstairs," he said.

Presently, a man came out, skinny in a rumpled shirt, balding. He took one look at Maria and said "Ooooh, you did good, Benny."

"Benno," Benno replied.

"Right," the man said, staring at Maria. He took a folded white envelope from his breast pocket, handed it to Benno, who quickly made it disappear.

"I'm Bucky," the man said, his hands in his pockets. Maria didn't say a word, frozen into place, emotion sharp inside.

"Well, go on," Benno said, and pressed Maria forcibly between the shoulder blades Bucky's tongue kept touching his lips, again and again, like a lizard. Before he could say a word, the car door opened.

"Hey, girlie," Joanne said from the back seat. "Go on, we're hungry. We'll get you later."

Benno's hand on Maria's back pressed harder, and she was pushed into a step, and then another. Benno got into the car, roared down the road, and the man took her hand. She put one foot ahead of the other, and walked through two glass doors into the man's building.

At the end of the hall the man pressed a button, stood in front of a closed door. Nothing happened. "How old are you?" he asked.

She understood the question but she couldn't answer, sorrow heavy in her throat. He tried it again, louder and slower: "How Old Are You?"

"Diez Anos." And then in English: "Ten years." The door slid open and an elderly woman stepped out of a small wooden room, walking a furry white dog. "Hello," the man said, turning bright red and looking at his shoes. He stepped quickly into the small room, pulled Maria in. The door slid shut. "I want to be your friend," he said as the room started to move.

An elevator. That's what this was. The door slid open and they were no longer where they had been. He held her shoulder down a hallway, opened a door, pushed her in. The apartment was messy, newspapers on the floor. He shut the door behind. "Can I get you a cerveza? That's beer, right?"

She shook her head 'no'.

"Then let's get to it." he touched her hair, took it into his hand, ran his fingers through it. She was shaking. "How old are you?" He'd already asked that. "Say it in English. Ten."

"Ten," she said.

"And you want to fuck me. Say it."

Maria was completely confused. "And you want?"

"No, no." He was getting angry. "Say: I'm ten years old and I want to fuck you."

Maria started to say: "I am ten years old? And—" she couldn't remember the rest.

"And I want–" he prompted.

"And I want?" she asked.

"Oh, Jesus Christ," the man said, abruptly impatient. "Take off your clothes."

It was involuntary: she was close to the door, and ran for it. He grabbed her arm, pushed her against the wall and crushed her to him. She hit his chest with her fists. His lips were pressing against her mouth, and all at once she knew what to do, and she bit down hard.

"Ahh, shit!" He tore himself away from her. "Oh God, you cunt." His lip was bleeding. He looked at himself in the mirror. "Look at that— look at that! You little piece of—"

And now she was wailing in fear of what he was going to do. He took up his phone, picked a piece of paper off the desk, shakily dialed a number.

"Yeah, Benno? Come back here and take this bitch away. I can't do a Goddamn thing with her. And Benno? Give me my fucking money back." And he hung up the phone.

*　　*　　*

Silence in the car all the way back. The radio was off. Angie and Stephanie hadn't met Maria's eyes when she'd gotten in, wouldn't meet them now. Maria tried to keep her crying quiet, but every sound she made hung in the air like smoke.

"Give you something to cry about," Benno muttered as he turned in the driveway. He stopped the car. "Go in, go upstairs, fill the tub with cold water, and wait for me."

"Shit," Steph said, and then: "Angie, let's go up to CVS and buy some makeup."

Benno peeled off four twenties, gave them each two. "Upstairs, I said," he told Maria.

Hours later, cuffed to the hot and cold handles, blue and shivering in the cold water, Maria could not believe she was still alive. Benno had cuffed her hands behind her back and held her under, pulled her out and shoved her head back, over and over until his clothes were soaking wet and there was water all over the bathroom. She'd breathed water, her face jammed into the floor of the bathtub. She'd coughed water and got it up her nose. Then he'd cuffed her to the taps, opened the drain and turned on the cold shower all the way and left, locking the door behind. That had been four hours ago, and still the ice-cold water hammered down.

Finally, the door unlocked and Benno stepped in. He had changed into a white sweatsuit. He was carrying a stack of dry towels. He turned the shower off, sat on the rim of the tub.

His voice was gentle. "You know what you did, don't you?" he asked.

Maria had thought of nothing but for the last four hours. She nodded.

"And you know I had to do what I did." He waited for her eyes to come around, make contact. When they did, he smiled. "I hate it," he said. "I hate it more than you do. Ask the girls— one time or another, I've done it to all of them. Some more than once. And they're all still with me. Think about that, Maria, okay? Now you want to come down, eat something?"

Maria nodded. Benno spent a moment uncuffing her hands. "That guy wasn't the right guy," he said as gently dried her hair. "Okay. We'll find you another guy. And then you'll do it, it'll go fine and you'll be that much closer to getting home."

* * *

Angelo's summation was masterful. He started slowly, even humbly: "Imagine that your brother is the biggest cocaine dealer in the world. And you are, from early boyhood, dependent on him. And as he rises, you rise. But at some point, you see the harm of what he does, and finally you break with your brother. You walk away, come to America and begin to build your own life." Angelo stood silent, let the wheels spin in the jury's minds.

When he started back in, his tone was different, his pacing quicker. "Many people come to America with empty pockets. My client did not do that. He had built a name as an exporter of flowers to the American market. He got off the plane with a business waiting for him.

"The government contends that this business is a front for Eduardo Nieto's cocaine business. If it was, how are the brothers communicating? No phone calls, not even on Christmas or birthdays, for four years. I assure you, if there had been one phone call, one email, one text message, Mr. Walker would have told you about it. But he couldn't, because Ricardo Nieto broke all contact with his brother when he left Colombia, and has had no communication since."

He paused, let the words hang, let the jury savor them. When he started again, his tone was softer. "This man—" he pointed at the mountainous Baby—"could live as a king in Colombia right now. He wouldn't have to do a thing. Just be awake for meetings and watch the money roll in. But he's here, ladies and gentlemen. He's a businessman. He sells flowers. He imports them—sometimes in truck boxes like the ones on that boat. But as you saw, when he imports flowers, the manifests say 'Agricultural Products.' Not floor tiles. Because his business is selling flowers. And he pays taxes on the money he makes— not a lot of taxes, as has been shown here, he's got a good accountant, but that's his right. The government tried to make this trial about my client's tax forms— remember that? Forensic accountants droning on and on? You know the bottom line? If the government believed my client had cheated on his taxes by a nickel, they'd've had counts of tax fraud in this trial. But they didn't, because my client is fundamentally an honest man. Every single thing they brought up, my client is entirely innocent. And that innocence—" Angelo's voice shifted in volume, "—includes having any connection—" now he was impassioned— "with any aspect of the importation of cocaine!" He said it so hard and so loud it rattled the windows.

"The man doesn't have flowers in his house— so what? You think petroleum CEOs decorate their houses with barrels of oil? You think CEOs of hospital corporations festoon their living rooms with stethoscopes? If you dealt with flowers all day in your business, maybe you'd like to look at something else during your downtime. Maybe you had asthma as a child, and you don't like the idea of breathing pollen all day and all night.

"All right, ladies and gentlemen. A boat was boarded by the cops, they found a lot of cocaine. They busted a customs agent, Barney Lind, gave him immunity to tell everything he knew. In his testimony he mentions Eduardo Nieto, yes. But Baby? Not once."

Angelo shook his head sadly. "No coke, no phone calls, no emails, no undeclared money, no connection to the boat, no plausible connection with anyone connected with the boat, no profit from the boat. My client is innocent. Let him go so he can resume his life here in America, and continue to import flowers."

When he stopped, the room was so quiet Tory could hear the individual jurors breathe. And then Sam got up, stretched to the full height of his lanky frame, and faced the jury.

"Been an interesting trial, hasn't it?" Sam's collegial off-handedness, smoothed by his silken Southern accent, managed to puncture Angelo's towering oratory. "We've created quite a record here, myself and Mr. Schwartz," he went on. "Quite a record for you all to judge."

He looked over at Baby; when he turned back, the genial affability had changed. "Now, ladies and gentlemen, everything I've told you— and will tell you— is in this record. In the wiretaps you heard, in the testimony of every witness, in the photographs and the exhibits you all saw. I'm not standing here making up some kind of fairy tale that has nothing to do with Mr. Nieto. I don't have to. The facts speak in the favor of the People of the State of New York. Every detail of the defendant's life tells the tale— the parties every night, the caviar, the Dom Perignon, the private chefs, the chauffeurs, the townhouse, the orgies— this is America. You can live however you want to live, if you have a legitimate business. But you heard the accountants say it: Mr. Nieto's extravagant lifestyle could not be supported by—" Sam snorted, "—a no-show partnership in a flower importing business." He shook his head. "Did Mr. Nieto pay any attention to that business? Nowhere in the record does it suggest that he gave it one iota of thought. And why would he, when that business was in no way the source of his great wealth?"

Sam smiled at the jury. "He was an importer, all right. On one boat he brought in just under 10,000 pounds of cocaine. That's five tons of coke, ladies and gentlemen. One hundred dollars a gram, a gram for an evening— how many evenings can you get out of five tons of coke? Over four million. What would have been the human cost of those four million grams hitting this city? Well, we see that cost every day around us, don't we? Drugs like cocaine and fentanyl are pouring into the country and this man, Ricardo Nieto, will stop at absolutely nothing to bring in even more.

"And make no mistake, Baby Nieto was the chief of North American operations of his brother's cocaine and fentanyl business. Like any good manager, he delegated. But he enjoyed the fruits of his criminal enterprise— one thing we've established is that Baby Nieto enjoyed the fruits.

"You hear the word plea bandied about a lot in a trial. Plea and plead. Noun and verb. How does the defendant plead? What is his plea? Well, right now, I'm going to make a plea that you look at the evidence and see that it is overwhelming— far greater than the standard Judge Parker gave you at the beginning, of proof beyond a reasonable doubt. To ignore this overwhelming evidence is to return this man to the daily importation of tons and tons and tons of his brother's soul-destroying poison. To respect it is to give meaning to the concept underlying our system of justice— everyone must be held responsible for his actions."

Sam sighed, something sad but inexorable in his demeanor. "This evidence cries out for only one verdict," he said. He looked at the jury, individual to individual. "I know," he said quietly, "you will see that justice is done."

Sam sat back down. Tory let the silence grow for a moment. Then, out of the corner of her eye, she saw the door from the robing room open, Anna standing there with a stricken look on her face. In her hands was a FedEx envelope.

Tory immediately knew what it was. She didn't let it faze her. "Ladies and gentlemen of the jury," she intoned, "I have some instructions I'd like to go over with you. The first and most important: from this moment on, this case is in your hands."

* * *

When Tory entered the robing room, Jerzy Poldak handed her a Xerox of the letter. It was laser-printed on white paper, in the same manner as the first had been.

> Augusta National declares we are serious. We have many more bombs, and we have no fear of using them. Release Baby and all will end. We even give you a way to save face: the charade trial will go to jury today. When the Jury comes with the verdict, they will give you a folded piece of paper. You open the paper, say "Not Guilty" no matter what verdict is there, and Baby goes free. If not, many bombs all over the country, all at once.
> BOOOOOOOOOOM!!!!
> The choice is yours.

Tory looked up. "They're watching the trial. Maybe even here, right in the courtroom." She felt a cold shiver run through her. "Where did it come from?"

"Miami," Poldak said. "Return address last time was fictitious. This will be as well."

"How long do you think the jury will take?" Leavall asked.

Tory shrugged. "Could be four hours, could be four days." She glanced at the calendar. "It won't go past Friday."

"How do you know?" Poldak asked.

"Jurors hate to spend the weekend." Tory smiled sadly. "You wouldn't believe how many verdicts we get late Friday afternoon."

"At least we have a little more time than with the last letter," Anna said.

Tory nodded. Time, yes, but what to do with it she had no idea.

* * *

Baby Nieto got off the bus with the other prisoners at Riker's, shuffled in his belly chain back into the cell block. After the Augusta bomb, they had put him in solitary. The guards cut him away from the other prisoners and marched him down grimy corridors to his new room. Two men unlocked his belly chain and shackles while another two stood with drawn shock clubs. When the cuffs were off, the men withdrew, slammed and locked the steel door behind them, and Baby Nieto was alone.

Solitary, he was finding, was bad for the mind. A bare room, no window, a sink-toilet fixture, a cement shelf for a bed. Nothing to do but let the terrors in your head come out to play.

Baby remembered his childhood as an endless series of toys being yanked out of his hands by his older brother. Eduardo had been a biter, a hitter, an angry little bastard. Baby had grown up hating his nickname, hating his brother, wanting nothing more than to get out. His father spoke of America as the ideal country— not the south, that had been his mistake, the south was no place for anyone with even mildly dark skin. Listening to his father, Baby had yearned to build a life away from Colombia, move to New York or Los Angeles and seek his destiny.

But fear had always been an inborn problem. Maybe Eduardo's routine terrorizing had torn something inside Baby, made him elect always to be lesser. His brother locking him in rooms, forcing him to eat rotting food, forcing him to humiliate and debase himself a million ways, and here he was all these years later, locked in a room, awaiting his tray of awful food, humiliated by the guards—and for what? To preserve Eduardo's innate sense of self-worth?

Baby had been there at the beginning of Eduardo's cocaine business, yes. Export, he'd decided, would be his ticket out, and to that end he had taken a job with a Colombian flower exporter. Thus, it was that Baby first went into the hill towns with cash, looking for farmers with orchids. The fact that his flower territories overlapped drug territories was simply a part of doing business.

But Eduardo had seen it differently.

Eduardo had already been in the drug business in Cartagena, but he didn't like working for anybody, and he saw that if he got the villages unified he wouldn't have to. Baby served as his intro to the territories, took him to all the different farm towns where he'd negotiated for orchids. Eduardo arrived with a road crew, promised roads in exchange for coca. When rivals appeared, they met untimely public ends, and Eduardo's business prospered.

Baby had never stopped selling flowers; the drug trade had always been Eduardo's machine. When Baby moved to New York, Eduardo asked him to keep one eye on the steady flow of traffic. Baby had long since delegated to Mr. Armstrong 98% of this dilemma; for this Eduardo threw him money with the same relish that he had grabbed his toys away as a child.

Now, in his windowless, featureless cell, he wished he'd been able to cut Eduardo out of his life completely. But Eduardo was more dangerous when he didn't control you than when he thought he did. So the emissaries shuttled north from Eduardo to Baby, never south, always north, with suitcases full of money. And in exchange, Baby had not given him, or his Mr. Armstrong, a Goddamn thing.

Baby hadn't known the details about that specific boat. He knew about Barney Lind, though, and a host more like him in harbors all over the country. He was connected, whether he liked it or not. And because of that, Eduardo was going to make everyone pay.

His reverie was interrupted by the distant thunk of the main door at the end of the hall. Nieto wondered if it was the man with the dinner cart. Then he heard a tuneless whistling.

Officer Frank! Nieto stood, hoping the whistling guard would stop to visit him, and sure enough, the little eye-level window on the door soon slid open.

"How's it going in there, señor?"

"It is a universe of boredom. Thank you for coming."

"I told you I'd stop by. Latino gang boys all miss you— they send their best."

"You watch your back with them, Mr. Frank."

"I always do. I figured you could use a little reading material." Frank bent down, opened the food tray slot, shoved in a magazine. Baby got down on one knee to pick it up.

Lusty Spanish lesbias. "Ahh!" It wasn't the thing itself, just a crappy porn magazine. It was the human caring that made Baby's eyes tear. "You are a good friend to me, Mr. Frank."

"Ahh, don't get all mushy on me. I just didn't want you to let your meatloaf."

"Wha—?" Baby didn't get it.

"It's a joke," Frank said. "All right, gotta run, I'll be seeing you 'round." He winked, slid the eyehole shut, and walked away whistling as Nieto called out: "Thank you, Mr. Frank! Muchas Muchas Gracias!" at the steel door of his cell.

* * *

At 10:45 the next morning, the jury foreman passed word through the bailiff that they had reached a decision. Tory, in her upstairs office working her way through FISA transcripts, closed her eyes and took a deep breath.

She was usually pretty accurate about how a jury would go at this stage of the game, but this time her compass was swinging wildly. The verdict had become a fulcrum for so much of greater import than the mere issue of Baby Nieto's fate. The NEST teams had been alerted and were on standby. She took up her secure phone, dialed the number she had been given, and told Dr. Michael Pappas, down in Washington, that she'd just heard from the jury.

"How much time do we have?" he asked.

"How much time do you want?" Tory replied.

"Two hours minimum. More like three," the man said.

"You've got it. I won't bring the jury out until I get a call that your team is in the air," she said. Then she went down to the robing room, looked at Anna and Thomas.

"We're getting a verdict," Anna said gloomily.

"Listen," Tory looked at the two of them. "There's a good chance we may be targets. If you want to leave the city, head upstate or wherever, seriously, go."

The room filled with a long silence. Anna finally broke it. "Nice try, judge."

"You're not leaving, we're not leaving." Thomas said.

Tory smiled at them. "Thanks, both of you," she said, and some part of her was surprised by the sudden emotion in her throat.

* * *

Tory, on the bench two and a half hours later, was always surprised how quickly word spread when a big-case jury reached a verdict. The courtroom was jammed, the press chatting like college buddies run into each other at a corporate function. Tory looked out at the faces, tried to figure out which one might be the conduit to Eduardo, which one would pull out his cell phone when the verdict was read and tell Eduardo Nieto's people what to do with their bombs.

Finally, Tory got the word that everyone was in place, offstage and on. She declared the court in session, brought in Baby from the cells, told the bailiff to bring in the jury.

Twenty hours. They had to have slept for at least 5. No questions about legal points to be elucidated, no requests for transcripts to be read over. For a judge, jury deliberations were the sanctum sanctorum; Tory was always curious what went on in those rooms, and she never ever would know.

This jury looked grim, no intercommunication between them, no stifled laughter, no glances out toward the prosecution or defense teams. The common wisdom was that that mean a guilty verdict, but the common wisdom was often wrong.

Tory waited until they were seated. "Has the jury reached a verdict?"

The foreman, a hygienist named Katie, stood. "We have, your honor." She handed the folded form to the bailiff, who carried it to the bench. Tory read what they had decided.

At no time did it cross her mind to change what they'd written. At no time did she even conceive of such a thing. What she thought when she read the verdict was: bombs away, Eduardo. As the gamblers say, it's to you.

*   *   *

At first, standing and listening to the jury with Angelo by his side, Baby Nieto didn't understand, and then he understood far too well. Guilty, the jury was saying it over and over on each count, it took forever. He turned to Angelo, whispered: "This is bad."

"I'm so sorry–"

"Not for me. For Eduardo. He will attack. People will die."

Angelo focused all his attention on Baby. "Tell me what you know."

"He once made the boast he could kill 20,000 people in one day." Baby snapped his fingers. "Like that. That was four years ago. Now it will be ten times that."

Angelo touched his arm to stop him, looked at Tory: "May I ask that the jury be polled?" "Absolutely," Tory said. The clerk polled the jury one by one, asking each juror if they concurred with the verdict. When each had, she gave her profound thanks for their work during this difficult trial, sent them back to the jury room and looked at the defendant.

"Mr. Nieto, this jury has found you guilty of fourteen counts of possession of a controlled substance in the first degree, and conspiracy. You will be remanded to Riker's Island until sentencing, which will be the 12th—two weeks from today."

Baby's voice came out forthright: "Your honor–"

Angelo turned to him. "Not now," he said in a sharp steely whisper.

Tory looked at the two of them. She never let this happen, but today was exceptional: "Mr. Nieto, do you have something to say to this court?"

"My brother will make us all pay for this." She would have thought it braggadocio, were it not for the raw panic in his voice. Angelo grabbed him. "Not now," he hissed again.

Baby pulled away. "I will tell everything!" He shouted. "Not for me! For all the people!" The corrections cops were forming a block around him. Tory had no idea what he was going to blurt next, but she didn't like all those reporters getting it on tape. "I will tell everything!" the large man yelled as the phalanx of guards took him away.

* * *

An hour later, Angelo stepped out of the lawyer-client meeting room in the courthouse prison complex, shook hands with Baby as they led him away, then took up his cell phone and dialed Tory. "I'm still in the building. I need to meet with you and Sam," he said.

"Come on up," Tory said. "The office upstairs, not the robing room."

For their part, Tory and her team felt none of the elation they usually enjoyed at the end of a long trial. No happy group lunches at Forlini's, no relieved postmortems and mordant jokes. Just a grinding anxiety about what would happen now.

Sam's rangy frame seemed to overflow Tory's office chair when Angelo arrived. "I'll tell you right up front, I don't like this," he said by way of greeting. "I don't care what kind of nuclear bullshit his brother's up to, Baby's not getting a pass."

"He's not asking for a pass," said Angelo. "He's mortified. He wants to cooperate."

Sam spat out laughter. "A day late and a dollar short. He could have flipped months ago, saved us all a lot of time and energy."

"It's absurd to see how your trial goes before offering to make a deal." Tory was embarrassed just saying it.

"He didn't think his brother would go nuclear," Angelo said. "And what he's got is major league— names of corrupt judges, Customs agents, detectives all over the country. He doesn't know where the dirty bombs are, but he knows who knows, and he's willing to tell."

Sam looked skyward. "He's pulling this out of his ass, Angelo. Granted, it's a big ass, but who knew there was this much crapola—"

"Look." Angelo's emotion was thick. "In Colombia, they corrupted everyone all the way to the top, and they're doing the same here. And your little case did nada to crack this thing wide, Mr. Prosecutor. This is bigger than Baby rotting in jail, and we all know it."

Tory cut through the testosterone. "What does he want?" she asked.

Sam waved his hand. "Witness protection program, a pile of money and a no-show job at an ice cream factory in Honolulu. What they all want."

"He'll do time," Angelo said, and that silenced the room. "He would prefer not a lot. And that's predicated on keeping him safe from retribution without keeping him in solitary the whole time. He knows he waited too long. All he wants is to stop his brother."

Tory wasn't immediately sure how to keep Baby safe from his brother's long reach in any American prison. "When he says all the way to the top, what does that mean?" she asked.

"He hasn't told me yet."

"Angelo—" Sam looked at him as if he was quite insane.

"it's the ace in his hand. He isn't going to lay it down until he signs a deal. But as a good faith gesture, he gave me this." Angelo took out a piece of paper, handed it to Tory.

Sam got off the chair, peered at the handwritten page. There, in Baby's own tight, crabbed handwriting, was a long list of names and telephone numbers. "Cops, customs agents and boats," Angelo explained, "in New York, New Orleans, Miami, San Diego and Los Angeles. Check out every one." He looked at Sam. "If there's a single clinker in there, I'm willing to take the deal off the table. But there won't be, because my guy's coming clean. And one more thing: Tory, he wants to talk to you."

"That's unheard of, Angelo," Tory said, "but everything in this case is unheard of. And if he's talking, I have a question I'd like to ask him."

* * *

When finally she was alone, Tory called Jack Riley's office, got voicemail. She called his cell phone, left a message, wondered where he was. Then she took up the securitized phone and called Drummond. Tory explained the situation, and Drummond considered.

"You were right to call," he said finally. "If I may, I'd like to set up an on-screen conference with all available FISA judges— sort of an unofficial working group, if you will." "Go right ahead," said Tory, and waited on hold. After long minutes and a succession of beeps, Drummond came back on. "That should do it," he said. "All right, Judge Parker, we have Judge Riley, Judge Hart, Judge Kottle, and Judge Clemente." There were murmurs of assent. "Judge Parker— Tory— please fill us in on the events in New York."

"First of all, Jack— where are you?" Tory asked. "I called you before."

"Down at the Potomac house, I was in the basement. Sounds like you've had it rough."

"You could say that," Tory told the story: the bomb threat, the verdict, the offer.

"After the trial's over?" Judge Kottle interrupted. "That's highly unusual—"

"The whole case is highly unusual," Drummond snapped, "or we wouldn't be here now."

Al Clemente piped up. "Are you sure there are gumballs in this machine?" he asked. "'Cause I'd hate to put in a quarter and not get a gumball."

It took Tory longer than it should have to realize Clemente was speaking metaphorically. For a moment she'd thought Drummond's call had found the man in a drugstore, sizing up vending machines.

"Well put," Drummond said. Tory, now that she understood it, supposed it had been.

Tory turned her attention to the list. "As proof of his sincerity, Mr. Nieto drew up a list of police officers and customs agents he says have been turned by his brother's organization. This is meant to be a taste of all the good things coming to us if we work with him."

"Cops and customs? After all this?" Fenton Kottle was baffled. "It's little more than a good beginning. We need a much higher level."

"Angelo insists his client says it goes all the way up. He's saving the big fish for after we sign a deal."

"Angelo?" Drummond asked.

"His lawyer, Angelo Schwartz."

"How high is all the way up?" AO Hart asked. "You get any sense?"

"Apparently up to the highest levels."

Drummond cut in. "It would be the Colombian model. Cops, judges, senators, legislators. If they could bag a president or prime minister, then they could run the table."

"But how far did they get here?" Hart asked again.

"They got to my DEA man," Tory said, "as you all know," An awkward moment of silence ensued on the hissing phone line. "Now the first issue," she went on, "is this list. There are FBI agents on it, so I'm reluctant to just turn it over to just anyone at the FBI. I do, however, have a personal relationship with Ellen Boettinger."

"Head of Homeland Security," Drummond said. "I knew her at Justice."

"She and I worked together when I was a prosecutor." Ellen was ambitious and, so far as Tory knew, incorruptible. And she had a sense of humor. "She hasn't tried to kill me recently," Tory said, "so I think she's a safe bet."

A couple of small chuckles over the cell lines. "Excellent choice, Judge Parker," Drummond said. "You may have noted that of the 11 of us, six are right now on the line–"

"I did indeed," said Tory.

"Which means we have a majority. Anybody have any suggestions or considerations?" No one did. "Then I think we all agree. Send that to Boettinger, let her get her people on it."

"Thank you, Mr. Chief Justice." As she hung up she realized: this was why America had FISA. This was the way it was supposed to work: Conscientious judges keeping checks and balances on the investigative power of the United States government, only letting it off its leash when the court agreed a target was worth chasing.

She was unabashedly thrilled to be a part of it. Then another idea bubbled up: Jack Riley had been uncharacteristically silent through that phone conversation. She wondered again what was going on with him, because in truth there was obviously something amiss.

* * *

Usually Tory was not part of the drawing up of a plea agreement; the prosecutor and defense would hammer it out. She'd only have to agree to go along with the deal.

But not today— time was too critical. Sam was typing in his laptop as Angelo and Tory debated language. Sam kept coming back to the mandatory prison sentence. "Five years? Ten thousand pounds of cocaine, and we're giving him five years? It makes my skin crawl."

Angelo cut in: "If he does nothing, he goes to jail for life. If he does anything we don't like, he goes to jail for life. He only gets the five years if he delivers what he promised. And. given Eduardo, he's worried he won't survive those five years. But he knows that's the price."

Sam finished typing the new changes in, handed the disk to Tory who printed three copies. They all spent a careful moment reading it.

"It's good?" she asked.

"It's good," Angelo declared.

"I can live with it," Sam said.

"Right, then." The two lawyers signed, and she did as well; she wanted her imprimatur right there on the paper, to allay any questions down the line. She stood, got her coat. "All right then, let's go to Riker's."

* * *

Riker's Island was a strange zone of limbo in New York. The island in the East River was part of the Bronx, but the only bridge to it went through Queens, and none of the residents wanted to call it home. Tory had been there once, years before, as an ADA. The thing she remembered was the ceaseless roar of planes from LaGuardia rising over the prison like angels in flight, screaming away from this dirty, stinking zoo.

On either side of the bridge the water was black and choppy. Ficht drove Tory, Angelo and Sam in one car; in another was Poldack and his team, and NYPD Counterintel in the third. At the main gate they were directed to the correct building; they made their way in, were metal detected and had their bags X-rayed, then led down endless hallways to a waiting room, obviously off-limits to prisoners, with nice leather seats and stacks of magazines.

"I hate this place," said Angelo.

"So do twenty thousand other inhabitants," said Tory. Mike Leavall from Counterterrorism entered, greeted Tory and Angelo. After a few minutes Lewis Clapp, the warden who had testified about the monitored payphone call, strode into the room.

"Everybody's here? We're ready," he said, and led the clutch of people to a surprisingly cold conference room with a heavy metal table. There they waited, Leavall, Jerzy, Angelo, Tory and Sam in the plastic chairs, Leavall's officers and the Corrections men stationed along the walls. Finally, after a lull, Baby Nieto was brought in. He was slightly abashed at the crowd.

"Thank you, Angelo, thank you, Judge. Thank you for coming." He seemed earnestly grateful. He sat on his side; Angelo took the plea agreement from his suitcase, slid it across.

Silence as Baby read it. Finally, he looked up. "Judge, you tell me what does this mean?"

Tory straightened her back. "It means five years in prison. Then you enter the Witness Protection Program. You'll be relocated— you don't get to decide where. You'll have a house, you'll have a job—a real job, where you show up every day and put in 8 hours. No champagne, no personal chefs, none of that."

"I don't care," Baby Nieto said.

Angelo jumped in: "You never leave the continental US without special permission. Your parole officer is the best man at your wedding, he's who you name your firstborn after. You don't take a dump for the rest of your life without him knowing where, when, and how."

Baby Nieto simply said "Okay."

Tory continued: "If, now or in the future, you withhold anything from us, you try to play some kind of game, then the deal's off, and it reverts right back to you being guilty of bringing in five tons of cocaine."

Sam cut in: "That's a lifetime in jail, and I don't see you ever getting parole."

"I don't withhold." He corrected himself. "I will not withhold." And then: "Okay, Judge Parker, but I want you to make sure I go to a prison where I will be safe. Whether it's nice, the country club, or not nice, I don't care. But wherever you send me, Eduardo can't touch me. Angelo can't make this promise, that's why I ask you."

"The safest way probably involves isolating you."

"As long as is not punishment, is safety. So I get books, I get to read." He grinned. "I never go to college, now I read all the great books, I give myself college. Is okay."

Tory smiled. "I will stipulate your safety be of paramount concern in my sentencing."

"Thank you, Judge. I did not expect you to be fair, but you are, from the start." As the correction officers drew close—prisoners had been known to pull all kinds of nasty tricks with pens— he signed the agreement, pushed the documents and the pen back across the desk.

Tory signed and dated the copies. Then she looked up. "Tell us about the bombs."

Baby hesitated, lips tight, trying to fight a lifetime of secrecy. "The bomb in the golf course was in a fire extinguisher," he said finally. "He had sixteen is what I have heard. Take away Augusta, that's fifteen. Take away a test down in Colombia to see if the design would blow up. Which I heard it all worked bueno, right on the first try. That leaves 14 bombs."

"Where are they?" Tory said.

"Exactly where, I do not know. But Washington. That is where they must be. He would put them all one place, when they blow up nobody can live in that place forever, it becomes a monument to him. Just like now in his mind the golf course is a monument to our father."

Angelo sighed deeply. "Thank you," he said simply.

Tory looked at Baby. "Did Eduardo order the deaths of the FISA judges?"

He looked stumped. "What judges?"

Sam let out a sigh. Tory and Angelo exchanged a glance. "The three judges in Washington, on the Secret Court," she went on. "They were shot, and then the building was burned."

"Aaaaah. Yes." Baby took a deep breath. "'Yes—that was my brother."

Tory leaned in. "Why?" she asked.

Baby said nothing for a long moment, lips tight together. Something skipped in Tory's heart: *He's not going to tell*, she thought. *This is all worthless.*

He eyed the agreement he'd just signed. "No lies, right? No lies." He let out a long breath. "The Americans spray the coca plants with a chemical to kill them."

"Glyphosate," Jerzy Poldak said.

"I think so," Baby said. "It kills everything. It kills the orchids, the flowers, vegetables in the gardens, everything. Eduardo has a scientist who makes the coca plants hardy against it."

"Invulnerable?" Tory asked.

"From inside. In the genetics. The spray does not kill them. It kills the weeds in the fields, but not the coca plants. There was a black man? On the court?"

"Judge Grant," Tory said.

"He found out. So everyone died."

Tory couldn't hide her surprise. Glyphosate-resistant coca plants. A frontline tactic of the war on drugs, millions of dollars and countless man-hours devoted to destroying Colombia's coca crop from the air, would have to be rethought. The ramifications were staggering.

"There is another judge." Baby said. "I don't know who—everything is separate, Eduardo keeps walls so no one knows everything except Eduardo. Eduardo sends him girls up from Colombia. Young girls. And is true, I don't talk to Eduardo in four years. But 1 know this: during the trial I learn the last girl run away. Usually they are dead, but this one run away, nobody can find her. This, for Eduardo— this is very bad."

Tory gulped. "There have been dead girls found in DC, and rumors—" she said.

"They are true," Baby said. "Every rumor you hear, with Eduardo, is true."

*　　*　　*

With Baby's signing of the documents, there was now officially no purpose or function Tory or Angelo or Sam could serve the man, and they left soon after. Baby was going to spend the next days and weeks in the hands of professionals, repeating his stories over and over as they looked. for inconsistencies and asked for elaborations. Angelo and Tory were quiet in the back seat, and Sam stared pensively out at the city as Josiah Ficht drove them back into Manhattan.

"Are you heading home?" Tory asked Sam. "We could drop you—"

"Leave me at the courts. 1 want to explain all this to the DA."

When the car rolled to a stop, Angelo got out with Sam. "I just wanted to say you did good work on this trial."

Sam looked at him, surprised. "You didn't make it easy," he said. "You kept me on my toes."

"We should do it again, someday," Angelo said, and they shook hands.

Angelo got back in the car. "So I have an advice column-type question."

Tory arched one eyebrow. "Tell me."

"Well, I remet this girl I really like," he said, "but she was the judge of this trial I was doing. But the trial's finally over, so can I ask her to dinner?"

Tory smiled. "Won't know unless you ask her," she said.

"Well then," he took her hand, looked her in the eye as if he were proposing. "Dinner?" he asked.

"Well, to be honest, I don't think I could take the whole formal restaurant thing, right
now."

"You mean waiters, menus, tablecloths, polite chatter—"

"Not up for any of that," Tory said.

"Neither am I." He considered. "How 'bout the world's greatest sandwich place?"

"Where's that?"

"11th Avenue. It's a place the cabbies go. Looks like crap, but they make their own bread, they have six kinds of mustard–"

"Perfect."

* * *

Ricardo Nieto had told everything he'd known about the bombs, and then he'd told it again, and again. Homeland Security had arrived and he'd told it all a third time. They'd asked him to make a formal statement in writing, naming every name, diagramming every relationship; he was exhausted, and he needed to eat. He asked if he could take a dinner break fill out the papers they'd given him in his cell.

On the way back, surrounded by the four burly guards, Ricardo Nieto found himself seeing everything around him in a new light. He had told American law enforcement his brother's worst secrets; now a whole new bunch were coming to ask him all the same questions again, and to get every name of every government official corrupted by his brother. He had a lifetime of things to tell them, and just the thought of saying it all made him feel lighter, filled with possibilities. And coupled with that came an idea he had never allowed himself to think:

He would no longer be Baby Nieto.

He would get a new name. He would be reborn an American, in America.

He would live his father's wish.

A rush of fierce joy filled him. He wanted to dance. He wanted to howl like a wolf right there in the prison hallway. He would have, but for the guards and their shock batons.

He would be thin. He would find a woman to love him whom he didn't have to pay for.

He would tell them everything, and by telling them everything, he would be free. He pictured himself working at a job in some small town in America, maybe doing gardening like his father had done, maybe working in a factory or a store. It didn't matter so long as it was work, and he went every day and he did it, and he came home to people he loved.

It had never been possible before, but suddenly, this minute, it was. And he couldn't help himself: tears leaked from his eyes.

Back at his cell, his cheeks were wet, his emotions bigger than the building. The corrections officers unbuckled him, stood back, shut the steel door without bothering to ask why he was crying. Their shift was almost over; they simply didn't care.

Twenty minutes later, the door at the end of the hall clanged open, and Baby distinctly heard whistling. He stood, went to the door. "Mr. Frank?"

The eye-level window slid open. "How ya doing, Baby?"

"Excellent, Mr. Frank. Very excellent."

"You got convicted today, I thought."

"The old me got convicted. The new me—" Baby spread his large arms.

"Well, it's excellent you're doing excellent. Listen, I got something for you, but I have to open the door."

"You get in trouble—"

"Naah, I wouldn't worry. Lie down on the bed, okay? I'm coming in."

Baby stepped to the far wall, lowered himself onto the thin mattress on the cement shelf. "I want to thank you," he said. "You have given kindness many times. Marzipan, magazines—"

"It's been my pleasure," Frank said, came through the door and shut it behind.

He didn't have a box. He didn't have a bag. Baby didn't understand. "So what is this—?"

Frank had the syringe in his hand. He shoved the long needle deep through the fat below Baby's sternum, emptied the contents as the huge man struggled to raise himself.

"What—? What—? Frank—?"

"Fentanyl. A whole lot of it. Little present from your brother."

All the blood had drained from Baby's face "Eduardo—"

"I think he liked the old you better," said Frank, as Baby Nieto crashed to the floor, his blood pressure plummeting down, his heart abruptly incapable of anything besides death.

Frank watched the fat man for a time, until he was sure it was over. Then he let himself out of Baby's cell, locked the door behind. He whistled a Zep tune as he stepped through the main door of the Solitary corridor, locked it up. He reentered the glass booth that contained the racks of digital recorders capturing the various feeds from the closed-circuit cameras, went back to the machine that monitored the Solitary corridor, hit the Record button, took the machine off pause.

There. Recording again. If, down the line, someone discovered the three-minute break in the time code of the tape, in his experience shit like that happened all the time.

* * *

Ned had never spent so much time in churches in his life. Not so much the upper rooms, where the pews and the altar and the windows were, but the basements, where they fed the young mothers and babies and the druggies who had once been hipsters but had rendered themselves useless and the seniors in various stages of decline. During the day Ned hit the soup kitchens; in the evening he would hit the AA and NA and other A meetings, DC had a zillion of them, and then at night he'd hit bars.

Bars were nice because he allowed himself one drink in each, just as a way of saying howdy to the bartender before showing the pictures around. Places he went back to, what with his pictures and his hard luck tale, often the barmen would knock him a free drink. Sometimes he'd run into people who had seen his pictures before, people saying he must be a very caring father, to come around again and again.

A very caring father who, if he found the girl, would immediately put two bullets in her brain and then get the fuck out of this country as fast and as far as he could.

He made a special point of stopping in shitholes. Your theme or sports or fern or food bars tended to get little groups of citizens, young people in clusters, hard nuts to crack. But shitholes, people came in alone to drink, and they were amenable to talk.

He was in one now, a stripped-down Irish joint, McSomethings. He'd been in before, but it had been a different bartender. He ordered a Boulton's straight up, knocked it back and showed the pictures. The bartender hadn't seen a thing.

He left the stool, started working his way down the sparsely populated bar. Nobody was helpful. He turned to the booths, approached a scratchy woman, gray hair, shopping bags, he didn't think he'd seen her before. Her teeth were a problem; so was her breath.

"Excuse me, ma'am? I'm looking for my daughter, these pictures were taken Halloween, we think she's on the streets, we're looking for any help—"

Alice Malice looked at the photographs. "Yup, same girl," she said.

Ned's blood quickened. "You've seen her?"

"She was real bad, sick, in an alley. I went to get her ginger ale– I used to get that for my daughters, when they were sick." She rubbed her nose, wiped her hand on her shirt. "Then, you know, shit happened, I didn't get back to her for a couple hours. Next time I saw her she was getting into a car with this pimp, he's an asshole, you see him around."

Ned slipped into the booth across from her. "What's his name?"

She shook her head. "I don't know his name. He's a pimp. He drives a big white Escalade. I see him around with his girls. You think I want to know his name?"

"You know where he lives?"

"Of course not."

"So how would I get in touch with him?" She stared at him. "I mean, if he has my daughter—"

"Can you look up plates?"

For a second he thought she meant Joseph Smith and the Mormon religion. "License plates?" he asked.

"Caesar, or Caesar 2. Like the emperor, or, you know, the salad."

"His plate said CAESAR?" She nodded. "CAESAR numeral 2 or CAESAR I-I?"

"2, I think, the number. Or maybe I-I."

He took the photographs from her hand, fished out his wallet, dug in and pulled out three $20s. "Here's my cell number." He handed her a card with the number pre-written. "You see her, or you remember anything else, you call me right away, you hear?"

The money disappeared into her bra. "Hey you should stay, have a few drinks." Under the table he felt her hand find his knee, roll it around.

The thought was beyond repulsive. "Uhh, right now I have to make a phone call," he managed, and stood. "Thank you, ma'am," he said, backing away. "Call if you see her!" he turned, walked out of the bar onto the street, opened his cell phone and hit the number for Armstrong.

* * *

The C&J Diner, on the far West side of Manhattan, was a place Tory had never noticed. The ceiling was pressed tin, the floor a black and white tile pattern that hadn't been seen in public since FDR's first administration. Angelo was right: there were taxis out front, roof lights off, doors locked, drivers inside at the counter. Tory and Angelo took a booth in the back.

Tory hated her reflection every time she saw it; she looked awful tonight, utterly drained. Looking at Angelo, she could plainly see he was too.

But even with all that, she was aware of a gathering quiet pleasure at being across the table from this man, regardless of their mutual bedraggled state. He was telling a story about a jazz club a client of his had started, and she found herself appreciating his humor as the plot twisted and turned. A thought bubbled up in her brain, came into place and locked, and she knew she was making herself a promise: *I want to see who you are when you aren't performing*. Then her cell phone started to ring.

"Judge Parker," she answered, and instantly Angelo could tell something was wrong. He watched her, waiting for their eyes to connect. Finally, they did and she said: "Baby's dead."

Angelo felt as if he'd taken a sharp kick. His mouth dropped open; no words came out.

"Right—" Tory said, and then: "They found him dead in his cell."

Angelo put one hand to his forehead, stared hard at nothing, anguish filling his chest.

"They think it's a heart attack."

"Bullshit," said Angelo. Tory felt exactly the same way.

She got off the phone. "That was Clapp." she said. "Baby was cooperating, his stories were consistent. Homeland Security was coming to interview him, he needed a break, they sent him back to his cell. The man was in solitary. How—" she said, "how on earth—"

"You're going to blame yourself."

"I promised he'd be safe!" She was shaking with intensity. "How in the name of God—"

"Tory—" Angelo was quiet, serious. "Who knew?"

"You, me, Sam— I have to tell Sam." she reached for the phone.

"He'll find out." His voice was hard. "Who knew?"

"Jerzy and his team, Mike Leavall and his team, FISA," Tory said. The video meeting. Something in her vision began to tweak with anxiety. "Drummond, four other judges, and me."

"Somebody acted fast," Angelo said. "Somebody did not want that man to talk."

Drummond, Riley, Hart, Kottle and Clemente. It wasn't Jerzy or Mike. It was FISA. It had always been FISA. One of them had made the call.

"I could subpoena phone records—"

"I like you breathing, Tory. It's very important to me to keep you that way."

"Right," she said, and then: "I don't want to go home." She saw it all at once.

"Then don't," Angelo said. "We'll stop, we'll get the dog, we'll go to my place."

Tory looked at Angelo across the table. "Thank you," she said at last.

"Thank you," he said back. And they both knew: there was no longer any reason on earth for them to be apart.

* * *

Siggy was sniffing around the edges of Angelo's vast loft; Tory sat on the couch with a 40-year-old scotch. Angelo fussed with the fire, sending showers of sparks up the chimney. Tory set down the glass. "I'm so scared Eduardo's going to blow those bombs."

"We've done everything we can, Tory." Angelo sat next to her. "The government got Baby's message. Right now, in ways we don't even know, they're mobilized. We have to believe the NEST teams and the emergency responders can do what they're trained to do."

"But I feel so powerless—"

He reached over, brushed her hair away from her face with his finger.

She touched his hand. At first it was a comradely recognition, a gesture of thanks. But then a spark passed between them, and it became something more. Angelo set down his drink, moved in close. Tory met him with her lips.

He kissed her back, and it was Angelo, he kissed exactly the way Angelo used to kiss, and somewhere deep inside, her heart said *here we go*.

They stayed like that, enthralled, needing more and more from each other, the warm orange glow of the fire shifting shadows over their faces. When the urgency between them became unbearable, Angelo pulled away, stood and extended a hand.

Wordlessly Tory accepted, and he led her into the bedroom. They stripped out of their clothes urgently, with no hesitation. Tory couldn't help feeling intimately familiar with his touch, his chest, his lips. This wasn't something new to them; these were familiar sensations, long held in check. Then the passion grew and an animal compulsion overtook them both. Tory pulled Angelo onto the bed, took him by the hand, lay back and guided him and the rhythms began, Tory meeting his thrusts with her own. Halfway through she flipped him, stayed in position, their eyes locked into each other as she rode him. Soon they were swept into a riot of sensation, excruciating unstoppable shocks of feeling melting into each other.

When they were done, they held each other a long, long time, neither saying a word. Somewhere out in the city, a fire truck's stuttering siren wailed in the night.

Finally, Angelo shifted. "I think we're better than we used to be," he said.

"I don't know—" Tory said. "That first time, back then, was pretty amazing."

Angelo smiled. "My office in the courts building—"

"We were working on cases."

"Trying to," Angelo remembered.

"But we were talking and talking. And you had to go into your office to get something."

"And you followed me in," Angelo said.

"And I never could look at that carpet again without smiling," Tory admitted.

"Are you kidding?" Angelo looked at her. "For a week, your perfume was in the carpet. I would get down on my knees and smell it for your perfume. Four, five, six times a day."

"You never told me that," Tory said.

"I didn't want you to think I was nuts."

"I knew you were nuts."

"Obviously it didn't work." They were very close. "When you're young," Angelo went on, "it's easy to sleep with people. You get older, it's tricky sometimes waking up with them."

"So?" Tory said.

"So I like the thought of waking up with you," Angelo said.

Tory pushed back. "Spoken like a serial dater of models," she said.

"Oy," Angelo said. "They're pretty, but you think it's fun, explaining everything to a 22-year-old who did the Paris shows every year instead of college? You know how old that gets?"

"You know how old we've gotten?"

"Old enough to know better," he said, and took her back in his arms.

* * *

The problem with searching for nuclear material in Washington DC is that the granite in the Capitol and many federal buildings contains enough natural radioactivity to set off detectors. To get around. this, the Nuclear Emergency Search and Tactics teams were using Cryo 7s, handheld digital scintillation Geiger counters that could sniff out a variety of radioactive isotopes and detect single radioactive particles through a variety of materials.

The first hit off a Cryo 7 was in a basement hallway in the Supreme Court building at 3:58 AM. It took four NEST team members clad in full protective gear to locate the source of the gamma rays, a fire extinguisher affixed to the wall. The bomb team used video and portable X-ray equipment to investigate the wall around the red extinguisher, sent the images back by secure link to the image translation team in a truck on the Washington Mall.

In the truck, Candice Brennan, the imaging leader, got the feeds up on two adjacent screens on her desk. "We have visual!" she said, as excited conversation broke out around her.

The X-ray feed was uninformative. "We're looking at a lead lining," Brennan said.

"So we can't see the triggering mechanism unless we get it open."

"Does it have a motion sensor?"

"Or a wire connected to the wall?"

"He's used single-strand connectors before."

Candice hit the talk button on her headset. "Dog team, X-rays aren't getting through. We're concerned about motion sensors and microwires connected to the wall. Over."

There was a short blast of static, and then, from inside the building, Terry Kurt's sardonic reaction: "No shit, Huntclub, we're concerned about those things too. Over."

On the screen they watched as a field-strength meter entered the frame, its wand held in a thick black mitt, and slowly probed the wall around the extinguisher. The voice on the transmitter came back: "We're not getting AC current, over."

"Feel like taking it down?" Candice asked.

The transmitter clicked back, "We're bringing in foam."

The video feed died, and then resurrected itself from a different angle. High-impact ceramic-steel alloy panels were brought in, quickly bolted together to create a dumbwaiter-sized case around the extinguisher. Hoses ran from the corners back down the hallway and out. The assembly was pushed flush to the wall, sandbagged into place.

"Looks good from here," Candice said.

"Foam on." A rumble of motors dinned. Within seconds, the box had filled with specially formulated explosion-dampening foam. It could do nothing about the radioactivity, but it would keep any explosion localized, or at least that was the idea.

"Now comes the fun part," Terry explained. A ladder was brought up, and Terry Kurt climbed on top of the large box. He flipped open access panels where the metal alloy plates met the wall, reached his black-clad arms down from above. "Huntclub, I'm reaching— I've made contact. I'm going to lift the extinguisher up and away from the wall." Inside the truck, no one was breathing. "Got it. It's in the air—" another breathless moment. "Okay, it's in the foam. Guys–?" On either side of the box, metal alloy panels were slammed into place, closing the box. "Okay, I'm going to set it upright on the floor of the box." Gently Terry slowly lowered the extinguisher until it was standing alone. "It's free. More foam, please?" The machine rumbled again as Terry pulled his arms out, covered with pink-pearl foam. "I don't think it's motion-sensitive, I kind of bumped it there and nothing happened."

Finally, he came back down the ladder. "One down," he said, "Thirteen to go."

* * *

The metal box was transported carefully out of the Supreme Court building, and there, under the shadow of the Capitol, transferred to a large military bomb squad truck. The truck roared to life and headed with its dangerous cargo northeast to Frederick Maryland, to Fort Dietrich, where facilities existed to safely neutralize and investigate the dirty bomb.

The sky was beginning to color gently in the east when Candice Brennan announced from the Huntclub command post that Bear Team had gotten a Cryo-3 hit at the Smithsonian, followed closely by another from Horse Team at the base of the Lincoln Memorial. By the time those bombs had been containerized and put into bomb trucks to Fort Dietrich, the sun had risen, and the morning commute had begun.

At Fort Dietrich, the truck containing the bomb was parked on a long elevator and lowered eight stories underground. There a bomb robot controlled from the sixth sub-basement floor opened the hatch and gently pulled out the fire extinguisher. Geiger counters on the robot's arms registered upticks, but whether these were from the extinguisher or from previous bombs that had been in this particular truck could not, at this juncture, be determined.

The robot carried the extinguisher through the spotless facility through containment doors to one of several booths. Techs on the sixth floor opened the door; the robot set the extinguisher between four spidery mechanical arms, then withdrew. The booth door shut, and on the sixth floor, two bomb techs in special suits on either side of an empty table got to work.

When they moved their arms, the mechanical arms two flights below did the same.

With a delicate turning gesture in the control room, the arms on the eighth floor could carefully remove the gears in a wristwatch. With various computerized controllers, the torque could be magnified to the point where the same mechanical arms would bend sheet steel.

In the sealed room downstairs, two of the arms spread their claws and held the body of the extinguisher. Two other arms began, at first gently and then with more and more force, to attempt to unscrew the head from the body. For a long time nothing budged, and then it did, and the scintillation units began registering radioactive particles. As the arm turned and the housing slowly unscrewed, the meters became increasingly more agitated, until finally the mechanism lifted free of the extinguisher, and every counter in the sealed room pinned hard into the red.

The arm lifted the nozzle mechanism straight up, and the camera could plainly see a central core of plastic explosive, a detonation pin pushed in, and three connected pieces of computer motherboard, each a half inch long,

Watching the feed, the techs understood the plastic explosive and the radioactive elements. But what those small boards were designed to do, whether or not it was a clock or a radio relay switch or something more complicated, they had no idea.

At about this time, the Smithsonian extinguisher arrived. It was inserted into a second isolation booth and opened by the robotic hands controlled by the techs two floors above.

Nobody expected it to be different, but it was. Instead of three small motherboards there were four. And the arrayed chips and components on the boards looked entirely dissimilar.

Hopefully the FBI would be able to make heads or tails out of this, because the bomb boys at Fort Dietrich were stumped.

*　　*　　*

In the Huntclub command post, Candice Brennan watched the feed as Fox team extracted the latest extinguisher from a first-floor women's restroom at the National Archives. It was 8:20 in the morning; ten down, and if their intel was right, four more to go.

She glanced at the screen that showed her direct message channels, saw a new one from Fort Dietrich. In it were several stills of videos made when they'd opened the bombs. When Candice realized their import, a thick wall of despair shot up around her throat.

The trigger mechanisms in the two bombs were different. The computer chips and transistors on their little motherboards looked nothing like each other. Hope, which had been cautiously flickering in Candice's chest, now sputtered and died.

Abruptly she felt with utter certainty the emotion she had managed to choke down in the last half hour: failure. In Colombia Eduardo Nieto liked to hit his targets at the beginning of the workday. Wait until everyone is in their offices, at their desks, and then unleash hell.

After the pictures came up, the DMs from various law enforcement bodies came thick and furious, and they were all negative. Candice clicked on message after message, heart sinking further with each one. She didn't want to know what it might not be; she wanted to know what it was. She had twenty minutes before all of Washington DC settled in to business, and right now she didn't like the odds.

* * *

Darren Mays had been at his desk at CIA Special Services since 8:15 this morning; his assignment this week was to create a smaller, better-disguised guided missile target homing device. The one currently in use, a half-inch-long GPS unit called a "battery cap" because it was designed to snap onto a standard square 9-volt battery, was too well known to targets; in various targeted strikes over the past few years, the US military had paid informants a hefty sum to put these in terrorist safehouses and drug labs, a policy responsible for a great many surgically targeted kills. But a radical group in Thailand had become familiar with the device, and publicized it all over the internet, and it was time for a new design. To that end, he had one guts-open on his desk. He was trying to figure out how to build around a flat coin-sized battery when he realized the steady stream of direct messages on his laptop seemed particularly busy.

Evidently the gnomes at Fort Dietrich were sending out an SOS.

Darren clicked, read the request, looked at the two contrasting video feed captures.

The wires to the firing pin told him he was looking at two different bombs; if it was at Fort Dietrich, it was either radiological or biological.

Not good, but at least they obviously had it, though they just as obviously didn't have a clue what they were looking at, or it wouldn't have popped up on his feed. He looked back and forth at the various electronic components protruding from the motherboards, knew immediately that some were decoys, there for the express purpose of confusing anyone who got close to them.

Darren Mays didn't like it when people tried to confuse him. He shifted his wheelchair, steered around his desk, went to the bookshelves on the far wall. He pulled down several loose-leaf binders, set them on his lap and rolled back to his computer. He spent a moment double-checking the configuration against various arrays illustrated in the binders.

He turned back to his computer, hit Reply and wrote:

> The common thread between these two pictures are the cell phone motherboard components in each. On the left, the second section from the top would appear to be from a Nokia motherboard; on the right, the bottom section is from a Phillips. Ignore all the other detritus intended to confuse. All that

is needed to trigger these mechanisms is someone somewhere dialing a cell-phone number.

He sent the text, went back to the problem of making guided-missile homing devices a more comfortable fit in the average terrorist compound.

* * *

Horse Team had found their third bomb of the morning. That made 11. And it was now 8:57.

The flow of DMs to Candice Brennan's machine had slowed to a trickle. When the one from DMays came in, Candace didn't recognize the sender, clicked on it without expecting anything helpful.

Then she read the simple explication of what the two bomb triggers had in common. "Cell phone," she said, and looked at the time. 8:58. She stood and shouted it: "CELL PHONE!" People stopped in mid-word, mid-gesture, pierced by the scream. "We need to shut down all cell service in Washington DC IMMEDIATELY. How do we do it?"

* * *

Two thousand miles to the south, Eduardo Nieto held the door open with a welcoming flourish as Reynaldo Torres slowly made his way into the office.

Fourteen cell phones were laid in a row on Eduardo's desk: various different makes and different designs, all unused, each with a single unique number programmed into its memory.

Colombia and Washington DC are in the same time zone, so as the men watched the digital clock on Eduardo's wall flash from

8:59 to 9:00, they could each picture the great engine of government to their north rumbling to life, begin its daily malfeasance across the globe. Eduardo Nieto knew he was striking a blow long in coming, the giant would be shown to be vulnerable, and for that alone he would be cheered by thinking people the world over.

And then maybe, maybe, the tide would turn, and Baby would not have died in vain.

At 9:08, Eduardo could contain himself no longer. "Let us begin," he said, took up the first cell phone, pressed the button to dial the single number in its memory. He set it down, took up the second, then the third, handed phones to Dr. Torres as he worked his way through each, until each was engaged and sending.

One by one, the recorded voice began its trebly message from the tiny speakers: At this time, the call could not be completed. Eduardo grabbed phone after phone; on each, the brittle voice babbled, repeated the same message over and over.

Eduardo, furious, looked over at Torres, who was busily redialing numbers, evidently to no effect. Eduardo grabbed the remote, flicked on his large television. A music video sprang forth, girls gyrating in a bullring. He changed it over to CNN, where a pretty red-headed reporter was standing in daylight on the mall in Washington, the Capitol in the distance.

Eduardo watched the Spanish translation at the bottom of the screen: Washington DC is on alert for a citywide bomb scare, but the authorities are confident they have blocked the mechanism by which these bombs were to be set off. Until the alert is over, there is no cellular phone service in or around the city.

Eduardo watched it all with an intelligent gleam in his eye, a man weighing the dispositions of fate. He turned to Torres, smiled, gave a slight shrug—that's how these things go sometimes. Torres nodded back, pleased to find Eduardo so agreeable under such unfortunate circumstances. Then Eduardo opened a drawer, pulled out a Ruger automatic, shot Torres six times, five in the man's chest, and once, very close, in the head.

He tossed down the gun just as soldiers burst in, terrified by the abrupt sound of gunfire.

"Clean this up, would you?" he said, and stepped over the man's body.

He would go to the stables and ride his horse. This unfortunate business had made him late for his morning excursion.

* * *

Trojo didn't know the deal with Armstrong, but for the past few days he'd been leaving them alone, some kind of special project, which was fine. Ned slept in in the mornings, and now with Armstrong momentarily out of their hair, Trojo had worked his way through the Air and Space Museum. Today he was looking forward to starting the National Gallery of Art; he had about two hours until Ned called his cell phone and the day's work began. But when Trojo approached the mall, it was filled with cops and emergency trucks and soldiers of every kind.

He watched it all, heart pounding. Something was going on. He turned, walked away into the city, found a breakfast diner, sat at the counter, wanted to order coffee but the waitress and the customers were all completely focused on the TV.

Reporter blaring on and on from the mall, emergency vehicles behind her, and finally Trojo heard it: "a plot possibly involving dirty bombs."

A collective groan shot through the room, and then the cook came out from the kitchen: "Everybody out, we're closed. Don't have to pay a thing, you want your stuff to go, we'll wrap it. But as of right now we're closed."

Trojo left the diner, his mind reeling, anxiety filling his chest. Esmeralda dead in New York. Baby's trial. Eduardo Fucking Nieto. Armstrong and his special project. He saw it all, and he knew.

Dirty bombs. That was it. He was done. He walked quickly back to the hotel, took the elevator up, unlocked the room and started to pack.

The hotel phone rang. He picked it up. "Dude," Ned started, "my cell phone's dead."

"There are dirty bombs in the mall," Trojo said. "Nieto nuclear shit. I'm out of here."

Silence on the line. "What about Armstrong?" Ned asked.

"Tell him to fuck himself. I don't do dirty bombs."

"Where are you going?"

"Canada," Trojo answered, meaning Mexico.

Long pause. "Can I come?" Ned asked.

"You're on your own." Trojo hung up the phone, finished packing, and walked out of the hotel.

* * *

The traffic out of Washington had been murder. Some kind of bomb scare, but there was always something, Svetlana thought as she got off the main road, took the lazy exurban two-lane along the Potomac to the judge's house.

She parked, found the key under the flower pot, opened the door and went in. Instantly, she knew things were not right.

The furniture was oddly positioned, as if it had all been knocked down and put back up by someone who hadn't known precisely where it had been. The kitchen had food on the stove, a big saucepan of chili, ice cold, hardening to brick.

She turned to the living room and there, hanging from a rope pitched over a wooden beam, was the judge. She ran to him, held him up to free his neck from the noose, but he was dead. She let him go, backed away as he swung, his face an inhuman shade of purple.

Only then did she see the magazines spread in a circle at his feet. At first she couldn't believe the photographs around the dead man– little girls naked, hands to their genitals, staring at the camera. Who made this? Who could photograph this? Who could do this—

She looked up at the judge swinging in the air. She found the phone, dialed the police.

Not Judge Hart. She couldn't believe it, but here it was, before her.

*   *   *

"First off, he wouldn't hang himself," Tory said. The trial was over, she needed a day off, and she was taking it with Angelo. They had been tucking in to green pea and shallot omelets at Elephant and Castle when Gar Burton called her with the news. "Arvin Hart was a Hemingway guy. He owned guns."

"He didn't hang himself to kill himself," Angelo shook his head. "He hung himself to make his orgasm better. Autoerotic asphyxia."

"And the child porn—" Tory wasn't so much questioning as angry.

"It speaks for itself, doesn't it? This is exactly what Baby said."

"But he wasn't a pedophile," Tory exclaimed. "He chased me!"

It took Angelo a moment to find his response, but once he did he was sure of it. "So? Chasing you and having a thing for porn and little girls isn't mutually exclusive—"

"It is if you have a ready supply of little girls." Tory was sharp, nose flaring. "AO Hart was a good man. He wasn't my type, and eventually I had to tell him that to make him stop—"

"When?" Angelo wanted to know. "After the night where that guy tried to kill you, right? Because I thought—"

"Yeah, it was that night." Men, Tory thought. No matter how strong they are, their ego always pops up just when you least expect it. "The point is, he pursued me, Angelo! Why would he do that if he had a steady supply of girls from Eduardo Nieto? Why bother?"

Angelo Schwartz had no ready response. “Okay," he finally said, "this is interesting."

Tory remembered with a smile: he only used that phrase when confronted by something he had not at all expected.

* * *

Penny could not wait to get out of the building.

A long day. They'd elected to keep the clinic open in case any help was needed, given the situation on the Mall, but all the bomb scare had done was make business quieter. Ten minutes to four on a Friday, an hour left before the weekend, and time so slow it was like the clock had a grudge against her.

She wanted nothing more than to get off that bus, march up to the door and get her rocks. She had a pipe in her purse— if caught, she was going to say she'd found it in the waiting room, threw it in her purse to show the cops— but a pipe was nothing without a rock.

Her fingerprints were beginning to get a little patchy. Over time, firing up rocks in glass pipes burned your fingerprints right off. They came back, of course, but that's what crack did to you. It removed your individuality so completely your fingerprints slid right off your fingers.

Her skin was itchy. Spread before her in the waiting room were the usual: some young idiot trying to get his herpes treated before his big date tonight, a large teenage girl brought in by her equally large mother for birth control pills, a smattering of earnest young couples in deep conversation, one man explaining, his woman in tears.

Just another Friday. And then a familiar face appeared at the door, and at first Penny couldn't place it, and then she did: Steph, one of Benno's girls. Penny looked to see if the rest of Benno's pack would come flocking in, make themselves the center of attention.

Evidently Steph was alone. Interesting—this was the kind of golden opportunity they taught you about in social work school. Penny stood. "Steph! Over here!" The young woman seemed hesitant as she stepped up to Penny's desk. "Sit, sit," Penny said. "What's going on?"

The girl was lovely, Penny thought, the prettiest of that crew. She was thin, willowy, with nice eyes and cornsilk-blonde hair. She opened her mouth, and no words came out. Finally in a tiny voice she said: "I want to go home, but I don't know how."

A well of gladness sprang up in Penny's heart. Steph had always been retrievable, she'd felt, not like some of Benno's harder cases. Penny checked the urge to jump in, let the girl have space to talk. "I can't make a phone call in that house," Steph went on. "He watches the cell phone bills, he sees something he doesn't like, he lets you know." Penny well understood the fear implicit in that statement. "I don't want to spend another Christmas here." she was about to cry. "I used to be a certain way, and I don't know how— to get— " she dissolved into tears.

Penny stood. "Come with me," she said, and led the weeping girl to the small office at the back. Penny sat the girl in a chair, handed her a box of Kleenex. "You have a brother—"

"I can't just go there." She wiped her eyes. "His wife's a bitch. I tried to call him, but she answered, and I hung up. Twice."

"And no other family?" Penny asked. Penny knew her history: mother disappeared, father entering the bedroom every night, having his way with his daughter. It was a pretty common story in Penny's line of work, but it always carried fresh pain.

"My cousin's got a dairy farm. If I could just go there to work— that's what I'd like. I don't want to live in the house with him and his wife, I'm not asking for anything but a job." She blew her nose. "I think working with cows would be good for me. It would be— real."

"Benno's going to be a problem."

"Benno can go fuck himself," Steph said, with sudden vehemence. "He's got this new girl, and she's just a kid, she's not even menstruating yet, and he's setting her up for the life." She shook her head. "It's disgusting."

Not menstruating? "How old?"

"She's 10."

Something in Penny's heart froze. "And she's turning tricks?"

"Not yet," Steph shook her head. "He found her on the street, she was real sick, he took care of her. And now she owes him—"

Penny remembered him asking for antibiotics. "He should just let her go home."

"Well, she can't," cut in Stephanie. "She's from South America, some guy kept her in his basement but she ran away."

Penny had a sick feeling. "Remember that body they pulled out of the Potomac?"

"I saw it on the news!" Stephanie said

"There've been a few of those. Ten or 11-year-old girls, sex crimes. They were all Hispanic." Penny remembered telling Tory that rumor about the Colombian pipeline. What if the whole thing was true? What if this girl could prove it? "You should bring her in."

"Benno's not letting her out of his sight."

Penny thought about leaving work and getting high. Every cell in her being wanted that, but this, she knew, was more important. Every cell in her being would have to stay quiet.

She got a sticky note. "What's your address?" she asked, and clicked open her pen.

* * *

Ned had been in this bar before, showing pictures around of the little girl. It was an office-crowd after-work bar down the street from a church, and he'd remembered it had a payphone, which a whole lot of other places didn't. Waiting on the long line to use it, he had Boulton's, and then another.

He needed them. Finally he got to the head of the line. Pulled a handful of change out of his pocket, inserted coin after coin and dialed Armstrong's numbers.

On the third one, he got him. "Pain in the ass, the cell phones being out," the man said.

"Trojo's gone AWOL," Ned said.

"Yeah, well, fuck him. Listen, my contacts have had a hell of the time dealing with the DMV, all this terror alert shit is fucking everybody up, but they got your white Escalade. It's registered to Benno Martinez–" he read off the address and phone number.

Ned jotted it down on a napkin. "So I do this and I'm done, right? I get a final payout and I'm out of here?"

"Whatever, kid. Whatever you want." He got off the phone.

Ned tried the number. It was a cell; he got the recording everyone in DC was getting
that day. He listened to it, hung up, took a seat at the bar.

"Another Boulton's," he asked the bartender, because until this cell phone thing cleared up there was nothing more to be done.

* * *

"I never believed those rumors," Drummond had called on a land line. "The fact that Hart—of all people, I knew Arvin Hart. I would have never thought..."

Tory, in Angelo's apartment on the securitized cell phone, said: "It is a surprise, sir." She hadn't expected the old man to be this affected.

"Times like this," Drummond went on, "it reminds me how little we really ever can know anybody else. So much is dependent on the social contract— so much is based on trust—"

Tory thought of shooting pool with him, how comfortable she had felt in his home. "Funeral's going to be in Texas," Drummond continued. "Hell of a thing to have a sober reputation destroyed in an instant, like that."

"It's a nightmare," Tory said.

"Apt term, Judge Parker. Now, I'd like to convene the court tomorrow— we have business, I think it's safe to say."

"Tomorrow would be fine, Mr. Chief Justice."

"Excellent. I'll see you then," he said, and got off the phone.

* * *

Ned had called every fifteen minutes, trying to make contact with Escalade Man. watching the news and drinking, waiting for cell phone service to be restored. He'd finally gotten a hamburger to soak up the alcohol. Eventually the TV said that some cell phone service was coming back outside of the central district. The next time he pumped change into a pay phone and dialed the number, the man actually answered.

Ned, fairly hammered, had had a rap ready, but now it went out the window. "I'm
looking for a little girl to screw," he said, eschewing all tact.

"How little?" Benno asked.

"Like a virgin. Somebody told me you could hook me up."

Long pause. "I don't have somebody who's like a virgin," Benno said, "I have somebody who *is* a virgin."

"What's she look like?" Ned asked.

"Brunette. Long brown hair. You like 'em young?"

"It's what I'm looking for."

"She barely has pubic hair. You want her tonight?"

Ned paused, considered how drunk he was, considered all he would have to do. He was in no shape right now to kill anyone. "Tomorrow," he said. "All day."

"A full day? 24 hours?"

"That'd be good."

"Five grand," Benno said.

"Four."

"Five. Half up front."

"Okay."

Benno silently cursed himself for not starting higher. "Where's your place?"

"I'll pick her up in my car. Noon?"

"Noon. You know the old Lyric Triplex? That parking lot," Benno said. "I promise you, she's for real. You won't be sorry," he said, and got off the phone.

* * *

Penny sat on the front steps of the house, thinking about how nice this neighborhood must have been. Now everything looked beaten; down the street two pit bulls paced back and forth behind a fence like caged tigers, pausing occasionally to urinate on a kid's plastic slide. Benno's house needed paint. No one had answered Penny's assaults on the doorbell.

She had come with the intention of staying as long as she had to, but sitting on the stoop as the evening faded into night she was having second thoughts.

She could leave right now, walk three blocks, get on the bus, she'd be high in half an hour. I'll give it ten more minutes, she thought, and, when that passed: okay, ten more. She'd been there an hour and a half when Benno's white Escalade pulled up. The gaggle of girls got out, it must have been a shopping trip, they all had plastic bags. Then Penny saw her.

She had big dark eyes and brown hair down her back, no bust and long straight legs. Benno came around the car, stopped when he saw Penny.

"Nursie–?" he growled. "What are you doing here?"

"Benno," Penny said, "you haven't introduced me to your new girl."

Benno was instantly furious, but he kept his equanimity. “Ain't no new girl," he said.

Penny walked to Maria. "¿Como te llamas?" Maria swallowed, looked at Benno and the other girls, anywhere but Penny. "¿Cuántos anõs tienes?"

"She's eighteen," Benno said sharply.

¿De dónde eres?" Penny asked. Maria started to answer but Benno barked over her reply: "She's my niece from Colombia. She don't speak English. She's just tagging along."

"She a virgin? ¿Eres virgen?" Maria nodded ever so slightly. "'Cause you can get a lot for a virgin, right?"

"Fuck you, Nursie," he exploded. "You leave us alone with this shit." He led his girls up the steps.

If somebody had been able to stop Penny when she was fourteen, her whole life would have been different. She ran up, forced herself in front of him.

"Benno, I'll buy her from you."

"Whaaa?"

"What would it cost to take custody of her? Take her off your hands?"

Benno laughed. "I didn't know you liked the girls."

Penny's fist struck his arm. "That's not it. I hustled on the streets when I was a kid, okay? She's too young. You're going to sell her, one piece at a time. Sell her to me whole."

Benno, for the first time in Penny's experience, was speechless. "Five hundred," Penny said.

She had no idea how she was going to get that kind of money. Benno looked at her and laughed.

"A thousand?" She hadn't meant to make it sound like a question, but it did.

Something flickered in Benno's eyes. "Ten thousand," he said.

Dizzying anxiety buzzed in Penny's head. "Somebody would pay that for her first time?"

"They'll pay a lot. But, you know, you gotta figure earnings over time—"

"If I give it to you tonight, will you promise to never see her again?"

Benno looked at the sky. "This is some fucked-up shit, Nursie."

It was too weird, Penny saw. It was out of his experience, it probably seemed like a trap.

She was losing him. "I've treated your girls because it was important to me they stay healthy. I've never given you problems, I've been good to you. Now I'm calling in my favors."

He stood, his body cocked belligerently; all at once she was aware she may have dissed him. She held her ground, unsure which way he would jump.

"Ten large," he said finally. "Right now."

"I need tonight."

He didn't like that. He dug through his coat pocket, came up with his keys.

"Just give me tonight," she could not hide the note of panic in her voice.

"She's got a date tomorrow, noon. Gonna keep her all day."

"I'll get it by midnight."

"You do that," he said, opened the door and walked into the house, followed by the girls. The beautiful child paused, looked at Penny with a mix of tarnished hope and despair, and then slipped into the house and closed the door.

PART THREE
Justice

Tory was at one end of the couch reading a wiretap transcript for FISA; Angelo was at the other, reading the grand jury minutes of a case he'd been asked to consider, when Tory's civilian cellphone buzzed. She looked at the screen, saw it was Penny, let it go into voice mail. she'd get back to her when she finished this transcript. Two minutes later Penny called again.

Something was up. Tory answered, immediately thought Penny was overamped. "Tory, okay, great, thanks so much for picking up. Let me have just one minute—" the phone clicked on hold, Tory mystified. She hadn't seen her friend this strangely nervous since— well, since an unfortunate period a few years back.

The phone clicked back on. "Tory, you still there?"

"Penny, what's going on?"

"There's this situation that's come up, and I need to get—a lot of money by midnight."

"How much money?"

There was a pause. "Umm, ten thousand dollars."

Tory closed her eyes, felt pain in her heart. "Penny—"

"It's not drugs, all right? You know those girls sent up from Colombia for government guys? I found one."

"What?"

"Tory, listen to this. This girl was flown up for some guy in DC, locked in his basement, she got away, walked the streets and was picked up by a pimp. She's ten, she's got long brown hair, just like the bodies in the Potomac. And the only way to save her is to buy her. But we have to do it tonight—he's got a date for her tomorrow, some freak's lined up to take her for the full day."

"So she's a working prostitute?"

"Right now she's still a virgin. Tory, she hasn't even started menstruating yet."

That caught Tory in the solar plexus. “Oh, God.” She stood. "OK. But I have to be there."

"Tory, of course. I want you here."

"All right," she said, "we can do this." She cupped her hand over the phone. "Angelo, we're going to DC. Right now."

* * *

Tory was insistent. "First of all, I'm not trusting anybody in the Justice Department. Second, Penny has to be there, the pimp knows her. But the standard FBI technique would be to put an agent in in my place—so it'll be Penny out there on the street, and me safe in a car. And if it goes wrong— hey, sorry Penny, but my ass is more important than yours. She called me for help, she gets me, not a stand-in."

"I understand that," Angelo said. "It comes down to trust."

Tory had bypassed the FBI, made a phone call to her old friend Ellen down in DC. Now they were in Angelo's doublewide elevator. "I'm nervous about your bodyguard," Angelo said, tapping his pockets to make sure he had everything. "We're meeting a pimp. We're buying a prostitute. What if he's got some kind of ties like Bart Alicia? What if they all do?"

"We won't tell him," Tory said. "We're going to DC, that's all he needs to know right now. It'll raise more questions if we try to sneak around him. And what if this is a setup? What if it gets weird?"

"It's already weird," said Angelo. Once in the Marshal's black Ford, the first stop was Angelo's office. They left Josiah in the car, took down all the pictures of Angelo with important Justice Department and governmental officials, put them in a large cardboard file box, bungeed it to a document cart. Angelo keyed into his law partner's office, worked a safe, came back with a thick wad of bills in a large vellum envelope. "It's a start," he said. Back on the road, they directed Ficht first to one bank, where Angelo got out and used the cash machine, and then to another, where Tory did the same.

Then they pulled up to her apartment. She packed a quick bag, walked Siggy, lined up the dog walker. Then, back in the car, she directed Josiah to the DC shuttle at LaGuardia Airport.

Angelo turned to Tory. "You sure your girl Penny isn't hustling you for drug money?"

"No," said Tory truthfully, "I'm not."

* * *

On the DC shuttle, Angelo gave Tory the window seat; Josiah sat on the same row across the aisle. He was reading a thick biography of Teddy Roosevelt; Tory and Angelo kept their conversation quiet. Something about being next to Angelo on this mission, cutting through the night skies toward the nation's capital, was enough to make Tory feel overwhelmingly attracted to him all over again. The fact that they had a chaperone made them behave, so that the fullest gratification of their mutual emotion consisted solely of holding hands. But the yearning implicit in his fingers intertwined with hers made the flight unforgettable.

Angelo had booked three rooms at The Inn at Little Washington; one ostensibly for each of them, Tory had specifically requested they not be met at the airport by the black Ford with tinted windows the Marshals always used. "It can be a tow truck," Tory had insisted on the phone to her old friend Ellen, "it can be an old crappy beater, as long as it's not a black Ford undercover car."

The plane landed. Waiting for them was an ancient green station wagon with fake wood paneling. Tory called Penny. "He wants," Penny said, "to do it at a movie theater parking lot in a shitty section of town."

"We'll pick you up," Tory said, clicked off and looked at Josiah, who was checking out the station wagon with an expression in between disbelief and distaste.

"Forget about the hotel," she told him when they got in. "We're picking up a friend of mine at this address," Tory gave him a piece of paper. "Then we've got a meeting uptown."

* * *

Tory and Penny were standing freezing in the cold. The Lyric Triplex had long been boarded up and defaced, and the parking lot where they were waiting was weedy and unlit. Under Tory's arm was the long vellum envelope with the money, mixed twenties and fifties all rubber-banded into ten $1000 packs. Save for the occasional straggling car blasting hip-hop into the night, Tory was unaware of any other living soul anywhere around her.

Penny stamped her feet to keep warm. "I'm sorry I got you into this," she said.

Tory shook her head. "I'm glad you called me, Penny. I just hope—" she let the sentence dangle as an enormous white car, a Cadillac Escalade, turned from the back alley into the parking lot. It pulled up to them with a swirl of dust in bright headlights. From somewhere behind the glare, an electric window rolled down.

Benno and the girl were alone in the car. Benno pointed at Tory. "Who's she?"

"She's my friend," Penny said. "She helped me raise the money."

"You a cop?" the man asked.

"Hell no," said Tory. "I'm a social worker. I work with Penny."

A long pause while Benno decided what to do. "Listen," Penny yelled over the roar of the engine, "if I'd gone to the cops, they'd've raided you by now, right?"

Benno considered that, found it reasonable, turned off the engine. "The money," he said, and stuck his hand out of the car.

Penny asked, "Can we say hello to the girl?"

In reply, the side window rolled down. Penny leaned in. The girl looked ten, and terrified. "Hola," Penny said. "Queremos llevarte de regreso a Colombia." The girl stared at her, wide-eyed. "¿Como te llamas?"

"Maria," Maria said.

Penny nodded at Tory, who stepped up, ripped open the vellum envelope, handed Benno the first rubber-banded bundle. "That's a thousand. Count it." She waited until he'd assured himself that it was. "Here's the second." She waited as he flipped through. "And the third—" Again she waited. "And the fourth— and the fifth." She handed them through the window. She held the envelope open, showed him there were five more. "You let her out of the car, and I give you the rest."

Benno nodded, hit the button that unlocked the door, told Maria "Vamanos." When she was away, Tory tossed the envelope into the car. Benno look at each bundle long enough to see they were real, then backed up, turned, started to wheel away.

Penny was kneeling with Maria, talking rapidly in Spanish. Tory stepped to them. "Let's go," she said, and the three ran to the street.

Within seconds, the green station wagon swooped out of nowhere, Ficht and Angelo in the front, and Tory and Penny pulled Maria in, slammed the door. As they rocketed around the corner, sirens began to fill the air around them, coalescing in furious squeals and snarls two blocks away, where Benno and the money in the white Escalade found himself hemmed in by Homeland Security agents in unmarked cars at every turn.

* * *

Tory had pulled up pictures of Judge Hart on her laptop. "¿Es este el hombre que te mantuvo cautiva?" Penny asked. *Is this the man who held you captive?*

Maria shook her head. "No."

Penny, Tory, Angelo, Josiah and Maria had been brought by Homeland Security to a safehouse. Tory thought Penny looked awful, now that she had a chance to see her in the light, too skinny with something daunted and wounded in her eyes. But right now Tory was concentrating intently on the young girl, Maria, who was talking quickly in Spanish.

Penny kept up with her. "The man who kept me was tall," she translated. "He spoke Spanish with an accent—"

"Or just bad Spanish," Angelo said, in Spanish.

"No, él conocía el idioma."

"No, he knew the language," Penny translated, and Tory immediately thought of Al Clemente.

Tory glanced at Angelo. "We brought some more pictures for you to look at," she began, and Penny translated. "We want you to have a very clear picture of the man who imprisoned you— it's easy to look at a lot of faces and forget the face in your head."

"Jamás olvidaré su rostro." *I will never forget his face.*

Tory turned to the box, opened the lid. Inside were framed pictures: groups, autographs, judges, senators. Not the full spectrum of the American political and judicial universe, but a fairly broad swath.

"I never thought I'd use my brag wall as a mug shot book," Angelo said as Maria began flipping through the framed photos. She glanced at each face carefully, stopped at a picture of Angelo in the oval office. "Him?" Tory asked, taken aback.

"¿Conocías al presidente?" Maria asked Angelo, something approaching wonder in her eyes. *You know the President?*

"I've met him," Angelo said in Spanish. "Is he the man in the basement?"

Maria shook her head. *No.* She set the photograph aside and turned to the next one, a group picture of smiling men at a reception. Her eyebrows jumped and blood drained from her face. "Es él," she said, and pointed.

That's him.

* * *

Maria told her story five different times, and it never wavered. Warrants were drawn up and signed. Food was delivered from a Mexican restaurant; Maria ate ravenously, went to bed, exhausted. Only then, with Angelo out of earshot, did Penny step up to Tory.

At first she couldn't give voice to the words, but finally they came. "I have a problem," she said, blinking away tears, "and I need help."

* * *

The next day was Saturday; by 9:15 AM all the FISA justices were in their seats, ready to begin the day's work, except Tory. Drummond had a stack of files on his desk, likely candidates to replace Judge Hart; he was waiting for Tory to arrive, gradually getting more and more impatient at the empty chair impeding the day's work.

Al Clemente found himself filled with sexual tension. He had recently learned of a brand new, very expensive private DC sex club, a place where anything was possible; he had paid his first visit the night before and had seen things he'd only imagined in his deepest, most secret fantasies. He'd stayed too late, he'd drunk too much; he was supposed to go to the track with the guys tonight, but he had a strong desire to blow them off and go back.

Fenton Kottle had spent the morning thinking about Judge Hart, but right now his mind had wandered. This weekend his niece was visiting from Albuquerque; seven years old, a brunette angel, she'd already done a bit of modeling, newspaper ads for local toy stores down there. Her younger sister, so far as Fenton could tell, had not inherited the same strong cheekbones and upturned nose—that was going to cause all sorts of complicated sibling rivalry down the line, he could see it now.

Jack Riley was thinking about the strange ways one's appetites changed, as one grew older. He had been single, searching for the perfect girl; he had been married, and had settled into docility punctuated by occasional trysts with women increasingly younger than himself. Now, as a widower, he could give free vent to any enticing proposition that came his way. Some of these were less than honorable, he knew; he didn't like himself some mornings, but he had learned to live uneasily with the man who'd wanted so much the night before.

At that moment the doors slammed open and a phalanx of Homeland Security agents and US Marshals, guns drawn, entered and filled the room.

Drummond was furious. "What is this?" he said sternly. "Get out of here at once—"

Tory stepped into the room holding Maria's hand. She knelt: "Which one of these—" but the child was already pointing.

Drummond turned pale, all his forcefulness withering as the girl said: "Him."

The room was silent. "That's the man who held you hostage?"

A female Hispanic DHS agent translated Tory's words.

Maria nodded. "Si."

"Who took pictures of you naked?"

"Si."

"Who tried to rape you?"

"Si."

"Who made you touch his penis?"

"Si."

"Who threatened to kill you?"

"Si."

Drummond had stood, was backing away from his chair. "FREEZE!" several agents yelled at once. Tory was surprised, more than anything else, by the tremor in his hand as he reached down into his bag, came up with a gun.

"NO!" Tory screamed as he put the gun to his temple, closed his eyes and tightened his finger on the trigger.

Out of nowhere, from the side, Gar Burton leapt at the Chief Justice, tackled him to the ground, twisted the gun out of his fingers. Instantly he was joined by a small crowd of agents and Marshals, pinning the man down, clasping his hands at his back, snicking on the cuffs.

As they led him out of the room, Tory looked into his eyes, and then turned away.

*   *   *

That evening, Al Clemente was at his table at the Skyline, over the oval of Aqueduct racetrack. Chuck Bellort and Herb Combover were with him and all was right with the world.

"Third race?" Herb asked.

"I got $50 on number 7, Turf Girl," Al Clemente replied.

Chuck Bellort looked up. "I liked that horse until Al mentioned it," he said. Then someone's cell phone rang. "Mine," Al said, seeing who it was. He stood hurriedly. "Yes," he said into the phone as he walked out of the restaurant.

"Al, it's Dirk Armstrong. I understand you're at Aqueduct."

"Indeed I am." He walked through the restaurant's glass doors into the hallway.

"Good, because we need to talk." And there, leaning against the wall, was Mr. Armstrong, taller than Al, not a hair out of place in his flat-top.

"Let's walk," Al said, putting away his phone. The two men went out to the grandstand.

Armstrong began it: "You realize, of course, that now you're the man," Al nodded. "Eduardo never liked Drummond personally,"

Mr. Armstrong went on. "He thought the guy was disgusting, and so did I. You were our insurance in case his bad habits came to light."

Al had expected this. "Too bad about Judge Hart," Al said.

"Had to be done," Armstrong said. "A shame, really, considering how it all turned out."

"More insurance, huh?" He took a cigar case from his jacket pocket, opened it and offered Mr. Armstrong a Monterrey. Armstrong shook his head. Al took up a cigar. "Well," he said, and fished out his cutter, "Whatever you were paying Drummond, I want more."

"We didn't pay Drummond in cash. We paid him in girls."

Al nodded "Well then," he said, "$25,000 a week ought to do it."

Armstrong didn't blink. "Done," he said. "But for that we get access to everything."

"Absolutely," Al said. "Everything that passes through FISA, you and Eduardo Nieto will get it within 24 hours. Less if it's time-sensitive."

"That sounds just about perfect," Armstrong said.

"Excellent," Al said, took out his lighter and lit the cigar. "Mr. Armstrong—" he exhaled a plume of rich smoke, "It's a pleasure doing business with you." He extended his band.

"Likewise," Armstrong said, and shook it.

That was the signal. Abruptly two of the railbirds yelled "FREEZE!" and instantly the two men were surrounded by men and women, young and old, all with guns and badges.

Armstrong looked around wildly, outnumbered. He pointed at Al. "This man is a corrupt judge!"

"Wrong, chuleta," Al said. "I'm not a judge anymore. But I'm not going to jail, and you are." He watched the small crowd of agents remove the man from the premises.

Al looked out at the track. Horses were thundering around the turn; he'd missed the start, but the number 7 horse was out in front, leading. She crossed the line with three lengths to spare.

Nice, he thought. See? Sometimes it works out.

* * *

Tory slept late, luxuriating in Angelo's enormous bed while her dog sighed in rumbly slumber on the carpet. When she finally disentangled herself from sleep, it took her a moment to decipher where she was, and then no time at all to be glad she was there.

She was alone; she heard Angelo moving about the apartment. She reflected on the night before, tested herself for worry, found none. She felt calm, pure, sure of herself.

Angelo. It was odd, how comfortable it all seemed. You can't go back in time, she knew, but they weren't.

She thought of Eduardo Nieto down in Colombia. He was a free man today, even after all he'd done. That might change someday, but for now there was nothing she could do about it.

She wondered if he blamed her for Baby. He was a sociopath, so he probably did.

She'd done everything she could. Maybe it would be enough. For now.

She heard the clicking of a computer keyboard from the other room; Angelo, no doubt working. It made her want to go interrupt him. She stood, debated what to wear, slipped into one of his white shirts. She padded into the living room; Angelo was sitting, staring into the screen. She put her arms around him and nuzzled in his hair, smelling his rich mix of smells.

He turned his head up, and they kissed, and kissed some more. When they broke, Tory noticed what Angelo had been looking at, saw billiard tables on his screen.

"I was going to surprise you," he said, "but I've been researching this for an hour, and I'm totally confused about what you would want."

Tory laughed. "You don't have to do that."

"Well, I have the space for it," he said. "So tell me: green or red?"

Tory draped her arms over his neck, put her cheek next to his, looked at the computer screen. "You're not going to buy me a pool table," she said.

"I'm not buying you a pool table. I'm buying me a pool table. I'm just hoping you come around sometimes and use it."

She shifted, looked him full in the face. "You don't have to lure me to hang out in your apartment. I'll be around a fair amount anyway."

"Promise?"

"Absolutely," she said, and they kissed, and the passion between them was immediately evident all over again. But more than passion— kissing Angelo, Tory felt at peace.

Here, with him, she felt happy.

Finally they broke for air. Tory looked at him. "Are you serious? About green or red?"

"I've never been more serious about anything in my life."

"Well then," Tory said, without any hesitation whatsoever, "red."

THE END